GRAVITY IS THE THING

GRAVITY IS THE THING

A Novel

JACLYN MORIARTY

HARPER

An Imprint of HarperCollins*Publishers*

GRAVITY IS THE THING. Copyright © 2019 by Jaclyn Moriarty. All rights reserved. Printed in the United States of America. No part of this book may be used or reproduced in any manner whatsoever without written permission except in the case of brief quotations embodied in critical articles and reviews. For information, address HarperCollins Publishers, 195 Broadway, New York, NY 10007.

HarperCollins books may be purchased for educational, business, or sales promotional use. For information, please email the Special Markets Department at SPsales@harpercollins.com.

Originally published in Australia in 2019 by Macmillan.

FIRST U.S. EDITION

Designed by Bonni Leon-Berman

Library of Congress Cataloging-in-Publication Data has been applied for.

ISBN 978-0-06-288373-5

19 20 21 22 23   OFF/LSC   10 9 8 7 6 5 4 3 2 1

To my son, Charlie,
to my sisters, Liane, Kati, Fiona and Nicola,
to Nigel, and to my parents, family, and friends,
because you are all the point, and the magic.

The motion of Animals is proportioned to their weight and structure. A flea can leap some hundred times its own length. Were an elephant, a camel or a horse to leap in the same proportion, their weight would crush them to atoms.

THE NEW SOUTH WALES JOURNAL OF RICHARD ATKINS, 1792

Two men are sitting—very quiet, motionless—one on either side of a gravel road. They are sitting on fold-out chairs. They face one another, across the gravel road. Their feet reach firmly to the dirt that lines the road.

Each man is pointing upward.

Pointing at an angle of forty-five degrees; pointing with a straight, taut arm; pointing at an upward that is somewhere high above the midpoint of the road.

GRAVITY IS THE THING

PART 1

1.

2010

A tall man at the airstrip took my suitcase.

He was tall in a long, lean, bony way, which he had tried to disguise with loose clothes. But at each gust of wind, the clothes clung fiercely, so that mostly he was out there on his own. A long, narrow flagpole of a man. He had a headful of curls, and these were unafraid. Crazed and rollicking, those curls.

"Snow," he said, smiling, as he took my suitcase from me. I stared.

I'll step right into my story at this point. Abigail Sorensen, but you can call me Abi, thirty-five years old, a nail-biter, former lawyer, owner/ manager of the Happiness Café on Sydney's Lower North Shore, mother of a four-year-old named Oscar—and this day—the day that I'm describing right now—well, it had started at 6 am.

The taxi driver was twenty minutes late but this made him wild-eyed with excitement. "You'll make your flight! I swear it on my mother's life!"

Traffic was backed up right across the bridge and his enthusiasm dimmed. He frowned quietly, moving his hands around the steering wheel. He'd been a little reckless with his mother's life: he saw that now.

Then, just as we got into free, fast road and his spirits picked up, eyes wild again, there was a random sobriety check.

"Can you believe this?" he said.

"I know," I agreed. "Who's drinking at this hour?"

But the driver's face darkened. "Who drinks at this hour? You do not know the half of it!"

He was still moody when we pulled up at the airport. He'd lost all interest in my flight.

At the Jetstar counter, a woman with sharp edges typed at a computer in a slow, measured way, my breathlessness filling up the quiet around the tapping. Without looking sideways, the woman tagged my suitcase and sent it away on a conveyor belt.

So there went my suitcase—nervous, proud, excited—starting its journey alone, ahead of me.

In Melbourne, I met up with my suitcase again. It's just your regular, black vinyl case that can stand on its own two wheels and roll along, but I felt close to it, and protective, anyway. We took the train across the city, my suitcase and I, to the smaller airport at Moorabbin.

The final leg of the journey made me uncomfortable, partly because I don't like the expression "final leg." Who started that, anyway? That dividing of rooms and people into feet, dividing of journeys into legs? The same person who tangled the ocean?

Also, it was the smallest plane I'd ever seen; I didn't know they made them that small. My suitcase would never fit, let alone me and that big pilot.

"My luggage won't bring the plane down, will it?" I joked.

The pilot turned a critical gaze on the suitcase. "Why?" he asked. "What's in it?"

He tested its weight with one of his big arms, laughed softly, and got on with checking over the plane.

It seemed like the kind of thing someone else should do, checking the plane—if we have to divide a journey into legs, we may as well divide it into fields of expertise. As it was, the whole thing seemed very Sunday-afternoon amateurish. He was saddling up his horse.

That plane is not a horse!

"She's a twin-engine Cessna," the pilot called, which was unnerving.

The letters *OWW* were printed on the airplane's side, and I was thinking that this was a mistake when the other passenger turned up.

"Don't you think that's tempting fate?" I asked her, as she put her suitcase down beside me. "Or defining destiny? At some point, that plane is going to have to say *oww*."

"Ha ha," said the woman beside me. Two words: ha ha. Difficult to interpret.

"It's going to fall out of the sky," I elaborated. "Or a missile's going to hit it."

"Hm," the woman said, noncommittal.

She was maybe thinking that missiles were unlikely. This was just a flight to an island in Bass Strait, the stretch of water dividing the mainland from Tasmania.

I will be honest with you: I had never once turned my mind to that stretch, nor to any islands it might contain, until just last week, when the invitation arrived. Turns out there are over fifty tiny, windswept islands in Bass Strait, including King Island (which I already knew: the cream and the Brie) and Flinders Island (where, in 1830, they exiled the last of Tasmania's Aboriginals). Taylor Island, where I was headed, is southeast of Flinders, has a population of three hundred, a lighthouse, and is "renowned" for its tiger snakes, muttonbirds, and yellow-throated honeyeaters.

After a moment of silence, the other passenger started talking.

She was oblong-shaped, this passenger, dressed in a tangerine suit, and she said that her name was Pam.

"Just plain Pam," she explained, "though wouldn't I have killed to be called Pamela?"

You wouldn't have to kill someone. You could just change your name by deed poll.

But I let it pass.

Pam, it turned out, was a local of the island heading home after a holiday.

Easily, her favorite part of her trip had been the Chinatown in Melbourne, because Pam was a lover of steamed pork dumplings, and a collector of bootleg DVDs.

It was a four-and-a-half-hour flight, and we all fit into the plane—the big pilot, me, Pam, the luggage—no trouble.

Sometimes the pilot spoke into his radio: "Oscar Whisky Whisky, how do you read?" his voice cool and low, and "how do you read" forming a single word, "*howdoyouread.*" Each time he said it, I would think: *How do I read? Well, I turn the pages, my eyes scan the letters, I . . .* even though I tried to stop myself. Even when the joke got old.

Pam kept shouting stories the whole way, only pausing when the pilot asked how to read. Pam told stories about chopsticks, and how she learned to use them, and strawberry farmers, and how they have bad teeth. ("Oh, the stories I could tell!" *But you are*, I thought.)

It's funny the way relationships can shift. Originally I had been the queen bee—making my humorous remarks about *oww*, while Pam was demure. But right away she had stepped up to take over the role. Maybe doubting my ability.

At first, I ranged around for matching stories, but the effort of shouting them over the roar of the plane—or maybe the air outside was roaring?—either way, it made my stories increasingly pointless, unworthy, so I stopped talking, the way you do at nightclubs, and it was all just reaction: smile, frown, exclaim, or laugh at Pam.

Pam seemed happy.

*

But now here I was, standing on the airstrip on Taylor Island, and the tall man was saying, "Snow!"

Just confusion, that was all I had left.

"Snow" could be a command. *All visitors, on arrival at the island, are required, please, to snow.*

Or it could be the tall man's name. In which case, I should shake his hand and say, "Sorensen. Abigail Sorensen."

There was a long, formal pause. The tall man's smile faded. Creases settled into the edges of his eyes. Something seemed to cross his face—a mild incredulity, I realized, at the fact that I was standing there, staring at him.

Then the tall man found his smile again and pointed to a sky that was heavy with clouds: "Snow," he repeated. "Anytime now." And he turned away, still smiling.

He swung my suitcase onto the back of a golf buggy, and gestured for me to climb aboard.

I called goodbye to Pam and to the pilot. But Pam was crouching by an open suitcase, drawing out a long, black coat.

The pilot was scratching at the plane's fuselage. Maybe he'd seen sense about the *OWW* and was scratching off the letters.

The path left the airstrip behind right away, leaning into curves like a yacht on a choppy sea. It carried the golf buggy through fields, sharp winds, and late afternoon.

We passed a letter box encrusted with dried starfish. A general store with an axe leaning up against its doorframe. A café with a chalkboard: FISH STEW AND MASHED POTATOES.

The ocean appeared now and then, gray and calm like an obliging old dog that shows up to walk by your side for short spells, but then disappears to explore.

We took a corner and, across a field, two men sat on opposite sides of a gravel road. The men were on fold-out chairs. Each was pointing up. Each was pointing at an angle just above the midpoint of the road.

The buggy turned another corner, and the pointing men were gone.

I looked sideways, but the tall man's hands were on the steering wheel, his eyes on the path ahead.

2.

The invitation had been printed on a shiny white notecard.

> *You are invited to*
> *An all-expenses paid Retreat*
> *Where you will Learn the **Truth** about*
> The Guidebook.

The "Truth" about *The Guidebook*! That made me laugh. A chapter from this book had been sent to me, out of the blue, when I was fifteen years old, and chapters had been arriving in the mail ever since. It was a self-help book that offered advice on how to live my life. I knew nothing about who was sending the excerpts (or why), other than that they called themselves "Rufus and Isabelle."

The invitation enclosed flight details and a promise that I would be collected from the airstrip and transported to the Hyacinth Guesthouse.

Now, here I was at the guesthouse, and a woman was handing me a form. She was the manager, she said, and her name was Ellen. A name of pleasing symmetry (almost), and a pretty lilt when pronounced, this Ellen had fine white hair, and glasses with a pale pink chain that swooped down from each of her ears like curtains on a stage. After I filled in the form, Ellen glanced at it and said, "You'll be turning thirty-six tomorrow, I see," which was quick—noticing my date of birth and adding up the years like that so fast.

Older people, I have noticed, are sharp-minded.

"We've home-baked cake and coffee every afternoon," she continued, "in the lobby here. You've missed it today, but it being your first day, well,

I set a slice aside for you, and I've just now put it in your room when I lit the fire."

She came out from behind the counter with a key.

"Here we are then," she said. "You're in room twelve." And she led me up three flights of stairs, my suitcase thumping behind me.

We paused at each landing so she could point out the rugs.

What? I almost thought. Do you mean me not to step on the rugs with my muddy boots? Or not to trip? Or do you just mean, *Look—look at those beautiful rugs*? But sometimes I get tired of my own confusion and overanalysis, and also I was fond of Ellen—the name, the birthday, the cake, the fireplace—so I was careful of the rugs, and smiled at them kindly, and I didn't bother thinking anything.

The room was warm and quiet.

Ellen's footsteps faded down the stairs, pausing at each landing. They slowed and paled into the distance, and so did the beating of my heart and the clamor of the day.

The window felt cold to my fingertips. It looked over the ocean, which blended into sky and into dusk. The wind rustled the waves and the trees, and slapped something sharp against the glass.

I stepped back and sat on the bed.

Here I was, unexpectedly, in a warm, quiet room with dark floorboards. A tapestry rug in olive green on the floor; framed antique maps on the wall. My suitcase stood in the corner, and it seemed content. By the fireplace, a tiny table with elegant legs offered a slice of frosted cake.

And the tall man had said there would be snow. Anytime now, outside this window, snow. Snow in December! But that's the way down south. Things begin to turn as you approach the poles; a giant hand tilting up the hourglass.

At least that's what I thought in my lyrical mood. I know that it's nonsense. It's just that it was unseasonably cold.

But at that point, happiness and calm were untangling themselves, all the way through my body, like a long, black coat drawn from a suitcase. At the same time, cold shots of excitement touched the back of my neck.

It was the first time I'd taken a break from the café in three years. It was the first time I'd flown in an airplane since Oscar was born.

It was not the first time I'd left Oscar with my mother overnight—but this was going to be for *three* nights, so it was the longest.

My lips felt dry—the cracking wind—but I was smiling anyway. A bird crossed the frame of the window, trailing night. I remembered the two pointing men we'd passed in the golf buggy, and had the sudden sense that I'd seen them before.

Or I'd seen that formation, or a piece of it: a man sits by the side of a road, pointing at the sky.

I realized I was in a dream state. I would call my mum, I decided, and check on Oscar, and then have a bath and sit by the fire in my pajamas and I'd make myself a cup of tea—there were tea bags fanned out on the sideboard alongside a shy electric jug and two upturned teacups; I could see chamomile and spearmint—and I'd eat that cake, one teaspoon at a time. I breathed in the strange happiness, and smiled my cracked, dry lips, and—

The door rattled.

A piece of notepaper slid beneath it. Footsteps hurried down the corridor, away.

I picked up the paper.

You missed three, it said. *Now what?*

3.

I didn't know what the note meant.

You missed three. Now what?

I felt irked.

Have you seen the movie *Bolt*? It's about a dog that believes it's a super-dog. The dog has John Travolta's voice and a quiet pride in its own super-strength and super-bark. The humor comes from the dog running around New York, believing in itself.

"*I am irked!*" says the villain, at one point in the movie, and Oscar turned to me and explained: "See that man? His name is Irked."

Kids! The world is so confusing, but now and then they think they've got a piece of it down: when somebody says, *I am* ——, they are giving their name.

You think you've got life figured out, you lean back on the couch—and then it hits.

You don't have superpowers. You haven't even got basic grammar.

So, this was me in a guesthouse with cake, towels, snow clouds, and I had figured out that *this* night was for happiness.

But no. Underneath the door, a cold truth. *You missed three. Now what?*

Who likes to be told that they missed something? Let alone *three* things. Who likes that accusatory tone?

I suppose calm, sensible people might raise their eyebrows: "I did? I apologize. Can you remind me precisely what I missed?"

But I am a person who will rise up: a student of Pilates *lifting*, puppet strings hooked onto my head, the puppetmaster *raising* my whole body. (You get taller and you get inner-core strength when you do that at Pilates.) But when the voice of authority addresses me in a singsong tone—*You missed three!*—I rise up, hackles up, claws out: *I DID NOT! I DID NOT EVEN MISS ONE!* Even when I haven't got a clue what they're on about. Maybe I did miss three? Maybe I missed fifteen.

I threw open the door, but there was nobody there so I slammed it shut.

In my irritation, I ate the cake. Without a cup of tea, without a bath, without a robe, without calm by the fire, just scoop, scoop, scoop with the silver spoon.

I saw what I'd done and became angrier. I considered calling the front desk to ask Ellen for another slice, please.

"On account of I accidentally ate this one."

But that was no excuse.

I called my mum instead, and she gave me a detailed recount of how and where she'd read *Where is Hairy Maclary?* to Oscar that day. Ten or twelve times *at least*, she said. She recited the story for me—as proof, I suppose. It has pleasing rhythms. It calmed me. Next she set out the complicated rules of each game she and Oscar had played in the garden. This also manifested as a form of meditative hypnosis.

I can't remember their other activities. She described them all; the day was crammed with them. Also, he'd had a good dinner, apparently: lamb cutlets, mashed potato, carrots, a slice of whole wheat bread with a little butter. All the food groups.

She was marking out the coordinates of her grandmothering for me, and they were excellent. They always are. From free-range mother to mindful grandma. Each time she takes care of Oscar, I think I should model my parenting on her. But when I take him back I return to normal life: go to work, collect Oscar from day care, get home, drop my bag and shoes on the floor before we eat fish and chips in front of the TV.

Oscar was asleep, which was sad, but was also, actually, a relief. I love hearing his tiny "hello?" on the phone, but then I don't know what to do with it. We have plenty to say in person, but on the phone? Well, all I can think to do is to reach down and hug his voice.

"Have you found out what it's all about yet?" Mum wanted to know. "Have you shaved your head and signed over your fortune?"

She was pretty sure it was a cult. She'd been joking to all her friends, "Abi's off to join a cult!"

But she'd also been saying, quite seriously, to me: "I think I should come with you, Abi. They might be going to sell you into slavery or turn you into a drug mule."

"They'd only do the same to you," I pointed out.

"Oh no," she said, "I wouldn't let them."

"Well, I won't let them either," I promised, and this seemed to cheer her up.

In fact, I knew what would happen here.

There'd be more of the same empty/weird stuff as in the chapters I'd received in the mail, only they'd keep making tantalizing promises that something better—the *point*, the *answer*, the **Truth**—was just around the corner! At the end, they'd tell me that this *really valuable* information would be available once I'd signed up for their two-thousand-dollar seminar and purchased this five-volume DVD.

But if they wanted to give me a free getaway and a boost of self-help? Well, great. I'd have no problem refusing to commit to anything further: I had my café and my kid. No free time and hardly any money.

And they couldn't *make* me do anything. I also have a law degree.

So I chatted with Mum on the phone, scraped myself into pajamas, dragged back the bedclothes and fell asleep.

4.

The next morning, I had a birthday room service breakfast in bed. It was excellent: crisp granola sparked with cinnamon and pecans, rich dark coffee with cream; the sky streaked with wind and gray through the softly rattling windows; the bed big and white. I took deep, shining breaths of it all, and let myself be both sad and glad, the way you're supposed to, and felt my lost birthdays, all the lost birthdays stacking up behind me, all the anger and the anguish, the terror and the hope, all the harshness and the sweetness, the spoon a silver glint against the white.

Then I went downstairs to learn the truth.

5.

It was the tall man; the man who'd collected me from the airstrip and offered *snow*. He was the teacher.

Or whatever you call the person in charge at a self-help retreat on an island in Bass Strait.

As I walked into the conference room of the Hyacinth Guesthouse, he offered me a manila folder.

"Don't open it just yet," he said. "Take a seat."

The conference room had much the same ambience as the guest rooms. Rugs, an open fire, framed prints of antique balloons on the walls. Narrow windows leaned into a cold, gray view of rocky slope running down to surly sea. Armchairs were scattered about like uncertain guests at a party.

A very slight woman sat in one of these armchairs, ankles crossed, manila folder resting on her lap. She was frowning to herself. She caught my eye, threw me a quick smile, then resumed the frown, deepening it now. Maybe making up for time lost with that smile. (Or had my face reminded her of something troubling? An unreturned library book, say, or soup she'd defrosted weeks before but never eaten.)

Across the room, their backs to me, two men stood at a table, each holding a large, white plate. One was broad-shouldered with red hair.

I'll tell you this for free. I like a man with broad shoulders and red hair.

The other guy, taller and darker, hovered over a tray of pastries with a pair of silver tongs. He murmured something in the tone of an uncertain joke, and the broad guy laughed, tipping sideways with his laughter. There was a note of golden warmth in his laugh (in my view, anyway), and in the way that he straightened up again so easily, ready for the next laugh.

I sat down. A few more people arrived, one at a time, some looking around in bemusement, others bright-eyed, or with grim expressions that seemed to say: *I'm suspending judgment but I won't suspend it long.*

At each new arrival, the tall man handed over another manila folder. "Don't open it yet," he said. "Take a seat." Again and again, the same phrases. I wondered why he didn't vary them.

But then he did. "Not to open yet," he said. "Please, for now, sit down."

Hm, I thought. Maybe stick to the original. The brief expression of distress on his face suggested he was thinking the same thing.

Eventually, his stack of folders was gone.

The room was all rustle and movement now. There were maybe twenty-five or thirty people, a mix of men and women, a scattering of races and accents. I heard American, something that might be Eastern European, and a New Zealand accent in there, but otherwise mostly Australian.

Some were at the table helping themselves to the pastries and coffee, chatting about pastries and coffee—and about weather, islands, breakfast, flights; a few at the windows, hands pressed to the glass; some sitting in the chairs, silent, or talking low-voiced. ("I like your shoes," I heard a man say to a woman. "Oh!" said the woman, and she swung her feet from side to side, admiring the shoes herself. I admired them too. Such a glossy purple.)

Nobody mentioned the strangeness of us being here.

I stayed quiet. It was my birthday. That exempted me from small talk.

Now came an unexpected twist in the day.

That's overstatement; it wasn't a twist. Only, the next thing took the mood around a curve. The tall guy strode to a sideboard, messed with an iPod, and music filled the room. "Read My Mind" by the Killers.

I love that song! It gives me this excited feeling like it has a secret message just for me. It's more the song's tone than its lyrics; I can't really figure those out.

Anyhow, the music starts and the tall guy stands there, expressionless.

Around me the chatter stops, the glossy-purple-shoe woman does a cute tapping thing with her glossy purple shoes, a guy with a goatee drums a quick flourish on his armrest.

And I have this surge of what my brother, Robert, and I used to call the *Breakfast Club* vibe. The feeling that something swift and strong is going to happen or unfold; that here, among these people, are stripes of energy, smoldering and poised, ready to snap into being.

Somewhere behind me, a guy sings along with a line of the song in a good, strong, unaffected voice. Another guy's voice, also strong, shoots back the next line, and people smile or chuckle softly at this, so then I know I'm right about the *Breakfast Club* vibe.

I felt happy-birthday good. People are going to tell secrets here, I thought. People are going to surprise themselves and one another. We will clash and cry and challenge one another; we may even change our appearances for the better—take down our hair or muss it up! remove our spectacles! tear off our shirtsleeves and use one as a bandana?—and certainly some of us will sleep together.

I hoped I'd be one of the ones doing the sleeping together and, in particular, I hoped I'd sleep with the redheaded guy.

Or that one over there with the flat cap and hipster beard. His smile was friendly.

I hadn't properly checked out all the men in the room, so there might have been further possibilities. I would certainly have been happy to sleep with either of the two men who'd sung along just then, although I couldn't quite see their faces.

The song ended.

Entertain me, I thought suddenly, looking at the tall man. Out of the blue, I felt supercool. I looked right up at him, with a challenge on my face. *Entertain me.*

The tall man waited. He let the silence carry on. He glanced back at me, like he was all set to meet my challenge.

Nice, I thought, in reference to his glance.

Then he spoke in a low, soft, reasonable voice.

"You might remember," he said, "twenty years ago, when you first received a letter in the mail?"

6.

He meant the letter enclosing the first chapter of *The Guidebook*.

We all knew what he meant. At least, I assume we did. There was a wonderful rush of goose bumps across the room.

"Open your manila folders," the tall man said next, same tone of voice.

Raised eyebrows, opening folders. Inside was a copy of that first letter.

"Touché," someone murmured.

"Um," a voice responded, "in what way?"

The tall man blinked at this exchange, then recovered. "Kindly read over the letter," he instructed, and we obeyed. People sighed, giggled, or swore as they read.

I looked over shoulders, confirming that the other letters were essentially the same as mine. Then I read it:

Dear Abigail,
Congratulations.

Of all the people, in all the world, you have been chosen to receive this.

Enclosed is Chapter 1 of The Guidebook. *One day, this book will change the world. In the meantime, it will change your life.*

We invite you, please, to read this chapter.

No. More than read it. Eat it. Devour it. Freeze it into ice cubes and place these in a glass of lemonade. (Drink the lemonade.) Dive into it! Swim through it. Love it. Embrace it! Wear it as a coat!

As you may notice, Chapter 1 is very short. Some might even say peculiarly short. This happens throughout The Guidebook. *Some chapters are just a line or two!*

But where is the rule that says a chapter must be ten to twelve pages?
Nowhere.

Would you like to continue receiving chapters from The Guidebook? *Do you dare to embrace this opportunity? Do you wish your life to soar to heights beyond your wildest dreams?*

If so, please write to us at PO Box 2828, Katoomba, NSW, with the single word: YES.

Yours with alacrity,

Rufus and Isabelle

PS It would be best if you kept this to yourself.

I looked up from the letter.

"Are *you* Rufus?" demanded a woman, pointing at the tall man at the front. A plastic frangipani flower was woven into this woman's ponytail; I tried not to judge her for this.

The tall man held up his palms. "My name is Wilbur," he said.

There was an interested silence.

"Not Rufus," he clarified, somewhat unnecessarily.

"So you're *not* the Rufus who sent us the chapters?" the frangipani woman asked, in a penetrating, cross-examiner's voice.

Good grief, I thought.

"I hope he's not that Rufus," I murmured, and people around me laughed. This warmed my heart.

However, not everyone laughed. Some, including frangipani-flower-woman, turned to me with reproachful expressions, as if I might have hurt Wilbur's feelings.

But honestly, the tall man appeared to be no older than me. If he was Rufus, he had started sending us *The Guidebook* when he was around fifteen. The idea that a teen had been "guiding" me was pretty unsettling.

"What I want to know," said a man with a wry and sonorous voice, "is why I ever agreed to keep *receiving* these chapters."

There was more laughter at this. I joined in. I tried to see the speaker, and he caught my eye—he had small, round spectacles; large mouth; high cheekbones—and he smiled at me. *Oh, I'll sleep with you too,* I decided generously.

"Of *all* the people in *all* the world!" a voice proclaimed, two seats along from me, and again, everybody laughed.

That speaker had a bland, pale-pink look. *I'm not going to sleep with you*, I apologized.

The tall man—Wilbur—nodded toward wry-and-sonorous. "This is precisely the question," he said. "Close your eyes. Are everybody's eyes closed? Good. Now, think back to the day when you first received this letter."

My eyes snapped open.

Wilbur caught this and gave me a stern look. Quickly, I closed them.

"Consider this." His voice dropped lower and took on a sway, like a voice on a meditation tape. Immediately, I grew sleepy. "Consider this. This letter was sent out to one hundred and twenty young people. Only forty-three responded with a *yes*. Over the years, that forty-three has slipped down to thirty-one. Of those thirty-one, only twenty-six agreed to come to this retreat. *You are those twenty-six.*"

That was good drama.

"Now ask yourselves," Wilbur continued, "why *did* you say yes? Why did you never *cancel* the subscription? Why are *you* the twenty-six?"

"Well, *I* think—" began a woman's voice, but Wilbur said, "Shhh. Close your eyes and think back."

7.

At our place, the mail was always in an old frying pan on the countertop. I don't know why.

It also contained a faded tennis ball, random elastic bands, and a little plastic Snoopy who got tossed about and clanged against the pan whenever you leafed through the mail. He seemed resigned to this.

On this particular day, I'd just walked up the driveway after school when Mum came tearing out of the house. She was shouting, "Robert! We forgot you've got that appointment!"

"What appointment?" I asked.

Mum ignored me. She threw open the screen door and ducked back inside. I could hear her shouting: "Robert! Come on! We've got to go right now!"

I waited in the driveway beside the car, interested to see what would happen.

The door flew open again and Mum was back. She ran down the steps to the car, opened the driver's door, registered me, and smiled a bit maniacally while she hollered: "ROBERT!" She was cradling something in her other arm, as if it were an infant. I can't remember what it was. Not an actual infant, I'm sure.

A couple of minutes later, my brother, Robert, wandered out onto the porch, squinted up at the sky then down at me and across at Mum. He'd stayed home from school that day, feeling dizzy. It seemed to me that you could just as well be dizzy at school as at home, but I kept that to myself. He was wearing his old tracksuit pants and a gray T-shirt, and his clothes seemed droopy and loose.

"What appointment?" Robert asked.

"You know, the thing with that doctor; the doctor who has the . . . he has the—"

"The elegant moustache?" I suggested. "The habit of stroking the porcelain cat on his desk?"

"The collection of elves locked in a box, pounding to get out with tiny bruised and bloodied fists?" Robert tried.

"The *fish tank*!" shouted Mum, relieved. "He has a fish tank in his office! Come on! We have to go!"

"Ah." Robert and I nodded wisely to each other. "Of course. The doctor with the fish tank."

Mum threw something at me—it was the object she had under her arm; I remember what it was now: a watering can. Droplets spilled out onto my wrist as I caught it. "Finish watering the house plants!" she said.

"Why?" I inquired.

She and Robert were getting in the car.

I studied the watering can: so twee and little, neat and efficient, tip, move, tip, move, tip.

When I looked up, they were driving down the road. Robert didn't wave at me. He was facing straight ahead. I watched them turn left at the T, and the car seemed to me to be a bright, little, twee, little, efficient, little watering can itself. I don't know why.

Inside, I opened my schoolbag and took out a bunch of notes about excursions and new uniform rules, and carried them to the rusty frying pan. (It wasn't just a place for stamped mail, you understand: it was the meeting point for all written communications.)

As I was about to drop in the notes, I saw a thin brown envelope addressed to me, *Abigail Sorensen*.

Right away, I knew it was a letter from a film producer saying they wanted to make one of my horror movie scripts into a movie.

Zing! Right up from my chest and across my face, I was so excited.

Even though I'd never actually *written* a horror movie script. Let alone sent one to producers. I just had a fierce intention of doing so, one of these days.

I opened the envelope, revising my excitement as I did, so as to keep it realistic. More likely, it was a film producer who'd *heard* about my fierce plans to write a horror movie, and now wanted to tell me that s/he admired such fierceness, and could s/he please offer me a million dollars to write a script?

But it was not from a film producer. It was the letter enclosing the first chapter of *The Guidebook*.

I remember I read the letter and laughed. *Of all the people in all the world.* I was hilarious with laughter. I couldn't wait for Robert to get home from the doctor with the fish tank so we could rip this thing apart.

Not literally. You know what I mean.

Then I read the enclosed chapter. It was printed on a single sheet of paper. I recall exactly what it said:

Chapter 1

Welcome.

We begin with a question and a reprimand.

The question:

Did you find this book in the self-help section of the bookstore?

The reprimand:

Why?

Sweet antelope, dear reader, what were you doing in the self-help section of your bookstore! Are you a fool or a baboon? Which? Do you think that the answer can be found in self-help? Do you think that the moon has a deficiency of iron and it is that which explains its wan coloring? If so, reader, get away! Do not scald this page with your plaintive, pleading eyes, do not blink your turtle tears upon this print!

We do not want you reading our book!

Get away!

Ha!

Just joking.

You can read it.

Now, tell us quick, did we alarm you? Were you scratching the back of your neck, embarrassed and confused? Well, sweet reader, let us offer you a warning: Here, in your hands, is a book that will keep you on your toes. This book intends to shock and jolt, and you, in turn, will kick and bite, but we (in our turn) will never let you down. The covers of this book—midnight blue and flecked in gold— these covers are our arms and they embrace you.

We do not mind where you found this book, though
we prefer not to call it self-help. For what is the
point in that? You can help yourself to the fish
in the sea, you can help yourself to a coconut
treat. You already know how to help yourself, yet
you do not!

So this is a we-help book.

It is we who plan to help. Not you.

That was it.

The whole chapter. Done.

I felt strange.

I mean, the first few lines, I laughed aloud. Then I stopped. The laughter hung around in the kitchen, growing uncomfortable, mumbling questions about when the party was going to start again. But I'd gone quiet. I had this sense that the authors of the book knew I'd come here to mock them, but they'd stuck out a foot for me to stumble over and were ready to catch me as I fell.

It is we who plan to help. Not you.

Partly, the strangeness was the cognitive disjunction: this was a sheet of printed paper that had been mailed to me, a girl in my kitchen; but, according to the words, this was a book, its covers midnight blue and flecked in a gold, and I was a girl in the self-help section of a bookstore.

I hid the letter and chapter in my bedroom, wrote *YES* on the back of a retro New York postcard and mailed it to the PO address.

I think I might have done this because it was so easy. I had a lot of homework to do, most of which seemed elaborate and tiresome. Whereas writing the word *YES*; taking a stamp; walking down the street to post it—that was a piece of cake.

Also, it struck me as supercool, superslick to use the retro New York postcard, so that was also a motivating factor.

Although I regretted this the moment I posted it. I'd had the postcard for years! It was from a street fair in Coolangatta, where I'd been on holiday, aged ten, with my best friend (and neighbor) Carly Grimshaw and her family. I'd been saving it for something special.

After that, I received chapters of *The Guidebook* regularly. No covering letters, just chapters, and in no particular order. The second one, for example, was Chapter 47. Then we skipped back to Chapter 11. Most were extremely short. I liked that about them. Again, they compared favorably to the reading I had to do for school.

I remember one:

Chapter 25

```
100 watts. But how many whys? How many ifs?
  And what about the whens?
```

That was the entire chapter, and I found it extremely profound.

Sometimes they sounded like a regular self-help book, but they always veered off-track in the end. Here's an example:

Chapter 9

```
It's simple, life. You just follow a rule or two.
Always keep an eye out for a fireworks display.
Don't brush your hair when it's wet. Teach your-
self to understand the wind. Never put a plastic
bag over your head. If you see a trampoline, jump
on it, jump higher! Never stick a knife in the
toaster. Do a thing you fear every other day. Raw
chicken? Avoid! Don't walk past a row of police
cars, snapping off the antennae one by one, and
```

gathering them into your arms like kindling for a
campfire. Never do that.

My parents noticed the envelopes eventually, and read a few chapters themselves, but quickly lost interest, finding them mystifying and
harmless, like my homework or my music. Sometimes the chapters gave
me instructions, simple tasks to complete: sign up for a martial arts
class, try this dance step, photograph the clouds, procure a dandelion,
eat a slice of cinnamon toast. Some of these I did, many I ignored. Also,
near the end of each year, a letter would arrive from Rufus and Isabelle,
urging me to write, and then send in, a few pages of "reflections" on the
year just past.

Alternatively, I was offered the option of canceling my "free subscription" at any time by sending them a note containing the single word *NO*.

I know exactly why I never did.

8.

Wilbur cleared his throat.

"You can open your eyes now," he said.

It had only been a few minutes, but people straightened, rubbed their
faces and yawned, like preschoolers waking up from nap time.

"Over the next two days," Wilbur declared, "I will lead you in a series
of group activities. These will be fun!" He hesitated, as if doubting that
assertion, then carried on. "Tomorrow night, I will share with you the
truth about *The Guidebook*."

Ha!

The *better*, the *answer*, the *promise*. But we won't get it tomorrow night,
I thought. There'll be something more. He will yank it from our grasp. "Listen—" Wilbur continued, but a sudden chuckle cut him off. I craned my
neck to see who it was. It was the guy with the red hair. I smiled at him.
His eyes crinkled in reply. Everything went hazy, and I hallucinated

ribbons and martini glasses. What I mean by that is, I wanted to sleep with him.

I turned back to the front.

"But listen," Wilbur repeated, his voice suddenly urgent, or pleading. "Only certain among you will be chosen to hear the truth. Please do not be sad if you're not chosen."

Sparks flew up in the fireplace. Everyone was silent and thoughtful.

"It is what it is," a woman suggested.

"Right," Wilbur agreed, brightening. "So it is!"

And the first day of activities began.

9.

My memory of that day has collapsed into the following glimpses. We are buttoning our coats, turning up our collars, tramping behind Wilbur into the bluster of the wind. Above us, skidding clouds.

Now we are in a field. Wilbur is handing out sacks that smell of horses and hay. He is shouting instructions. We are climbing *into* the sacks, lining up side by side for a sack race. Unexpected! The strange awkward loping of a sack race. (I am winning the race for a moment! Then tipping sideways into rutted grass. Bruising my hip. Coming in last. Oh well.)

We are tying our feet together for a three-legged race! My ankle is tied to the leg of the man with the sonorous voice and round spectacles! One minute, he's not there, and then he is. Beside me, leaning down, his hand brushing mine as he loops the rope around and pulls it tight. He looks at me and shrugs. "Okay?" His eyes, behind their spectacles, are smoky gray. We both laugh and I'm thinking, *He chose me for this race! He chose me!* Now we're running together, the heat of it, the panting breath, an even rhythm, a jagged rhythm, the pull of his body, his leg against mine, our legs scissoring back and forth!

We don't win; we come in maybe fourth.

Now our legs are free again, strange to be loose and free after a three-legged race! The smoky-gray-eyed man has drifted away, much like smoke itself.

Wilbur is pointing out a long, low, brick wall. He is telling us to walk along the wall. Single file, we walk, arms out for balance. Somebody stumbles, jumps smartly down and climbs up again, all in a flash.

We are racing down a grassy slope, arms outstretched again, eyes tearing up in the wind, leaping onto the sand dunes. Everybody laughs.

"This is a fitness camp!" somebody suggests.

"No," says Wilbur. "No, it's not." He seems disconcerted.

We are on a long stretch of empty, cold beach. A lighthouse on a cliff. Someone shouts over Wilbur's voice, "There's a whale!" Pointing fingers, squinting eyes, a distant haze rising out of the gray. The pale, pale pink cliffs.

Wilbur wants us to play leapfrog. Firm hands press against my back.

"It *is* a fitness camp!" people shout.

Wilbur frowns.

There's an urgent life and laughter to the day, I remember. It's a day that has leaped out of its bed and is dancing around its room. A vibrancy, an intensity—which is *strange*, because this man, this stranger, is making us race up hills, across fields, along walls, for no *apparent reason*, and yet, rather than querying this, refusing, demanding explanations, we are laughing, joking, and delighting in it—and I realize why.

It's a competition! *Only certain among you will be chosen to hear the truth.* Everybody wants to be chosen. Not only do we not complain, we *embrace* the day. Personalities are varnished. Voices rise, laughter arpeggios. It's like a reality TV show, and I find myself peering around, looking for the hidden cameras.

But how do we know the criteria for selection? I wonder, watching a woman flaring out her hair as she offers chewing gum around. She collects the gum wrappers back, and presses these into her pocket.

Could the criteria be the furnishing of chewing gum combined with the thoughtful collection of litter?

Probably not, I decide.

Most people seem to have reasoned that *vivacity* is key. They are speaking in bursts to each other, their words flying out in the wind, their words not the point. Like extras in a film, *chatting animatedly in the background.*

A woman turns a cartwheel! It's the small woman who had frowned when I arrived this morning. She's sparked up now! Turning cartwheels! She's even smaller than I thought; she's teeny tiny! Perhaps that's why she was frowning? She was thinking to herself: *Why, oh why, am I so small? How can I grow?* Whereas now she has come to terms with her size and thus is turning her cartwheels.

A man, seeing the cartwheel, climbs a tree. He clambers at high speed and then pauses, considering the next branch, fine, twiggy, thin. He decides on a lively leap back to the ground instead. Takes a bow. People applaud.

We are back in the conference room, faces wind-pink, eyes bright, shivering to warmth by the fire. The fruit and pastries are gone; in their place are trays of sandwiches and sushi. My hands are cold.

Wilbur splits us into groups of five or six. He seems to do this in a rapid, random way, grouping people who happen to be standing near each other.

The man with red hair is in my group, as is flat-cap guy with hipster beard.

Also in my group is a wiry little man with a disgruntled scowl, who seems to have an issue with his shoulder. He keeps stretching it, shrugging it, wincing. His shoulder has all his attention.

I worry, on his behalf, that he will be eliminated from *the truth* for inadequate shoulder health.

Wilbur is handing each group a long thin stick, like a cane. "This is a team-building exercise," he says. "Each group must place the stick along outstretched fingertips, and work as one to lower it to the floor."

"Why?" calls Flat-cap, beside me. "Why are we doing team-building exercises when we are, in fact, not teams?"

Others gaze across at him. His friendly smile makes his question perfectly reasonable. Yet it is also a risk. I see that in many faces. You don't get chosen for *the truth* if you're insubordinate!

Wilbur smiles.

Oh. The faces falter. Maybe you do? Maybe he *wants* us to ask questions?

"How do you know," Wilbur responds, "that you are *not* a team?"

Redhead looks directly at me and widens his eyes. *You're the kind of guy I like!* I think directly at him. But then he widens his eyes at the others in our group too.

We lower the stick to the floor. It keeps rising back up! (It's something to do with the collective pressure of our fingers being stronger than the weight of the stick, Flat-cap explains.) Everybody laughs and laughs, and then everybody works together *as teams* to make the stick hit the ground. The wiry guy with the shoulder issue does not appear to enjoy this game and, at one point, almost barks at us to *stop lifting it up*. No way he'll get chosen.

But it doesn't take long for us to sort it out and we feel proud.

Now we are back at the beach, kicking along in the sand, and people are pointing out seals in the whites of waves. Wilbur is handing out blank sheets of paper, which flap violently in the wind. We chase them. Wilbur's face flashes with mild panic. He wants us to make these papers into airplanes, he yells.

We're sitting on rocks, folding paper. We're tossing our planes and our shouts into the wind, where they're turned, turmoiled, dashed against rocks, skimmed along sand, bedraggled by foam.

Wilbur, I notice, stands perfectly still, eyes closed, wearing a strange sad smile, while the wind beats his face, wrenches at his hair, flutters his lashes; a leaf rushes up against his cheek and away and he does not flinch. These are the Roaring Forties, I remember, the strong westerly winds that urge sailing ships around the world and that, farther south, grow even angrier: the Furious Fifties, the Shrieking Sixties.

"I forgot!" Wilbur shouts abruptly, eyes flying open. "You were meant to *write your names* on the paper and *then* make them into airplanes."

He slaps his own knees and bursts out laughing. This is the first time Wilbur has laughed. He seems ecstatic with his laughter. Also, for the first time, people regard him with uncertainty.

"Let's go inside," Wilbur bellows into the wind, "and introduce ourselves!"

The sun fades and tumbles, clouds darken. We gather all the paper planes. It seems a little late in the day for introductions.

10.

Here my memory calms again, so I can return to past tense. We were back in the conference room and this time the food table was bare. I felt sad. I'd been imagining coffee and cake. It seemed rhythmically natural at this point of the day. Specifically, I'd visualized coconut-raspberry-chocolate squares. I had no grounds for visualizing these, I just like them.

At least it was warm in here, and we moved toward the fire, a shivering group again, but Wilbur told us to sit down. He was very quiet: his strangely heady excitement about the paper planes seemed to have fled, leaving him a shell of a man.

I exaggerate, of course. It's another flaw of mine. I just mean he seemed subdued.

Shedding our coats and scarves, we gravitated toward the same chairs we'd chosen earlier. School classroom training: those chairs were our new homes.

Wilbur spoke at serious-information level. "I'm going to invite each of you to come forward and tell us your name and a little about yourself."

He expanded on this a while, but I was thinking about the fact that it was my birthday, and that I had spent the day very oddly, jumping along inside sacks or with my leg tied to a stranger's leg, walking on walls, running down sand dunes, making paper planes. I'd done all this with a group of slightly hysterical yet good-natured strangers, under the tutelage of a tall, lanky man named Wilbur.

My mind wandered to Rufus and Isabelle, authors of *The Guidebook*, and I felt a sad yearning. Where were they, anyway? Too important to be here? Probably American. Vaguely, I wondered how significant our introductions would be, and whether they might determine whether we were chosen for *the truth*.

For the first time, I felt a jolt about that. Now, I didn't think *the truth* would count for much, but I'd been assuming I'd be chosen. Of course I would: It was my birthday! I'd been receiving these chapters for the last twenty years! Tomorrow, however, would no longer be my birthday, and every other person in the room had *also* been getting these chapters for twenty years. In addition, most had been *lively* today, whereas I'd been mild and quiet. I'd laughed and smiled, of course, chatted now and then, but without really having much to say.

If this were a reality TV show, I'd be eliminated. Not right away. The quiet ones slip along unnoticed for a few episodes, but they never make it all the way through. I needed some pizzazz!

"Also," Wilbur was instructing us, "explain *why*—why you said *yes* to these chapters."

"It's my birthday today!" I said suddenly, and to my own surprise. (I don't mean I was surprised that it was my birthday. I knew that.)

There was a sort of uprising of laughter and turning heads.

"So it is, Abigail," Wilbur agreed warmly.

People began exclaiming, "Happy birthday!" The red-haired man said, "Happy birthday, Abigail," in his lovely, broad-shouldered, red-headed voice. I liked how he took my name from Wilbur so effortlessly and adapted it to his own purposes. This struck me as resourceful.

The woman with the frangipani flower in her hair spun around and scolded, "Why didn't you say so *earlier*?" I tried to see beyond the criticism to the humor, but could not locate this in her expression. I smiled, trying to come up with an answer, but I didn't have one. Eventually, she swung back around, still frosty, to face the front again. Why did it *disturb* her so much?

She's jealous! I realized. *She thinks I have an* unfair *advantage! She wants to be chosen for the truth!*

I hoped she was right to think that I had an advantage. It seemed a good sign, the warmth in Wilbur's voice when he said: *So it is, Abigail.*

Wilbur took the reins again. "Introductions," he said. "Let's begin with you." And he pointed at someone just behind me.

11.

Introductions. They seem like a fascinating idea at first, and then, what are they? Just a bunch of names and résumés.

I started off ready to listen carefully, and ended up gazing at a series of vacuum cleaners. (By this I mean they seemed to me to drone.)

A commercial litigator, an admin assistant, chief . . . I don't know, someone was the chief of something. There was also an ENT surgeon whose family had come to Australia from Nigeria when she was twelve years old, a project manager, and everyone else was in IT.

Initially, I was quite interested to hear people's explanations for accepting *The Guidebook.* But people never really know why they've done a thing. Everyone seemed to have first received it in 1990 or 1991, like me, and they'd all been around fifteen or sixteen at the time, again like me. A few talked about being lost as a teenager—depressed, overweight, lonely— so *The Guidebook* struck them as a gift from the universe (or from God, two participants declared). But I had the sense that this was a contrivance, a post hoc reinterpretation, or possibly sycophancy.

Some talked about being plain curious, which was probably more honest, but dull.

A few acknowledged they had no answer. The disgruntled guy with the shoulder seemed incensed to be asked at all. "Why did I accept this book?" he demanded, as soon as he stood up. He frowned fiercely. "How should

I know?" He was in pest control, he added. Pete Aldridge. That was it for his introduction. He sat down right away, which made me like him.

The man with the sonorous voice, spectacles, and smoky eyes also claimed he had no idea. But he claimed this in a friendly, gentle way. When he rose, ready for his turn at introductions, I realized I'd forgotten all about him. Earlier, I'd been willing to have sex with him, but then he'd completely slipped my mind. I felt ashamed at my lack of commitment.

Now I took the opportunity of his introduction to reassess.

Beautiful, wise, self-deprecating smile . . . *Okay, I remember you now. I'm in.*

"My name is Daniel," he said. *Daniel*, I thought, pleased. That's a fine name. Just step into the lion's den, Daniel. Daniel Boone was a *man*, he was a *big man*. I tried to think of a third Daniel and came up with Daniel Day-Lewis, and what an actor he is!

Also, Daniel said that he restored stained glass for a living. That struck me as very limited, and I worried about how he paid the bills, but he went on to explain that there was plenty of work around Sydney—many old houses have leadlight windows, he said—and that he loved the freedom, the solitude, the craft of his work. His passions included his volunteer work with some environmental agency and his brother's yacht. (Chuckles.) Everything he said was thoughtful, as if he was very interested in where his sentences might go next, and then gently pleased with where they went. I saw that, if we made love, it would be one of those beautiful, slow, tender experiences and he would treat me as a fine piece of fragile window glass. Which, when you're in the mood for that sort of thing, is brilliant! The best! If you're in that sort of mood.

One person said her mother had instructed her to say yes to *The Guidebook* chapters, because she (the mother) was highly suspicious about the whole "endeavor," and wanted to keep an eye on it.

This was the petite, cartwheel-turning woman. Her name was Tobi, which made me jealous. I love a boy's name for a girl, especially a girl who does gymnastics.

"Yeah, Mum was ready to report it to the police the moment it took a step wrong," Tobi told us, grinning—she was very self-assured and forthright for one so petite, I thought, but that was petitist of me.

"But the letter told us not to tell *anybody* about *The Guidebook*," frangipani woman called—urgently, smugly, triumphantly—all three of those things. "And yet you told your *mother*!"

Whoa. Frangipani made a good point. Petite Tobi had just admitted she'd broken the first rule. If this was a test, Petite Tobi had just blown it. Of course, I'd told people too. Probably we all had. But I wasn't *confessing* to it.

One person who stood out in the introductions was the glossy-purple-shoe woman. She walked to the front in a lively, bouncing way that made me think: *That must be good exercise, walking around like that all the time!*

Her face matched the bounce, freckles scattered everywhere. She wore a huge knitted jumper and she twisted her hands into this as she began to speak.

"About me," she said, with a suddenly shy smile. "Well, my name is Nicole and when I was sixteen years old, a fortune teller at a fair told me my future."

She paused, and we waited with interest.

"She told me I would meet a man with golden hair, have two children, develop a serious illness in my early thirties, and raise goats."

That got a laugh. She had a good, straight-faced delivery.

"None of those things happened," she continued. "Although, of course, I've *met* men with golden hair. They're around!"

Some laughed again; others were a little too intense and/or confused to laugh.

"But the implication of the fortune was that I'd *marry* the golden-haired man and have two kids with him, right? But no, I did not. I married a Polish guy with black hair and brown eyes, and we have four kids. Again, you could say I fulfilled the prediction, in that I did have two children—but then I had two more. Still, the implication . . ."

People nodded, agreeing. Others stepped up their puzzled expressions, anxious for the point.

"My early thirties have passed without an illness more serious than a cold or swimmer's ear," Nicole carried on, still ticking off predictions. Now she might have been stretching the point. But she was so friendly and warm, I found that I loved her. "And no, I don't raise goats, although we do have a guinea pig."

She assumed a dreamy expression. "Whenever I feel low, I google *raising goats*," she said. There was more laughter, but she continued in the same distant tone: "I have this strange feeling that if I just implemented *that* part of my fate, I could unravel the last twenty years and have them again: the golden-haired man, the two kids, even the serious illness—I've never been properly sick, so I'm drawn to that idea."

Wow, I thought. Watch out, fate might be listening. I admired her recklessness, though.

"But which of your children would you give back?" called a voice. It was disgruntled shoulder guy.

Nicole gave him a startled look.

"If you are going to unravel your life and have only two children, you must return two of the four, no?"

"Right. No. I'm kidding. I wouldn't give any of them back, obviously."

"You wouldn't want to get sick," someone else said. "It's not all it's cracked up to be."

"I know," she said. "I mean, I get that impression. It was a crazy thing to say. Sometimes I just speak without thinking."

There was a knock on the door. Wilbur, who was standing to the right of Nicole, took a sharp, surprised breath. "We're out of time!" he said. "We'll have to finish introductions tomorrow."

So I had a reprieve. There was a minor commotion in the doorway.

It was the hotel manager, Ellen, with a giant birthday cake on a tray. Candles were alight, tiny flames swaying madly together, as she strode in. *Oh, it's somebody's birthday*, I thought, and then I saw people smiling at me, glancing from the cake to me and back, and Ellen and Wilbur both started singing, Ellen in a high, sweet voice, Wilbur in a low rumble: *Happy birthday to you!*

I was, too. Happy, I mean.

12.

The next day, Wilbur forgot about continuing the introductions. So we never heard from me. We also didn't hear from the redheaded-broad-shouldered guy, or Frangipani.

I know those were the missing ones because the first thing that happened that morning—while we were still drifting in, tired and hungover, helping ourselves to the fruit and pastries, relaxed and friendly in the manner of people who have been drinking and joking until late the night before—the first thing that happened was this.

Wilbur began to list the activities he had planned. They were along the same lines as the previous day, so I wasn't concentrating—I was standing at the table, studying the fruit platter—but halfway through Wilbur's speech, Frangipani raised her hand and called, "Don't forget we haven't finished introductions!"

"Oh yes," Wilbur said. "Thank you, Sasha."

Why is he calling her Sasha? I wondered, but then I recalled that frangipani was the flower in her ponytail, not her name.

"It's just, a few of us haven't had a turn yet," Frangipani/Sasha expounded (redundantly).

She still wasn't finished. "There's Abigail, for one," she said. "The birthday girl!" And she turned and pointed. I had a slice of honeydew melon gripped in tongs now, and I felt as if she'd caught me stealing it, the way she pointed. She beamed in a truly alarming way. I assumed she was implying that I was *no longer* the birthday girl? Which made her mad with delight?

Her beam settled into a smirk and she shifted her pointing finger toward the redheaded guy (whose expression, in response, was a master-work in blank) and then she paused, gasped and pointed at herself: "Oh yes, and *me*! We haven't heard from me!"

I suspect she had planned this speech and, in her head, the pause and gasp had sounded genuine. Also, I suspect she'd been working on her introduction, finessing it, all through the night.

"I won't forget," Wilbur promised.

But he did.

At that point, however, he lowered his chin so he was looking at the floor—rather than at us—and spoke in a quick, almost breathless voice: "Between three and four pm today, you will each receive a notice under-neath your door. The notice will tell you whether you have been chosen."

The room grew still. Wilbur's voice had been so quiet and quick that we were waiting for his words to settle into themselves.

He looked up. "Or not," he added.

"Not chosen to hear the truth," Frangipani clarified.

"Right." Wilbur frowned down at the papers in his hands. "If you are *not* chosen, you may prefer to go home at once, rather than to wait until tomorrow. That is your choice, of course. A shuttle will be available to take you to the airfield, and a few flights are scheduled to depart around five pm. For those who *are* chosen, we meet here at five thirty for the truth."

There was a thoughtful pause.

"Out of interest," someone—Daniel—asked, "how many will be chosen?"

Wilbur's face was suddenly profoundly sad. "Come," he said. "Let's begin our program for today."

13.

The night before, there'd been the birthday cake. I'd been handed a large silver knife and told to slice it.

High pressure: everyone watching, slices tipping sideways, inconsistency in portion size, anxiety about whether there'd be enough to go around, and so on. I felt offended by a woman who said, "No thanks," to a slice, then ashamed when I overheard her mention she was diabetic.

Life! It's just a series of humbling lessons.

Over cake, we chatted in our bright-eyed voices. Then Wilbur wished everyone a grand good night (that's what he said, "Have a grand good night"; it put me in mind of both leprechauns and pianos), and he left the room. A moment later, Frangipani also darted from the room, calling over her shoulder: "Bye, everybody! Happy birthday, birthday girl!"

We watched the door close behind her.

"She's sleeping with the teacher?" the guy with the flat cap mused. "Well *played.*"

There was a beat of shock, and then everyone fell about laughing. That was the moment that cracked open the charade, split the day from night. We laughed so hard! Honestly, it was a smooth transition from Flat-cap's joke to phoning in an order to Lola's Woodfired Pizza and uncorking several bottles of wine.

It's a beautiful thing to peel a slice of pizza from an oily cardboard box and realize that you are not alone in being bemused about what the *fuck* you are doing here. That's a quote. "What the fuck are we *doing* here?" someone said, and everyone laughed even harder.

A lot of people swore! This added to my elation. Maybe you tense up when people use bad language, but my whole body relaxes. *Lean back, slouch, there are no rules, these are my people.* Also, people who curse tend to be funnier than those who don't.

(Although swearing every second word? That's swagger, or power play, or lack of imagination.)

Everyone was joking about our teacher, Wilbur, and how he seemed just as confused as we were.

One guy confessed he'd thrown away *every single* chapter of *The Guidebook* he'd received the moment it arrived, and the only reason he'd never canceled was because he could *not* be arsed. So he was here under *entirely* false pretenses, he said. "Am I right?" And everybody agreed, very happily, that yes, he was right.

Others told funny stories about the tasks they'd tried to do—I can't really remember the stories, so possibly they weren't that funny and it was more the wine and the relief. Nicole, the friendly, glossy-shoed woman who had four children (not two), and did not raise goats, said that, when an early chapter instructed her to teach herself to juggle, she'd used fresh eggs.

What?! we all said. *You taught yourself to juggle with eggs?!* We laughed and laughed, but the story wasn't done. She'd taken them out on the balcony, she said, and most had smashed, causing a slippery mess to form, so that she'd skidded, at one point, the egg in her hand flying over the balcony railings *and landing on the head of a passerby.* No joke. Smack onto a man's head.

She had a good, deadpan delivery, Nicole.

A few people said they had read the chapters but never did the tasks, and also, what was up with the notes pushed under our doors the night before?

So then I felt even happier. It turned out almost everyone had got a note like mine *(You missed three. Now what?),* only most had "missed" more than three. Redheaded-guy-with-broad-shoulders, whose name turned out to be Niall, said he'd missed *nineteen*!

It could have been the wine, but we laughed uproariously at that. He warmed to the story, saying he got mad as hell about the note. *"I missed nineteen?! I did not! I did every single one!"* he insisted, without having a *fucking* clue what it was about.

Which was exactly *my* reaction, I said, and I'd only missed three; others laughed at both of us, and said they'd just shrugged, assuming the note was meant for someone else.

Oh, it was like a therapy group for people who get notes under their doors.

We all agreed we'd only come here for the free holiday. Or out of curiosity. Somebody said she was tweeting the whole thing. Somebody else said he was considering writing a piece about it for BuzzFeed.

Then everyone had a theory about what "the truth" was going to be.

"It'll be nothing," someone said. "It'll be your usual self-help hogwash."

Hogwash. We talked about hogwash then, the origin of the word, and somebody got out a smartphone to look it up, but the guy I liked with the beard and the flat cap—his name was Antony; I decided I would remember this by thinking of Cleopatra and snakes—anyway, Antony shouted at her to put it away. "Instant access to answers is *killing* conversation," Antony explained, so the person with the smartphone put it away, ashamed, and everyone fell silent, considering this.

"You see?" Antony grinned. "Conversation killed."

Then his grin broadened and he told us about how, when he came out to his family, at his nineteenth birthday dinner, his mother had said, "Now there's a conversation killer."

So Antony was gay. It was lucky I hadn't told him my plans to sleep with him.

When I tuned back in, everyone was talking about parents, coming out, smartphones, technology, answers, truth, hogs, cars, laundry. I don't know.

"Let me tell you, I will be pissed if I don't get chosen for the truth," somebody announced. "Talking about access to the answers."

"It'll be a pyramid scheme," Petite Tobi declared. "Watch this space."

We made fun of her about *watch this space*, which she took in her stride.

Niall said he thought it would be something about extra-sensory perception.

"What? Why?" we all asked, and he reminded us that Wilbur had played us the song "Read My Mind." "Why else would he have played that?"

"Huh," I said. "I thought he was just setting the mood."

At this, Niall turned his chair slightly so he could face me, consider me.

"I agree with birthday girl," Antony put in, and Niall inclined his head ever so slightly, but kept his gaze on me.

"I bet you a thousand dollars," said a voice, "that we *all* get invited to find out the truth."

It was Daniel. *Oh, Daniel*, I thought, *why do I always forget you?* On the outskirts of the group there, leaning forward with his stained-glass-repairing fingers interwoven. They must be so careful, those fingers.

"Wilbur looked sad, though," Nicole pointed out, "when somebody asked how many would be chosen. Who was it who asked that?"

It had been Daniel himself who asked. So others forgot him too.

"He didn't answer," I remembered.

"Exactly," Daniel said. "Because he knew it would be all of us."

"I bet you a thousand dollars the truth will be something we find out in a series of upcoming seminars," Antony declared, "and I bet you a thousand dollars the seminars will cost a *mint*."

"I haven't got a mint," Niall announced, "but I do have some chewing gum."

"I'm losing track of the thousands," Petite Tobi complained. "Are these separate bets?"

"All bets are off," someone said, but they were just drunk.

"Watch this space!" a voice threw in, to make us all laugh again, and Tobi continued to take the laughter in good grace, although she looked a little bored by it now.

I can't remember what happened after that. Someone stoked the fire and called himself a *fire doctor*. Fire whisperer. We moved our chairs closer and spoke intently. Someone was in love with a woman named Zelda. I told the group that I'd once been married to a man named Finnegan. It seemed connected, somehow.

We talked about sociological jurisprudence and string theory. We took grand statements and illustrated them with amusing anecdotes, so that we never had to explain or even understand the grand statement. Chitchat was thereby elevated, given a theoretical framework.

"I was suspended from high school," I announced, late in the night, sleepy with wine, "for almost blinding a teacher."

But when the others leaned closer, enthralled, I asked if anybody played a musical instrument. I think there was a seamless transition then, to the dialogue inherent in music.

14.

So now it was the day after the birthday cake, pizza, and red wine, and we were following Wilbur's schedule.

First, we undertook further team-building exercises on the beach. These involved balloons, and the balloons either blew away or burst, so it was mostly hilarity rather than team building.

Next, Wilbur announced a yoga class in a field.

Someone asked why couldn't we do the yoga right here on the beach?

But Wilbur explained vaguely that the field he had in mind was "a very good field." A little harried, he swung around and led us off the beach and along a dirt track.

I found myself walking beside a woman named Lera who had beautiful posture and a way of reaching out each foot as she walked as if to test the ground ahead of her. Like someone fearing cracks in the ice. She did this rapidly so it didn't slow us down. Her hair was also interesting to me, cut as it was in a short, sharp style.

Lera spoke about her daughters—I remembered her mentioning them when she introduced herself, but I was scrambling to recall what *else* she'd said. She was from Nigeria originally, I remembered that. And her girls were ten, eight, and six.

"Your girls are ten, eight, and six," I said. Just to show off my memory.

"Right," she said kindly. "Exactly."

I asked if they got along.

Mostly, she said, but sometimes they fought like nobody's business.

She asked if I had kids myself and I told her about Oscar and she said, "Oh, four, that's a cute age."

So far, people have told me that all of Oscar's ages are cute. "He's eight months old." "Oh, such a cute age!" "He's two and a half." "Oh, the *cutest*!" Each time, it troubles me, because I think: *So he stops being cute after this?* But so far he's kept up his cute.

I said, "Yeah, pretty cute, except when he's sick," and Lera, looking worried, asked, "Is he sick a lot?"

"Just the usual," I reassured her, but she still seemed concerned, so I began to list his ailments. "Just, you know, colds, conjunctivitis, that kind of thing. Ear infections. He gets those all the time."

"All the time?"

"He's had seven ear infections in the last year." I may have sounded proud.

"Really?" She seemed so intrigued now. "Because that's what I do. I'm a pediatric ENT surgeon."

Of course!

I felt a rush of embarrassment, as if I'd been caught out in a lie. Seven ear infections? Impossible! But it *was* true. Oscar *had* had seven ear infections in the previous year. I could prove it if required: it was all in his medical records. I calmed down in time for a second wave of embarrassment: she'd think I was mentioning the infections *because* she was an ENT doctor! And I could only escape this charge by admitting I'd forgotten who she was. Your regular catch-22.

"Who's looking after him?" Lera asked.

"My mum."

Lera nodded slowly, walking along in her careful way. "It's good he can stay with your mum."

I told her that my mother was only in Sydney for a few days, house-sitting a friend's place in Crows Nest.

"Crows Nest?" Lera said. "That's where I live!"

But I wasn't finished. I told Lera that my mother actually lives up north, in Maroochydore, having moved there to be close to my grandfather after he had a stroke. While there, she'd fallen in love with an old school friend named Xuang and married him. So usually, I said, she could *not* look after Oscar. *Usually*, she was nowhere near Crows Nest.

I didn't know why I was telling Lera all this, except that I wanted to set the record straight. I wanted there to be no confusion about the availability of my mother to babysit my child.

"Which is a shame," I said, "because she's great with him. And so is Xuang."

Next, I told Lera about the nutritious meals my mother and Xuang provided for Oscar and how, *by contrast*, I feed him so badly! But then I recalled she was a doctor, and regretted saying this. It wasn't even really true: fish and chips sometimes, sure, but I give him five servings of vegetables a day. More or less. And small servings. But still! I'd only talked about feeding him badly as one of those things mothers say to each other: oh, my place is a *mess*; oh, I let him watch *way* too much TV! The other mother is supposed to engage in reassuring competitiveness: You think *your* place is a mess! Or else, *My* children *live* on fairy floss! At which, you both feel better.

But Lera was only nodding.

I tried to backpedal. I mentioned that Oscar *loves* bananas—and avocado on toast? Can't get enough. And he really likes salmon!

Lera was growing very bored here, I believe, as she didn't say much, just murmured a sort of congratulatory, "Oh!" about the salmon. There was a moment's quiet and then Lera asked, "And his ears? Who's looking after his ears?"

Oh wow, I thought. She thinks we have to split a child into separate body parts and distribute them among carers. We're going to have to go through his nose, toes, fingernails, and I'll have to reply, "My mum. My mum. Yep, my mum has that too. You know what? My mum has *all* of him." I worried about her career as a surgeon, given this misapprehension.

"His ears?" I repeated, stalling.

"I mean, just the GP or does he have a specialist?"

So then I saw a couple of things: first, that I'm an idiot, and second, that this was what she'd meant by her original question about who was looking after him. Only, she was one of those kind-hearted people who instead of saying, "No, I mean . . .", just follows the trajectory of a mis-communication, waiting for a chance to gently reel you back.

"Dr. Koby," I told her.

"Oh, Tom," she said. "Yes. He's good."

"Last time I saw him, he told me that Oscar is cured," I offered. "That the ear infections will stop now because his skull has caught up with his tonsils."

Usually I mock Dr. Koby at this point in my narration, the hundreds of dollars I'd paid to sit in his office, have him peer at Oscar's tonsils, and eventually declare him "cured." But Lera had just called Dr. Koby *Tom*.

"Do you watch *Grey's Anatomy*?" I asked, to change the subject.

She seemed surprised but told me she'd watched an episode or two.

"And is it like that for you?" I said. "The way they love surgery? They really want to *cut*."

Now she smiled. "No." With tonsils and adenoids, she said, you just do them. There are so many. Hundreds, she's done. Thousands. "But with the other ones," she said. "The life-threatening ones . . ." She stopped and crouched—maintaining her beautiful posture—to tie her bootlace.

I waited, thinking about tonsils and adenoids, hundreds of them, thousands.

At this point, Niall caught up to us. Redheaded, broad-shouldered, as per usual. He'd been walking a few steps behind and, as he reached us, I felt grateful for bootlaces. He looked down at Lera, still double knotting, and he smiled at me. I could see pale freckles, the same color as his hair, on white skin. I could see the shape of his nose, a big, rounded nose. Neither of us spoke.

A strange thought crept across my chest. *You're not just the kind of guy I like, you* are *the guy I like. I know you!* But I didn't know him at all. Confusing.

"Those ones," Lera said, carrying on our conversation, "the life-threatening surgeries—I come out of those bathed in sweat."

The three of us walked on, and Lera continued to talk about her work.

"It's those little round batteries," she said at one point. "The button batteries. Kids swallow them. They stick them up their noses. They'll burn a kid's esophagus irreparably. Right away, they start burning through, those lithium batteries. If we don't get to them in time, the kid will die. Or never talk again. Never breathe on their own again."

And the drownings, she added. The water in their throat. "I don't ever want to get a swimming pool," she said. "And when I see little boys running with lollipops in their mouths . . ."

Niall and I listened and asked questions.

We walked and, in the distance, there they were again: the two men sitting opposite one another, pointing at the sky. This time, as I watched, one lowered his hand and scratched the back of his head.

A moment later, we passed a girl flying a kite in the center of a field. A man rode by on a bicycle, brrringing his bell so that we all stepped aside to let him pass. We passed a house with a garden in which a woman pushed a child on a swing.

Each of us noticed, in silence, the pointing men, the kite, the bike, the child on the swing.

"And grapes," said Lera. "I'd cut them in half until a child is eighteen."

15.

Between 3 and 4 pm, I was in my room, as instructed.

The fire had been lit, and there was a slice of cake on a plate again. I wondered if this was in everybody's room, or only those of the winners.

Or losers: a consolation prize.

Everyone would be chosen, I remembered. This was not a game; it was a hoax, a scam, a con.

In order to demonstrate that I wasn't waiting around for a note under my door, that I had not fallen for this elaborate recruitment exercise, I called my mother. *Look at me getting on with my life.* However, she didn't answer. That was a relief. I could not have paid suffi-cient attention to another recitation of *Where Is Hairy Maclary?* while

I tilted the phone away from my ear, straining to hear footsteps in the corridor.

I leafed through the guesthouse information folder. I boiled the kettle, poured water into a cup, opened a tea bag, made tea, and forgot all about it. I ate some of the cake: coconut and lemon.

It was raining outside, and there were other sounds: a clattering, a door slamming, a motor running. I stood at the window, wiped the mist with my sleeve, and looked down.

A golf buggy stood in the driveway, motor running, door open. Wilbur leaned against it, holding a black umbrella. He called something in the direction of the guesthouse door. Somebody laughed in reply.

A man stepped toward the buggy now, pulling a suitcase behind him, head bowed against the rain.

He turned slightly as he climbed into the buggy, and I saw his face.

It was Daniel.

My face went cold. *Not chosen*, I thought.

Even though he fixes glass and the environment.

Even though I had planned (when I remembered his existence) to sleep with him.

He wasn't chosen so he's leaving.

Yet he seemed composed, and cheerful.

Now a second man strode toward the buggy and hoisted his suitcase into the back.

Oh no, I thought. *Oh no, not Niall! He's my other option!*

But the man at the buggy turned his head and it was nobody important—an unshaven, unkempt look, the sort of look I sometimes find attractive, other times exasperating. He was the one who'd climbed a tree, I remembered.

So! Tree-climbing was not, after all, a criterion.

I turned toward the door of my room and studied the carpet. So far, I myself had not been chosen. Neither was there any guarantee that Niall would choose *me*. *Let me keep my fantasy*, I argued violently.

After tree-climber came the petite cartwheeling woman, Tobi, her head bowed. It was beginning to seem that physical prowess might, in fact, *preclude* you. *Interesting.* Lucky I hadn't won the sack race, after all.

I looked toward the door again. I felt fluttery. I hadn't packed my suitcase. I'd been thinking I'd stay on even if I wasn't chosen, to show that I didn't care. Also for another night of sleep, reading, and cake. (And I'd persuade the actual chosen ones to just *tell* me the truth, over wine and pizza, later tonight.) But all those people downstairs were busy climbing into the buggy, so maybe we were *expected* to leave? Maybe it was one of those unspoken assumptions and people would look at me aghast if I stayed, or would wince, embarrassed on my behalf. What if the chosen people shunned me? Apologetically, of course. Explaining that they'd signed a confidentiality agreement, or they'd made a promise not to tell: they'd sworn.

I'd be so *irritated* if they did that. I hate people who get ethical on you.

My eyes wandered back to the door. A piece of folded paper lay on the carpet.

How did *that* get there?

My heart thudded wildly. Ice ran down my spine; a blast of heat hit my face. Honestly, suspense is just the weather.

I turned back to the window. Outside, three more people were trundling their suitcases toward a second buggy. I didn't recognize the first two particularly, but the third stepped in a careful, considered way— back straight, legs reaching out—and *oh*, I thought. Lera!

I felt crestfallen. *My crest just fell*, I thought.

Lera seemed okay, though: she was climbing into the buggy, speaking to the person beside her. They *all* seemed fine. Cheerful even.

But I *liked* Lera. There was something good about her, something good and complete, and she'd done hundreds of tonsils, thousands. She deserved to hear the truth.

I looked back at the paper on the floor by the door. Now I felt hostile toward it. It was a folded piece of white that could keep me from the truth.

Two quick strides across the room, and I pounced.

Congratulations, it said, *you've been chosen for the truth.*

I'm deeply ashamed to say that I burst into tears.

16.

Everything felt different in the conference room.
There were empty chairs and a complicated hush: curiosity, pride, and a determination not to be curious or proud. Also, we felt sad and strange about the missing people. All this added up to a desperate, low-level embarrassment.

I looked around at the "chosen ones," and felt suddenly annoyed by that phrase. Chosen ones. As if the missing people didn't deserve to be chosen! As if *we* were really up for Jedi training!

But Niall was here. Antony with the flat cap, whose mother had been cruel when he came out; the disgruntled guy with the shoulder, who muttered now under his breath; Nicole, who did not raise goats or meet a man with golden hair; Frangipani.

Of course, I thought in relation to Frangipani.

She beamed at me in a way that suggested she was equally annoyed to see me here.

I looked around, counting quickly. Fifteen people.

Wilbur was the last to arrive. He rushed in, tousled with wind, cold and rain. He must have just come back from the airstrip. He was more outdoors than all of us now, and therefore somehow superior. He carried a stack of folders, and he began to hand them around.

"Here it is," he said. "Inside this folder. The truth."

That was unexpected. His voice was distracted, offhand. His eyes remained lowered.

Once we each had a folder, Wilbur stood back, rocking on his heels. Nobody moved. It was as if the group understood the importance of ritual better than Wilbur now. We disapproved of his failure to build drama.

"Inside this folder," Wilbur repeated, frowning slightly, "is the truth. It's the original prologue to *The Guidebook*. Go ahead and read it."

He sat on a table, swung his legs like a boy, and turned toward a window to look out. Here's what was inside the folder.

Prologue

Tell us. Do you yearn for the uneasy balance?

Do you seek out the fine shred of moment when the seesaw hovers and stills? Does the principle of lift—based as it is on two pairs of sneakers hitting the dirt at the same time—does the principle of lift raise up your heart?

When you close your eyes, do you see scales? (We don't mean fish scales, by the way. We mean the scales of justice! Or the scales you use to measure your fruit in a supermarket.)

If you have answered YES to any of our questions, then this book is for you!

You see, this book rests on the principle of lift. The principle of lift, based as it is on two pairs of sneakers hitting the dirt at the same time, the principle of lift, let us assure you, is the principle of *life*!

The Wright brothers, tiring of the effort of balance, cut out a section of the wing of their plane and they found it: the principle of lift. It had been there in the wing all the time.

Read all the chapters, complete all the tasks, and you will be ready to fly—primed for your lessons in flight.

We, your authors, already know how to fly.

```
    Isabelle learned first. Later, she fell in love
with me (Rufus), and taught me the secret.
    For Isabelle, it started simply enough, as all
great things do. One day, when she was four years
old, her father found her playing in the garden.
    "Do you know, Isabelle," he said, "I think you
could fly if you put your mind to it. You have such
lovely little bones."
    He said, "We'll start on the small hills in the
snow."
```

That was it.

I finished reading, and looked up.

Wilbur was still swinging his legs.

Around me papers rustled as others read, finished reading, and looked in the folders for more.

There was the sort of silence in which people sniff or cough. Drop something, pick it up. Clatter of a pen. Creak of chair.

"Wait," I said suddenly. "That's it?"

Others murmured similar doubts.

"*That's* the truth?" The speaker's voice twisted with contempt. "That we have to have *balance* and then we can *fly*?"

Wilbur was frowning. "Well," he said. "Not . . . It's the principle of . . ."

"I'm not sure they've quite got the principle of lift down," Niall contributed, reasonable. He read from the paper, a smile in his voice. "Based as it is on two pairs of sneakers hitting the dirt at the same time."

Others were talking among themselves, in a tone of raised eyebrows and sighs. Oh, the dreary predictability of self-help.

"They're always on about balance."

"Wow, I'm glad I didn't pay for this."

"See, there's never anything new because there *is* nothing new."

"Good to be reminded, I suppose. I do need to get more balance in my life."

Wilbur, meanwhile, had stopped swinging his legs and was looking around at us, his expression perplexed.

"Oh!" he said, standing suddenly. "Oh, you're thinking it's a *metaphor*! No! No!" His face had cleared. "It's not metaphorical flight, it's actual flight. The book has been teaching you to fly." He smiled warmly.

"To fly a plane?" someone asked.

"No. To *fly*." Wilbur spoke the next words slowly and carefully, as if he'd just realized that we weren't all that bright. "Assuming you've been reading *The Guidebook*, and you've carried out *most* of its tasks and exercises, you can fly now. All of you can fly."

17.

"**O**h, *brother*," somebody said.

A tide of laughter moved around the room, snagging on one or two silent people with gaping mouths.

Wilbur's eyes panicked. He saw the division falling swift, a rapid descent of boom gates, dividing him from us. He raised his voice. "Listen to Nietzsche," he almost shouted. "*The higher we soar, the smaller we appear to those who cannot fly!*"

"Yes, well, that's an issue of perspective," someone said mildly.

"I'm not a fan of Nietzsche," another voice declared.

"In the year 1002, or thereabouts," Wilbur tried next, "the Turkish scholar Ismail ibn Hammad al-Jawhari climbed to the top of a mosque with wooden wings, and said: *The most important thing on earth is to fly to the skies.*"

There was a brief, impressed silence.

"What happened next?" somebody inquired.

"Well," said Wilbur, "he jumped to his death. But that's not the point; the *point*—"

But he'd lost us again. Not everyone was laughing. Some scowled.

Some shook their heads in disbelief. Some—well, Frangipani—were wretched, bright-eyed, bewildered.

"I haven't done *any* of the exercises," one woman said, pretending to be fretful. "So *I* certainly can't fly."

The laughter revved up again.

Niall grinned. "This is brilliant," he said.

Nicole was sitting with her head at an angle, studying Wilbur, her expression all compassion.

Oh, I thought. Of course. She's got it right. Yes, poor Wilbur! Poor mad Wilbur.

I tried to imitate Nicole's expression, but quickly grew bored, wanting to look around instead.

"Think about it," Wilbur said, more urgently. "When people are asked what they would choose if they were granted just one wish—"

"World peace," Frangipani declared. "I'd wish for world peace."

"Other than world peace . . ."

"I'd wish for my family to be happy and safe," somebody said. "And for an extensive property portfolio."

Wilbur frowned. "One *superpower*," he tried. "If you could have one superpower?"

At once, people began thinking aloud, weighing possibilities. "Invisibility?" someone tried, and someone else said, "Super-strength!" while a third confided, "You know, I've always wanted to be able to turn myself *really, really* tiny, but with a—" and Wilbur snapped: "Flight! Everybody wants to fly!"

"Oh. Right." We all sat back, nodding.

"And therefore we can fly?" Niall now smiled broadly. "Because everybody really, really, really wants to fly?"

"It's a symptom, rather than a cause," Wilbur said distractedly. "I need to explain better. What I'm *saying* is—"

"What you are *saying* . . ." The disgruntled shoulder guy stood up, dropping his folder. Everybody turned to look at him. His face was watermelon but more ferocious than the fruit. "What you are *saying* is, if we all go up to the roof right now and jump, we'll be able to fly."

"Well, no," Wilbur said. "Please. I wouldn't advise that."

The cranky guy was shoving his way through seats, using his knees. "You get *fifteen-year-olds*. You get *children*—children who are unhappy, vulnerable—you get them signed up, invested. You *shape* their *lives*! You ought to be *ashamed* of yourself," he half shouted at Wilbur. "You ought to be *shot*."

He flung open the door, pulled it closed behind him, opened it again and slammed it so hard the room vibrated.

I worried about his shoulder, doing that.

Wilbur looked at the door. "We'll start on the small hills in the snow," he whispered.

There was an embarrassed quiet. I began to think we all ought to follow cranky guy out, one at a time, with the same drama. *Slam! Slam! Slam!* It would lose its impact, though, the slamming. There might be structural damage.

"So we *can't* fly?" Frangipani asked, still trying to figure things out.

"You can!" Wilbur insisted, cheering up.

"But you just said you don't advise us to jump off the roof, *ergo* . . ."

(Ergo. That's what she said. I am not kidding.)

Wilbur sat on the table again. "Everybody has a sense of flight," he began. "Now, you know how you have a sense of smell, of sight, taste, touch, and so on?"

"Not me," Niall put in. "I have no sense of smell."

Wilbur nodded at this, curious, then returned to his theme. "The human being also has an innate sense of flight."

Flat-cap—Antony—raised his hand. "Are you talking jet propulsion? Artificial wings?"

"No," Wilbur said. "Neither. Flight, like I said, is a *sense*, only lost to human memory. And yet we *know* it's there. A part of us *knows*. Consider your dreams of flying. Consider the long history of the human quest for the secret to flight. Consider the yearning way we watch a bird soar. Or simply gaze at the sky: cloud-gazing, stargazing. We are enamored by the sky."

"That's true," Frangipani said hopefully.

Niall chuckled.

"Now think about babies and the way they develop," Wilbur continued, warming up. "At first, they are helpless and lie perfectly still. Then they learn to roll over. To sit up. To rock on their hands and knees, to crawl, to pull themselves to standing position and eventually to walk. The next step?"

"An education? A job?" somebody hazarded.

"Flight! The child is supposed to learn to fly! But the young learn by example, by watching the adults of their species. Adults today *are not* flying, so what do children do?"

People were quiet, fascinated by this new turn in Wilbur's insanity.

"Children *sense* that there is more, something *beyond* mere walking. The child's body *needs* to fly. Why do you think babies flap their arms and legs? Why do you think children never stop running, jumping, climbing? Why do they love a bouncy castle? A trampoline? They are always clambering onto furniture, rolling down hills!"

"Playing," Antony put in softly.

"Right! No. No, actually. They are expressing their frustration at their failure to employ their innate sense of flight."

People were too dazzled to laugh: a long silence of amazement.

"Are you saying children would be well behaved if we taught them how to fly?" Niall asked eventually.

"Yes," Wilbur said. "Or better behaved, anyway. We teach children to swim. We understand that our bodies need to move through water. Yet we forget that we should also move through air! We are doing children a disservice, not teaching them to fly."

"Ten Things You Must Do for Your Child If You Truly Love Them," Nicole reflected, grinning now, her compassion done. "Give them a hug. Turn off your phone. Teach them to fly."

I thought about teaching Oscar to walk. "So one adult holds the baby in the air," I suggested, "and another stands a short distance away and reaches out their hands—*Come on! You can do it! Come on! Fly to me!*—then the first person kind of *tosses* the baby toward the second?"

"Makes sense," Nicole nodded, while everybody else laughed. Nicole and I smiled at each other.

Wilbur pushed on. "*The Guidebook* has been developing your sense of flight. All these years, we've been awakening it through the exercises. Now we need to show you how to use it."

"Right now?" someone asked, interested.

"Well, no. In Sydney. We will hold a series of seminars during which we will consolidate your knowledge. By the end of that series, you will fly."

The laughter took on a jeering tone.

"Of course you're holding a series of seminars," somebody said. "Need our bank account details, do you?"

"No, no," Wilbur said, helpless. "The seminars are free. We *want* you to fly."

Around me, others were standing, stretching, gathering their things. We'd been compliant, patient, ready to play, to take a break from life, but now? Now we were grown-ups looking at the clock, at the setting sun, at the real world of families and jobs, schedules and appointments. It was time to pack the game into its box, to wind elastic around the cards, gather up tokens and dice, press down the lid, set the box back on its shelf. We were somewhat mortified by having allowed the game to come so far.

"You see, we all *need* to fly," Wilbur was urging. "We just don't *know* that we need it."

Flat-cap began explaining aerodynamics to him, his voice kind and apologetic. "Human arms are not *strong* enough to carry the human body. Even if you rigged up artificial wings, they'd need to be eighty feet long."

As I left the room, I heard Wilbur launch into the benefits of flight: *Practical benefits, of course—you avoid traffic! And health benefits. The fresh air, the physical exercise . . . Why do you think we all have these issues with our joints? Knee reconstructions, hip replacements, lower back pain? It's because we never spend time in the sky! Now, the benefits to the human spirit—*

18.

On the stairs, my dismay was contained in a framework of resignation. My dismay was tired, cynical, amused, adult. A wry smile, an arched eyebrow.

I opened the door to my room, paused, ran my gaze across the rugs, the pictures, the bed, and here came my dismay, tumbling out from behind the wry smile, splintering its frame, lighting itself into wildfire, to fury.

This, I raged, *this life! This waste! These promises! These chapters in the mail!*

I wrote "reflections" for these people every year!

Outside the window, the wind was blowing strong. Trees were ducking down fast as if something dangerous were hurtling overhead.

This pathetic fallacy, I sneered.

There went Lera, I remembered, rolling her suitcase behind her, and of *course* she had not been chosen for the truth! Lera, the pediatric surgeon, like Daniel, the glass-repair man, was sensible, separate, good and complete.

They chose the fools like me. The people left behind. The incomplete, the broken, the children still trapped inside their childish years.

Little boys with lollipops inside their mouths, Lera had said. *Those tiny sticks.*

I am a half-person.

Also: *You have to be so careful—you have to be so careful, because you can push it down, out of reach—and you can't fix a burnt esophagus.*

I flung my suitcase open and began to throw clothes into it.

"Is there happiness in truth, or only beauty?" a chapter of *The*

Guidebook had once mused. "When the glass becomes clear, the truth shines through and everything jumps gleeful at your face."

Well, sure, truth is like a bright light at a window, but truth is also hands on your chest shoving you backward, and truth is your esophagus burned beyond repair.

Snow, Wilbur had promised, and it hadn't snowed either.

Wilbur was a liar and a cheat.

19.

Yes, I *know*.

What did I expect?

I'd laughed at the invitation. I'd known it would be a scam.

But I had thought—a secret part of me had believed—that this retreat would take me back to the year that I first received *The Guidebook*, which was also the year we lost my brother.

Somehow, I had thought, this would bring my brother back.

I didn't think this *consciously*, of course, but if you want to get beneath the surface of my rage, there it is. If Nicole can turn back fate by buying goats, if she can unwrap her husband and her children and start over, then I can unwrap 1990, unwrap all the years between, take us back to Robert, Robert heading out to a doctor's appointment, *The Guidebook* in a rusty frying pan.

I've said goodbye a hundred times, a thousand, yet I'm always on this carousel, turning and turning, and he'll always be there, my brother, Robert, always there, and always gone.

The Guidebook was absurdity: inexplicable, inscrutable; and so was my brother being gone. Hence, the two must be connected.

That is why I never canceled my subscription: a part of me never stopped believing that, eventually, the one mystery would unravel the other.

But Wilbur wants to teach us how to fly.

PART 2

REFLECTIONS ON 1990

By Abigail Sorensen

The first time I had sex I was like, excuse me?

This was around a year ago now with my boyfriend of the time, Samuel McKew.

He was seventeen and I was fifteen, so I wondered if the problem was right there, in those two years.

Afterward, we went into his backyard and grilled sausages on the barbecue. We didn't say much. Just looked at the sausages, rolling around. I was thinking about getting a new boyfriend, one closer to my age. Samuel was wiping smoke out of his eyes.

"Sorry about that," he whispered.

I got a humorous expression on my face like, *Yeah, so you should be,* but replaced it right away with: *Ah, it's not your fault, never mind.*

But was it his fault? His equipment was too big was the problem, as far as I could tell. (When he first called it his "equipment," I laughed, thinking it was a joke, but he looked at me like, *What? What?* so I stopped laughing and respected his equipment.)

Anyway, but can you blame them for the size of their equipment?

Do they exercise, eat a lot of Weet-Bix, to build it up? Was it that size because he was seventeen years old, or because he had *made it that size*?

That ridiculous size.

I was just feeling hostile about the number of bananas he ate—he used to bring seven or eight to school with him every day—when his mother tapped on the kitchen window.

We turned to look, and there she was, waving at us from inside the house, smiling like she knew we'd just had sex for the first time, and she thought it was funny and sweet. We both waved back, thinking: How did she get her car into the driveway and herself into the house without us noticing?

"I was too quick," Samuel explained in a low, cracking voice, while he waved back at his mother. He promised he'd never be that quick again.

I smiled at him, but I was thinking: That's *what he was sorry for*?

And I was thinking: *Did he even* know *how much that hurt*?

The sausages hissed, and I was thinking: *It's supposed to go for longer than that?*

*

My brother thought it was funny about the sausages. That we grilled sausages afterward. He kept laughing about that.

Then I asked if eating a lot of bananas might have given Samuel extra-big equipment, and he laughed so hard he was practically sick.

My name is Abi, and my brother's name is Robert, and I tell him almost everything. Robert and I are both fifteen years old.

So you're thinking that we're twins. But we're not. He's eleven months younger than me—we're just in the overlap time. See, he's a fresh-faced fifteen, whereas I'm a weathered old fifteen. Been sailing this here fifteen-ship a whole lot of year now, me hearties.

Just about to say goodbye to it, in point of fact. Tomorrow is my birthday and I turn sixteen, and that's when I leave Robert behind. He'll be home any moment, and we'll have our farewell ritual. We always have it, just prior to midnight, the day before my birthday. He'll miss me when I leave him for sixteen, but someone's got to break the new ship in.

*

The second time I had sex was also with Samuel. This was the thirteenth of April. It was a Friday. So, Friday the thirteenth. Black Friday, which I did a speech about in year seven, and the reason that thirteen is black is—actually, I forget why. In my speech I told a story: *there were thirteen demigods, and the thirteenth demigod . . .*

Was full of mischief.

I think that's what I said.

Anyhow, that's why I remember the date.

Luckily, Samuel was quick again, but that made him depressed, so afterward he played *Larry* at his computer. I sat on his bedroom floor leaning up against his bed and did my math homework. When his mother opened the door, I was pleased about the picture she must have got: her son at his desk, me on the carpet, both of us working like young scholars. But it really worried me, how quietly she arrived home.

*

So now you're thinking: *Can this girl talk about anything else besides SEX?!*

I can. However, as requested, I'm reflecting on 1990, and sex featured.

But so did many other things! For example, I did year ten, and that's not a walk in the park. I started writing my first novella (I've started novels before, but never novellas). I babysat for the McCabes, the Pulies, and the Picellos. I would also have babysat for the Holtzmans, but they never go out, cheap fuckers.

I went on two family skiing trips: the first one there was no snow, so we skied on the rocks, dirt, and grass; the second was two straight days of blizzard and one perfect blue-sky day.

I played in a doubles tennis tournament with my brother and we got to the semifinals.

I watched forty-seven horror movies. I wrote the titles of all of them in my exercise book and gave them star ratings along with statistics such as victim count/authenticity of blood, etc.

I waited for Mum and Robert to get home from doctors' appointments.

Also: this last year, strangers named Rufus and Isabelle began sending me chapters from a self-improvement book called *The Guidebook*. But you already know that, obviously.

It's true I tell my brother everything, but I've never said a word about those chapters to him.

*

It's 9 pm. I'm going to get a coconut biscuit. Mum made some earlier.

Okay, I'm back, but I ate half the biscuit on the way here, so it didn't count, and now I need to get another one.

Wait.

Back again.

Mum and Dad are watching a video. They're concentrating hard; you can see that through the frosted-glass door. Their sweet little heads are leaning forward, and now and then one turns to the other and asks a question and the other replies in a voice of doubt, and then they turn back to the screen.

Robert will be home any moment, like I said. He's been staying in Glebe, at the squalid student house of his eighteen-year-old girlfriend named Clarissa, for the last few days. He hasn't been going to school. Too far to commute.

My friends are all like, "Are you *serious*? Your parents are *okay* with this? He's fifteen and he's staying with an eighteen-year-old? Is that even legal?" etc., etc.

(My parents are as relaxed as a couple of beanbags, but they don't know that Robert's been staying with his girlfriend in Glebe. They're not *that* relaxed. They think he's at his friend Bing's place so that he and

Bing can work on their piano duet for the upcoming eisteddfod. They're relaxed in that they have no issue with Robert staying at Bing's without talking to Bing's parents about it.)

*

Some of my favorite words:

Windcheater.
Skyscraper.
Wolkenkratzer.

Wolkenkratzer is German. It means skyscraper but, *literally*, it means cloud-scratcher.
Cheating the wind, scraping the sky, scratching the clouds.
Cool, right?
I'd like to cheat the wind, among other things.

*

Wait till you hear what my novella is about.
I started it in this Workshop for Young Writers that Robert and I did in January.
Robert plans to be a poet, and I plan to write horror movies, that's why we did it.
It went from 9 am to 5 pm, which is too long, you get exhausted.
There were seven other people besides Robert and me, and the teacher counted us silently. "Oh, there's supposed to be three more," she said, and turned expectantly to the door. She waited until quarter past nine before she gave up.
Then she introduced herself and said she had published a book called *Peach Stones*. Nobody had heard of it, which made me feel a bit sorry for her. Robert said he already felt sorry for her, because of the expressions that crossed her face during the minutes we waited for the missing students.

I can't actually remember the teacher's name.

Anyhow, she went around the room and asked us all our names, and why we were here, and when we felt most imaginative, and what our favorite food was, and she wrote all this down on a notepad. Which was either a red herring or bad plotting, because she never used any of that information again, not even our names—she just pointed at us when she wanted us to speak.

I don't remember any of the other names either except for this red-headed guy named River, like the actor, who was cute. His favorite food was Special Fried Rice. There was a girl with tiny wrists who said she was there because she wanted to test the waters. I noticed River raising his eyebrows at that, and we had a moment, because he caught me also raising my eyebrows.

A guy with curly hair and a longish nose said he was not sure that he *was* there. That made me feel a bit complicated, because I was partly thinking, *Stupid thing to say*, at the same time as: *Oh, cool, let's talk*. He also said he felt imaginative when he pressed his fingertips together—he showed us what he meant, his knuckles were knobbly—and that his favorite food depended on the ocean. Again, I wanted to enter discussions with him, mainly to get an explanation. And because I liked how he pressed his fingertips together. It made me feel spooky in a good way.

A girl who was way too blond and pretty to be a writer said her favorite food was chocolate sultanas. Robert turned right around and smiled at her when she said it. She kept trying to get his attention for the rest of the day, but he'd forgotten her. He's a handsome guy, my brother, and forgetful.

Robert himself assumed his (excellent) Italian accent, said that his name was *Roberto*, that he was from Montepulciano, Italy, where they race barrels on the last Sunday in August, and that he felt most imaginative when he was standing on the ice.

"The ice?" said the blond girl, almost breathless now. "What ice?"

Roberto shrugged and smiled. "Any ice."

The only ice I've ever seen him stand on is the rink at Macquarie

Centre. We've never even left the country, let alone been to Italy. We laughed about all this later.

*

I just went to get myself more biscuits because Robert's *still* not back. It's fine; he just has to be here before midnight.

Dad was in the kitchen microwaving popcorn and as I walked into the room he shouted, "PUT IT ON PAUSE!", which made me jump. He apologized. He was shouting at Mum because most people, when you walk out of the room, they'll pause the video, but Mum always forgets and merrily keeps watching.

That's Mum's words, by the way: *Oh, look at me merrily still watching!*

*

It being 11:35 pm, you're going to want to get a move on, Robert.

*

I have that excited feeling because it's my birthday tomorrow, and it's like colors are brighter. And like everyone else, every*thing* else—my OMD poster, my chest of drawers—they're all looking at me lovingly. Like, with Dad in the kitchen now, little words pranced in the air between us: *Tomorrow is Abigail's birthday!*

Strange that it's all in my head. Dad was probably just thinking about the popcorn. I mean, he *knows* it's my birthday tomorrow, but it's not likely to be foremost in his mind.

It means I'm growing up—the fact that I recognize this.

*

I like Rufus and Isabelle, and I like their chapters from their guidebook because they seem insane. (The one I got yesterday told me to study the clouds for an hour, draw pictures of them, and tape them to my bedroom ceiling: *In such a way, you will learn to see that the sky is* not *the limit.* What? Excuse me, *what?*)

I'm finding it hard to imagine sending these reflections.

I'm obviously not going to send them tomorrow. That's my birthday, and a birthday is no place for a post office.

So, it'll have to be after the birthday, but that seems impossible. How can there be anything beyond a day as important as a birthday?

Maybe I'm not as grown-up as I think.

*

One day, Robert said to me, "Do you know where your right foot is?"

We were watching a movie. *Raising Arizona.*

I stuck my right foot in the air. "There."

We kept watching the movie.

"But do you sometimes *not* know where it is?" Robert persisted.

"My right foot?"

I looked over at him. He had his serious frown.

"It's always at the end of my right leg."

"Hm."

"Not yours?"

He laughed, but a non-laugh. The sort of laugh Mum uses when we make a joke mid-crisis, say she's microwaved a tin of soup. She's not focused on our humor, see, she's focused on the blacked-out microwave.

*

Robert complained about aches in his calves and his neck. Mum took him to a physiotherapist who gave him exercises and advice about posture. Playing Pictionary, he said, "Wait. My eye's doing that thing where it blacks out for a second."

Also, he kept talking about how tired he was. "I just need to lean against the wall here," he'd say, and once, walking along the edge of the ocean, he fell face-first into the sea. He scrambled up and carried on walking.

*

Well, it's beyond midnight, which means we're in the land of my birthday. My bedroom light is on and my room's at the front of the house, so Robert will see it when he gets home. It will shine out at him like a rebuke. He'll see it, remember, and his face will fall. Trip right over and fall.

The way he does himself, actually, all the time. Which, sometimes, I think he should just try to be more careful.

*

Okay, about my novella.

There's a bunch of people in a life raft in the ocean.

The people come in various shapes, sizes, and flavors, shoulders sometimes oblong, sometimes droopy.

There's a man in a gray suit and gray felt hat, and everything about him is thin: his fingers, toes, his briefcase, *which he never lets go of because it's handcuffed to his wrist.* His opinions tend to be thin like him, and he squints toward the horizon, and nobody knows what he's got up his sleeve, other than the handcuff.

An old woman in a lilac cardigan wears a broad-brimmed straw hat with a matching lilac ribbon around it.

A wise boy, about seven, sits in the boat making astonishingly wise observations.

The older characters turn and look at him.

"Such wisdom," whispers the woman in lilac, "from one so very young!"

I have to fill in the wisdom, though. So far, I've just got: *[wise statement] said the small boy.*

Here is the thing that will blow your mind about my novella.

The people in the life raft were *originally* in a novel! Not a novella. It was a novel about a cruise ship, and they fell overboard—possibly during a storm or pirate attack—and were lost. In the world of the novel, they were minor characters. Shadows. No names, no personalities. The protagonist in the novel never gave them a thought except to say sadly, "Oh, the lost souls."

But, guess what? I rescued them in my novella. Just as the moon is a piece of the earth that has broken away, a novella is a piece of a novel. My novella is a metaphorical life raft. So that's why they're in a life raft.

*

My best friend, Carly Grimshaw, lives two doors down.

She's from New Zealand, which makes her a slightly exotic friend, and she's always got a little packet of travel tissues in her pocket, which makes her a handy friend. She wears her hair in a plait that she keeps at the *front*, over her right shoulder. *Just toss your plait over your right shoulder there, Carly.* (That's what Robert says to her sometimes, because he's noticed that she places it there. She looks annoyed/embarrassed/sort of pleased when Robert says this.)

Also about Carly: she's got a four-poster bed in many shades of pink (the canopy, the quilt cover, cushions), and she's got an older brother named Andrew, who is useful in that he is nineteen. So Carly sometimes steals his licence from his wallet and lets Robert borrow it for ID.

Otherwise, he's pretty pointless, Andrew. He gets terrible acne and that's his identity.

(I expect he has thoughts and dreams beyond his acne; he probably sees himself as having more scope than his skin.)

Also, Andrew and Carly have a baby sister named Rabbit.

Not really. The baby's name is Erin. Rabbit's one of those nicknames people pick up.

My family attended Rabbit's first birthday party this year.

Afterward, Robert and I talked about how, when you turn one, it's the first time you have a birthday, and everyone's making a big deal out of it. So you get socialized into thinking birthdays are a big deal. But they're not. They're *no big deal* (we agreed).

I see now that this was a stupid discussion to have. Birthdays *are* a big deal. The day you're born? I mean, come on, *what bigger deal is there?* That's your *existence* on a *plate*.

I pointed out that maybe Rabbit didn't know it was her birthday. All she might have noticed was that everyone was suddenly paying attention to her.

"And so she's trying to figure out: *What did I do right today?*" Robert said. "*How can I do it again tomorrow?*"

We agreed that that's how we become the people we are. Let's say we're quiet people, well, it just happened we were being quiet, having a think and a reflection, on the morning of our first birthday, and then—*bam!*—people were bombarding us with presents and cake! So we decided to be quiet from then on.

Same with people who were wild that day, or fretful, or giggled, or slept a lot, and so on. Tiresome people, you know? Trace it back to the source.

The first birthday is the key to identity.

*

Have I told you what the birthday ritual actually is?

Well, it was supposed to happen just before midnight, as you know, *but that ship has sailed.* Still, I don't see why it shouldn't happen at 12:47 am, if he would just *walk up the front driveway.*

Anyway, when he does, this will happen: Robert will clap his hands onto my shoulders and say, "Godspeed," and he'll say, "Thank you, Abi, for taking the road ahead, the unpaved road of sixteen—and paving it for us."

He'll start getting hoarse as he says, "If I could come with you, I would, you know that, don't you?" and I'll say, "I know it, Robert," and we'll shake hands, tears in our eyes, and he'll say, "Oh, to heck with it," and give me a quick hug, then I'll say, to cover the awkwardness, "One last drink before I go?" and he'll say, "Why not?"

We'll pour ourselves some of Mum's single malt whisky, then we'll toss it back, making our eyes tear up even more, clasp each other's upper arms, and I'll say, "We will meet again in eleven months, my friend, I swear it."

Then I glance at the clock and, right as it hits midnight, I open the door. Then, *without looking back*, I walk out of the room.

But again, I guess it doesn't have to be midnight.

Usually, I go right back in, and we both go, "Oh, hi, how are things?"

Funny.

Anyway, very funny to us.

We've done this since we were ten. And we drink a bit more whisky every year. It gets better with age. By the time we're twenty, we'll be chugging a bottle each, I predict.

Our parents were not distressed when they found us with the whisky a few years back. That's a good example of the kind of parents they are: we're supposed to make our own mistakes. I remember they did suggest we try a different drink—Dad thought that billy tea would be just the ticket—but we disagreed.

"Just the ticket," he said. "In keeping with your explorer theme."

We made a lot of fun of him about that. *In keeping with your explorer theme.*

*

They're those kind of parents, like I said—they believe in letting us find our own way. When we were babies, they used to let us crawl off into the distance, and we always came back, they said, except for one famous incident when I crawled under the fence of a park, crossed a soccer field, and was heading up the embankment toward a highway. Somebody rescued me, and Mum and Dad say they rethought their parenting strategy for a while after that.

But they decided that that was just a glitch, and reintroduced it.

Anyway, my parents are fine about our secret whisky ceremony. They like it even. They're happy about how close Robert and I are, and they attribute our closeness to their freedom-in-parenting philosophy.

*

This one time that Samuel and I had sex, his mother was in the sewing room down the hall. We were just kissing, me thinking it would not lead anywhere because, well, his mother was down the hall. Then Samuel went to the cupboard and got out the condoms.

"I don't *think* so," I said, laughing. I thought it was a joke, like we were sharing a joke.

But he put on a sad face and mouthed, *Please*, and I shook my head, still smiling: no way. His mother was about to come to the door and offer to drive me home—she always did that at exactly 6 pm—no way was I going to have sex.

Then Samuel got a strange expression on his face and came over to the bed in two strides and he said in a low voice, "I'm going to do it anyway."

I had enough time to feel a bit confused, like—*wait, he's allowed to just do it?*—and next thing he was on top of me, pushing my dress up and my underpants aside. I could shout, "NO!" but then his mother would hear, and anyway, now he was kissing me, and getting on with things, and then he was done.

"See?" he whispered. "That was fine." Because there were still a couple of minutes before his mother would jingle her car keys on their little Smurf key ring.

*

After that, I was cold with Samuel and he kept going, "What's *wrong* with you?" and I would say, "If you don't know, I'm not going to tell you." He got so angry about that. It's a girl thing to do, apparently.

A couple of weeks later, he broke up with me because he wanted to have sex with other people. I couldn't expect him to only have sex with *one* person in his entire life! Actually, I didn't have that expectation of him. I hadn't really thought about the next few *months*, let alone life.

But I'd imagined he'd be there, in my life, for, you know, *the next day*.

I was pretty sad. We were sitting on his bed, and he had his arm around me, and he was rocking me back and forth. It was romantic. Yet also a bit strange. Then he got up and put on Roxy Music's "Angel Eyes," looking back at me with tragic (rather than angel) eyes, as he tried to line up the start of the song. He did a lot of rewind, stop, play, rewind, stop, play. He became a bit frustrated but got it in the end.

Then he sat back on the bed and rubbed my back while I cried. At the same time, I was thinking, "He's put on 'Angel Eyes'! He's changed his mind about breaking up!" Because "Angel Eyes" was his song for me. Also his nickname for me. Two for the price of one.

But it turned out he was just playing it as part of his strategy to comfort me. So then I cried a bit more, and went home.

*

That was the day my brother got the news from the doctor.

He didn't tell me about it straight away. To be honest, I *forgot* he'd been going to the doctor's that day to get the results. I was too upset about Samuel.

Mum had gone out to the shops. I told Robert that Samuel had broken up with me, and Robert was so mad! He was going, "*What*? Why would he do that? Samuel? You mean *your* Samuel?"

I was glad that he said *your Samuel*. Like he still believed that Samuel belonged to me, even though Samuel seemed to have forgotten it.

He was really pissed off with Samuel. He promised me I'd meet someone better tomorrow.

"Tomorrow?"

And he nodded seriously. "Tomorrow you will meet someone better."

He was so sure about it, I believed him and felt excited. I wondered if the new boy would be cute.

"Cuter than Samuel," Robert promised.

Then Mum got home, looked in at us, and fixed her tender gaze on Robert for a bit longer than necessary, so I remembered.

I said, "Oh yeah, what did the doctor say?"

That's when Robert told me that he had multiple sclerosis. (It's a misdiagnosis, I am sure.) Mum stood at the bedroom door, watching him tell, and watching me tell him that it must be a misdiagnosis.

*

After Samuel and I broke up I was depressed for a while, and then I got more depressed because I remembered something.

I'd been planning to have sex for the first time with someone I truly loved! I had a whole plan for that! I'd just forgotten about that, getting caught in the heat of the argument.

We'd been arguing about it pretty well since we started going out, in fact. Samuel was worried about the fact that he was seventeen, which meant he could easily turn eighteen and he'd still have his virginity. Imagine if he was able to drink and vote and be an adult but still had his virginity! He didn't want it. "How do I get rid of it without your help?" he demanded.

"What d'you want me to do?" I said. "Chuck it over a bridge for you?"

But he said I should take this more seriously.

Sometimes I'd wake in the night at home and go, *Wait a second, why is his virginity my problem?* But during the arguments I'd forget that, and get caught up in how to solve Samuel's problem. Also, I didn't like him using the word *virginity*; it made him sound like a girl or like the Holy Mother of God.

I think that's why I agreed in the end. I was just worn out, and wanted him to quit using that word.

*

It is now 2 am.

*

One day, Mum and I were in the kitchen talking about the person who invented multiple sclerosis.

She'd been reading about him, apparently. His name was Jean-Martin Charcot and "he ought to be shot."

Robert and I agreed.

He was French, Mum added ominously, as if being French explained a lot.

"What's wrong with French people?" I asked.

"Oh, you know, they're always wearing stripes and eating croissants," she said, and then she raised her voice over our hysterical laughter to explain that Charcot went around inventing things *all* the time—"well, *naming* them," she admitted. In addition to MS, there was Parkinson's and Tourette's, for example.

"All we need to know about *him*," she finished dramatically, "is that, after he died, his son gave up medicine and became the world's first polar explorer. That's about all we need to know."

At this point, Robert and I looked at each other, and then at Mum, and we squinted hard, to illustrate just how bewildering our mother was. She was lost in thought at the stove now, but noticed our squinting and got annoyed with us.

Robert was stringing beans, I was peeling potatoes. Mum put her hands on her hips and said, "The son *had been* a doctor because his dad *wanted* him to be. But the moment his dad died? He ran off and became an explorer!"

So then we understood that the dad had not allowed the son to be free. As our parents allowed us to be free.

"The son named an island after his father," Mum added listlessly.

"So at least he liked his father," Robert said.

"Of course he didn't," Mum protested. "The naming thing was an effort to compensate for his hatred of his father."

"Well," I contributed, "his dad named diseases; he named islands. That's what that family were all about. Naming."

I was also thinking that maybe he did want to be a doctor, but changed his mind and thought, *polar explorer!* right after his dad died.

Or maybe he felt so desperately sad about the loss of his dad that his heart turned to ice, and he ran away to the polar regions, looking for someplace even colder.

I didn't say any of that.

"Maybe he did want to be a doctor," Robert said, which gave me the strange feeling I get sometimes that maybe we have a psychic connection, like actual twins. "And when his dad died, he felt so sad he just wanted to go as far away as he could, like running away from his grief, as far as the North Pole."

"Hm," said Mum, but she didn't sound convinced.

*

2:49 am.

*

Robert was having a bad day on Tuesday, and he stayed home from school and just lay on his bed.

When I got home, I went into his room with a glass of lemonade and a packet of chips, plus some homework a teacher gave me to pass on to him, plus three different notes from friends of his at school.

He was looking a bit pale. He said, "I've got a joke for you. You want to hear it?"

"Sure," I said.

"What did Tarzan say when he saw the elephants coming over the hill?"

"What?"

"Here come the elephants!"

I looked at him a bit sternly.

"Wait—it's a two-part joke," he said.

"Okay."

"What did Tarzan say when he saw the elephants coming over the hill wearing sunglasses?"

I thought about it. I wanted to come up with a humorous answer of my own. But in the end I just said, "What?"

"Nothing," Robert said. "He didn't recognize them."

I looked at him for a while.

"So Tarzan saw the elephants coming, and they were wearing sunglasses, so he didn't recognize them?"

"Right."

"Robert," I said, "that's not funny."

His face fell.

"Part one of the joke isn't funny," I said, "and part two doesn't save it."

Robert frowned, thinking it through. He played with the corner of his pillow. Then he straightened up and said, "I see your point."

"I mean, I don't even really *get* it," I admitted.

He nodded.

I elaborated. "And if I did get it, it still wouldn't be funny."

The fact is, just because you've been diagnosed with a serious, possibly even life-threatening disease, doesn't mean you can let your sense of humor slip. I didn't say that, but it was implied.

*

He went to Clarissa's place that night, so he can't have been that sick. I haven't spoken to him since. I can only hope he's out there gathering better jokes.

*

I don't know if you've noticed this, but I'm using a technique that I learned in the creative writing workshop. It's called impressionistic glances.

At least, I think that's what I'm doing. Maybe I need to be more fleeting. My impressionistic glances might be more like impressionistic, long, unnerving stares.

Anyway, you just write quick scenes/moments/thoughts that come out of nowhere. Like silver fish darting by in an aquarium (the teacher said). You put dots between them—the dots could be fish food, someone in the class suggested. It was a belligerent guy with square-framed glasses and when I looked back at him, the light hit the glasses and made me think of a fish tank. "Okay, yeah," the teacher said to that, "but let's not . . ." and then she petered off.

*

I have a new boyfriend now. His name is Peter. He falls asleep listening to the Cure each night, and he wears black eyeliner.

*

Meanwhile, here *I* am *petering off* . . . Ha ha.

*

Anyhow, Peter's crazy. Not in the technical sense, more in the wow, he doesn't fit into any category sense. He says we're *stepping out together.* Not "going out," but stepping out. Which makes him sound like he's sort of a dork, but no, he's the opposite. He and *cool* are also stepping out together, if you see what I mean. (I mean he's cool.) He's got the mod look, so he's all slick black hair, black pointy shoes, thin black tie, smudgy eyeliner, and his eyes themselves look like he's about to say something hilarious. Those sort of eyes. And he says things from other eras.

Stepping out. It's funny. The image of Peter and me, our feet lined up side by side. Like the start of a tap dance. Like a sunny day and me in a yellow dress which billows out like an umbrella.

*

One final thing about my novella before I fall asleep.

The wise seven-year-old boy?

He's going to be *sucked back* into the cruise ship novel. Because the author of that novel will decide s/he wants to resurrect him. The boy will be seen from the deck of the ship, bobbing up and down in one of those rings—and everyone in the novel will shout in disbelief: "HE'S ALIVE! HE'S ALIVE!"

He'll wave, lethargically, from the water. He'll be suffering from exhaustion and hypothermia. There'll be a tearful reunion with his mother.

*

Going to sleep. Robert still not here. Very mad at him.

It's 5 am.

Happy birthday to me, and to all a good night.

PART 3

1.

I flew home from Taylor Island—ha, I mean I flew *in an airplane*—reconfiguring my rage back into wry amusement. Life, I said to myself, smiling faintly. Life!

It was late by the time I reached Crows Nest, and Oscar was already asleep. Mum and I had tea, and she told me, as usual, that Oscar is the spitting image of Robert. I never see the resemblance. I see Oscar's father in his face, flashes of it, and sometimes, alarmingly, my own soft cheeks and puzzled gaze. But: "You're a little Robert!" my mother says to Oscar. And to me: "When he's concentrating, he gets the exact expression Robert used to get."

I worry that this is a weight on Oscar's tiny shoulders. There are photos of Robert on my mantelpiece; Robert's childhood artwork is framed on my walls. We all tell stories of Robert to Oscar, for the pleasure of it, and because he belongs in our family. An imaginary uncle, a hero, an enigma, watches over him, and this is who my mother expects Oscar to become.

I told Mum the hilarious story of the weekend. The sack races, the balloons, the paper planes, the competition for selection, and then the punchline: all this time they'd been teaching me to fly!

She laughed in surprise, and then fell about laughing properly, although I think this was partly relief that I hadn't joined a cult.

Eventually, her stomach was hurting so she had to stop. She grew thoughtful instead, and asked me how I felt about having read the chapters for "all those years," never knowing that the writers were "bonkers."

"All those years," she repeated wistfully. "Bonkers."

I assumed my wryly amused expression and explained that I'd mostly thrown the chapters away, or mocked them. It wasn't like I'd constructed my life around them. I told her about Frangipani—only her real name was Sasha, I explained, and Mum said "yes, yes," understanding that here was a woman with two names—and said I had the impression that she had taken every word of *The Guidebook* seriously, that it had been the framework for her reality. We shook our heads sadly at how she must be feeling, the crack running through her existence.

"But still," Mum said, "I'm thinking of you, too. All those years you've been getting those chapters in the mail? And didn't you write out your thoughts—or what was it, reflections?—for them at the end of every year and send them in? All those years!"

Then I got a bit testy and said it was time for me to go. I gave her a jar of honey, a slab of King Island Brie and a little book of sudoku puzzles, to thank her for looking after Oscar.

Oscar stayed asleep when I carried him to the car, but he woke abruptly during the drive home to announce that it was a "boat, not a helicopter."

"What was?" I looked in the rearview mirror: dark shape in car seat, gleaming eyes. I thought he must be dreaming aloud. I kept my voice dreamy so he could reenter sleep at any point.

"My Batman boat. It's a boat, not a helicopter."

"Of course it is," I agreed.

"Grandma thought it was a helicopter," he said, "and it's not."

It seemed we were awake, discussing life.

Several times, he repeated: *It's a boat, not a helicopter!*

Each time, I agreed wholeheartedly. *Yes. Your Batman boat is a boat. No question.*

I saw this could go on indefinitely. As we turned up Kurraba Road, I said: "Oscar, did you tell Grandma that it was a boat?"

"That's easy," he replied. "Every time Grandma say-ed it was a helicopter, I say-ed, *I see what you mean.*"

"Um?"

"I kept on saying *I see what you mean*, but she just kept on saying, *Got your helicopter?* and, *Oops, you dropped your helicopter!*"

"So what you're telling me," I said, as I maneuvered into a parking spot, "is that Grandma has been referring to your Batman boat as a helicopter for the last three days, and instead of saying, *Grandma! It's not a helicopter! It's a boat!* you've been saying, *I see what you mean*, and hoping this would make her stop?"

"She didn't stop," he told me grimly.

I had been looking forward to carrying a sweet, sleeping boy inside, placing him ever so gently onto the bed and covering him up, hearing him do a little snuffly thing, holding my breath until he relaxed into sleep again, gazing down at him with a surge of love—*he's so exquisite!*—stroking his soft face with my fingers, wishing he was awake so I could hear his little voice, and then creeping back out of the room and getting a cup of tea and some chocolate.

However, we walked up the stairs side by side, arguing about whether I should call Grandma *right now* to tell her it was a boat.

Eventually, he was in bed and I had to do the whole routine: "Twinkle, Twinkle"; "Mary Had a Little Lamb"; "Lullaby and Goodnight"; and "Hush, Little Baby." (I don't know the words of that last one, I just make it up. *Hush, little baby, don't you cry, Mumma's gonna bake you a lemon meringue pie. And if that lemon meringue pie's too flaky, Mumma's gonna play you music that's groovin' and shaky.* That's just one example. It varies a lot.)

"Oscar," I said, when I'd paused to find a rhyme for *If those parrots sing a bit raucously* (*a friend who behaves tortiously?* But would he want the gift of such a friend?), "you know how you kept saying to Grandma, *I see what you mean?*"

"Yes."

"Well, what do you think it means when a person says, *I see what you mean?*"

Oscar widened his eyes at me accusingly. "Stop it," he commanded.

He was right. The question was too complex.

I returned to our traditional songs, then scratched his back, patted his back, told him I loved him so, so, so, so much, engaged in a brief discussion about how much, and about whether Batman would defeat Spider-Man in battle, walked out of his room and into my own, unpacked my suitcase, and went to bed.

2.

In bed, I smiled my wry smile and found myself weeping. I tried to make my tears quiet and amused, a sort of chuckling of tears, but soon the pillowcase was wet and my body was shuddering, the sobs taking on an alarming momentum of their own. I had to bury my head under the quilt.

I cried for my fifteen-year-old self, standing in the kitchen looking at an envelope inside a rusty frying pan. I cried for my self of two days earlier, standing on an airfield, staring at a tall man and wondering if I was supposed to snow.

I cried for my happy, hopeful, righteous, wise teenage self, peering through a window at a darkened, empty driveway on the eve of my sixteenth birthday.

For the self that keeps accepting, and hoping, accepting, and hoping, like quitting cigarettes and then reaching for another, the loop of magic smoke around the coincidence of dates.

If he disappeared on the eve of my sixteenth birthday, he will reappear on the eve of my thirty-sixth. The men pointing upward, the cake on a plate, the promise of snow, a note pushed underneath the door.

*

Next, I cried for Antony in his flat cap, for his story of coming out at a birthday dinner, for Daniel with his smoky eyes and broken glass, for Niall standing with his back to me at a table of breakfast pastries.

I kicked out my legs so the sheets got in a state, and cried for the empty space in my bed.

One.

Two.

Three.

One, two, three, I thought, the sobs tearing through the numbers, one, two, three, Robert, Finnegan, *Guidebook*, one, two, three, my brother, my husband, my *Guidebook*.

I cried for Oscar and his Batman boat. *I see what you mean*, I thought, although I didn't see at all, so I cried harder.

I had held myself together, laughed at *The Guidebook*, but all the time, secretly, there it was: the promise of truth, of answers, a reason to keep living with the absence of knowledge, this immense knot of silence and mystery, the loss of Robert, the loss of Finnegan.

But now even *The Guidebook* was gone.

That night, I dreamed that I was climbing a tree, picking leaves as I climbed, placing these into the pockets of my corduroy jacket, climbing, picking, climbing, picking, the leaves small, ordinary leaves, sharp-edged, dark green, tear-shaped, and then I sensed something odd, a spreading all around me, and I was in a forest of trees! Other people were busy climbing the other trees, only they were plucking fruit: mulberries, peaches, plums. None, as far as I could see, were taking leaves.

3.

The next morning, I dropped Oscar at Blue Gum Cottage, his day care center, and drove to the Happiness Café.

My café is on Blues Point Road in McMahons Point, a block down from the main stretch. The path is wide here and runs up the hill past cafés and restaurants with al fresco dining beneath golden robinia trees, a post office, a bookstore, an artisanal grocer (shiny fruit in tissue paper, chocolate in fancy wraps), eventually darkening to the railway station, the office towers, the crowds more purposeful, the closer, grayer, shadowed streets of North Sydney. In the other direction, the path narrows, bumping down alongside stone houses, brick walls, side streets, and gardens, before stopping abruptly at a pocket of green grass, a pocket of bright blue water, the Harbour Bridge and Opera House posing for a photograph, a ferry boat crossing one way, a speedboat the other, their threads of white foam intersecting.

I started the Happiness Café after my marriage broke up.

Despair, eh? One moment it sends you scuttling under the covers; next it makes you open a café.

The idea is happiness immersion. We have mood-enhancing light and colors, chairs that make you say "aaah" as you relax into the cushions, quirky cutlery and napkin holders to elicit chuckles, newspaper clippings of feel-good stories, puzzles that are pleasantly easy to solve, audio loops of happy sounds like kookaburras laughing and brooks babbling, and indoor plants recommended by NASA for drawing toxins from the air. The walls are decorated with framed prints of misty cities or mountains piercing clouds, and framed lines of uplifting poetry rendered in calligraphic swirls.

The menu is a masterpiece of happiness-inducing foods.

But it's tricky.

For instance, not all foods that trigger serotonin are particularly tasty.

Also, it turns out that the effect a color scheme has on your mood depends on factors such as childhood and cultural background.

If you have lower back issues, you don't say "aaah" as you sink into the chairs, you frown: "Where's the lumbar support?"

Images of Paris in the mist might only remind you that you went there in the summer of 2002 (say), slipped on a cobblestone, broke your arm, and then discovered that your partner, who had promised to organize travel insurance, never did.

Swirly poetry makes some people physically ill.

And so on.

Another thing. The café is next door to a beauty salon that does hair, skin, and facial treatments. I remembered this now, as I approached. (I forget sometimes.) My heart sank a little. It had been propped up by anticipation—seeing Oliver, my chef, and Shreya, my waitress, my regular customers, setting the weekend aside—but now it readjusted.

I worry about the effect the salon might have on my customers' happiness, you see. A woman leaves the café, brimful of joy, notices Hair to the Throne next door, its signs offering *Anti-Aging Microdermabrasion* and *Hair Removal Laser Treatments*.

Her footfall, which had been animated, slows. "I *am* getting old," she sighs.

Or: "I *am* kind of hairy."

Or: "Hair to the Throne. Stupid name."

Her joy spills and evaporates.

Anyway, there it was. The salon.

Inside, Jennie waved at me with both hands. She's friendly and warm, Jennie. I like her. I just want her business to fail.

I pushed open her door, calling, "Hey!"

"Hey yourself!" she said. "How was your weekend away?"

That's how well Jennie and I know each other. She was aware that I'd just been away for the weekend.

"Great!" I replied.

So not that well, I guess. I mean, I didn't say, "My weekend shattered the illusions that have held me together for years. This was predictable. And yet it did so with an unexpected twist that has left me both fragile and bereft—although, in all honesty, that could also be because I was smitten by two different men simultaneously, neither of whom I will ever see again."

I just said: "Great."

We did chitchat not worth recording, while Jennie used some kind of pump to spray her client's hair, and the client sat quietly, like an obedient child. Then I stepped back out of the salon and turned toward my café.

Happiness, I thought. It's a complicated thing.

I've thought that many times before, of course. But now the thought sprouted tendrils. It rose up inside me like Jack's beanstalk. It twisted up my chest, down each arm, and pierced the fingernails!

The beanstalk thickened, grew to the circumference of a tree, and there I was, inside my dream, climbing up the branches, reaching for leaves while others plucked at plums and peaches.

I saw what the dream meant.

I saw what I must do.

4.

Later that night, I set to work doing what I knew I must.

By now, it was so obvious to me I felt embarrassed by my subconscious for dreaming with such transparency.

Here it is.

As you know, self-help is a vast and thriving industry. It spans books, movements, religions, communes, therapies, diets, psychics, philosophies, life-changing novels, and exercise regimes. From the earliest civilizations, people have been trying to sort out how to live, the point of it all, the key to happiness, and how to interact in a way that makes everybody like us.

Yet I had only ever read *The Guidebook*.

Seriously. Although I'd often skimmed, ignored, or mocked its pages, *The Guidebook* had been my only reference point. I'd never read another self-help book, never enrolled in an aura-healing class, never even been to see a motivational speaker!

Of course, it is impossible to live without coming into contact with self-help. Essentially, life is the river in which we all tread water, sometimes flailing, sometimes swimming a steady freestyle, maybe a leisurely breaststroke (and so on). Now and then a flotation device bobs by—a boat, a buoy, a candy-pink inflated castle—and people grab it and climb aboard. At last, they can have a rest.

They float along the river for a while (or forever), riding on the device. (Some are hoisted up when they are born and later jump off, to the distress or chagrin of the family and friends left aboard.)

Sometimes, the same style of flotation device is suddenly everywhere, crowded with excited people, and they call out to you, "Here! Come try this! It's brilliant! My sister told me about it! If only I'd found it sooner!"

They're in the zeitgeist; they *are* the zeitgeist. You catch the lingo, you read the articles, your friends go off to the courses and describe them to you, embarrassed by their conversion, or they babble, not embarrassed at all.

So, I knew some of the basics. I had sampled various religions over the years, trying to get a navigation system to God, or whoever was in charge, so that I could put in a request for the return of my brother. I knew about living in the moment and the value of yoga. Movies had taught me how therapy works: the therapist tells you to set boundaries, and that nothing is truly your fault.

Also, I knew that there was something called chi which you—well, you wanted it. It belonged to another culture, but it was good.

But I had never climbed aboard anything! I was living my life, missing my brother, searching for my brother, I was studying law, I was falling in love, I was losing my husband, I was being a parent, and whenever I saw, say, a giant inflatable swan floating by, I waved it on! No, no, I said, I'm okay, I've got my *Guidebook*.

There was so much I didn't know, because all I'd ever known was *The Guidebook*.

Yet here I was running a Happiness Café!

To be clear, and to get out of the river and back to my dream metaphor: I had been plucking leaves from the pages of *The Guidebook*, and had never tried the fruits of other trees.

So I'd sped to Stanton Library after work and taken out a number of self-help books. These were now stacked on my kitchen bench.

I took the top one from the pile and started reading.

The Celestine Prophecy, it was called. I'd heard of it and knew it was connected with coincidence, and with messages delivered by strangers.

The book turned out to be the story of a man who travels around Peru eating soup, sleeping here and sleeping there. (People were amazingly hospitable.) He learns that we can direct our energy at plants and they'll grow really well, but then we eat the plants. So, in the end, they lose. But *we* win, in that, following our consumption of the plants, we grow happy and healthy. Chew food very slowly, the man also learns—I suspect the author was suffering from indigestion at that point—and be nice to other people and open to conversation because anybody might have a message for you. You don't need to think hard, or weigh up factors; you just keep an eye out for coincidence and messages. Easy. In the end, we will stop working because we'll make money by selling our messages, and next we will vibrate madly and disappear.

5.

The morning after I finished *The Celestine Prophecy*, I felt very wise and floaty.

I wondered if Oscar had a message for me. He had just woken me by jumping onto my bed and shouting, "GET UP!", so that might have been his message. But I checked for another.

"Oscar, do you have a message for me?"

"Yes!" he said at once.

This made my chest flutter.

"What's your message?" I asked him carefully.

But he scrambled off my bed and ran from the room. His footsteps pattered down the stairs.

Oh well, I thought.

I lay in bed, stretching my arms above my head and looking forward to the time when nobody would need to work and we'd all vibrate invisibly. Although, how would I keep an eye on Oscar when he was invisible?

And he's so cute! It would be a shame not to see him anymore.

Oscar was singing downstairs. Footsteps on the stairs again. Now he was back in my room, something cupped in his hands. "Hold out your hands," he instructed, and he filled my palms with Honey Nut Cheerios. Many fell onto the pillow. "Here is your message," he said.

"Oh," I said. "Surprising!"

"No, no," he chided, disappointed in me. "You say this: *Thank you for my message*. You say: *I love my message.*"

He ran back down to the kitchen to get me another message.

This went on for a while, trails of Cheerios up and down the stairs. Then *I* had to give *him* a message, and it had to be something from the fridge.

Eventually, I drove him to day care.

I kept glancing at the trees we passed, trying to tap into their energy, so I wouldn't steal Oscar's. I worried about just how much of Oscar's energy I had taken in the last four years, before I had read *The Celestine Prophecy* and knew I was supposed to get it from the universe.

I felt the energy from the trees! Seriously! It kind of tipped into my head through my right ear and tunneled its way through my body. It was very good. It was so good I wondered how I'd missed it before. I felt the energy clogging up around my shoulder, so I used my imagination to scoop it up and pour it into the essence of my being.

After that, I just had to break off a piece when I needed it. For example, I took a piece to help me find a parking spot, and to remember the security code at Blue Gum Cottage, and to push the gate open—it gets jammed. It was good to let the universe deal with that jam.

I signed Oscar in, read a notice about proposed Mandarin lessons for the children, felt grateful to the universe for offering my child lessons in Mandarin, and said goodbye. Oscar considered whether to weep at my departure or to get straight on with playing. I could see it in his face, the weighing up of factors. But then his friend Lachlan ran by, calling, "Oscar! We need you!" so that was decisive. I left him busy trying to catch Lachlan to find out what was needed.

Arriving at the Happiness Café, I asked Oliver, my chef, if he had a message for me, and he said, "Yes, the Schweppes guy called to say he was running a couple of hours late, but no sweat, we still have plenty of soft drinks in the fridge."

"No, no," I said. "I mean a message. Like, a *message?*"

"Hm." Oliver squinted.

"Like an insight?"

A sharp intake of breath through Oliver's teeth, his eyes bright. "For sure I do!" he said. He clicked his tongue quickly, thinking, thinking.

Eventually he admitted that he was not completely sure what his insight was, but it might be something to do with the color of my dress, which wasn't the ideal shade for my complexion, and he'd need to consider overnight. Was that okay?

"Sure," I said. I'm an easygoing boss.

Our waitress, Shreya, had been listening to our exchange, and now she raised her eyes to the ceiling and exhaled. I knew better than to ask her for a message.

"Don't worry," I told her. "You'll give me a message without even realizing you're doing it."

She rolled her eyes. "I have zero interest in happiness," she had told me when I originally interviewed her for the position, which I found so funny I hired her.

*

I spent much of the day eavesdropping on customers' conversations, in case they contained messages.

A man sat in the corner, at table seven, making call after call about insurance policies. As far as I could deduce, he'd recently separated from his wife and wanted her name removed from his policies. An open manila folder lay before him and, as he talked, he fanned out paper after paper until the table was covered.

At table four, two girls in their twenties were drinking green tea. "Oh, his photos!" one enthused. "His *photos!*"

The other said: "No, it's just his equipment. He's not that good."

I would have liked to see the photographs myself, to decide. Also, I can't hear the word *equipment* without thinking of my first boyfriend, Samuel.

Meanwhile, at table twelve, a woman sat alone, a map open on the table before her, her hand covering her mouth.

Shreya approached insurance guy at table seven, a plate of banana bread in her hand. She paused and studied the scattered papers: "Let's clear a bit of real estate here," she said.

6.

I arrived home weary from my floaty search for messages.

There was a letter in my mailbox. The envelope was white. A pair of leaping dolphins on the stamp. Addressed in blue handwriting. No return address.

Probably another letter from a real estate agent offering to value my house and pointing out that there are motivated buyers in this neighborhood. These always make me uneasy, imagining small crowds of motivated people loitering outside my front door, ready to pounce. They'll be so mad, I always think, when they find out I can't sell. (I don't own this house. I'm renting.)

Oscar tipped his toys out of their box onto the floorboards, with a sound like shattering glass. I put the envelope on the side table and peered through the front door glass. *Give me energy*, I requested of the magnolia on the nature strip outside, *please.*

The tree didn't answer, only waving its leaves around in the breeze.

It wasn't just trees, I recalled. You could also get your energy from stars. I reached for a blue marker and wrote *Remember stars* on the back of my hand.

Next I ran back over the conversations I'd overheard in my café, looking for messages.

Insurance, photography, equipment, maps. They did seem connected! They meant I was supposed to go on a trip somewhere, buying travel insurance first, using maps to find my way, taking photographs!

I was pleased. I like a road trip. The logistics, however, would be complicated.

Taking a break from my thoughts, I picked up the envelope from the side table and opened it. Inside, there was a single typed sheet. I ran my eyes down to see who was talking.

Wilbur, of all people. *Best wishes, Wilbur*, it concluded.

Here is what the letter said:

Dear Abigail,
I have made a serious error of judgment.
    I invited you and the other recipients of The Guidebook *to a weekend retreat and told you that you knew how to fly.*
    Not surprisingly, each of you is now either angry or heartbroken— or, anyway, annoyed—and all of you consider me insane. Or, at the very least, inane. I don't blame you.
    I should have been open and honest from the start. I should have told you, for example, that Rufus and Isabelle, the authors of The Guidebook, *were my parents.*
    Those same chapters they mailed to you were placed, by my parents, on my bed.
    My parents died last year, within a few months of each other. They left instructions for me (their only child) to complete the venture

they began when they first sent out the chapters. A portion of their estate was allocated for this purpose.

Out of a sense of loyalty to my parents—also befuddled by grief, I guess—I followed their instructions precisely. I sent out invitations, arranged the accommodation, carried out the weekend activities, and selected the "chosen ones."

Instead, I should have told you this: until my parents died, I had no idea that they believed in human flight. I loved my parents. They were kind, funny, and eminently reasonable. In fact, they were more sensible, more rational than many of the parents of my friends. I feel gutted by this absurdity I've uncovered: it's completely inconsistent with my memories of them.

And yet, I cannot bring myself to abandon my parents' plans.

Now I am going to say something you will find preposterous. You'll laugh aloud. Here it is: Would you consider coming along to the flying seminars?

I will hold them on Tuesday evenings from 6:30 pm at my apartment, 3/17 Engalwood Street, Apartment 3C, Newtown. We will begin next Tuesday. Please meet me in the lobby of the building.

Listen, I know that human flight is impossible. I'm not a fool. I have pages of detailed instructions on how to conduct these flying seminars, and I am profoundly aware that every word is nonsense. But the pages were written by my parents.

I mocked The Guidebook *often, or ignored it, but all along I sensed it was leading somewhere. I've waited for some answer, some explanation or conclusion. Without one, I feel incomplete.*

Perhaps you feel that way too? If we undertake these seminars together, carry out my parents' plans (as a game, an exercise?), perhaps we might begin to see the point?

Thank you for listening.

I hope to see you next Tuesday at 6:30 pm.

Best wishes,

Wilbur

I put the letter down.

"Tuesdays at six thirty pm," I scoffed, looking over at my child. You see there, Wilbur? I have a child! And who do you think will look after him while we carry out this whimsy, this tribute to your parents (good and kind, I'm sure, despite being unhinged)?

I did feel a profound yet paper-thin (mismatched adjectives, I realize, and yet . . .) sadness for Wilbur and his lost parents. Also, I liked that Wilbur seemed to write from his heart (even if a little fancily). But mainly I was busy with my rage and despair—mild rage, mild despair, but nevertheless there it is, whenever I'm invited to an evening event.

Tuesdays at 6:30 pm.

The preposterousness! The insurmountability!

I know what you're thinking: Easy! Get a sitter!

See how you even shorten the word *babysitter* like that? The casual, the abbreviated, the breezy: pop it in the freezer! jump in a cab! bang it in the microwave! shoot me an email! throw the kid in the car! Easy, breezy, *bung-it-all-in-there*, Jamie Oliver–style. As if the words themselves, the quick breeze of them, will do the job for you, will themselves tackle this relentless, this exhausting life.

Here is what a night out means to me:

Choose a babysitter; make the phone calls; send the texts; choose a different babysitter because that one just replied: *Sorry! I'm busy!* ☹; find money for the sitter—*or* ask for a favor from a friend, take on the debt, the guilt, the gratitude, the logistics, the complexities; sort out Oscar's dinner; sort out sitter's dinner; resent having to sort out sitter's dinner; figure out how late the sitter or favor can stay . . . and that's all before I have to tell Oscar: *I'm going out tonight!* and see his smile flip away, panic parachuting in, the pleading or defiance, his hands on my sleeves, little footsteps chasing me, determined, down the hall, dragging me away from the front door, his tears and snot and wails, the babysitter standing back, uncertain and judgmental—*don't fall for it, he's manipulating you*—the favor moving forward, wincing and judgmental—*oh, how can you leave the little one, you already leave him so much to go to work, what could be more important than the little one, he's going to grow up before you know it, stay at home!*

My phone was ringing somewhere.

I moved toward my handbag but the sound drifted away. It was coming from upstairs. No, from the kitchen.

The phone was on the bench beside the bananas.

Missed call.

Dad.

My dad almost never calls me! He never calls anyone!

(He has a wife named Lynette. I suppose he calls her at times.)

I waited a moment and then *ding!*

Voicemail.

"Mummy?" Oscar called from the living room.

I looked at my stack of library books on the counter. The next one in the pile was called *Tuesdays with Morrie*.

Tuesdays at 6:30 pm.

"MUMMY?" Oscar shouted.

"Yes, Oscar?"

"Mummy? We need to get a cat."

I picked up the phone, to listen to the message.

"Hello, Abigail," said my father's voice. He speaks carefully when he does call and avoids contractions. "It is your dad. I have a proposition. Well, Lynette has a proposition. She says there is a new play center that has opened up next door—I beg your pardon, next door but one—to the printing place where she works in Erskineville. Now. Lynette thinks it might be fun if she and I took Oscar to dinner at the pizza joint and then let him have a play in the play center. To give you a break. This coming Tuesday, Lynette thought, and then every Tuesday if you like, depending on how it works out. As a regular thing. Anyhow, think on it. It would be Tuesdays," he repeated. "Tuesdays at around six pm."

"MUMMY!" Oscar shrieked. "We need a cat!"

7.

If you have a map, you know that Erskineville is just down the road from Newtown, where Wilbur intended to hold his seminars.

You may have pieced together all the Tuesdays flying at me—the book on the bench, the letter on the side table, the voicemail from my dad—and you will have realized that my babysitting issue, which you probably thought I was making too much of, was here beautifully resolved.

Finally, if you have read my rental agreement, you will know that I am not allowed a cat.

Setting aside the cat issue, the universe was clearly sending me a message: I should go to the Tuesday flying seminars.

8.

It turned out that one of Oscar's day care teachers had told him he had to get a cat.

I found this unlikely.

"Which teacher told you that you had to get a cat?"

"The orange one."

"Leesa?"

"Yes."

When he says "the orange one," Oscar is referring to the color of Leesa's hair. She is not otherwise orange.

"Leesa told you we had to get a cat?"

"Yeah. I forgetted but I just me-membered."

I like how he says *me-membered*. On the other hand, I'm happy to correct *forgetted*. A speech therapist visited Blue Gum Cottage once, and addressed the parents. *Rather than pointing out a child's mistakes*, she instructed us, *you should repeat the word yourself, correctly.*

"Three times," the therapist said. "Say it correctly *three* times. So if your child refers to his friend Thomas, but pronounces Thomas's name with a lisp, you should reply, 'Yes, and wasn't it nice to see Thomas? And hasn't Thomas done a lovely painting? It would be good to visit Thomas, wouldn't it?'"

By which time, I thought, the child will regret ever having mentioned Thomas. He will be backing away from you slowly.

"You forgot to tell me that we have to get a cat?"

"Yes. I forgotted."

"If Leesa told you to get a cat," I said, giving up on *forget*, "she was only joking."

"No." He was adamant. "It was not a joke. She didn't laugh. She telled me we have to get a cat."

"Well, it's not up to Leesa whether we get a cat or not!"

This led to a long, exhausting argument. I should have just shown him the rental agreement.

9.

In the bath that night, Oscar wanted to talk about Spider-Man.

"Let's talk about Spider-Man," he said.

This is a conversation we have often.

"Okay," I said. "What do you like about Spider-Man?"

"I like that he shoots webs," Oscar declared.

"I like that he helps people who are in trouble," I said promptly. Always trying to teach him something.

But he seemed unimpressed, and switched to a game in which the bath toys engaged in battle. The plastic boat could shoot fire and lava. The rubber duck, ice. The seahorse left a trail of poisonous spiders. The bottle of bubble bath was a crack shot with a rifle. And so on. He urged me to participate, offering the washer and soap for my team. They had no particular powers, he explained.

This is a world, Oscar's world, of fire, ice, lava, shooting webs.

*

On the landing outside the bathroom, Oscar stopped. He looked up at me, his hair damp, eyes big, draped in his white towel.

"You can have any wish you like," he whispered.

"I can?"

"Yes. Right now."

Quickly, I flicked through options, sensing somehow that a four-year-old *could* do it; that if anyone could, he could. Mansions on the harbor with guesthouses and tennis courts; world peace; a chain of Happiness Cafés around the globe.

"For you to be happy and healthy, Oscar," I said.

He nodded curtly. "That's your wish?"

"Yes."

He leaned forward and slapped me fairly hard on the face three or four times with a small cupped hand, the firm slaps of the bishop at a confirmation. Then he stepped back and said nonchalantly, "You might get that wish—or you might not."

He fell asleep while I sat on the edge of his bed, singing and rubbing his back, and all the other rituals and then, just when I thought he was breathing into dreams, he murmured, "Don't forget we have to get a cat."

10.

In bed, I thought of my wish and how, if I could have a supplementary wish, it would be for a beautiful man who would sing in my heart and listen with his eyes. The man would be lying beside me in this bed right now, and his hands would be reaching for my body. In the moonlit room, I could see him almost, the shadow of this man turning toward me.

I felt a rush of rage then, the rage of longing, its violent ache, but more than that, rage at a world that cheapens, dismisses my need for sex and love. That labels it women's fiction, rom-com, chicklit. The sneering at the happy ending, the pursed lips intoning: *You don't need a partner! You must be happy with yourself, content to be alone!*

I don't want a man to save me; I *am* happy with myself. Only, this longing for physical contact is real, a shape with dimension, and it's all on a continuum with longing for closeness, for friendship, connection, for love. It's a yearning that reaches back to lost best friends, lost brothers, lost birthdays, lost birthday wishes.

11.

A strange, grim calm changed the contours of my room, the tone of the moonlight.

I don't deserve a wish. The chain of causation is clear.

PART 4

1.

The driveway, the front door, the hallway, the house, all crouched beneath a heavy silence.

This was back in 1990, the night before my sixteenth birthday.

I was writing my "Reflections on 1990," but every second sentence I stopped to listen out for Robert. Footsteps on the porch, creak of front door, key clatter in ceramic bowl on hallstand, footsteps down the hall, the puff of my door opening, Robert's voice, *I'm here*—all those sounds were waiting, poised, on the *edge* of happening—but the silence just sprawled into the blackness of the night.

So I carried on typing.

Sometimes the silence was puzzled and friendly, a comical puppy with tilted head, but other times it would turn sly and slither onto my lap, coil itself deep into the pit of my stomach.

Fangs! A flare of terror! *Where is Robert?*

(I was pretty interested in horror movies back then.)

I didn't mention my concerns in my "Reflections on 1990." Once, I settled my fingers onto the keys, ready to type: *Seriously, where is he? Has he had an accident or what?*

But instead I typed: *I have a new boyfriend now. His name is Peter.*

I went to bed about 5 am. The silence coiled down under the covers with me.

But I woke at noon and it was my birthday! I lay still in the summer light and listened, and there was silence, but *completely different.* Now it was misty and calming, like yoga.

Because I thought it translated into Robert being fine. If something had *happened* to him, I reasoned, there'd be noise. Something would have woken me earlier: phone calls, police fists pounding on the front door. Shrieks and cries running up and down the hall.

But the house was quiet.

There were *some* sounds, Saturday sounds like birds and lawnmowers, but these were consistent with Robert being fine. I got up and pushed open the door of Robert's room. It was empty, the bed made, so I wandered the house, looking for him.

I opened the sliding door and found my parents on the terrace smiling about something. They were sitting at the outside table with cups of tea and newspapers, an opened packet of SAO biscuits, butter, jams, knives, crumbs, and orange peels.

"Birthday girl!" they said. "Welcome to the land of the living!" That kind of thing. "Happy birthday!"

"What time did Robert get in last night?" Dad asked.

"Is he up yet?" Mum said. "We should have your birthday breakfast and do presents!"

They both looked at me, waiting.

"He's not home yet?" I asked.

They continued to look at me, but now blinkingly.

"Oh yeah, I forgot," I said, smooth, covering for him and his secret girlfriend in Glebe. "He's staying at Bing's an extra night because they needed more practice."

"What! So he missed your farewell ceremony last night? I can't believe it! You always do that!" They both seemed mildly outraged on my behalf, which made me realize: Yes, they were right! It *was* outrageous!

I started to feel angry.

"I'll go phone him at Bing's," I said, turning back toward the house, "and see what time he's coming home."

"You have Bing's number?" Mum called, and I said, "Yeah."

Actually I didn't have Bing's number, and, more to the point, I didn't have Clarissa's number either.

Once I got into the kitchen I decided I was going to track him down somehow. *It's just not good enough,* I thought, in a teacherly voice. *Just because you're sick, it doesn't mean everything should fall apart. Actually, that's a reason not to let it fall apart. It makes our traditions even more important!*

That's the sort of lecture I was drafting as I searched for Clarissa's number in Robert's bedroom. I don't really know if I was right—I mean, *are* traditions more important when you're sick? Shouldn't sickness actually make us all more flexible?—but I chose to believe it passionately as I looked.

I was trying to remember Clarissa's last name so I could find her in the phonebook, but when it shot diagonal into my brain—Clarissa *Armstrong!*—well, she wasn't in the book. Plenty of C. Armstrongs, but none in Glebe. She was sharing her place with other students; the number must have been in one of their names.

I went back to opening drawers in Robert's bedroom, and flicking in a random way through papers on his desk. I found his homework diary and turned pages—and there it was. On 7 July, right next to details about an English essay on *Romeo and Juliet, CLARISSA* in Robert's happy handwriting, a phone number beside it.

I took it into the kitchen and dialed the number. A boy's voice answered.

"Robert?" I said.

"Who?" said the boy, and of course it wasn't Robert. I asked if I could speak to Clarissa and the boy said she'd moved out of there three months ago to a place on Glebe Point Road. I recalled something about Robert taking a day off school to help her label boxes.

He'd illustrated each label, he told me, and had taken an interest in the art of classifying possessions.

The guy on the phone was obliging. He tracked down Clarissa's new number for me. I found his voice sexy, warm, and supercool. University student, I thought. If Robert can have one, why can't I?

Then I remembered my boyfriend, Peter. I smiled suddenly, thinking of him. He ought to call for my birthday soon.

I dialed the number that the sexy, warm, supercool guy had given me, resuming my angry thoughts about Robert having missed our ritual last night. I was ready to be strident, to really *explain* to Robert that it was, well, it was my *birthday*. I was going to tell him I'd stayed up until 5 am waiting. I was excited about that part, and felt it fevering away, the climax of my speech.

Clarissa answered this time. I recognized her voice. I'd met her a couple of times at parties, and once at the train station with Robert.

"No," she said, "Robert's not here. We broke up a couple of months ago, actually. Didn't you know?"

I told her that now I was mad at Robert for two things: one, for not being here on my birthday, and two, for not telling me he'd broken up with Clarissa. She laughed like I was being witty, but I wasn't, I really was mad. I couldn't piece together from her tone why they'd split up. She said we should hang out sometime, and I thought: *Really? That depends on the story here. Could be a loyalty issue.*

But out loud I said, "Yeah! We should."

I put down the phone.

Mum and Dad were coming in from outside, carrying their cups and stacked plates.

"Any news?" Mum asked.

"Oh, he and Bing had walked down to the shops," I said. "Bing's mum said she'd get him to call me when they're back."

Mum nodded vaguely. Dad opened the fridge to put the milk away, then stopped. We used to have this list of words on the fridge, Robert and I. We were working on our vocabulary, so each week we'd write down five words along with their definitions. I seem to remember we'd lost the *L–Z* volume of the dictionary at that time, so the words were all from *A–K*. I think *frangible* was there that day.

Also *incipient*.

So Dad paused with the milk in one hand, the other hand holding the fridge door ajar, and he studied our list.

"I have *incipient* anxiety," he said.

I looked at him, startled. "What?"

"Well." His brow crinkled. "It's just this strange sense of foreboding that I have."

Then he put the milk away, closed the fridge and grinned, his expression like: *It's cool! I'm just fooling around.*

2.

Much of my sixteenth birthday was wasted being furious with Robert, at the same time as secretly thinking that his absence meant a surprise party for me, at the same time as being faintly frightened that something was wrong.

If someone is not where he says he is, is he a missing person or a liar?

Peter phoned and said, "Many happy returns," which was his quaint way. I took the call in my parents' room, with the door closed, and told him all about Robert. He seemed to think it was awesome.

We didn't use the word *awesome* in those days: I'm translating his reaction for the modern reader.

Basically, he laughed with delight—he's not at Bing's! he's not at Clarissa's!—as if this were a magic trick Robert was performing, or a detective story with unexpected twists. Peter instructed me to call him if anything else unfolded but said that otherwise he'd see me tonight.

We were going out for Chinese for my birthday: Mum, Dad, Robert, Peter, and me.

"What if Robert doesn't turn up for that either?" I asked.

"Whoa," Peter said, like that was the coolest suggestion ever. Or like he needed his horse to slow down. One or the other. Then he hung up.

I played with the phone dial, spinning it and letting it fall back, thinking angry thoughts about how Robert was confusing my birthday, and happy thoughts about my upcoming surprise party.

If he didn't turn up in time for the birthday dinner, was I meant to cover for him again? I mean, how far did he want to take this thing? Also, what if he was now lost at sea and about to be eaten by a shark? Shouldn't I tell my parents so we could swim out and save him?

But if this *was* part of a surprise party plan, I'd feel such a fool for worrying. I should just play it cool.

But the shark! Or maybe a lion?

Back and forth I went, all the time heading grimly toward my birthday dinner, where I feared I would have to tackle the ultimate moral dilemma.

It turned out I didn't have to tackle it.

I was getting ready for the birthday dinner when Mum knocked on my bedroom door, a glinty look in her eye. "So I'm down at the shops picking up your birthday cake," she said, smile growing like she's heading for the punchline, "when who do I run into but *Bing's* mother!"

That's when it started to unravel.

Afterward, I sometimes thought that everything would have been okay—that Robert would have skidded up the driveway on time for my birthday dinner with a black eye, arm in plaster and a story about having secretly entered a skateboard competition, and stacked it doing a three-sixty—if only Mum hadn't run into Bing's mother down at the shops.

But she did, so now she knew Robert had not been at Bing's, so now I admitted he'd told me he was at his girlfriend's place in Glebe, so now there was fanfare about the girlfriend in Glebe—which was a red herring, I kept telling them, irrelevant, barking up the wrong tree—because they'd *broken up* and he wasn't there at all . . .

Once I had them back on track, there were many phone calls, always circling back on Bing and Clarissa, the false stories, the false trails, and me trying to get people back on course, and now it was the next day, and we were searching his bedroom, and his favorite coat was gone—and now Mum was sure we'd given that away to Goodwill a year ago, so it *wasn't* gone, or not really gone, and now we were arguing about whether he'd have done that—whether he'd have given away his favorite coat—and now my dad was calling the police.

3.

My mother likes to recite conversations; she's a human listening device. *So he said, and then I said, and then Robert pointed out.* When she told me about Robert's MS diagnosis, it was as if I were in the doctor's office with them, Robert in one chair, Mum beside him, Dr. Lee across the big desk, the window lit behind him, a framed photograph of his two grown children on his desk.

"You might have been feeling extremely tired," Dr. Lee said. "You might have been confused, your arms or legs might have felt numb, you might have tripped or stumbled, you might have felt dizzy. Does any of this ring true?"

All the symptoms, scrolling out across the doctor's office, across Robert's room as Mum talked. And here they came! All the little moments: Robert falling asleep at Grandma's eightieth birthday party, Robert sitting astride the brick wall at the skate park and slowly tipping sideways, Robert rubbing the feeling back into his arm. Falling down at the edge of the ocean. I could see it in my mother's eyes, my brother's eyes, my own eyes—to the extent that you can see your own eyes.

It was like when they open a new register in a supermarket, and here come the shoppers swarming right to it. It's pleasing, at first: Like a question and a rush of answers. A magnet drawing pins, a collection, a list, a robust set of examples.

But then it's just a waiting crowd and one tired cashier.

When the search for Robert started properly, it was similar: A Swarm rushing at the problem. People and suggestions gathering. He must be with *another* friend, *another* girlfriend! Everyone had ideas: his friends, our relatives, my dad's two brothers, my mum's sister, the cousins, they all knew exactly where he was. The police heard the story and smiled in their wise, grim, world-weary way and promised he would be back.

Then the crowd of suggestions became restless, rowdy, and, quite frankly, ridiculous. Maybe he'd had an accident! His MS symptoms *caused* the accident—vertigo made him trip or fall over a cliff— No, the MS made him clinically depressed and suicidal, made him run away from home!

We chased the wild-Robert angle, the post-Clarissa-break-up angle, the depressed-Robert, the sick-Robert. We chased accidents in hospitals across the state. We spun around and chased the wildness of my parents' parenting, its wilderness.

Sometimes I thought MS was getting *way* too much attention, at other times I thought not enough. We kept racing down streets that curved back on themselves; following intertwined mazes.

After a while, the police paid attention. They finally agreed to file a missing persons report—only they called it a Person of Interest form, which we all found unsatisfactorily vague. "He's *more* than interesting! He's lost!" Later, we found out that Robert, being fifteen and unwell, was technically a "person at risk": they should have circulated his details immediately. But until we met Officer Matilda Jakopin, who took the details for the report from us, and therefore automatically became our caseworker, all the police we spoke with were languid, dismissive. One officer lectured us on the scarcity of police resources, and the wasteful-ness of employing police to hunt for recalcitrant teens who *always* made their way home. On the one hand, we wanted to tear this guy apart; on the other that phrase—*always made their way home*—was beautifully soothing.

4.

Our caseworker, Matilda Jakopin, had a bland face and thin, fair hair. She was asthmatic and always seemed to have a catch of phlegm in her throat. It made me want to cough for her. At first, we complained to each other that she was useless, weak, insipid, and ought to use a Ventolin inhaler. I secretly wished we'd got a big, burly man.

But it quickly emerged that Matilda was a straight talker with a colorful, profane vocabulary. This reassured us.

She swore most vividly about the officer who'd lectured us on wasted resources. "Bullshit," she said. "It's the hours right after they disappear, those are the *crucial* ones."

We knew that Robert's report had been sent to the Missing Persons Unit, which I found encouraging, but Matilda explained that this was basically five plainclothes officers who kept records of missing people. "If you're lucky," she said, "your liaison from the unit will go to bat for you— get out on the street, do the interviews." She knocked on my mother's shoulder. "*I'll* fight for you," she promised. "I won't quit. But you've all got to get out there yourselves. It pisses me off, I tell you. The whole thing."

We all fell in love with Matilda.

At everyone else, we were mad. We were madly searching, and we were mad at the *concept* of searching. Mum and I had good, intense exchanges about that.

"How do you search for a *person*?" we kept demanding, focused and angry. "It's not like you can look behind the couch!"

We wanted to be walking up and down streets, opening every door, searching behind *everybody's* couch. But you can't. You're not allowed.

If you knocked on a stranger's door and said, "I'd like to check if my brother is in here, please," they'd say, "Uh, no. He's not."

But you want to shove them out of the way, head down their front hall, check their closets, the top of their fridge, under the workbench in their garage.

*

We asked people, phoned people, everyone we knew and everyone *they* knew. I called a second cousin we hadn't seen since we were three. "Just wondering if you've seen Robert?" And I felt stupid, like asking was admitting to carelessness but, worse, it was exposing my own desperation, which itself made the desperation real.

My grandfather lived in Maroochydore, on the Sunshine Coast, and it seemed like an obvious place for a boy to run away to, so everybody kept suggesting Grandpa. I called him every day for a fortnight to see if Robert had turned up yet, until Grandpa *swore* on his black opal, which he'd won in a bet back in '63, that he'd phone me the second Robert got there.

The lies to my parents about being at Bing's, or to me about being at Clarissa's, cheered us up. It meant he must have had another plan. There was a strategy at work behind the scenes. Any moment he would pounce with his denouement.

"He must be *somewhere*," we said to one another, whenever we remembered the lies, as when you know that the keys are *somewhere* in the house, because you *used* them to get yourself inside.

We put leaflets in letter boxes, ads in the papers asking him to please come home. Signs on telegraph poles: HAVE YOU SEEN THIS BOY?

You're a lost cat, I told Robert in my head, ready to laugh with him about it.

At first I chose photos in which he looked supercool, so he'd be grateful, but sometimes I chose pictures of him looking dorky, tea towels knotted around his biceps, or blowing a mediocre pink bubble.

See what you get for doing this! I thought vengefully.

Also, I thought it would make him come running to tear the pictures down.

Mum called that radio guy, John Laws, one day and told the story, and he was nice to her, as were the people who called in afterward. For two days she was happy, thinking John Laws was on the case.

Matilda came by for coffee and talked to Mum about the media angle. "You want to remember that he'll probably come back," she said, stirring three heaped teaspoons of sugar into her coffee. "So there's his privacy to think about. His health is an angle, but is it an angle we want to use?"

She got us a double-page spread in the *Women's Weekly*. "It's good he's such a beautiful kid," she said, smiling and wheezing at the photographs we'd chosen. "That helps a lot. With boys, the problem is, people think they're tough, indestructible. We worry about girls, but we think boys can take care of themselves. Kind of sexist, to be honest. But your boy has such a sweet face. He's a handsome one, that's helpful."

We loved her even more.

We spent the summer looking, including Christmas Day, and then school started again.

I had no plans to go to school, but Mum said maybe somebody there would know something. I should keep an ear out, she said, ask questions. So I went back to school, but only as an undercover cop.

I remember seeing Bing crying in the schoolyard. He was crying for his missing best friend, for the eisteddfod that had come and gone without him, or he was crying because he'd agreed to cover for Robert, without knowing why, or because, when Bing's dad found out about the cover-up, he'd shouted at Bing in Malaysian and pointed upstairs, so that Bing bowed his head and disappeared upstairs to his room. I was there when that happened, my parents and me in their living room. I was amazed, and also deeply embarrassed for Bing.

I don't know. I guess that's why Bing was crying in the schoolyard. Maybe he'd just failed an exam. I know it really bothered me, seeing him take off his glasses and wipe his eyes with his shirtsleeve, and then wipe them again and again.

5.

There's a movie you might know called *Horton Hears a Who!*—it was a book first, by Dr. Seuss, before it was a movie—and I was watching it with Oscar at home last year.

An elephant finds a speck of dust. That is the movie in a nutshell.

About ten minutes in, I couldn't watch another minute. I had to leave the room.

"Oscar," I said, "I have to make you an avocado sandwich."

"Yes," Oscar said agreeably.

But I had to leave the room because inside that speck of dust—well, inside it there was a world of zany, happy people living busy lives in curly houses—but for *me*, inside that speck of dust was myself, aged sixteen, standing in my kitchen howling.

Three months after Robert's disappearance, I was home alone, staring at the phone, waiting for Robert to ring, urging him to ring, sending fierce or polite or ice-cold-James-Bond-villain-style messages out into the universe—and I let my gaze wander. An envelope sat in the frying pan.

Another *Guidebook* chapter. I opened it.

Chapter 56

```
Say you are a teapot.
   No.
   Say you are a china teapot on a ledge, faint
crack running around your base, so faint it might
not be a crack, it might be a tea stain or a hair,
and—
   No, no, no.
   Say you are the dust on a butterfly wing, and
say that the butterfly's in flight; now, say that
```

the butterfly is banking steep and say that you
feel yourself slide. Can you cling to the butterfly wing? Or will you slip, speck of dust, through
the still kitchen air to the bubble wrap happen-
stance below? The bubble wrap abandoned on the
kitchen floor, which once wrapped a teapot on a
ledge?

Say what you are.

That's our point.

What are you, dear reader? What exactly are
you?

Tell us what you are.

I howled. I read those words and the howl crept up my spine, and out through my throat and wrenched itself out into the world before I noticed it. The words were an arrow, they got me in the chest and tore a handy hole for the howl.

I was howling words: *What am I, what am I, what am I? What exactly AM I?*

Because that was the point, exactly. Who was I? Who was I? What was I?

Now, interestingly, I was sixteen, and maybe that's a question that all sixteen-year-olds ask themselves, from time to time. Maybe they also howl and sob, enjoying the drama of their existential crisis and the shaping of identity and whatnot.

But for me, there were only two answers to the question.

(a)   I was Robert's sister, which is to say I was Robert's best friend, the other half of Robert, so close to Robert that he'd never ever leave without telling me exactly where he was going.

(b)   I was Robert's sister, but it turned out we were not all that close, I was not all that important, I was irrelevant to him, he was indifferent to me, maybe even hated me a little, and so he'd run away without a word.

If (a) was true, Robert must be dead. If (b) was true, my life had been a lie.

I was standing in the kitchen, staring at my palms, each palm holding an impossible identity, asking myself which one was me. It came to me that everybody else had already seen this dilemma: everybody knew that I was the yardstick, the touchstone, benchmark, barometer. My parents often looked at me, and now I knew they were actually assessing: *Which one are you, Abigail? What's the truth?*

The police, Grandpa, Auntie Gem, the Grimshaws, my mother's best friend Barbara, my boyfriend Peter, all of them staring at me, wondering, calculating.

So I don't know how that movie, *Horton Hears a Who!*, finished up. I made a giant stack of avocado sandwiches and then baked chocolate-banana muffins. ("What is going *on* out there?" Oscar called now and then. Sometimes he sounded stern, sometimes wistful.) I don't know whether the people on the elephant's speck of dust are safe or not. I expect they're all fine in their happy, curly houses.

6.

There was nothing. Not a single clue. Robert had taken an overnight bag, his toothbrush, and a few clothes, but nothing else. Enough to stay at Bing's to practice piano; enough to stay at Clarissa's in Glebe. Nobody had seen him. I mean, *heaps* of people had seen him; they were always calling up, breathless with the news. But it was never him, or if it was, he was gone before we got there.

Meanwhile, the chapters from *The Guidebook* arrived every other week.

Sometimes I stared at them, astonished, or I laughed bitterly. Here's an example of one that made me sneer:

Chapter 12

```
I want to begin by recommending the apple.
   Honestly, it brightens the mind.
```

The apple. I looked around to tell Robert how preposterous it was, these people offering an *apple* when Robert was missing.

Again, I had nothing but contempt for these two chapters:

Chapter 87

```
Learn French or Spanish. Or maybe Japanese? You
can get a set of tapes at the library.
   Write a daily letter to yourself (in English)
explaining just how wonderful you are. Seal it in
an envelope. A little later, open it!
```

Chapter 33

```
Listen to music, play music, keep music in your
life at all times! Also: water. Immerse yourself
in water, run your hands under water, drink water.
Also: color. Listen to color, look at color, keep
color in your life at all times. And finally: con-
versation. Stand beneath the eaves and let them
drop. That is to say, listen in to conversations.
Try not be noticed doing this, as it is considered
rude.
```

I ignored the instructions and advice, shredded the pages, but now and then a chapter made me howl again.

Chapter 26

Oh God, and sometimes you miss somebody. And your
body aches, restless with it. The window is open,
the rain-green grass outside, and his shirt is
over the back of the chair and it's shifting, ag-
itated by the wind.

7.

We found out that Robert been working the night shift in a
twenty-four-hour supermarket near Clarissa's place. Whenever
I thought he was at Clarissa's, after they had broken up, and my parents
thought he was at friends' places, that's what he'd been doing. He must
have saved hundreds of dollars. So he had cash. This struck us all as good
news. He wasn't starving on the streets. He was in a youth hostel somewhere, we decided.

But he didn't telephone or send a postcard.

One day, I arrived home from school in a daze because Mandy
Kirkerwal had walked by my desk in math and whispered: "I know how
you feel. I've lost my cat."

I opened the front door and, as usual, tore around the house looking
for Robert. Or for signs of Robert: his bed rumpled, his backpack on the
floor, big shoes kicked across his floor.

Then I played back the answering machine even though the light
wasn't flashing.

Next I checked the mail in case he'd written.

He hadn't, but there was another envelope from *The Guidebook*.

I was glad to see the envelope. It would be something I could slowly,
methodically destroy. I opened it, low-level snarl carved into my face,
and I read:

Chapter 62

We want you to think about the number 3.

Close your eyes and count to 3, count *back* from 3, reflect on 3, write the number 3 on a piece of paper and stare at it a while.

And now tell us this: Do you know the Rule of Three?

You can survive for 3 minutes without air, or in icy waters.

You can survive for 3 hours without shelter in a harsh environment.

You can survive for 3 days without water.

You can survive for 3 weeks without food.

Take the number 3. It is survival.

That was *The Guidebook* and its sleight of hand again. I'm standing there, dazed, ready to shred it, and it leaps at me with grabby hands and shreds my daze instead.

I was hyperventilating. Shivering so hard my muscles hurt.

I was appalled that this hadn't occurred to me before but here it was: *I could not survive without my brother.*

Couldn't do it. Not a chance.

Not for 3 weeks, not 3 days, not 3 hours, not 3 minutes.

The number 3 bounced around my vision, flashing lights and pixels.

I stumbled. I let myself fall to the floor, ready for the logical conclusion. I spared a moment's thought for my poor parents, one child missing, and now they'd come home and find me dead. My breath came in rasps, and sometimes alarming silences. I was repeatedly convinced that my windpipe had snapped.

Then I caught sight of something sitting on the kitchen bench. It was small, blue and white.

Oh cool, I thought. Bounty.

I stood up from the floor, reached for it, and ate it. *Robert will be fine*, I thought, *Robert will be back*, as I smiled and ate, enjoying the soft sweet melt of coconut.

Which I suppose was a survival mechanism in itself: the ability to be cheered by a minor, unexpected pleasure, a chocolate-covered coconut treat, while on the very precipice of death.

Or it was some deep flaw in my character, I decided, coupled with a fondness for Bounty bars.

8.

Six months went by.

I was suspended from school for nearly blinding a teacher.

Speaking generally, I became ruthless and so did my parents. The three of us tore all over the state putting up posters, and tore through our friends like tornadoes, snatching them up and tossing them aside.

But they deserved it.

First, Mum stopped speaking to her best friend, Barbara. They'd been friends since high school. They'd hitchhiked to the Gold Coast together as seventeen-year-olds, been each other's chief bridesmaid, godmother to the other's first baby and so on. Barbara had been coming over almost every day since Robert disappeared, bringing packets of strawberry sponge fingers, and talking a lot about her sister-in-law. This sister-in-law was related to the attorney general in some remote way, and Barbara's plan was to *use* this *access point* to speak directly, personally, to the attorney general and demand that every police officer on the *force* get out there and look for Robert.

The first time she said this, I felt confused: *Well, aren't they?* (I thought). *Isn't every police officer in the country looking for Robert right now?*

Even though I knew that wasn't true. Then I felt glad that Barbara was going to make it true, at the same time that it struck me as wildly unlikely. The police had other things to do. I knew that much.

Nevertheless, she continued promoting her intended *personal* conversation. It was always future tense. Eventually I saw it would never take place.

One day, walking down the hallway to the kitchen, I heard Barbara say in a low voice: "Do you ever think this is maybe for the best?"

There was a *clump* sound. I think Mum was putting the kettle on to boil and she'd plonked it down quite hard.

"Um . . ." Mum said, almost a teasing tone in her bewilderment.

"I mean, because of his illness. If he'd gone downhill quickly, you'd be having to reconfigure your whole house. You'd be building ramps down the front porch steps."

I was in the kitchen doorway at this point, staring at Barbara, who was looking through the front window at the steps.

Mum was silent. She was reaching for the teacups.

There was a lot she could have said. For example: *MS affects people in many different ways, Barbara, and Robert might have been fine for years, forever even. He might never have required a wheelchair.*

And she could have said: *What kind of a breathtakingly fucked-up world do you think we live in, Barbara, where we'd prefer Robert to vanish from our lives rather than to have to build a* fucking *ramp?*

I was predicting the second option.

But Mum's voice was thrillingly polite. "Yes, good point, Barbara," she said. "It's far better that he's out there on his own, building his *own* ramps."

Then she asked Barbara to leave.

Actually, even before Mum started speaking, Barbara was apologizing, backtracking, trying to reel her words back in: she didn't know what she was saying, she was out of her mind with worry, she was clutching at straws.

I think now that Barbara had been coming over so often, and saying the same thing about her sister-in-law and the attorney general so much, that she was sick of herself. She was trying a new angle. She should maybe have tried it out in her own mind first, before saying it aloud.

But Mum never forgave her. Neither did I. This was annoying because she stopped sending me checks for fifty dollars on my birthday, *from your godmother, Barbara.*

A day or so later, Dad came home from work and said he'd got into a shouting match with his best buddy at work, Tony Stabback, because Tony had mentioned that it was a waste of police time to be hunting down drug-addicted teens.

Dad had told him to eff off.

Tony said, *No, no, you misunderstand, I'm not making a reference to Robert here!* But he knew that Robert went to dance parties and took ecstasy, because Dad had *told* him about this not long before, so Dad was not convinced, and he came "this close" to taking Tony out.

They didn't make up until years later, when Tony got stomach cancer and was dying. Dad visited him in the hospital and apparently they hugged.

Meanwhile, I stopped speaking to exactly three-quarters of my school friends, broke up with my boyfriend, Peter, and fell out with my best friend, Carly Grimshaw.

The school friends I stopped speaking to because it turned out they were stupid. That really surprised me. I'd always thought I had smart friends.

They got merit awards and knew who the prime minister was and worried about rain forests.

But Tina Amagetti said, "Look. About your brother. You *know* in your heart where he is, Abi. You have to trust your instincts. So . . . where is he?"

Vicki Livingstone said, "It's been six months. You have to let it go. It's time."

And Mia Sun, who got high distinctions in the math and science competitions every year, suggested we hold a séance to see if we could get in touch with him. "At least that way you'll know if he's dead or alive, right? You'll get *closure.*"

Idiots.

I couldn't even look at them.

Interestingly, that left me with a couple of girls I'd always thought of as the daft ones. Mish Choo, for example, never knew *what* was going on at school. "Wait, we were supposed to *read* that?" she would gasp, about a book we'd been studying for half a term already. Whenever a teacher issued complicated instructions, we'd all look around at Mish because we knew she'd be doing her hilarious thing, her face swimming in circles of confusion.

But Mish kept saying the right thing. "He'll be back, Abi. I promise."

Kirrily Palmer had recently been diagnosed with dyslexia, so we were only just becoming accustomed to the fact that she wasn't daft at all, but actually very intelligent. She would say, "You still don't have any news, do you? Holy mother-freaking *cocksucker*!" She looked up dictionaries of profanities, found expletives in other languages and curses from medieval times, all for me. That was also perfect.

I broke up with Peter because he used the word *heel*.

Whenever I saw him, he'd give me a brooding, tragic look, wrap me in his arms and say, "The latest?" I'd shake my head, and he'd hug me tighter. *Stop it*, I'd think, *you're hurting me*. Or: *Stop it, I need to be free to look for Robert*.

After a few minutes, he would stop hugging me, relax his hold on tragedy and initiate regular conversation about music, books, movies, philosophy—the things I had previously loved conversing about with him. Once, I saw him glance at his watch while in the brooding, hugging segment, and it occurred to me that he had allocated himself a five-minute slot for sadness and was checking whether the time was up.

Meanwhile, he continued using peculiar historical phrases like "chip chip." Possibly it was "pip pip." Either way, I wanted to kill him for that phrase. I was going to take that phrase and snap it over my knee. In addition, his tennis was erratic. I kept shooting scowls at him on the court, then quickly pretending I was only joking.

One day, he said something about wearing jodhpurs and I said, "You are a walking anachronism," and quickly assumed my cute, *just joking* look. He laughed as if we were having a good, flirty moment. Meanwhile, I made a decision that the next time he used a historic phrase or word I would break up with him.

Exactly one minute later he said, "I feel like such a heel, I left my—" I never found out what he left, or where, because I said, "Peter, this isn't working out."

He cried!

It was a shock, and I felt bad for him. But then he squeezed my hand, which hurt because I'd ripped off a hangnail with my teeth and made it bleed, and he started saying that he knew this was about Robert, and that *he* wasn't going anywhere, he promised.

"No," I said. "This has nothing to do with Robert. You might like to think that, because it makes you feel better, but you have a right to know the truth—and the truth is, I just can't stand to be with you."

And I walked away.

That brings me to my best friend, Carly Grimshaw. Around this time, Carly and I would hang out on her four-poster bed and come up with explanations for where Robert was. We knew he was *somewhere* because of the lies about Clarissa and Bing, and we lay on her bed eating Twisties and inventing narratives. Usually, we gave him amnesia. He was always safe and comfortable, and his memory was elbowing its way back at *that very moment*.

Then we discussed exactly how we'd feel when he returned. *Euphoric acid* would course through our veins, we said. Then we would start a band of the same name. Quickly, we'd learn musical instruments—Carly played the flute and I played the piano but neither was hard-core enough; we were going to learn electric guitar and sax, and Robert would be on drums.

I loved how Carly got right to the heart, the absolute truth, of Robert coming back.

Only, one day she said to me, "Well, it's like they say, Abi. Every cloud has a silver lining."

"Huh?" I said.

It was good for me to find my independence, she explained. Sometimes, she said, she used to *miss* me, because Robert and I were so often together, as if *Robert* was my best friend instead of *her*, so this absence of Robert was giving us space to—

I don't know. I missed the next bit. I was spilling Twisties everywhere trying to get up off her bed, to get away from her, and I was shouting—using the curses that Kirrily Palmer had taught me—and running out of her bedroom.

That day was the first time I wondered if *The Guidebook* might actually be a manifestation of my own thoughts. Because when I got home, crying angrily, I saw an envelope in the frying pan, opened it, and the first thing I read was: *Every cloud has a silver lining.*

My chest did one of those dramatic tumbles down a flight of stairs.

Chapter 79

```
Every cloud has a silver lining. No. Every cloud
does not. Because, look, I've seen clouds without
a single trace of silver. I've seen clouds of pure
white. Or violent purple. Clouds that are nothing
more than lethargic wisps.
     Also, if you see a silver lining, it's actually
just a shot of gray.
     Silver linings merely indicate the possibility
of rain. Too bad if you're hoping to go fishing.
Or if it's your wedding day.
```

It carried on in this vein, querying the origin of the phrase (Milton), defining "linings," and discussing skirts.

This was also the first time I realized that the authors of the book, Rufus and Isabelle, were taking it in turns to write the chapters. Two days later, Chapter 80 arrived (which was surprising: they never usually turned up in consecutive order) and it specifically referred to Isabelle having written the previous chapter, whereas now (the chapter said), it was "my turn."

For some reason, the coincidence with *The Guidebook* made me go to Carly's place and make up with her. She apologized and we hung out with her cute little sister, Rabbit, helping Rabbit to make a cubby house under her cot, and introducing all of Rabbit's toys into this cubby house, until we were crowded with teddy bears and hard-edged trains, and we looked at each other, Carly and I, tears running down our faces, and we cheered right up.

9.

My mother had a job at the Department of Education and her boss permitted her extended leave to look for her son.

After about a year, he seemed to think she'd looked for long enough.

"What, you think I should give up?" she demanded.

"Of course not! Never! Just, maybe, look in your spare time?"

That was how the conversation went, according to my mother. "As if Robert being missing is a *hobby* of mine," she said.

She resigned. Her days were too full for work: she spent them at support groups and libraries, at the printers and "pounding the pavements." She traveled right up the east coast, staying in caravan parks and youth hostels, asking questions, handing out leaflets. Now and then people would agree they'd seen him, and there'd be a flourish of hope. A clairvoyant called to say she'd seen Robert in a pinball parlor in South Australia and Mum followed up on this, until another clairvoyant swore he was in a treehouse in Brisbane. Eventually, she learned to ignore the spiritualists and crank callers. She became extremely skinny: her skin was tightly fitted to her face now, releasing many new wrinkles.

Dad agreed that she should make finding Robert her full-time job, but she wanted to cover the costs of advertisements and private detectives herself, so now and then she'd get some kind of part-time work.

For a while, she tutored children with a *b-d* reversal problem. I'd come home from school hoping for Robert and, instead, there'd be a stranger's child sitting at the dining room table alongside Mum, eating green grapes and thinly sliced pear from a saucer ("Natural sugars bring the brain to life," my mother said), and leaning over an exercise book with a pencil. They'd do *b* for pages, then pages of *d*. They'd decorate *b*'s and *d*'s, color them in, give them dragon wings, before they got down to the brass tacks of words: boat, bat, butter, ball, dart, dim, down. They all learned the difference in the end, the kids, the difference between *b* and *d*.

It strikes me now that they'd probably have figured it out eventually, with or without my mother's help; also, that this was a fairly narrow field of specialization she had going on, my mother.

Around this time, Mum sent me to see her counselor, a woman named Éclair . . . no, that can't have been her name. I'm thinking of the chocolate éclair I had after my session with her. Her name was *Renee*, and she wore a lot of makeup, including purple lipstick. Renee sat in an armchair and a shaft of sunlight, and said: "You're holding on to two truths, aren't you? It's like your heart is split in two."

I was quiet, thinking about that, and then I decided to speak my mind. "It's more than that," I said. "It's like I've got *two* hearts, and both of them are full—like, absolutely full, so full they sometimes spill. Because I know *absolutely* that Robert will be back, and I also know for sure that he won't. He never will."

Renee nodded, her eyes very sad, and I burst into tears. I sat there crying, crying.

I told her about all the many stupid things people said, and she shook her head, exasperated with these people. I told her about the friends who said he must be dead, and she became stern and said, "*Nobody* knows. Nobody can say that for sure."

Afterward, I was starving and ate the chocolate éclair. I'd have liked to go back to see Renee again, but Mum never suggested it. I think she thought I was done now: *b-d* reversal problem *solved* in a single session.

But they still sat there, side by side, *b* and *d*. The exact same thing but opposite, facing one another and pointing to the truth, which was nothing but a giant blank.

10.

You hear people talk about how it's a turning point when you realize that your parents are human.

It's also a turning point to realize that they're *not*. The sounds I heard my parents make when they thought they were alone—rasping wails like animals, or something else not-human, lacerating sounds. I made sounds like this myself, too, when I thought my darkest thoughts, like *Robert is never coming back*, and vicious thoughts, the secret, terrible thoughts about Robert having been stolen, taken, starved, attacked, raped, about Robert slipping over a cliff's edge and dying a long desperate death, about Robert pleading for us to rescue him, about—I will stop this here.

When I was eighteen, in my last year of high school and studying for the HSC, my parents were fighting.

People seemed to think this was natural, for them to fight, which irritated the hell out of me. Apart from anything else, I felt embarrassed by their predictability.

For a while, they circled the issue of their liberal parenting—reassuring each other that Robert's disappearance had *nothing* to do with that, or holding each other close and saying, "Why weren't we more strict? Why? Why?"—until Mum said she'd opposed it all along. Free-range parenting had been *Dad's* idea, she announced, and she'd only gone along with it for his sake.

"First I've heard of it," Dad said.

She said it again the next day, and she kept on saying it, in a soft, sad voice, or a friendly, regretful voice, or a low, resentful voice, and Dad continued to proclaim that this was the first he'd heard of it.

"It always troubled me," Mum asserted. "I wanted to keep a closer eye on them."

I was thinking: *Well, why didn't you then?* I was thinking: *Stand up for yourself, Mum; you were a parent too!*

This was more or less Dad's position as well. "If you disagreed, why didn't you *say* something?"

I began to feel sorry for Mum, given the flimsiness of her angle. One day a chapter from *The Guidebook* arrived and it said this:

Chapter 42

```
Raising teenagers is all about deception.
     Give teenagers the illusion of freedom. It's like
when you're playing the triangle. If you clutch
the bar, it will make an ugly clang. However, if
you dangle the triangle in the air from a fine,
fine string, it will chime out its sweetness. It
believes it is free, you see, even though you've
got it by the string. Convince the triangle it is
free.
```

I showed this to Mum, thinking, in some bizarre twist of my mind, that it would comfort her. Because Robert had a sweet voice when he sang, a little like a triangle perhaps, and so giving him freedom had been the right thing. I was going to say that I honestly thought Robert running away had nothing to do with us having freedom. In fact, I planned to say, kids were more *likely* to run if you tried to restrict them. Robert's disappearance was an aberration.

I didn't get a chance to say any of this because Mum read the chapter and said, "Throw it away. Just *throw* it away," and she flung the page. I could see that it was not satisfactory to her, the flinging, as the paper moved lethargically, drifting toward the ground. I caught it and took it away.

Later that night, I read it again and realized that my parents had forgotten to give us the *illusion* of freedom: they had given us *actual* freedom. Urgently, I thought: *They need the string—they should be holding the string! If they'd just tied a string around Robert's ankle, they could drag him home right now!*

I saw it so vividly, the string, and here came Robert, cartwheeling home like a wayward kite.

Then I was filled with rage toward my mother for not having insisted on a string, and I wondered why I'd ever wanted to comfort her.

11.

Time carried on. You can't divert it from its tracks.

I myself was walking alongside the tracks, however, not *on* them, and I despised everybody who used the word *miss*.

I missed the bus.

I miss my grandma—she's gone back to Scotland now.

You know what I miss? That milk bar on the corner of Clyve and Scott Streets.

As if anybody knew the meaning of the word *miss* other than me.

I finished school and started Arts/Law at Sydney University. My ambition to write horror movies had dissolved. Instead, I was going to be a lawyer and fight for justice for the families of missing people.

I felt strongly about that, without knowing exactly what I meant by it.

PART 5

1.

Early English settlement of Sydney started on the south side of the harbor, and spread west, east and south from there.

I live on the north side of the harbor. *Warung*, the Aboriginals called it, meaning "the other side." There's a powerful *otherness* here, the Harbour Bridge a psychological barrier. Those across the water are contemptuous or mocking of the protected, golden life of the north (so that I rush to say that I grew up in the west, in Stanmore, to give myself street cred). Embraced a century ago by a bohemian community of painters and authors who built Arts and Crafts houses and planted gardens, the Lower North Shore is now a collection of suburbs: McMahons Point (where I work), Kirribilli, Lavender Bay, Waverton, North Sydney, Cremorne, and Neutral Bay (where I live).

Leafy doesn't cut it for my neighborhood. There are great swathes of green: apple green, lime green; green swept up and over fences, massive established trees, figs, and gums, spreading extravagant branches; camellia, magnolia, bougainvillea, jacaranda, frangipani, bird-of-paradise, and everywhere the cascade palm, cabbage tree palm, and golden cane palm. When I first moved here, I used to walk Oscar in his pram along the cracked and lopsided footpaths, climbing steep hills that would startle me with sudden glimpses of city skyline, harbor blue, the cartoonish curve of the bridge. There are beautifully maintained children's playgrounds, lost toys propped on letter boxes by friendly passers-by, happy people walking dogs or babies. The architecture is a curious collation of styles: terraces, bungalows, blond-brick apartment buildings crammed with families here for the school districts. Twigs fall, sticks fall, a mess of seeds and berries, golden orb spiders strung on webs, kookaburras laughing, magpies murmuring; the astonishing bright white wings of a sulphur-crested cockatoo on a stormy day, the clamor of chatter from rainbow lorikeets at dusk, possums crossing wires in the moonlight.

Even my father makes fun of me for living here, and old school friends joke: "It's so *nice* over here, everyone's so pretty! And they're *all exactly the same.*" There's diversity here, but it's concealed behind uniforms. There are broken people here, but they're pinned together with therapy, Botox, hair dye, and designer clothes, rage pegged down with hot stone massages, soothed by high-functioning alcoholism.

Across the Harbour Bridge, beyond the tourist district and the central business district, the diversity, especially in the inner west, is flamboyant and proud. There is wealth there, too, but it's cooler, hipper, more working class somehow. The broken people there are scarred and pockmarked with dirty teeth, their cracks open, deep fissures showing, their dependencies visceral. They'll shout at you from parks littered with broken bottles and graffiti, or they'll sell you crystals.

All this is to say that, although the drive from Neutral Bay to Newtown in the inner west was only twenty minutes, it was like crossing to a different dimension.

Here I am, I thought—as I always think when I walk the streets of Newtown, elation rushing at me, along with the sensory cacophony of crowds, pubs, restaurants, secondhand bookshops, traffic jams, horns, buskers, the anger open, the loss visceral. Here I am, at last, in the world.

I found Wilbur's building and there he was in the lobby, the shape of him uncertain through the frosted glass.

2.

The guy with the hipster beard was here.

I remembered his beard, and the fact that he had come out at his nineteenth birthday dinner, but not his name. For this, I blamed the man himself. He'd worn a flat cap each day of the retreat, but not tonight. Just brown hair and beard tonight. If he'd been wearing the cap, I was sure I'd know his name.

We were in Wilbur's apartment. Wilbur himself had disappeared down the hall into a room that sounded like a kitchen. That left four of us standing in his living room: Guy without his flat cap; Frangipani, whose real name I had also forgotten but then it sashayed back to me (Sasha); disgruntled man with problem shoulder (Pete?); and me.

I was not surprised to see Flat-cap. He seemed like one of those affable types who hadn't yet found his gang of pals. So he floats around, taking social opportunities, just in case, you never know, life is for living. Nor was I surprised to see Frangipani: her investment in *The Guidebook* was substantial.

Disgruntled man, however, was so astonishing, such a wild card, that all of us were surreptitiously staring at him. On the last day at the retreat, he had shouted his way out of the room and slammed the door—yet here he was!

Wilbur's apartment was on the top floor of a three-story block in a Newtown side street. Dark red brick, narrow corridors, blistering paint, graffiti on the fire extinguisher. The staircase and the corridors had been low and claustrophobic as we'd filed behind Wilbur, after meeting him in the lobby, and then Wilbur opened the door of his apartment and *shazam!*

"Shazam" might be extreme. I just mean that the front door opened direct onto his living room and it was bright! One wall was lined with windows. These were old, framed, rectangular windows, each splitting the summer-evening sky into six squares.

"Just a moment," Wilbur had said, and he'd disappeared down the hall. So we'd formed our ragged circle in the living room, and looked around us.

First, your eyes were drawn to the bank of windows, and then to the rich dark wood of the floorboards. These were battered, with wide cracks between: I saw pins, staples, coins and dirt in the cracks.

Next, you realized that the room appeared to have been recently, haphazardly decorated, as if by a teacher who has rushed to display the children's arts and crafts in time for Open Day.

For example: miniature hot-air balloons dangled from the ceiling. A fan spun slowly so that the balloons tipped and swayed. You could imagine their occupants shrieking in alarm, the balloon pilots sweating and grabbing at ropes.

Origami butterflies and birds perched on the TV, coffee table, bookshelf, and even on a stack of CDs. (I studied the CD titles: some I didn't know, some I liked. He had Joni Mitchell's *Hejira*, which is one of my mother's favorites.)

The wall opposite the windows was crowded with posters, many askew or slipping, of hang gliders, dragons, antique planes, griffins, and dancers caught mid-leap.

"I sense a theme here," Flat-cap announced.

"What?" said Frangipani, uneasy. "What theme?"

We waited as she gazed around at balloons, butterflies, birds, the pictures of airplanes and people in midair.

"What?" she repeated, almost scolding.

"Flight," Flat-cap told her gently. "Everything here is in flight."

"Hmm." Skeptical.

We were all deliberately quiet then, careful not to catch each other's eyes.

Wilbur returned from his kitchen with a huge platter of sushi. His arms were stretched wide to carry it, and he kept ducking to avoid hot-air balloons, now and then hitting one and swearing in a quiet, friendly manner. "I should have asked people to RSVP," he said, "instead of leaving it open like this. Didn't know how much sushi to make."

"I don't eat sushi," Frangipani declared.

If we were still on the retreat, I reflected, she'd never have said that. She'd have been a giant sushi fan.

Wilbur said, "That's okay!" as if he forgave her for not eating sushi. His identity had also changed. It's funny when you meet someone and you think, *This is what he is like*, and then you see him smiling in his own apartment, in his own favorite, loose and comfortable clothes, in his own bare feet, and you think: *Ah. No. Here he is.*

He was wearing a T-shirt with a faded, soft look and old jeans, and his feet were bare, as I just now hinted, and his hair was shorter than it had been, and he seemed perfectly happy with his height.

He set the platter on a low coffee table before dragging this into the middle of the room.

Next, Wilbur pushed and shoved armchairs and kitchen chairs until they formed a ring around the coffee table.

While all this happened, the four of us stepped back and forth, getting out of his way, silent, not offering to help. We were all reserving judgment.

Wilbur didn't seem to mind. He stopped, wiped his forehead, and counted us. Then he counted the seats he'd set out. There were enough.

"Would everybody like to sit?"

We were still in our circle, slightly displaced. Nobody moved. Wilbur twanged an elastic band around his wrist. Lines crossed his forehead. I was reminded suddenly of the moment I first met him, tall guy smiling, "Snow!"

His face cleared now, just as it had then.

"Please," he said. "I'm extremely grateful to you all for coming tonight. Like I told you in the letter, my parents wrote *The Guidebook*. They left me instructions to invite you on the retreat, and then to teach this course. If you decide to keep coming each Tuesday, I'll follow their outline—maybe it will even be fun." He hesitated. "I *hope* it will be fun, but not in the sense of making fun of my parents. Do you see what I mean?"

Flat-cap nodded. "You don't want pure irony," he suggested.

"Right. Exactly." Wilbur seemed relieved. "I *could* run this course with a smirk. We could roll our eyes at each other. We could be consciously meta. We could analyze my parents step by step, and pity them. But I think we have to play it straight. It's a game, sure, but can we all agree to step inside the game?"

There was a strange pause then, the moment poised. Frangipani cleared her throat as if to speak, then changed her mind. Outside, someone in a car hit the horn hard and long. The blaring faded, started again, then merged with the sound of an airplane passing overhead.

Flat-cap grinned. "You arranged the airplane?" He pointed up.

This made us laugh again, only in a quiet and thoughtful way. I was thinking about Wilbur's question. This charade: Was it safe, was it a lie?

Unexpectedly, disgruntled guy spoke up. So far he'd been silent except for grunts and a low-level scowl, eyes darting about.

"I'll say something here," he said, intensifying the scowl. "Pete Aldridge, as you might recall. Pest control. I won't beat around the bush. I came tonight because I don't trust you, Wilbur. No offense"—he stopped and glowered at Wilbur, who nodded graciously—"no offence to you, I say, but I believe this to be a scam. Quite possibly you want to start a cult, Wilbur, and you want to take these good people for everything they've got and then have them jump off a cliff." He ran his gaze around the circle. "What they do with their money is their concern, I suppose. However, I will *not* have them jumping off a cliff to their death. To their respective deaths. Therefore, Wilbur, I will play your game. I will play it just as you ask. But so help me, the game is done the moment I think you've gone too far. And do you know what I'll do then?"

"What?" Wilbur asked.

"I will snap you over my knee. Is that a deal?"

Here I felt a sweet surge of gratitude toward this Pete Aldridge, pest control, because he was here to take care of me and prevent me from jumping off a cliff, and was prepared to back that up with violent threats against a man considerably taller than he, a man on a larger scale than himself—a man whom he might have considerable difficulty snapping over his knee. We all looked at each other, contemplating this—but gratitude was immediately followed by irritation because the guy seemed to think the rest of us were idiots.

"Deal," Wilbur agreed, cheerful. "Now, shall we sit?"

At this, a buzzer rang in a sharp, important way.

Wilbur reached for a phone on the wall, said, "Third floor, apartment 3C," pressed a button, then hung up.

He remained standing as the rest of us took seats. "Drinks?" he said. "Sasha? Red or white? Mineral water?"

He poured wine for each of us in turn, so eventually I had Flat-cap's name again: Antony. I decided to think of Cleopatra as a way of recalling his name, Cleopatra and snakes, but then I recalled that I'd decided that before.

Somebody knocked. We swiveled, glasses in our hands.

Wilbur crossed the room and opened the door.

It was Nicole!

She wore an orange, polka-dotted scarf around her hair, and a full skirt with bobbled edges, and her cheeks were pink: she really did look as if she'd come direct from leaping over rocks with goats. Her beam seemed to propel her toward us, exclaiming, as she came, at the floating balloons and pictures and paper cranes, then at each of us in turn. She said all of our names, and when she got to Pete Aldridge, she said: "Pete! How's the shoulder?" to which he replied, "What shoulder?" frowning fiercely. Then she bobbed up and down on her heels, chatting an apology that had to do with one of her children having brought home the wrong homework. She admired the sky through the windows then stopped abruptly, her smile faltering. She touched her scarf, uncertain. I remembered that about her: the energy always chased by self-consciousness.

Wilbur offered Nicole a seat, and sat himself. A long pause.

"Shall we get on with this?" Pete Aldridge demanded.

Wilbur laughed. "I'm nervous," he admitted. "I apologize. I've memorized a script that my parents wrote for this first lesson. But now I have stage fright."

The buzzer rang again.

Pete Aldridge shook his head, his expression suggesting that there were many things he could say right now, but would restrain himself.

This time, it was Niall.

Red hair, broad shoulders.

He stood in the doorway and looked across at us, face serious, smile in his eyes. He wiped his feet on the mat.

"Am I too late?" he said.

Nobody else arrived that night. That was the group.

We sat in the circle. We drank wine and ate sushi. (Frangipani, I noticed, had four or five pieces, each time reaching out in a reluctant way, as if engaging in a small battle with herself and then surrendering.) Wilbur repeated his wish that this not be ironic. Nicole and Niall both agreed. More chatting.

"Are we ready?" Wilbur asked. He was holding a manila folder.

We all became still.

"Then let's play."

3.

He handed out forms.

I hereby promise that I will not attempt to FLY unless and until WILBUR informs me that I am ready to FLY. I hereby agree that we will start on the small hills in the snow.

"There is no snow," Frangipani pointed out. "It doesn't snow in Sydney."

"We'll go on a field trip," Antony told her comfortably. "I love a good field trip."

Wilbur shook his head. There would be no field trips, he said. He explained that *small hills in the snow* was a metaphor. It meant that we would only fly in safe conditions. "At least, I think that's what it means."

He blinked. For a moment I thought he might break character, but he shook himself and carried on.

"Before I say a word about flight," he said, "you need to sign these forms. Look at me."

Obediently, we looked.

"Our arms and chests have insufficient muscle power to fly," he said. "We will *never* fly by flapping our arms. Do you understand? If you jump off a skyscraper, you will *die*. If you make yourself wings out of cardboard, you will die. If your wings are made of wax, they will melt in the sun and you will crash into the ocean and *die*."

We stared at him.

"None of you will fly until I tell you," he declared. "And then *only* in the safest of conditions. Yes?"

Nobody answered. We carried on staring.

He handed around pens and we signed the forms. I was thinking that this was kind of fun. Pete Aldridge raised his eyebrows as he signed. He seemed impressed, but in a provisional way.

Wilbur collected the forms and placed them inside his folder.

"Every single one of us," he said, looking up, "is born with a sense of flight."

A pause. I was impressed by his sense of the dramatic.

"Can I quickly ask a question?" Nicole stage-whispered.

Wilbur considered, then nodded regally.

"It's only, I'm wondering if your parents put *everything* in their lesson plan, including your tone of voice? Because this is *really* good. I'm kind of *believing* it!"

"*Nicole*," Wilbur said, annoyed rather than regal, "remember what we said about how we're going to play this straight? That's the ground rule."

"I know," she said. "That's why I was whispering. I'm *offstage*. Sorry. It's just, you're doing a good job."

"Thank you," he said, and frowned. "Where was I?"

"We are all born with a sense of flight," Niall prompted.

"Right. We are. Only we lose it. Thousands of years ago, people stopped using their sense of flight. They considered it sacrilegious: only angels should fly, they reasoned. Or perhaps there were too many accidents? Anyhow, they stopped. Over time, human flight disappeared. It was forgotten. It fell into the realm of impossible. Now we continue to be *born* with the sense, but it quickly fades. If children approach an edge, they are scooped up, warned, reprimanded. They learn to fear flight. The sense falls dormant."

Antony spoke up. "I see a number of holes in your thesis. Now, historically, angels—"

"Hush," Nicole said. "We're playing this straight."

"I *am*," Antony argued. "Playing it straight doesn't mean we have to go along with it. It means we don't make fun of Wilbur's parents. I'm being exactly who I would be if *they* were saying these things. I'd question everything."

"Save your questions until the end," Frangipani suggested. She ran a finger around the rim of her wineglass.

Wilbur's eyes had been darting back and forth between the speakers during this conversation. He appeared to decide not to respond at all.

"We no longer believe we can get into the sky," he said, "without such trappings as airplanes, helicopters, hang gliders, and cliffs."

"Cliffs!" barked Pete Aldridge.

"In the sense that you need a cliff to use a hang glider," Wilbur apologized.

Pete Aldridge accepted this. "Go on."

"Now, my parents reasoned that it would be too late to revive an adult's sense of flight: they needed to start earlier, with young people. Children, preferably—but what parents would allow it? They require sufficient youth combined with independence. They settled on teenagers. On you."

He began to refill glasses. It was a very nice Peppertree Shiraz, I remember.

"And on me," he added, as he poured. "*The Guidebook*, of course, is full of flight."

"No, no!" Frangipani was irritated. "*The Guidebook* said *nothing* about flight!"

Wilbur raised an eyebrow. "*The Guidebook* is full of flight," he repeated. "Kites, remote-control helicopters, cloud formations, gravity. Just to name a few."

We all frowned. Had I been sent the wrong extracts? I had no memory of kites, helicopters, clouds—then I laughed, realizing. "No," I said. "Those were self-help metaphors."

"Lessons in flight," Wilbur declared, "disguised as metaphors."

We all took a break in the form of a sip of our wine to consider this.

"By reading *The Guidebook* extracts," Wilbur went on, replacing his glass on the table, "and doing the exercises, you have tuned yourselves to flight in all its grandeur."

"And if you haven't been reading it?" Niall wondered aloud. "I mean, if you only read it occasionally, and did maybe *two* of the exercises, you're completely out of tune?" He chose a piece of salmon-and-avocado sushi. "Speaking hypothetically, of course."

Everybody laughed.

"No," said Wilbur, which surprised us. "My parents knew they couldn't expect teenagers to read it *all* or do *all* the exercises. But by reading *some*, we have been changed. Its stories layered themselves into our beings. We are now composed, in part, of its words."

Wilbur stood abruptly. "If everyone's done with the sushi," he said. "I've got dessert."

He took away the platter and returned with a tall chocolate cake and a jug of cream.

Frangipani surrendered to her own nature and helped him to slice it, passing the bowls around, adding cream if people wished.

"In this course," Wilbur resumed, "we take the next step. *The Guidebook* has triggered your sense of flight, but it only flickers. Our lessons will fan the sense into its fullest vitality. There are five units. First,

Meditation. Open your mind to flight. Second, *Flight Immersion.* Imbue your consciousness with the idea of flight. Third, *Sensory Development.* Flight is a sense, as I've mentioned. It lies just beyond your other senses. Fourth, *Practical Flight.* The physical aspects of flying. Once we have completed those four units we move to the fifth and final unit: *Emotional Flight.* By that point, your sense of flight should positively blaze."

"But what *is* a sense of flight?" Frangipani complained through a mouthful of cake. A crumb spilled onto her chin and she wiped it away.

"I'm glad you asked," Wilbur said smoothly. "Who here knows what *aerodynamics* is?"

"Aerodynamics is the study of the motion of air, and the movement of objects through air," Antony said. "This cake is very good, by the way. Where'd you get it?"

Most of us murmured agreement. I said that this was exactly the sort of cake I was looking for in my café, and everyone said, "What café?" So I told them about my Happiness Café. They were very interested and Frangipani said that she regularly had her hair done in Hair to the Throne right next door to that café!

"I've even thought about going *into* that cafe!" she told me, as if it should both amaze and delight me that she had considered my café.

"Actually," Wilbur said eventually, "I made the cake myself." He pointed to his windows. These were dark now, sprinkled with stars. "There are waves in the ocean," he said, and for a moment I thought this was cake-related. Had he folded salty waves into his cake? Or was it some kind of commentary on life and its possibilities: *Much as I baked this cake, so too are there waves in the oceans.* But then I realized he was getting back on track.

"The waves in the ocean can carry you, yes?" he said. "Well, you can ride on a surfboard, of course, but you can also simply ride."

"This is true," Pete Aldridge accepted. "Body surfing."

Wilbur seemed encouraged by the unexpected approval. "There are also waves in the air," he continued. "These waves carry light, sound, color, messages. They carry images, both moving and still. Light waves, radio waves, infrared, and so on. There are also waves in the air that can carry *you.*"

The room had grown quiet. Except for the clinking of teaspoons in bowls and the sound of Nicole saying, "Can you pass the cream?" and Frangipani pointing out, "You told me you didn't *want* cream," and Nicole apologizing, "I thought I shouldn't, but it looks so *bright* and *white* against the chocolate, and—"

"Shush!" Wilbur ordered. "Give her the cream, Sasha! This is the dramatic finale!"

"I think that was self-referential." Antony smiled. "And breaks the ground rules."

"No, it doesn't." Wilbur stood, raised both hands and spread them high and wide. His fingertips almost touched the ceiling. "There are *waves out there that can carry you through the sky,*" he said, and lowered his voice to an almost-whisper. "If you could only see them, feel them, *know* them, you could ride them, my friends. They are everywhere."

"In this room," I asked, "or just outside?"

Wilbur looked confounded for a moment. He cupped a hand around his mouth and lowered his voice: "I'll have to check my notes. But I think just outside?"

"Those other waves you were talking about," Antony shout-whispered, "they're electromagnetic rays from the sun. Are these flying waves part of the same spectrum?"

"Good question," Wilbur whispered. "I wondered that myself."

"Maybe just get back to the script?" Nicole suggested.

"Flight waves!" Wilbur cried, giving Nicole a quick thumbs-up. "You simply leap aboard the lowest one that you can see. You ride it! Fling yourself from wave to wave." He was gesticulating madly, to demonstrate. "To an extent, you can even *steer* the waves. Ever so gently, and just a little. You can *fly,* my friends. There are *flight waves* in the sky!"

"And that's what our *sense* of flight is for?" Frangipani breathed. "So we can see these flight waves?"

"Exactly," Wilbur said. "*Aerodynamics*. From the Greek. *Aero* meaning air, and *dynamics* meaning powerful. *The air is powerful, my friends. The air will carry you.*"

He stopped. His hands dropped to his sides.

There was a faint rustle around the circle. Nicole raised her hands as if to applaud but then quickly replaced them on her lap.

At this point, Pete Aldridge spoke up. "You know you've got an ant problem, right?" he said to Wilbur. "See them tracking right along there?" He pointed. "Up from the skirting board, across that frame, and right along the ceiling." We all followed Pete's pointing finger up behind the standing lamp, across the picture frame, and right along the ceiling. A thin trail of moving blackness.

This was the first time I'd seen Pete Aldridge smile.

At the end of the night, Wilbur asked if we'd like to come the following Tuesday, and everybody said, "Sure," or "Why not?" while Pete Aldridge growled, "Of *course*."

Wilbur took our phone numbers so he could let us know if he ever had to cancel a class. There was a brief uneasiness at this, but then I suppose we all recalled that Wilbur already had our home addresses and—if his parents had kept the files—access to any annual "reflections" we had sent in to *The Guidebook*.

4.

I read *Tuesdays with Morrie*, and it was about a nice old guy. He's quite a character, and he's dying. A former student, who has not stayed in touch despite having promised to do so, comes by to leech the remnants of the old man's wisdom.

Ha ha. No, he comes by to chat with the old man and keep him company while recording his final, wise words. The old man appears to appreciate this, and to enjoy the idea of himself as wise. And he does say many thoughtful things! However, I cannot now recall what they were. I have a sense that the two men passed abstract nouns between them—regret, death, family, aging, love, marriage, culture, and forgiveness—but there was probably more than that.

The next book in my stack was *I'm OK—You're OK*.

I had heard of this book, and looked forward to reading it: there is something very soothing about you, me, everyone being okay. (Previously, I had *not* been okay, because *The Guidebook* prevented me from reading this book, but now I would be.)

However, it was more complicated than that. The book explained that everybody is a Parent, a Child, and an Adult. The Parent is bossy and thinks in absolutes; the Child cries and falls apart; and the Adult reasons things out and is very dull and sensible. So, when the bus runs late, the Parent says, "Isn't this *always* the way!" and the Child has a tantrum and punches the bus shelter, but the Adult says: "No. In my experience, buses are not always late," and sits on the seat to wait.

Buzzkilling Adult. Takes everything literally.

The author mentions group sessions he runs in which, when anybody grows angry or upset, he reminds them to "keep being their Adult." People must want to strangle him.

And he tells a little story about what you should do if your husband writes, *I love you*, in the dust on the coffee table. The husband is doing this to point out that you are failing as a housekeeper. You *could* be a Child and shout at him. But better to be an Adult and meet him at the door with a clean house and a tall, clean drink. Like the people in his group, I want to strangle him.

5.

When I started the Happiness Café, I placed a ceramic pot just inside the entrance. A stack of notecards sat next to it, along with a pen and a sign:

HOW TO LEAVE YOUR SADNESS AT THE DOOR:
WRITE DOWN THE THINGS THAT MAKE YOU SAD OR ANGRY
  TODAY,
FOLD THEM UP, PLACE THEM IN THIS POT
AND, AT THE END OF EACH DAY, WE WILL BURN THEM
  FOR YOU.

At first, this seemed ingenious and people loved the idea, filling in many cards. But pretty quickly I started to find *names* on the folded papers. I felt like a witch doctor, practicing voodoo. I wasn't at all keen on burning names, burning people.

Also, all this anger, this bitterness, in a pot by the door. Was it toxic?

And there were days when I didn't feel like lighting a match over the sink, and days when the smoke alarm went off, and more generally there were the fire risks associated with, well, fire.

So I replaced the pot with a mat. *Welcome!* it says. *Wipe your feet here and you will wipe away your tears.*

Simpler, more civilized, and less sweeping up.

Today, everyone seemed to be wiping their feet assiduously. We were in the flat space between morning coffees and lunch. Two tables taken.

One was a group of older women talking Europe, vegetables, parboiling, and rental cars. "He's the sort of man who has two strong coffees and a cigarette to start the day," said one, and I felt a powerful yearning for that sort of man. But when I returned with their coffees, they had moved on to bypasses, cancer, the price of bok choy, and the smell of cigars in the upholstery. "You cannot get it out," said one. "Not ever."

I wondered if she was playing the Parent. Should I approach the table and, speaking in a reasonable Adult voice, say: "Never? Are you certain? Surely there are home remedies that could assist in these circumstances. Perhaps you should consult the World Wide Web?"

I also wanted to verify whether the man who started his day with two strong coffees and a cigarette was responsible for the cigar smoke in the upholstery. He struck me as a man who knew how to stride about the world, a man who smoked cigars in his stylish car, a man who would be excellent in bed. I don't mind the smell of cigars, I would tell them.

At the other table a young couple sat, dividing up their property. This was one of the ironic uses of the Happiness Café: the venue chosen as a sharp and bitter joke. They each had open notebooks before them, pens in their hands—he kept clicking his; she gripped hers tightly—and across the table came calm politeness, or bristling intensity, back and forth, ducking or colliding, each taking turns at both. The young man thought he deserved a greater share of the property. Because if she hadn't done this, if she hadn't taken off, if she hadn't met . . . this never would have . . . and here, the young woman rose up and rode on her sentences: "Do you *really* think that *that* is how it works?"

I sidestepped toward an empty table, wiped it over, straightened chairs. When a marriage breaks up, does the brokenhearted one become the Child? Pleading, desperate, sullen, sobbing, stamping feet, seeking consolation and reward, all the time secretly appalled at this loss of self. While the other is the Parent: contemptuous, self-righteous, terrified by guilt and so stepping up, up, up to this position of authority, laying down the rules, declaring that this is how it works!

I collected plates and crumpled napkins from the women's table. "It works with lymphoma," one of them was saying, "to get your own bone marrow? While you're in remission?"

Nobody seemed very happy in the Happiness Café today. I felt my usual desperate sense that it was my job to cheer them all up. After all, this was what I promised. I should switch on upbeat music, do a belly dance, get the whole place in hysterics! I should run next door to Hair to the Throne and return with a pretty girlfriend (with shiny new hairstyle) for the sad-young-newly-separated man! Phone the grocery store and arrange for a box of bok choy! Find a cure for cancer!

The door opened.

I looked hopefully for a new conversation, but it was a man alone.

He paused in the shadow of the doorway, shuffled briefly on the welcome mat, took a step forward, and it was a man with red hair and broad shoulders.

Niall caught my eye and smiled. "Hey," he said, with a laugh in his voice. "So you *do* own a Happiness Café!"

At both tables, the conversations paused, and faces turned to watch my response.

6.

Niall and I went a block up the road to Billi's Café where, it turned out, you get a little round chocolate covered in colored sprinkles—a Freckle—on the saucer with your coffee. It made me happy, the Freckle.

"This," I said. "It's all you need for happiness. And I try so hard."

Niall studied the Freckle leaning up against his own latte. He lifted it across to my saucer, using his teaspoon. So now I had two.

"You're not happy?" he asked.

"Yeah, no, I'm happy."

"But you . . ."

"Oh, I get it! No, I just meant I try hard with my café. With the menu and the ambiance and the cushions and all that. Did you notice the cushions?"

"Yes," Niall said. "I noticed them." He raised an eyebrow, teasing.

Now, although we had spent a weekend together on an island in Bass Strait, and although we had, a few days earlier, attended the introductory course on flight at Wilbur's place, Niall and I had never sat and faced one another. There had always been others around. Even when we walked from the beach to the yoga, Lera, the pediatric ENT surgeon, had walked between us, a midpoint, a bridge.

Now we chatted at our table on the pavement. I told him the story of the Happiness Café. He asked where I'd grown up. His family had come here from Ireland, he told me, when he was ten. He was in property development, by which he meant he bought cheap flats, fixed them up himself, and "flipped" them. He liked to mountain climb.

"This flight course," Niall said eventually. "What do you think?"

He stirred sugar into his coffee and tapped the spoon on the side of the cup. His hand was big around the spoon. His forearms were freckled and the pale orange hairs on them listed sideways in the breeze.

"I don't know what to think," I said. "I mean, it's a sad story about Wilbur's parents, and I see why he wants to run the course, but why are we going along with it? The guy's a stranger! It's nice of us, isn't it?"

Niall leaned forward, folding his arms on the table. It rocked. Startled, he sat back and studied the ground. Then he shifted the table slightly and now it was steady.

"It is," he agreed, smiling. When he smiled, his eyes disappeared almost completely, leaving just cracks of bright blue amid deep patterns of lines. This was unexpected: when not smiling, Niall's face was long, steady, solemn, almost somber.

"Do you think you'll keep going?" he asked me.

"So long as he keeps giving us sushi."

Niall nodded. "And cake."

We both smiled.

"Plus I want to see what happens," I said.

"You want to see what happens," Niall echoed, considering this carefully. He looked up at the leaves of the tree standing beside us. A golden robinia, shining lime green. The blue sky bright above it.

A car pulled up beside us, and we both watched a woman climb out, open the boot, pull out a stroller, and set it up. Next she opened the back door of the car, reached in, and emerged with a baby.

"Is that why you went to the first class?" Niall asked, turning back to me. "To see what would happen?"

The woman was now clipping the baby into the pram. She handed over a stuffed toy caterpillar. The baby accepted the toy in silence. A business transaction.

"Well, no," I said. "I went because it was on a Tuesday night."

Niall's eyes disappeared into another grin. "On a Tuesday night?" His intonation made me think of an Irish accent now, but only the shadows, the traces of it.

I told him about my reading plans, *The Celestine Prophecy*, the letter from Wilbur, the message from my father, the confluence of Tuesdays.

He smiled faintly as I talked, and drank his coffee, looking to the side, the crinkles around his eyes deepening now and then. He seemed to find the story funny, so I drew it out, but eventually I finished.

"How about you?" I said. "Why did you go?"

He tipped back the last of his coffee, put the cup down, glanced at me then turned sideways. He was facing the tree. "Why did I go?" he repeated. "Because I hoped you might be there."

7.

Oscar seemed wild that night: wild curls, wild eyes, laughing loudly at my jokes about the dinosaur.

They weren't jokes so much as a performance. We were eating dinner on the couch, watching ABC for Kids, and I picked up the latest toy dinosaur that my mother's husband, Xuang, had mailed to us. Xuang was obsessed with dinosaurs as a child, he says, and he wanted to encourage the same in Oscar, phoning him now and then to ask after his favorite. "T-Rex!" Oscar always says, and I can hear Xuang's voice urging a less obvious choice: "Diplodocus? Brachiosaurus?" "No," Oscar says patiently. "T-Rex."

Anyhow, tonight I picked up Xuang's latest gift (a triceratops) and had it rise up behind the cushions and express surprise to find us there. "I'm just walking around on my mountains here, and—Oh! What's this? Who are you?" The dinosaur kept lumbering around the couch and discovering us. It was a riot. Hilarious. Oscar's wild eyes, wild laugh. We both fell about laughing. Some peas slid from Oscar's plate to the floor. "What are those?" the dinosaur shouted. "Falling green boulders!"

Oscar couldn't breathe, he was laughing so hard. The dinosaur leaned over, trying to get a closer look at the falling green boulders. He toppled to the floorboards. He survived but with various wounds.

We bandaged him up with torn strips of paper towel and he was fine.

"What a day," Oscar said, as I put him to bed.

8.

The following Tuesday night, I returned to Wilbur's place, and he held a class in Flight Meditation.

Before we started, however, we lined up side by side at Wilbur's windows and stared into the evening blue. We were looking for flight waves.

"We'll start each class with this exercise," Wilbur explained, striding up and down behind us, and instructing us to keep our eyes on the glass. "Don't expect to see anything tonight, of course. It will take weeks, months even, before the flight waves appear. We just need to get into the habit of looking."

"Wait, so this isn't part of the meditation?" Frangipani frowned.

"No."

His "no" was emphatic, but in fact I did find it meditative, to stand at a window and stare. Through the glass I could see roofs, chimneys, pipes, wires. A bird swooped. I turned to Niall, who was beside me, and smiled. He smiled back. I stepped forward and looked down at the road. A parked car, a garbage bin lying on its side.

"Not too close," Wilbur said. "You're not looking down at things, you're only looking out at the air."

I looked up again. "Sorry."

"Never apologize," Wilbur told me kindly. This seemed like bad advice. Sometimes an apology is just the thing.

Antony tapped on the glass. "Flight waves? Can you hear me?"

Pete Aldridge winced and massaged his own shoulder. It must have been playing up again. He was paying almost no attention to the windows.

"Is it like looking at those pictures?" Antony inquired. "The Magic Eye pictures with the hidden 3-D images?"

Interested by this idea, everyone turned to Wilbur.

Wilbur considered. "It might be," he hedged.

"Well, that's it for me then," Niall said. "I've never been able to see those images. I've stood and stared at one for half an hour or more, and it was always nothing but the pattern." He sketched squiggles in the air.

"I've never looked at one properly," Nicole announced. "Every time I try, the word *priorities* comes into my head. *Priorities!*" She pronounced the word in a fluting, Scottish accent. "So I stop, because is life long enough for us to stare at patterns? No, it's not. Not that I'm judging you, Niall. The fact that you tried for half an hour shows commitment."

Niall laughed.

"Got one in my living room," Pete Aldridge put in, bending his elbow and forcing it upward with the other hand. That's a good stretch. It made me want to do it, only that would have seemed like I was imitating Pete Aldridge. He was still speaking. "Dolphins hidden in mine. I see them instantly now."

"You have to look through the pattern," Frangipani told everyone. "Blur your eyes and relax, let the image come to you." She turned to Wilbur. "The same way you see auras. I expect that's how we'd see flight waves too. Make our eyes passive, rather than active."

"Yes." Wilbur was warming to the idea. "Yes, that's exactly how you do it."

We all looked back at the windows. I sensed the others working to relax and let images *come* to them. The blue outside was darkening.

"Right," said Wilbur. "That's probably enough."

He gestured toward a stack of purple yoga mats by the front door. "Everybody take one and find a place on the floor."

There was a moment's pause while we measured the living room floor with our eyes. Then Antony and Niall began pushing furniture back against the walls. Frangipani and I handed out the yoga mats.

"Perfect," Wilbur said cheerfully, assisting Antony with the coffee table. The muscles in Wilbur's forearms were pronounced. "Thank you. Yes, I wondered about space but Antony and Niall are problem-solvers. And wait." He headed down the hall and I saw him pivot on his heel as he turned into a doorway.

When he returned this time, you couldn't see his face for the cushions in his arms. He peered around them. The cushions were the big, puffy sort, embroidered with silvers and golds, tasseled edges. These, he flung about the floor.

We were instructed to lie flat on our backs on the yoga mats and cushions. There was jostling for place, and my feet ended up dangerously close to Pete Aldridge's head. He didn't seem to mind. He groaned as he lay down on the mat, grasping his shoulder, but once flat he exhaled noisily and said, "Just the thing."

Wilbur wove between us, turned on some low, mystical music, sat down on the floor, and requested that we close our eyes and breathe.

9.

Incidentally, for his thirteenth birthday, my brother Robert received a Magic Eye picture. He Blu-Tacked it to his bedroom wall. It rippled like water, shades of green woven with yellow in vertical shimmers. Late one night, not long after he had disappeared, I went into his room and stared at this picture. I had never bothered with it before, but now I stared until a woman appeared, riding a bicycle. She was not the person I was looking for, of course, but I was pleased enough to see her.

10.

"Eilmer of Malmesbury," Wilbur said, low and gentle, into the quiet of our breathing, "was an eleventh-century English monk."

I opened my eyes.

"Keep your eyes closed," Wilbur murmured. "Breathe in. Breathe out. Don't try to listen to the words that I'm saying. Simply breathe them in."

I breathed deeply. My arms and legs felt heavy on the mat. Niall was two mats over. I could hear him breathing.

"Eilmer of Malmesbury jumped from an abbey watchtower," Wilbur said, "one hundred and fifty feet high. He was wearing wax wings. He broke both his legs. Afterward he said he failed because he wasn't wearing a tail."

Nicole snorted.

"Shhh," Wilbur said. "Breathe in. Breathe out."

"Which?" Pete Aldridge complained. "In or out?"

"Both," Frangipani clarified. "Or I assume so. Wilbur?"

"The father of King Lear," Wilbur continued, ignoring the question, "King Bladud, died leaping from a tower. According to legend, he was attempting to fly: wings he had constructed himself were attached to his arms. He was smashed to pieces."

There were puzzled, distressed murmurs from around the room.

"Shhh," Wilbur said again. "In 1519, a Portuguese man named João Torto attempted a flight from a cathedral wearing calico-covered wings and an eagle-shaped helmet."

"What happened to him?" Nicole asked.

"Hush," Wilbur said. "Breathe. He died."

Antony laughed aloud.

"Paolo Guidotti crashed through a roof wearing wings of whalebone and feathers," Wilbur added, "and broke his thigh."

Niall spoke up. "I'm not sure," he said, "that these stories are quite the thing."

Giggles rose and fell. Wilbur raised his voice but sustained his lulling tone. "Otto Lilienthal first attempted to fly a glider in 1891. In 1896, his glider stalled and crashed. He broke his back and died."

The stories continued. People jumped, leaped, fell, and broke their limbs. People crashed balloons into the sea and drowned. People flew and fell, flew and fell. All the time Wilbur spoke in the same singsong voice.

Eventually, he couldn't be heard over our laughter. "It's in the script," he pleaded. "I'm reading from the script." And now our laughter grew and ascended until we were rolling around in it, sitting up, falling sideways, hurting with it, weeping. Wilbur shrugged, set down his notes, and we laughed even harder.

After that we ate lemon and ginger cheesecake and drank sherry.

"We were getting to a point," Wilbur said eventually. "The point was that all these people thought they had to use wings of calico, or whalebone, machines, cloth, motors and gas, and *that* is why they crashed."

"It's a reasonable point," Niall conceded, "but it's not really meditation."

11.

That night, I collected Oscar from my father's place and drove home while Oscar chatted, from the back seat, about Grandpa and Lynette, and how Lynette couldn't find any socks for him, and you cannot play at Firecracker Soft Play Center if you don't have socks. You need socks. And Lynette said, "This is a disaster!" but then she found them.

"They were in the exact same place I put them last week!" I said. "The front pocket of your backpack! I told Lynette they were there!"

But he only repeated the story of how Lynette could not find them, until she could. "So very lucky," he added to himself in Lynette's voice, shaking his head at the car window.

Lynette had bought Oscar a baby doll from a vending machine in the play center, and this now lay across Oscar's lap, alongside one of his toy swords. The gift of the doll pleased me because I like the idea of Oscar having a doll: it is consistent with my principles of parenting, many of which I keep forgetting to apply. But was it an implied criticism of the three plastic swords in his backpack?

"Did Lynette get you the baby doll before or after she looked in your backpack for your socks?" I asked Oscar.

"She couldn't find my socks at all!" Oscar declared. "But then she find-ed them! So very lucky."

Which was no answer.

In any case, you can't call up your father's wife and say, "Was your gift of the baby doll a commentary on my parenting? Because, just so you know, he already has plenty of non-gender-specific toys. He has a pink fairy wand at home! I bought it for him in the two-dollar store *the moment* he asked for it. The swords in his backpack are not representative."

Just as you cannot ring and say, "His socks were in the exact place I told you they would be!"

I was excited about naming the doll, and suggested several possibilities, but Oscar was dismissive. He preferred to call her "the baby."

"Pretend the baby tries to get my sword and we don't notice," Oscar instructed me. "And pretend you see the baby with the sword in her mouth and you say, *Oh no, what's going on here?*"

"Oh no, what's going on here?!" I obliged, with much drama and dismay. It seemed to me that a more sensible course would be to remove the sword from the baby's mouth. But these were not my rules.

"Pretend the baby has to go to sleep now," Oscar said next. "And so does the sword. Now I'll sing a tweet for them. Do you know what a tweet is?"

"Oscar!" I said. "You have a Twitter account?"

"A tweet is a song you sing for a baby to make them never wake up," he explained. He strummed the sword and sang one of our lullabies.

"That was lovely!" I said.

"I know. I can do a tweet for you now, Mummy."

"Thank you," I said. "I hope I wake up eventually."

"You will."

He strummed the sword and sang:

Rock a bye, baby,
the lightning's falling down,
the sky is singing to hold Mummy in her cradle,
the sky keeps Mummy safe, keeps Mummy safe, for Osca-a-a-a-r.

He knows how to fade out a song.

I thought: *This is the happiest you can be.*

At traffic lights, I looked at my phone. The day he'd visited me at my café, Niall had not asked for my number. He had looked at his watch, scraped back his chair, paid the bill, and left with one more smile.

I looked at my phone, but of course nothing happened. The lightning falls down, I reminded myself, the lightning falls down. I wasn't sure exactly what I meant.

12.

The next book in my stack was *The Secret* by Rhonda Byrne. I'd heard of this book too. In his job interview, Oliver, my chef, told me it had changed his life. He seemed to think my Happiness Café was directly related to the book. When I admitted I hadn't read it, he breathed, "Do it. Today," and he guaranteed that it would change my life.

I laughed and promised to read it, but did not. I still had *The Guidebook* then.

Now I picked up *The Secret* and felt a frisson. It's a great title. Secrets can be so tricky to uncover, but this one I could just read!

The key to this book seems to be that we're all magnets. That is, we draw good things to us by thinking good things. *Demanding* good things of the universe, with great enthusiasm. So easy!

The catch is that the reverse is also true. Think bad thoughts, bad things will happen. As soon as you think, *Oh, I hope this car doesn't crash!* the universe understands that we are asking for the car to crash. It sets to work crashing it. The universe could use some lessons in grammar. It struggles with the negative and subordinate clauses.

Catastrophic incidents, meanwhile—plane crashes, earthquakes, tsunamis—are all the fault of the victims. They were thinking worried thoughts.

I closed the book and considered it.

By analogy, I decided, anxiety, superstition, knocking-on-wood, locking doors, bringing an umbrella or a coat or extra water, basically anything you do to prepare for the worst, will make the worst come true. When I used to draft contracts, negotiate settlements, advise on Y2K, these were always based on the hypothetical, worst-case scenario. By doing that, I was *inviting* the worst-case scenario! By worrying that I would lose my brother to MS, I made him disappear; by worrying he'd never come back, I manifested that destiny. By fearing it had to be too good to be true, that I had found a perfect man named Finnegan, I triggered the dissolution of our marriage.

Books like *The Secret*, I reasoned, along with lotteries, basketball scholarships, and happy-ending movies about impossible dreams, all help to maintain the inequitable system. You are not poor because of entrenched privilege, race, class, oppression. You are poor because you emit negative thoughts. If only you allowed your light to shine, glowed with positivity, you could have anything you wanted! This is government by false or faint hope.

I found the book ridiculous. I despised it.

Simultaneously, I panicked with excitement.

I walked around carefully obeying the book's instructions, sending out messages to the universe (rather than waiting for the universe to send them to me), asking politely for more customers, please, for an unexpected consignment of quirky coffee cups, for a glowing review of the Happiness Café in *Spectrum*, for Shreya to clean the coffee machine without me asking her, for my telephone to ring, for it to ring, for it to ring, even though he didn't have my number. (An easy problem for the universe to fix.) Meanwhile, I rigorously censored negative thoughts.

For weeks, I asked the universe repeatedly for this and that, beaming at it fondly. I took great care to rephrase all negative thoughts in the positive. *Oh God, I hope Oscar doesn't wake up in the night again*, became, *Dear Universe, please let Oscar have a beautiful sleep tonight. Thank you, and goodnight.*

I did not believe a word of that book, but I wanted to so badly that I played as if I did.

13.

There was also this.

The night before my weekend retreat to the island, I had a dream. In the dream, I stood on a balcony and reached my arms out to the sky. A strange, powerful surge ran through me and out into the blue.

That was it, the entire dream: a question sent out into the blue.

I saw now that I had asked the universe, please, for love. In my secret, quietest heart I saw that the universe had answered. Redheaded, broad-shouldered man in jeans and rumpled T-shirt reaching for sliced honeydew.

14.

Our third class, as Wilbur had promised, was in Flight Immersion.

Beforehand, I imagined we would all be required to climb into large black boxes, have the lids clipped shut, and then crouch quietly, thinking about flight for an hour. I don't know where I got this idea, but I was convinced it would happen. I planned to refuse.

Anyway, I arrived at Wilbur's building at the same time as Nicole. She seemed happy to see me. "You want to ring the bell?" she offered, even though she was right beside it. Then she laughed and said she's so used to hanging out with her kids that she thinks any kind of button is a treat. "I actually felt a moment of relief," she said, "that there was just one of you, so no fighting over who gets to do it."

We both laughed and I said she could do it, and she said no, you can, and we went back and forth, still laughing. Then she pressed the button. It made such a sharp *brrring!* that I half wished I'd got to do it. "I want a turn," I said, and pressed it myself, and there we were laughing again.

So we went upstairs in a good mood.

In Wilbur's apartment, the armchairs circled the coffee table. Frangipani and Pete Aldridge were already there, sitting the farthest distance from each other that could be managed in a close circle. For the first time, I noticed that their frowns matched. In the center of each of their foreheads, between identical parallel lines, was a triangle without its base—a pointed hat, a circumflex.

On the coffee table was a bottle of red wine and a platter of cheese and crackers. "So fancy!" said Nicole as the buzzer rang.

Niall and Antony arrived together. I wondered which of them had pressed the bell.

There were three different types of cheese on the platter—a blue, a cheddar, and something ripe and gooey—and all three, for the record, were excellent. Throughout the evening, people kept interrupting Wilbur to praise his choices in cheese, or to confer with one another about which was the favorite. Pete Aldridge only ate the cheddar. He cut himself huge chunks of it and I noticed that Frangipani flinched each time he did. Then she would quickly slice herself a wafer-thin piece.

Wilbur opened the proceedings by announcing that Flight Immersion classes were designed to "accustom" us to the sky, to "accept" that we belonged there.

"We belong in the sky?" Pete Aldridge pounced, shoulders tense.

"When you're ready," Wilbur hastened to clarify. "Not a moment before."

I could see by Antony's grin that he was warming up to make a joke, and Wilbur must have sensed this too because he coughed loudly and flourished his hands. "Look around you! See the hot-air balloons! The cloud paintings! The hang-glider prints! You've already done some flight immersion just by spending time in this room."

"Is your apartment not ordinarily decorated like this?" Frangipani demanded.

"No," Wilbur said firmly. "It is not."

Frangipani slumped back. Her eyes roamed the room. "That card over there has nothing to do with flight," she said fractiously.

A card stood on the TV table. *Happy Birthday to the Greatest Guy to Walk the Planet*, the card declared. The print looped around a cartoon Earth.

Surprised, we all turned back to Wilbur. Here he was, our teacher, and we had never for a moment suspected that he was the greatest guy to walk the planet. Nor that he might have a circle of acquaintances outside this circle of armchairs, or a friend or even partner who considered him the greatest guy on earth. I'd never even thought he might have birthdays!

Wilbur waited patiently, his elbow on the arm of his chair, chin on his hand, spark in his eye, allowing us time to adjust.

"Neither does cheese have a thing to do with flight," Pete Aldridge snapped suddenly, "and yet, here it is!" He slapped his hand on the table.

We all jumped.

Then Niall said in his reasonable voice, tracing his long-lost accent: "Well, and this chair I'm sitting on, does it fly?" After which we all began pointing out objects unrelated to flight in the room. We kept turning to Frangipani for a reaction. An interesting thing happened. Her irritable expression faded and an impish grin appeared. That is exactly the word: *impish*.

Wilbur breathed in deeply and his voice soared above our chatter: "For today's class in Flight Immersion, I will tell you how an airplane works!"

And, quite honestly, that is what he did.

Or, rather, he outlined the basics of airplanes. I cannot remember much of it now, but I know he took a large sketchpad and drew diagrams to illustrate his words. He sketched a childish plane with arrows all around it, and he labeled these arrows: THRUST, LIFT, GRAVITY, and DRAG.

Thrust is what you need to get the plane going. If you have a glider, you start high—that's the key—and gravity provides the thrust. Otherwise, you need an engine.

Lift is what keeps it in the sky, I think. You get it by shaping the wings a certain way. They should be flat underneath and curved from the front to the back on top. As you travel forward, air passing over the top has farther to go because of the curve, so pressure above is reduced. High pressure below and low pressure above generates lift. The faster you go, the more lift you get.

"The principle of lift," Niall stated.

"Yes," Wilbur agreed.

"Nothing to do with two pairs of sneakers hitting the ground at the same time."

"No." Wilbur shook his head. "I think," he admitted, "that my parents may have been confused."

He carried on.

Gravity is good if you have a glider, and it's good when you want to come back down, but otherwise is something of a nuisance.

Drag is caused by the frame of the airplane itself as it tries to push its way through the sky.

Wilbur spoke in a relaxed, conversational voice, leaning back in his chair. He reminded me of a German literature professor I'd had in first-year university, who used to smoke a pipe in tutorials. Only Wilbur did not have a pipe.

He also talked about the Wright brothers, and praised them for having figured out how to control an airplane. Here I recall that Wilbur used words like *roll* and *pitch* and *yaw*, and he confessed that he himself had been named after the Wright brothers.

"Which one?" Frangipani asked.

Everyone turned quickly to look at her.

"Well not Orville," Pete Aldridge grumbled. "Obviously."

"Oh God, I'm an idiot," Frangipani announced, which surprised us all.

"No, you're not," Nicole soothed, falling into mothering again. "Don't ever let me hear you saying that. Here, have some cheese."

15.

The next book in my stack was a little manual of happiness. It was full of sensible, snappy advice about being cheerful and friendly, getting enough sleep and exercise. But I was mostly struck by the Chinese proverb used as its epigraph.

If you want happiness for an hour, take a nap.
If you want happiness for a day, go fishing.
If you want happiness for a year, inherit a fortune.
If you want happiness for a lifetime, help somebody.

I'm not one for naps. I wake feeling cranky.

Fishing does not interest me at all. It would certainly not cheer up a vegan.

Inheriting a fortune: Well, that depends from whom I inherit it. My mother? That would not make me happy for a year; it would make me want my mother back.

Help somebody: I suppose this refers to charity and digging wells. It would feel good to dig a well. But would you carry that feeling for a lifetime? Only if you kept on digging. You'd get so tired. Weighed down by problems surrounding well-building—ground too hard, ground of clay, broken spades, insufficient funding—and you can never dig all the wells you need, help all the thirsty people, so you are constantly faced with moral quandaries about priorities, and you just keep on helping, helping, and the sand sucks up your help, your skin dries in the sun, your bones ache and crack, and nobody ever helps you back.

I helped my friend from university Natalia and her sister Tia move house once. This was not long after I'd met my eventual-husband Finnegan at a party at their place, so I felt affectionate toward the sisters and the house itself. I spent a long day packing up their kitchen for them, wrapping bowls and glasses in newspaper, Spray-n'-Wiping the cabinets, running up and down flights of stairs with cardboard boxes. It was fun at first, but I grew increasingly weary. Finn came by and hefted bookcases and beds, even though he had lower back issues at the time. I remember seeing him wince and pause, right as Tia pivoted around a corner and sang, "TV next, please!" Here, I experienced a flash of fury, and recalled that both girls earned good wages and could have paid movers. Also, I did not find either of them sufficiently grateful, they were so caught up in the tizzy of their move. I kept hearing them on the phone, telling people they were "Doing it all on their own!" while I was there on their kitchen floor, scrubbing away, thinking: *What am I, chopped liver?!*

Helping Natalia and Tia to move did not make me happy for a lifetime.

16.

Oscar came into my room at 5:23 am, waking me from a pleasant dream. I can't remember the content of the dream, only that it suffused me with pleasantness. I know that it was 5:23 am because the first thing I do, when Oscar wakes me, is look at the clock. That way I can determine whether I should feel bright and awake, or desperate and weary. I reserve my response until I see the clock.

5:23 am. Not desperate, but weary.

Oscar had Baby tucked beneath his arm. "Mummy, can you take me to the toilet?" he asked.

"Oh," I said into the gray light. "You can take yourself. It's not dark."

"No," he said. "I'm scared."

"Baby will keep you company."

"Baby's scared too."

So we walked across the hall to the bathroom. Then he climbed into my bed, cheerful, chatty, bright, and cuddling, the sharp bends of Baby pressed against my chest, and I said, "Okay, let's go to sleep now," and closed my eyes, but each time I drifted his voice drew me back. Sometimes I thought, *This is lovely, this is how it's supposed to be, chat with him, cuddle him*; other times I thought, *Oh God, please let me sleep.*

Eventually I opened my eyes to the day: *Choose happiness!*

I *breathed in the happy*, and *breathed out the sad.*

I scrambled eggs for a healthy, protein-rich breakfast, and chopped grapes in half. Oscar shared his grapes with Baby, which seemed a waste.

He announced that today he would bring Baby to day care.

"But what if you lose Baby?" I asked.

I meant: What if the children tease you, a boy with a baby doll, and the strides we are making in gender-neutral play slam into a brick wall?

Don't worry! I exhorted myself. *Go with the flow!*

"You want to bring Baby along? Sure! Why not?"

His face lit up and he grabbed my forearm and kissed it.

I drove Oscar to Blue Gum Cottage.

At the gate, I paused. *Be in your life!* This was a good thought. Far better to be in your life than outside it.

I looked through the fence to the slopes of artificial green, the raised wooden paths, the little girl named Amber who was leaping, exuberant, from the path.

Look at her leaping into life! I thought. I encouraged my heart to leap in sync with Amber, but then she fell and began wailing, and I hastened to get my heart away from her.

I signed Oscar in, hung his satchel on its hook, and led him back outside. The children were now sitting in a circle and a teacher was handing around SAO biscuits. Another teacher, Leesa, was quietly teaching Amber, still tear-stained from her fall, how to have a thumb war.

This is beautiful! I thought, pausing to consider the roses (by which I meant the children eating SAOs). Leap, fall, but then learn thumb wars!

Beside me, Oscar adjusted Baby in his arms. The children turned toward us, chewing, slow gazes falling from me to Oscar, from Oscar to Baby in his arms.

"One, two, three, four, let's have a thumb war," Leesa chanted. "Now we have to bow our thumbs to each other. Like this. See?"

Approaching my café, I thought: *So great to have a hairdresser next door! So handy!*

Inside the door, I paused to appreciate the marvel of my café. I started this café, I designed this café, I chose the furniture, I composed the menu, I employed these people!

Xuang helped, of course.

When I returned from Montreal, pregnant and broken, and announced my Happiness Café plan to my parents, they laughed gently, clicked their teeth, said, "Maybe one day," and, "What a lovely dream." Then they asked if I'd confirmed my start date with my old law firm yet and how much maternity leave I would take.

But Xuang squeezed his eyes tightly shut, flung them open and shouted, "Yes! I love it! Let's do it!" My parents were pretty annoyed with him.

He's an enthusiast, Xuang, who always has a scheme, an investment, a real-estate deal, an enterprise in hand, and he has opened several restaurants. Most of what he does is successful: he's shrewd, relentless, and now very wealthy. He has told me, quite seriously, that he thinks he might be mildly bipolar, and he does get into very low moods. But when he's upbeat, he's intoxicating. He told me my Happiness Café was ingenious, that it would go global. I planned to use the inheritance I'd got from my grandfather for start-up costs, but Xuang insisted on bankrolling my first few years, and covering Oscar's day care.

I was unlikely to make any real profit for a year or two, he explained, and he advised me on payroll software, and helped me search out a location. It's because of Xuang that I live on the Lower North Shore now, that there is plenty of storage space in the back room of the café, that our espresso machine is the best available.

But I applied for council permissions! I did online courses in the Food Service Industry, Retail Management, and Café Ownership! I consulted with psychologists on happy color schemes! And so on.

Now I felt faint with joy at my achievements.

Every table was full!

My café is a hit! A success! (More or less. It does pretty well, anyway, and Xuang hardly ever has to subsidize now.)

It's always full at the breakfast hour. Three people waited for takeaway coffees at the counter. No one was drumming fingers on the counter impatiently or frowning at their phone. No one was holding out a leg to trip up other customers.

Many cafés offer stacks of coloring books and crayons for children. At mine, we have boxes of CRAFTS FOR EVERYONE: HELP YOURSELF! The boxes contain stickers, pencils, and complex coloring-in sheets of a superior quality, because playing makes adults happy too; creativity stimulates endorphins. It only ever seems to be the children who play with these boxes of crafts, however, which makes me feel resentful in the same way that I resent it when I get a box of Paddle Pops for the kids and Mini Magnums for the adults, and the kids all demand a Mini Magnum, please.

Today, however, three young men in their twenties leaned forward, shading and coloring, sticking and gluing.

My heart leaped at this, without me asking it to.

All day long, conversations made me smile.

"How've you been?" a guy in a suit asked his companion.

"I've been well," the companion replied, then reconsidered. "Never better!"

At another table, a woman confided in her friend. "It's a cake that looks like a boot," she said. "But I want it in different colors."

Her friend nodded thoughtfully. "Like a boot?"

Later, a couple sat and planned their wedding with a civil celebrant. A different couple had once sat at that very table sorting out their divorce. You see, there is always balance. After the dark, there is light.

"Sometimes people like a poem read," the celebrant informed the young couple.

"And you will read this poem?" the young man inquired, uncertain in his English.

"I will if you want me to, or you can have a friend."

The celebrant told the young couple: "I've had weddings with the string quartet, the butterflies, the flowers in an arch, everything! And weddings where they've just had a handful of people sort of gathered"— she cupped her hands together, gathering the guests—"in a spot."

The couple nodded, pleased. "We will actually be facing the view," the young girl said.

"So the guests have their backs to the view?" the celebrant confirmed, making a note.

When I collected Oscar from day care, I read the daily report.

The children lay on the floor with their eyes closed today, it said, *and thought about colors. The children looked at mirrors to see what they looked like on the outside. Then they looked at kaleidoscopes to see what they looked like on the inside.*

That startled me. I thought: Is there something . . . is there some scientific truth here that has passed me by? Is this, after all, what a kaleidoscope is? A vision of one's own internal organs? Or, more metaphysically, a vision of one's soul?

On the drive home, I asked Oscar what he had thought when he looked at himself through the kaleidoscope. He didn't appear to know what I was talking about.

"Why is it dark?" he asked instead.

"Because it's late."

"Why is it late?"

"Well—" But before I could answer he'd asked his next question.

"Where's Uncle Robert?" He asks this now and then, although the answer is always the same.

"We're not sure," I said. "He's lost. He's not coming back."

"How do you know?"

"I just know."

"Why is the moon there?" Pointing through the window.

I used to hear people complaining about the questions children asked, all their *whys*. And I thought: *So easy! Just answer! What's the issue, you strange, complaining parents?*

That's what I thought.

Now I want to claw out my eyes sometimes, at the questions, the days and days of questions. Life is a constant pop quiz, and I'm always failing. The cognitive dissonance, the limits of my knowledge, the exposure of those limits when the four-year-old demands answers in a lift, say, a quiet, crowded lift, everyone waiting, with interest, for my reply. To be left with *I don't know*, to slip listlessly into *I'm not sure*.

I don't *know* why the sandblaster can knock Spider-Man off the wall!

And definitions! "What does *serious* mean?" he asks.

"Not funny," I say, but you can't define words by their negative. "Serious, it's just, you know, *serious*." Or I define it with words that themselves require definition. "Solemn, grave, earnest . . . you know, *serious*."

Once, he was walking down the stairs and he said, "Nobody is ugly except you."

"Oscar!" I said, reeling. "Really?"

And he looked concerned, uncertain, and asked, "What does *except* mean?"

Try defining *except* to a four-year-old.

"Why can ghosts go through walls?" he asked once.

"Because they have no material substance," I said. "They're mysterious, misty, intangible, without form."

He giggled. "Why is there no such thing as monsters?"

17.

At "Flight: A Practical Approach" we learned the best positions for flying and how to avoid cricks in the neck and cramps. We stood in a row, our heads tucked down, our arms outstretched, and Wilbur studied us in turn, consulting a chart, adjusting our positions ever so slightly with his large, firm hands, moving up and down the line.

Nobody laughed. We were deep in the game.

Afterward, we stood on a street corner and now we did laugh, but softly, almost mystically.

"I mean, why are we doing this?" Nicole asked.

Pete Aldridge was unusually cheerful. "Ah, well." He shrugged.

Everyone dispersed, waving and smiling, toward their cars, but Niall and I stood on the corner.

Choose happiness! I thought. *Keep it simple!*

This man standing beside me had sought me out at my café. He had suggested coffee. Looking sideways at a tree he had informed me that the reason he was doing this course was that he hoped I might be doing it too.

In response, I had sent a message to the universe requesting that it please arrange for Niall to ask me out.

"Hey," I said now on the street corner, "can I have your number? You want to get a drink sometime?"

PART 6

1.

While I was studying at university, and still living at home—it was a seven-minute train ride from our place in Stanmore to Redfern, followed by an easy walk to campus—my parents separated.

They'd stopped fighting about parenting techniques by then: now it was more a hideous, intransigent dichotomy. That is to say: Dad claimed that Robert must be dead; Mum said he was alive and coming back. She baked Robert a cake each year on his birthday, in preparation. She still took trips, visiting police stations all over the country, distributing posters and pamphlets. She still met with our caseworker, Matilda, for regular updates and to devise action plans.

Obviously those two positions were inherently incompatible.

I hated both my parents, and both their positions, but especially Dad's. I could hardly look at him. I glowered at him when I did.

The day that my dad moved out, I ignored him. He was going in and out with boxes and suitcases, pushing them along the hall floor, and I was walking past him to the kitchen to get myself a snack.

"I hate that smile of yours," he said suddenly.

I didn't even know that I was smiling. I had thought my face was blank.

But he stopped and said, "That weird half-smile you do. It's so vindictive. It's so insouciant."

"Which?" I said. "Which is it?"

He started shoving the big box down the hall again, using his knees, and I shouted, "Because those two words mean *opposite* things!" But he didn't answer.

I visited him at his new flat a week later and we didn't mention that conversation, or the fact that they're not really antonyms, *vindictive* and *insouciant*; I guess you could be both at the same time.

2.

Mum tried to buy out my dad so we could stay in the house, but she couldn't get a bank to lend her enough money, even though she told various mortgage brokers, bank managers, people in the post office, and her hairdresser that we *had* to stay there for when Robert came back. The banks didn't seem to find this relevant. (The hairdresser did.)

There were more, bigger fights then, because Mum couldn't believe that Dad would insist on selling and Dad laughed an awful, scornful laugh, or else roared that she was being *ridiculous* and Robert was *never* coming back, get it *into your head*.

Mum and I moved to a rental place in Petersham, which had issues with mold. She asked the people who bought our house to pass on our address to Robert if he ever turned up. She left them a stack of laminated cards containing our new address.

Meanwhile, chapters of *The Guidebook* kept arriving because I filled in their change-of-address form.

The first to arrive at our new place was disconcertingly apt.

Chapter 99

If you are a pilot, you cannot fly in cloud unless you have an instrument rating.

Flying in cloud is an illusion. You can *feel* the plane turning right, you can *see* the plane turning right—you can see the movement of the wing! But you are not turning right. The instruments tell you that the plane is going straight ahead.

You have to believe the technology despite what your senses tell you.

Once you've lost your horizon in cloud you have only 30 to 40 seconds before you become completely disorientated.

Once, *The Guidebook* told me to swim a thousand laps. Another chapter instructed me to climb walls. They said that I should breathe in, and then out. (That was an easy one.) They informed me I should pretend I was a certain animal: a flying fox, a butterfly, a frog, many others.

Chapter 144

Visualize yourself as a bush turkey. Get into character as a bush turkey! Impersonate a bush turkey! Strut about, darting this way and that, peck at an insect on the side of the road, get into a flap!

Study these diagrams of a cat posing and stretching. Try them out regularly!

I did not pretend I was a bush turkey. Or maybe just the once, alone.

Sometimes, as I fell asleep at night, I imagined myself to be a dolphin or a dragonfly. This was soothing. A cure for insomnia.

The cat stretches were good: like free yoga classes.

Chapter 52

Seek out the following objects and inhale each
deeply: vanilla, coconut, cinnamon, nutmeg, frangipani, freesia, roses, mint, glue, tar. Next,
sign up for a wine appreciation class.

I did not set out to locate the fragrant items but I did take a whiff if I happened on one. Not the glue or tar. I'm pretty sure sniffing them is dangerous.

I signed up for a wine appreciation course. But that was only because I saw a notice for one, and a cute boy stood beside me reading the notice too. He reached up and tore off one of the number strips, so I tore off one for myself.

When I got to the course, the cute boy wasn't there. Why had he wasted one of the number strips?! But I made friends with a girl named Natalia who was studying electrical engineering and skateboarded everywhere. It's easy to make friends when you're both throwing back one glass of wine after another. We paid no attention to talk of how to swirl the wine, or to hints of sesame or strawberry, we just chatted and drank.

3.

I finished my arts degree with first-class honors in English, finished my law degree, went to the College of Law.

What I remember about getting my arts degree was Natalia. We often met for lunch, either at the Holme Building or at Manning Bar, and one day I said, "Where should we go today?"

"Well," she replied, "I myself am Holme-ward bound, far from the Manning crowd."

That took my breath away, it was so clever. I loved Natalia after that. We lost contact for a while when I went to law school, but reconnected later and, now that I think about it, maybe *all* students at Sydney University say that clever Holme-ward thing?

Also, I had a boyfriend. Carl. He was kind of mean. "You are unbelievably stupid," he'd say, smiling like he was sharing a joke with me, when I did something like parked over somebody's driveway by accident, or got lost on the way to a party.

I told him about my missing brother on our second date. He seemed fascinated, as if this was a puzzle I'd been unable to solve, but he was pretty sure he'd solve it for me. He asked a lot of questions. When I told him about the MS diagnosis, I could almost see him drop the puzzle onto the table, his expression suggesting we'd just squandered his valuable time. "Oh, right," he said. "So he'd be dead anyway by now."

"No," I said. "No, no, no. MS isn't usually fatal."

"Well, but," he said, shrugging, and he changed the subject.

Around the time I started law school, my grandfather had a stroke, and Mum moved up to Maroochydore to be close to him. She carried on her work of tracing Robert from there.

What I remember about law school is that some guy had been framed by the police, apparently, and everyone wanted to get him out of prison. It seemed to me they should get a *lawyer*, rather than pinning up posters. This was before I *became* a lawyer, remember, so I believed that the legal system worked.

Graffiti on the inside of the law school toilet doors said: *Do something shocking. Vote blue stocking.*

Okay! I thought obligingly, every time I saw this. But I have no particular memory of voting anything.

I had a boyfriend named Lachlan at law school. He was fine. He used to tickle me a lot, though, which makes me squirm now, thinking of it. It was his version of foreplay.

Also, he liked to read imaginary survival guides. They made him laugh out loud. *How to Survive an Alien Invasion. A Guide to Life on the Planet of the Apes.* He gave these to me as gifts and said, "Trust me, this is hilarious," and I would flick through them and no; no, they were not.

The College of Law was fun. You do six months of practical legal training there, which means you play-act being a lawyer, and then you get admitted as a solicitor of the Supreme Court of New South Wales, and you can be a lawyer.

4.

My grandfather died, and he left me thirty thousand dollars. I'd only ever visited a few times, when I was a kid. I hadn't paid much attention to him on those visits, being busy on the beach. So, at first, this seemed like a bargain: inheritance without grief.

But the rest of the estate wasn't worth much—even when they sold his black opal—and my mum and her sister, Auntie Gem, ended up with twenty thousand dollars each. None of my cousins got a cent.

I think Grandpa must have meant my thirty thousand as a kind of consolation prize because I'd lost my brother, whereas the other cousins still had their siblings. But it was more trouble than it was worth: the cousins made brash jokes about how I was the rich cousin now and I'd better throw a *massive* party and invite them, and buy them trips to Europe and jewelry and pay off all their student debts. Actually, these were confusing jokes because sometimes they seemed deadly serious. And with a really inflated idea of how much thirty thousand dollars buys you. But I laughed anyway.

They also made jokes about how I was the favorite granddaughter, and what did I *do* to make Grandpa love me best? No, seriously, *what*?

Meanwhile, Auntie Gem smiled politely, but in her slightly squishy way, while her *husband*, my Uncle Bob, became heated and wanted to challenge the inheritance in court. I read back over my notes on succession and prepared arguments, but felt mortified, and thought I would probably just hand over the money. Certainly, if anybody deserved the money, my *mother* did, since she'd moved up to Queensland to be with her father when he had the stroke. This added another layer of tension, because she reminded her brother-in-law, Bob, of this one day, adding that she was happy for me to get it so that should be an end to it. My mother had fallen in love with Xuang by now, and was sunny.

Uncle Bob responded: "Yes, right, of course. That makes sense. And that summer I went up there and retiled his bathroom means nothing, does it?"

Sometimes, in the middle of the night I would wake and think: *But I do deserve it. I did lose my brother. I do.*

Nothing happened in the end, but Uncle Bob took me aside one day and said in this half-smiling, half-serious tone: "Half of that money belongs to your brother, I suppose. So you'll put that aside for his return?"

Which I think was meant as pure malice.

I gave the money to a financial adviser and forgot about it.

I got a job at a big Sydney law firm, in litigation. This was the 1990s. The main thing happening then was that we were *en route* to the year 2000.

That's what we were up to in the 1990s: tipping slowly, steadily, wide-eyed, terrified, elated towards that big, heady, ugly year 2000.

5.

There were two important things about the approaching year 2000: first, the pressure that the artist formerly known as Prince had placed on us by defining the ultimate party as that which takes place on the last day of 1999; and second, the fact that the world was going to be wiped out by the millennium bug (presumably *while* throwing Prince's party).

I am honored to say that I was a member of my law firm's Y2K Action Response Group. This meant that I was on the firm's email list for Y2K updates, and received weekly reports about such things as the six thousand firefighters who would stand guard over the first few uncertain moments of 2000 in riot gear, and the air traffic controllers who used paper and pen to monitor all flights in England and Wales while a computer was being upgraded to overcome Y2K compliance problems.

I spent a lot of time writing letters of advice on the Year 2000 Information Disclosure Act. If I remember correctly, this legislation protected you if you told people you were prepared for Y2K but then it turned out you were wrong. A lot of countries had this kind of law. It was known as Good Samaritan legislation. As if reassuring your customers that your system wouldn't crash when the calendar changed was exactly the same as crossing the street to help somebody who has been beaten up, robbed, stripped, and left half-dead, bandaging his wounds, pouring on oil and wine, and hefting him up onto your donkey.

6.

It was 1999, and I was sharing a flat in Balmain with a pair of strangers, a self-contained couple who were always at the theater. I was taking the ferry to work in the city each day, arriving home late at night. *The Guidebook* kept right on turning up, because I kept right on sending in change-of-address notifications. Sometimes I threw it away without opening it, but one night I opened it.

Chapter 72

Is there happiness in truth or only beauty?

Keats is the one to ask, I suppose.

But *I* think—in my view—there is some chink or gleam of happiness in truth. The radiance of understanding?

And when truth becomes clear, it comes shining through. Like the window you think is clean, but it's not, and then you wash it and everything outside jumps forward, jumps through, jumps glee-fully right at your face.

One of my flatmates was a draftsman or a town planner—I don't know; I never really concentrated when he spoke, as he was indescribably boring—and he had this stack of rolled papers on the dining room table. I remember reading the chapter about truth jumping forward at your face, looking up, and seeing the rolled papers, the *o*'s in the center of each roll, little round mouths, gaping black mysteries, *o*'s of anguish, silent wails for help.

PART 7

REFLECTIONS ON 2000

By Abigail Sorensen

In February this year, I had lunch with an old friend, Carly Grimshaw. Carly and I grew up as neighbors and best friends. But I had not been in contact with her for several years. We had "drifted apart." No animosity.

Her email arrived in my inbox at work. My heart smiled at her name. She must have searched for me online, located me on my law firm's website. She introduced herself as a "blast from the past!", congratulated me on having "become a lawyer!!!!", reminded me that she and I had planned to grow up and become "rock stars!!!" Next, she informed me that she was now in retail, working at Country Road in the Queen Victoria Building, and that we should "defo" meet for lunch at the café in the General Post Office building in Martin Place, "as that's about a halfway point!!"

The "defo" confused me for a moment, since we refer to defamation law as "defo" in my firm.

*

The lunch with Carly did not contain as many exclamation marks as Carly's email, but there were a few.

We exclaimed at how happy we were to see each other. She exclaimed at my new hairstyle. I exclaimed at hers. (She used to wear it in a single braid over her shoulder, now it's a pixie cut.) We exclaimed about how long it had been.

Then we settled into sentences ending in question marks or full stops. Essentially, an exchange of information about our families. How's your mum? How's *your* mum? How's your dad? How's *your* dad? I asked after her brother, Andrew, and her sister, Rabbit.

"Rabbit!" She smirked, as if I'd used the wrong fork. "I forgot we called her that!"

Surely not. Rabbit had been Rabbit for years.

But no, now she was Erin, apparently, in year five and winning tennis comps. I almost said, "Year five! I can't believe little Rabbit's in year five!" but felt weary, suddenly. Also, it made sense that Erin would be in year five. Time passes. People grow.

Andrew had studied Japanese at university, Carly said, and spent a year living in Kyoto.

"Seriously?"

She nodded, serious, to match my *seriously?*, then her face lit up, and she told me an amusing story about how Andrew had missed his flight to Japan because he couldn't find his passport. He'd had to get an urgent passport replacement and fly a few days later.

I laughed. We both laughed. "It was *hilarious*!" Carly said. "He's standing at his open drawer going, *I know it was in here!* and we're all going, *When did you last see it?* and he's like, *It's just, it's always there!* and it turns out he hadn't checked! He couldn't actually remember seeing it since we'd been to Tahiti! And we were all going, *Andrew! Tahiti was years ago!* Because it *was*—you remember when my family went to Tahiti? And it rained the whole time? His passport had probably expired! And the taxi's waiting outside to take him to the airport!"

"Oh, that's *so funny*!" I said.

But it wasn't that funny.

I tried to think of something else to say about it. "Typical Andrew," I tried, although, in the time I knew him, I had never been particularly conscious of his absent-mindedness pertaining to identification documents.

"Just hysterical," Carly said.

At this point, I had run out of things to ask.

I wanted to inquire whether Andrew's skin had cleared up, but that seemed inappropriate. Flute! I remembered Carly played flute. "How's the flute going?"

"Oh, the *flute*!" She frowned. "I haven't played for years. Forgot I played that."

Her braid, Rabbit, her flute: these were essential elements of Carly.

"Who *are* you?" I considered asking next, but I suspected she would be defensive rather than amused.

There was a silence and Carly ate her focaccia with roasted vegetables. A piece of chargrilled eggplant spilled onto her plate and she looked at this with intensity.

I began to feel uncomfortable. It was too much intensity for a single piece of eggplant. Several pieces maybe, or the entire range of roasted vegetable, but this was just one.

She's going to say something about Robert, I thought suddenly. She's going to say something wise and philosophical, or tragic, or hopeful, or sympathetic.

I honestly couldn't stand it. Don't, Carly, *don't* mention Robert's name.

Despite my silent pleas, she spoke Robert's name, but what she said was completely unexpected.

*

She said that she'd been having a secret relationship with Robert right before he disappeared.

A relationship.

That was the word that she used.

"A relationship?"

She clarified. She and Robert had been going out for two weeks.

"That's not a relationship."

She shrugged.

"Going *out*?" I asked.

"Well, not *going out* out. I just mean we were together. But we were keeping it secret. Until we were sure."

I stared at her.

"He would sneak into my place late at night," she said. "And then sneak back to your house in the early morning."

"This was happening right before he disappeared?"

Carly nodded. Her face was now grim. Her expression made me laugh.

"It's just—it's not true," I said. "You'd have told the police about that. You'd have told *me*!"

"It is true." Now she smiled tragically. "I didn't tell the police because Robert and I had agreed to keep our relationship secret. And I thought he would come back."

"But he *didn't* come back," I said. "So *then* you could have told. At some point, you must have known that it was time to tell!" I was still half laughing in disbelief.

She shrugged. "Maybe now's the right time."

I gave her a look.

"It's just, I kept expecting him back," she said. "Remember how we used to spend hours figuring out where he was? I *believed* that. And time kept going by. And I started to think I should say something, but it was, like, why now? It would have sounded so weird! Like, *oh, by the way, there's this.* It might have seemed like I was lying."

She was lying right now, I was sure of it. Or she had fabricated memories based on a teenage crush.

"So when did you last see him?" I asked, playing along to test her.

"The Tuesday night, three days before your birthday," she replied promptly.

"You did not."

"I did."

She used her fork to eat the fallen eggplant. This struck me as odd.

"Are you saying you were the last person to talk to him?"

"I suppose."

"And you still didn't think it was relevant to tell the police? Or at least me?"

She shrugged again. "It wasn't like it changed anything. He was gone! He was gone whether I told you or not. It's not like he'd told me where he was going! I had no relevant information."

"But, Carly," I said, "he disappeared three days before my birthday, re-member? I mean, I thought he was at Clarissa's, and my parents thought he was at Bing's. But he wasn't at either place. Don't tell me he was at *your* house. You didn't hide him under your four-poster bed for three days!"

"I did have that four-poster bed, didn't I?" Carly smiled nostalgically.

"Oh, do not tell me you've forgotten *that*, too!"

"He told *me* he was at Bing's. He knocked on my bedroom window about midnight, talked about how piano practice was going, and how he had to sleep on a really thin mattress on the floor of Bing's room, and how Bing had a Yoda night-light. I told him I wasn't sure about us—about our relationship. He left at about three in the morning. He *said* he was going back to Bing's."

"You broke *up* with him?"

"No. I told him that I wasn't sure. I said I needed time."

"And he climbed back out of your bedroom window and told you he was going to Bing's?"

"Right."

"But he didn't."

"I know that. Don't you think I know that?" She sounded wounded.

*

I returned to the office after lunch and found a memo in my in-tray from a senior partner.

> *Dear Abigail,*
> *A client has raised an interesting issue with me today. What if he wanted to publish an article on a website, and include a hyperlink to a different website? Would he be liable for anything defamatory contained in that other site?*
> *Could you give me your thoughts?*
> *Regards,*
> *Stuart Reevesby*
> *PS Cliff's instincts are clearly right: the internet is going to create a minefield of legal problems before we can figure them all out.*

There was no client name or file number on the memo. Non-chargeable work.

Ordinarily, this would have made me angry. I'd have been annoyed by Stuart's informal tone, particularly his use of a *postscript*, and the content of the postscript itself.

Everyone was talking about the net as a legal minefield: Why give Cliff's "instincts" the credit? Cliff Maybridge, another partner, had used the line in a meeting the previous week.

But that day I was elated by the memo.

Yes, I thought. *Yes.*

Can you hyperlink to a defamatory article? Can you *contain* someone else's defamation within your own frame? I began to research.

*

I do not mean to suggest that I forgot all about Carly's revelations and buried myself in work.

I called Matilda, our caseworker, and shared Carly's story, noting my reservations.

Matilda took it more seriously than me. She interviewed everyone again—with a focus on Carly, obviously.

My mother, who had started working now (part-time: her real job was finding Robert, keeping his name in the public eye, following every lead), took leave and flew down from Maroochydore to meet Carly for coffee. Apparently they both cried.

I met with Carly a few more times myself. Each time, Carly cried.

I still thought she was making it up.

In the end, all we really had was another reason for Robert to have run away, or to have taken his own life: a broken heart.

"I just said I needed *time*," Carly insisted, crying again. "I didn't break his *heart*."

Nobody saw that distinction as relevant.

"I didn't even want to break it off," she added, small child's voice. "I was trying to keep his interest."

"But now we know *exactly* the moment he disappeared!" my mother said. "He was heading from the Grimshaws' place to Bing's, and he never got there!"

She seemed to find this exciting, as if we could go to that place now, reach through time and pull him back.

*

Also this year, *The Guidebook* has, as usual, offered sporadic advice, asked strange questions, and instructed me to undertake extracurricular activities. These activities have included, but have not been limited to, ballroom dancing, deep-sea diving, and parasailing.

Generally, I disobeyed.

One or two chapters surprised me as reasonably pleasing. For example:

Chapter 13

You think that a helicopter does not have wings?
You are wrong.

The helicopter's blade *is* a wing. A rotary wing.
Wings come in all shapes and sizes, you see. The
helicopter's wing just happens to go around.

(Of course, if the blade falls off a helicopter,
it immediately takes on the aerodynamic configu-
ration of an express train.)

Listen: You have wings yourself. You just don't
recognize them yet.

*

In March, I did sign up for a class in Italian cooking, as instructed.

Thursdays at 7 pm, Leichhardt.

I was held up in a meeting with a barrister, and arrived at the first class an hour late to find the other students seated around a table, about to eat the food they had prepared.

The teacher kindly "borrowed" a little from everybody's plate. "I'll just borrow some of this chicken here? I'll just borrow a twist of spaghetti?"

"No, no," I kept saying, "please don't," but she continued borrowing. The faces around the table were blank. "They'll be mad at me for stealing their food!" I said. Most faces *remained* blank, which confirmed my hypothesis. A few smiled wanly. All but two were women: the men included a chatty guy who growled when the teacher tried to steal his food, and another guy who laughed at this.

I missed the second and third lessons because I was working eighteen-hour days preparing for a hearing. (The case settled just outside the courtroom, minutes before it was called.) I missed the fourth because I was exhausted. I was determined to go to the fifth. However, my mother, who was visiting me at the time, called to tell me she had hurt her ankle climbing onto my kitchen bench to reach the flour. "I feel very strange and faint," she said. "I can't think why I wanted the flour now, except I had in mind making gingerbread men."

I took her to the hospital to get the ankle X-rayed. It wasn't broken, only sprained. She apologized. "Now you've missed your cooking course! And my ankle wasn't even *broken*!" She glared at her ankle.

"It's good it isn't broken."

"Well," she said, unconvinced.

After that, only two lessons remained, and there seemed no point in going. Nobody would recognize me. Or if they did, they would guard their food.

*

In April this year, I received the following chapter from *The Guidebook* in the mail:

Chapter 16

```
Consider your peripheral vision. Always be look-
ing for things out of the corner of your eye.
```

This was amusing because I'm already looking. I look for my brother through windows, at bus shelters, down corridors. I'm always turning my head quickly, catching at shadows and reflections, reaching for glimpses, cupping my hands around corners.

*

In May this year, I attended a party in Glebe.

It was my friend Natalia's twenty-sixth birthday.

She was a programmer now, renting a large house in Glebe, which she shared with her sister, two cats, and a fish.

I arrived with a bottle of pinot in a brown paper bag. Natalia embraced me. We looked at the pinot and pretended to admire it, imitating the teacher from our wine appreciation course. In fact, it was a very good wine with heady notes of summer fruits, but I played the same ironic, mocking games we'd played back in our university days.

Other than Natalia, I knew nobody at the party, but she introduced me to a small group standing in a circle by the fridge.

I tried to join their conversation. They were discussing recycling. I did not find this particularly entertaining, but I joined in anyway. They welcomed me.

I drank several glasses of wine. Natalia found me again and introduced me to her sister, Tia, who was like an elongated replica of Natalia—the kind of sibling resemblance that is almost humorous: genetics on display. The three of us had a good conversation about the Human Genome Project, law, life, Java, time, TV, and drank more. A young man walked by.

I stared at him.

I knew him.

I was drunk now, so I carried on staring, although I was not so drunk that I didn't know this was impolite.

The young man stopped. He had thick eyebrows and dark eyes. A watch on his wrist. Forearms thick with dark hair. A beer in his hand.

He stared back at me.

"I know you," he said.

"I know you too. That's why I'm staring."

We were both silent, studying each other.

"But why?" I said. "Why do I know you?"

He nodded. "Why?"

Natalia and her sister were excited by the puzzle. They quizzed us both. We shared our occupations, our educational history, employment history, favorite holiday destinations. None of these matched. Between questions, we stared. Now and then we laughed. Then we grew serious again. It was suspenseful.

"You're like someone I saw once on TV or something," I said eventually. "Are you on TV?"

"But he knows you too," Natalia pointed out.

"Are *you* on TV as well, Abigail?" Tia wondered. "Or in movies? You know each other from red carpet events, Oscars after-parties, greenrooms."

"No, I'm not."

His name was Finnegan. He worked with Tia at a graphic design studio in Lilyfield. They had stayed back tonight to finish a project, and Tia had invited him along to the party.

Finnegan and I both took sips from our drinks, and gazed at each other.

*

At some point later that night, I found myself in the front room of the house. A sitting room: a couch, a piano, a huge sack of cat kibble.

Finnegan sat beside me on the couch.

The room was dark, the only light from the street outside. I do not know why we had not turned on the light. I think we couldn't find the switch.

We were facing the piano.

"You play?" I asked.

"A bit. You?"

"Used to."

We slouched on the couch.

"Scales are funny," I said, remembering. "Your fingers run up the keyboard, and you keep putting your thumb under so you can reuse the same fingers. You can go forever because your thumb finds an ingenious way to recycle." Recycling was on my mind.

"But you can't go beyond the keyboard," Finnegan pointed out.

"No, you turn around and come back down," I agreed. "So you cover the same ground. It's back and forth, it's up, full of hope, and back down to the bleak, then up, then down. And so on."

"I used to make up stories on my piano," Finnegan told me. "The low notes were scary, the dungeons and woods. The high notes were like happy little elves."

"Me too."

We tilted our heads back, stared at the dark ceiling.

"Kierkegaard thinks that music begins where language ends," Finnegan said. "Beyond language—or when language reaches its peak—you get music."

I considered that. "I can't believe we're talking about Kierkegaard," I said.

"You're not. I am. And the same is true if you go in the other direction," he said. Because the simpler words become, the more they're just sounds, and sounds are music."

"So music is like parentheses around language?"

"Exactly. Or music is everything. This small segment of everything is language. Our conversation. Everything outside it is music."

I sat beside Finnegan in our small segment of language while everything else was music.

"I like that," I admitted.

In the moon glow, or maybe it was streetlight glow, you could see that the piano was shadow-dusty. There were ornaments on top of it, and framed photographs. On the lid, a bowl of chips and a jacket.

"Shall we play?" Finnegan suggested.

He stood and put the chips on the window ledge. I lay the jacket on the couch.

We sat side by side on the stool, and lifted the lid.

The white keys glowed strangely. The black merged with the darkness. We squinted down.

First, we played scales. I played down the scary end, he played at the fun pitch, but our hands kept meeting and entangling, his hands over mine, mine over his.

This reminded me of games that children play, clapping hands together, holding hands to form rings. Piling hands like a stack of pancakes, a continual stacking, as endless as scales.

Other people's hands. So intimate, so tangly and strange.

I was thinking all this while we were playing.

Somebody came to the door and watched us, leaning against the frame. A big guy. He wanted to say something funny. The alertness in his cheeks and eyes told me this. But after a minute, he turned and walked away, leaving us to it.

We stopped playing. Sat on the stool, hands resting on the piano keys.

"I know you," Finnegan said.

"Yeah, yeah, we've done this. I know you too."

"I know where I know you from."

"You do not."

"I do," he said. "Italian Cooking for Beginners."

It was a deep-breath moment. "No," I said. "No way."

"You came late to the first class," he said. "Everyone had to share their food with you."

Astonished, I pressed middle C.

"But you never came again," he continued.

"No way," I whispered.

I thought about the people in that class eating their food, casting resentful glances my way. I looked sideways at him on the piano stool. His profile in the shadows, eyes bright.

"Where were you sitting?"

"Down the end of the table," he said. "There was a guy beside me who talked a lot."

Now I remembered the chatty guy, his sentences, his cadences, and here came Finnegan, sidling into the memory, an elbow on the table, a profile, a nose, a shape, a darkness, a quick laugh, a hand on a fork, the flash of a memory, that's it.

"The only reason I signed up for that course," Finnegan said, "was because I thought I might meet a girl."

I laughed.

He played an arpeggio. "Do you want to know a secret?"

"Okay."

"I knew who you were as soon as I saw you tonight."

Now I turned on the seat to properly stare.

He stopped playing. "I looked for you each week," he said. "You never came again."

"You looked for me?"

"I know you," he whispered, tilting his head so his voice became an action, a gesture, a touch. "I told you that."

*

If you want a jury to believe that something is true, say it three times.

A barrister explained this to me once. Find a way to state your assertion *three* times in your opening address, he said. Three times before the case is even underway. It becomes fact.

Three, this barrister told me, *is a very powerful number*.

This is the Rule of Three.

*

For our first date, we saw a comedy show at the Enmore.

For our second, we ate Korean barbecue in Surry Hills.

Next, Finnegan invited me to his place to watch a movie and get takeaway Thai.

He lived in a redbrick apartment building in placid Artarmon, which surprised me. I'd imagined someplace grungy and artistic like Chippendale.

We watched *Forrest Gump*. His mother had given him the video for Christmas the previous year, he said, and he hadn't yet watched it.

"Life is like a box of chocolates," Finnegan announced, when the movie finished.

"It's not," I said.

"It's not," he conceded at once.

I elaborated. "With a box of chocolates, you don't know what you'll get, but you can be pretty sure it's going to be chocolate."

"And not, say, a scorpion."

"Exactly. Whereas you reach your hand into life and you can pull out a boiled egg, a scorpion, or a parking ticket."

"Any of those things," Finnegan agreed.

I told him that I had felt claustrophobic, driving to his place along the Pacific Highway.

He swiveled to face me, excited. "I know! Those narrow lanes."

We slept together that night. The third date is the right time to sleep together, according to the Rule of Three.

*

At work, I read an 1894 case about boilermakers.

Two boilermakers started a business not far from the cottage of one Mr. Hird.

Now, Mr. Hird did not like their boilermaking. He got an injunction, shut them down.

Understandably, the boilermakers were boiling mad.

One day, a placard appeared, suspended between two poles on the roadway. MR. HIRD IS MEAN, is more or less what it said.

Nobody could prove who wrote the words, or who erected the placard.

But a certain man sat on a stool on the side of the road, smoked a pipe, and pointed at the placard.

Which is more or less the same, the court concluded, as putting the thing up.

*

Chapter 188

It is probably time for us to embark on a survey
of Western philosophy.

   I shall begin.

   Socrates.

   He wandered around asking people questions.

   Where is the help in that? He sounds insufferable. Always coming up to pester you, demanding
answers.

*

Finnegan had never been to Taronga Zoo—he grew up in Melbourne—so I took him for his birthday.

A woman walked past with her hand on the shoulder of a tiny boy. The boy's face was smeared with chocolate ice cream, and he was sobbing. The woman was shouting. "And if you *ever*, *ever* do that again, so help me, I will *smack* you!"

The woman and boy walked on, wails fading into the distance.

"These are the memories," Finnegan said.

I nodded. "Exactly! How can she not *realize* that? You bring your kid to the zoo for a special day out and it's like, can you not just be calm and patient for this one day?"

"For this one day."

"Days are rare," I said.

Finnegan nodded. "Days. Collect them. You might only get a handful." He was holding open the palm of his hand to demonstrate.

We were standing in front of the giraffe enclosure now. They're so tall, giraffes. The view behind the giraffes was Sydney Harbour. Sky was blue.

I looked at the open palm of Finnegan's hand.

"My brother loved giraffes," I said.

"You have a brother?"

*

Chapter 189

Question everything and all that you believe, Socrates said. Are you really so brave, are you really so wise, are you really so virtuous?

Rather than making people happy, he probably made them disconcerted, disorientated, unhappy, in the knowledge that they were *not* so brave, so wise, so virtuous as once they had believed. Foundation shifted beneath them.

Did Socrates really wander around asking questions? We only have Plato's word for it.

It seems to me that Plato may have had a lively imagination. Certainly, many of Socrates' conversations seem implausible.

*

Finnegan and I took two weeks off work and went on a trip to Paris together, my first time leaving the country.

Finnegan's mother is French Canadian, so he grew up speaking French with her. Handy companion for Paris.

When we boarded the plane, there was a technical difficulty. We sat on the tarmac for three hours.

During those three hours, Finnegan and I did all the things you ordinarily do during a flight. Read books and magazines. Discussed whether we'd remembered to pack various things. Said, "Yes, please," when they offered snacks. Ate the snacks. Watched the inflight entertainment. (They switched that on, eventually.)

"We're getting on with the flight," I said, "without getting on with the flight."

"Right?" Finnegan said.

After a moment he added: "That must be what it's like to have a brother missing." He turned to me. Opened a bag of pretzels. "Getting on with life but life's not moving. Is that what it's like?"

*

Chapter 190

Aristotle strikes me as important! One of the Father Figures, I believe.

Aristotle said that the world and all that is in it is determined by the number three.

Surprising! The number 3, behind it all!

I had no idea.

Why, Aristotle? What's your reasoning? Please.

Well, part of his reasoning seems to be that when you have two things, say, or two men, you refer to them as *both*. Three is the first number to which the term *all* applies.

Hence, three must be all. It must be everything.

I understand that Aristotle is famous for his logic, but I do not find his reasoning at all convincing here.

Nevertheless, he finds *himself* convincing.

Necessarily, he says, and *on all of these grounds*.

We may infer with confidence, he says, and: *fire moves in a straight line*.

*

In Paris, we stayed in Hotel Le Relais Montmartre. Our room was very small, of course. That's the way with Paris hotel rooms.

One night, while lying in bed, we talked about our previous relationships. I like that conversation. I like hearing the man's stories, feeling tiny twists of jealousy. These twists are manageable: *Look, he's beside me right now. We're in Paris. Our hands are intertwined.*

Finnegan had been in two long-term relationships. One had started when he was in year nine and ended when the girl's family moved to New York when they were in year eleven. The other had ended when the girl got a scholarship to do a masters at Cambridge.

"So girls move away," I said. "That's what happens to you."

"That's what happens. Where do you think you'll go?"

"I'm not going anywhere," I promised.

I told him about my teenage boyfriends, Samuel and Peter, and how I'd broken up with Peter when he used the word *heel*.

Finnegan found that hilarious. He asked me to draw up lists of trigger words, and vowed to consult these often.

I told him about my university boyfriends, Carl and Lachlan, and how Carl had been sort of mean.

"Sort of mean, how?"

"Well, he used to call me stupid."

"He *what*?"

"And when I told him about my brother, he kind of shrugged it off. He found it irrelevant that Robert was missing because he said MS would have killed him anyway."

"So Carl was the stupid one."

"Yeah."

"How long were you seeing him?"

"I don't know. About a year?"

Finnegan thought about that. "Even if MS *was* always fatal," he said, "what, so if Carl's house burned to the ground because of an electrical fault right when a bushfire was approaching, well, no sweat, they cancel each other out? It's just your house, Carl. It was going to burn down either way."

I laughed. "Exactly. Exactly."

Finnegan went on: "We'll just smile sanguinely down at the ashes, Carl. 'Cause one way or another, that fire was coming. It was destiny. High five, let's have a drink."

I looked at the ceiling of our Paris hotel room. I said, "But it was stupid of me to keep seeing him. That was like contributory negligence."

*

Contributory negligence is a doctrine at common law. If you have contributed to your own injury through carelessness, this can be used as a defense.

"I don't have a law degree," Finnegan said, "but Carl can't use that defense." He turned sideways in the bed. "Still," he said to my shoulder, "you ought to be shot for putting up with him."

*

Around this time, I finally relented and began to call Finnegan *Finn*. I'd been so attached to *Finnegan*. The syllables.

"This is a terrible thing to say," I told Finn one day, "but sometimes I think it's worse losing my brother than it would be to lose a child."

When you speak to Finn, he becomes still. He stops what he is doing.

He was scooping ice cream from a tub, and he stopped. The spoon in his hand. His face still.

"Because you already have your*self* before you have a child," I explained. "And so you have that self to go back to. But I had Robert all my conscious life. All of *me* is me-and-Robert. Without Robert, I'm just making it up. Inventing myself as I go along."

"Not a terrible thing to say," Finn said. "Anyway, a terrible thing happened to you. Say what you like." After scooping ice cream, he added, "Do you think it's been harder for you to lose Robert than it has been for your mother?"

"No!" I said. "Definitely not. It's been worse for her."

Finn waited.

"Oh, well, but that's different," I said. "This is *Robert* we're talking about."

To change the subject, I told Finn about the Rule of Three. How the barrister told me that if you say something three times it's true.

"Do you know what I did while I walked back from counsel chambers that day?" I said. "After he told me that?"

"What did you do?"

"I whispered to myself: *He'll come back, he'll come back, he'll come back.*"

Finn put the ice-cream scoop down. He wrapped his arms around me and crushed me against him. I could feel him trying not to cry, trembling with it.

"He will," Finn promised. "Your brother will come back."

*

Finn spent a lot of time at my place in Balmain. Closer to his work. Closer to restaurants and bars. My flatmates, the theatrical couple, had moved out, and I'd taken over the main bedroom and made my old room into a study with a futon couch and desk.

I gave him a key. He began to let himself in and dinner would be waiting when I got home. Mostly pastas. Fettucine boscaiola. Penne puttanesca. Ricotta and parmesan ravioli. He learned the recipes in Italian Cooking for Beginners.

We talked about beauty and truth: whether one really is the other. He told me his grandmother had once been clinically dead for two minutes.

"Did she see a tunnel of light?" I asked.

"No. But she had this wonderful sensation that she was about to know everything. On the verge of understanding it all."

The CD had just ended. The room was quiet.

"Knowing everything," I said, "that seemed like a good thing to your grandmother?"

"Wonderful. I think she used the word *elation*."

"The truth is a good thing?"

He took both my hands in his. "Exactly," he said.

*

Matilda arranged for a forensic artist to create an age-progressed image of Robert.

"He's been growing up without us," Mum whispered, tracing his face.

I thought the artist had rounded his cheeks too much, made him too jowly. This was a stranger, not Robert.

But I posted the age-progressed image on online bulletin boards. If the internet is a legal minefield, it's also an ocean of buried treasure; you just have to dig in the right place. Nights, Finnegan would find me in the study, clicking on links and comments. "Come back to bed," he'd say, rubbing his eyes.

*

Chapter 192

This digging and digging for answers.

You uncover something shiny, turn it over on your spade, and your chest hurts with the joy of it, the sun-catch.

You uncover something rusty and mundane, an old chain link, a tin, and it's a different hurt. The ache of the mundane, of useless, predictable, dirt-encrusted things.

Or you uncover maggots and skulls, bloodstained clothes, and now your chest collapses in your body.

Even when you uncover the shiny, the gem, you cannot be happy because the next turn may be grim. The context sullies the shine, makes it false. An incomplete truth is an untruth and there is no happiness in lies.

Always the shadow of the spade lying diagonal on mud. Can we go downstairs, watch a film, eat salted caramel, knowing that it's out there, more truth, unturned, unearthed?

*

If you want to convince a jury that events did not unfold the way evidence suggests, you need a compelling alternate narrative.

MS can cause cognitive difficulties, including memory loss. In Robert's case, it has caused amnesia. Robert is out there somewhere, happy and forgetful.

Robert got hit by a truck. He's in a coma. In a small country hospital. They don't have—they don't have a telephone. (That one needs work.)

His face has been damaged beyond recognition!

But don't worry. Once we find him, we'll get him the best plastic surgeon.

MS can also cause difficulty paying attention or making decisions. Robert can't focus long enough to get home. He can't make up his mind whether he wants to come home. Once we find him, we'll fix this with appropriate medication.

Robert is lost in the bush. He is fending for himself.

Robert is trapped in a cave somewhere but has food, water, sunlight, and books.

Robert ran away to make his fortune.

To see the world.

He fell in love with a girl in a witness protection program.

He himself is in witness protection.

He got into an underground crime scene. He's in trouble! When we get him back, we'll sort that out. He didn't actually do anything bad. Mostly it was all a misunderstanding. I have friends who are criminal lawyers!

He developed anger management issues. Went into therapy. They wouldn't let him out! Once we get him back, I'll talk him through his anger. He'll calm down.

*

"And where is your grandmother now?" I said.

"Well, she either knows everything," Finn replied, "or she was wrong."

"Oh. I'm sorry. Were you close?"

He shrugged. "She used to give me Scotch finger biscuits when I visited."

I asked if he liked Scotch finger biscuits, and he said yes, the pleasure of breaking them in two, splitting them down the middle.

This was Finnegan's paternal grandmother. His maternal grandparents live in Quebec, along with various uncles and cousins. His father met his mother while doing a semester of a medical degree at McGill in Montreal, and lured her back to Melbourne. She hated it, Finn told me.

"Melbourne?"

"Australia. All of it. She was always homesick. Still is."

How could that have been, growing up with a mother who despised your own city, your own home, a part of you?

Finn shrugged, paused mid-shrug, reconsidered. "Sometimes I argued with her," he said. "Sometimes I thought maybe she was right."

"Does she go home often?"

"Never."

I dropped the remote control. We were watching TV at this point, and I'd just picked it up to change channels.

"If she ever went back to Canada," he continued, "she was pretty sure she'd never return. She still owns an apartment in Montreal. She could chuck out the tenants and move in."

I shook my head at all the memories, the strangeness inside him. "Tell me your secrets," I said. "I want to know *all* your secrets."

And he laughed and said, "Look, that's the ad I was telling you about, the one with the disconcerting color scheme," pointing at the TV.

*

Now and then I say to Finn: "Tell me one thing about you that you have never told anybody else." And he comes up with a commonplace series of events that happened that day, let's say while he was waiting to cross the road at the traffic lights or had just ordered a sandwich.

"I swear, I never told a soul that," he says, "before now."

At night, I watch him sleep, trying to see into his soul. I lift his fringe and kiss his forehead in case it's there.

*

The lease on Finn's place came up for renewal.

He packed his things into boxes and moved into my place.

*

At work, my assistant's name is Judith. I talk to her on my dictaphone. *Please open a new file under the name— This is a letter on—*

I like how everything falls into folders and lists. *Terry—Correspondence. Terry—Pleadings.*

"Interesting," said Finn, "that you're so drawn to order at *work*, and yet . . ." Indicating the apartment. He said, "Do you mind if I sort this out? Tidy up a bit?"

"I do not mind in the slightest."

*

Chapter 193

```
Epicurean means chocolate and silk sheets, the wind
in your hair in a sports car, but no, it doesn't.

    I just looked it up. According to Epicurus, the
key to joy is in three things: friends, freedom,
and a moment to think.

    Also, something to eat, something to wear, and
a roof over your head.

    Well, that's cheating, isn't it? Six things, not
three.

    Oh, and you need people to chat with. And you
can't have that miserable Sunday night feeling:
tomorrow I have to go there. And your friends can't
be talk, talk, talking all the time, making you
crazy.
```

*

"One thing that really bothers me is strict liability offenses," I said to Finn.

We were eating his parmigiana di melanzane. I love eggplant.

"What's a strict liability offense?"

"It's where you get busted even if you didn't mean to do it. Like speeding, say. You get a ticket even if you didn't notice you were going so fast."

Finn nodded. "Strict liability offenses bother me too."

Finn collects speeding fines like a hobby. He listens to "loud, bitchin music" while he drives, and this makes his foot pound on the accelerator. Any more fines, he'll lose his license. The other day he got a fine from a camera. I signed a form to say that I was driving. Took the fall for him.

"They offend my sense of justice," I explained.

"Mine too."

He poured me another glass of wine and I told him about a conversation I once had with my brother.

*

In the conversation, Robert told me that he was depressed.

"What do you have to be depressed about?" I asked. "Look!" I pointed to the sky, which was clear blue. We were in our backyard. Shooting goals. We had a freestanding netball ring, pegged to the grass.

"Well, I've got this disease," Robert began.

"No," I said. "No, you do *not*. You don't have it."

"But what if I do?"

"If you do, they'll find a cure. I've told you this before. You can't be sad about that. It's ridiculous. Just be happy."

Robert nodded. We continued playing. I scored considerably more points than he did.

*

Finn listened and chewed on his food. When I got to the part about me scoring more goals, he smiled. "That's my girl," he said.

"I played A-grade netball for years; I was shooter," I explained.

"You never told me that!"

We breathed in the happiness of stories still untold.

I returned to the issue at hand.

"I should have let Robert be sad," I said. "I did it wrong. I kept shutting him down!"

"You thought you were doing the right thing," Finn argued.

"But it was the wrong thing. I did it and he disappeared. It doesn't matter that I didn't mean to do anything wrong. It's a strict liability offense."

Finn listened. He allowed me to be sad.

Then he said, "Actually, I think you did exactly the right thing."

"Now you're shutting me down!" I said. "But okay. How?"

"Here's how. You were yourself. You didn't let Robert score more goals than you. You didn't let him wallow. If you'd been somebody *other* than you, *that* would have been wrong. You did the right thing and a wrong thing happened. The two are unrelated."

*

Chapter 195

Isaac Newton.

Gravity, the apple, the orchard, the moon. Windmills, flux, parabolas, curves. Of course, gravity is not a thing. It's just a way of describing the fact that things fall.

Everyone was busy in the seventeenth century, not just Isaac. Deposing kings, inventing clocks, pinning down nature and continents, fighting fires and plagues.

Did this make them happy? All this pinning? Oh, I think it made them desperate with excitement.

*

Finn and I were in a café.

"Complete, complete, complete," said a man at a nearby table.

The man's companion asked: "What do you mean by that?"

Finn raised his eyebrows. I raised mine back. We waited.

"You let it wash over you," explained the man. "Everything that worries you. That's how I meditate. Complete, complete, complete."

Now we raised our eyebrows in a considering way.

I scooped chocolate foam from my cappuccino. Finn had a blueberry Danish. Mine was lemon and poppy seed.

"Even if Robert comes back," I said, "it won't be him. He'll be different. He might even be *bald*. He might not call himself Robert anymore. He might be Rob. Or Robbie. Or Biscuit-face."

Finn nodded. "Could be."

"And we'll be scared that he'll do it again. We'd have to tie him down somehow. Lock him up."

"Complete, complete, complete," Finn confirmed. "Listen, how do you feel about marriage proposals?"

"It's okay if the woman does it," I said. "Why does it have to be the man? Unfair to the man, demeaning to the woman. And the balance tips. The guys are like, *Wait, is she really the one?* And the girls are drumming their fingers, hoping: *Will it be on my birthday? Maybe he'll do it on Valentine's Day?* And when he does it, she has to burst into tears and call her mum."

"Huh," said Finn.

"So yeah, never propose to me. I take that responsibility off your shoulders right now. I might propose to you one day. You might get lucky."

Finn smiled.

"See that?" I said. "Now I have the power."

"How do I indicate to you that I'd like you to use your power?"

"Like a code? No! That gives you the power back!"

"But it's your rule," Finn argued. "You propose whenever you like. You don't have to wait for my signal! I'd just like to have a signal. Say I turn a Danish upside down? That could be a signal."

I thought about it. "Okay," I decided. "We can use that. Because we'll forget."

Finn turned both our Danish upside down.

*

Chapter 196

Anytime you try to impose a template on life
there will be leaks. Every theory, eventually,
is debunked, undermined, turned over with the
spade.

Until you understand that things are *not*
connected, until you see there is *no* universal,
why happiness will never be yours.

*

One night, I cut an orange open and saw that it was not, as I'd assumed,
a Valencia. It was a blood orange.

The vibrant excess of that red: leaking into the rind, staining my
palm.

*

Chapter 19

All we need to know is that beauty is truth, said
Keats, and I'm sorry to sound callous, but what he
actually needed to know was the cure for his general malaise and for the illness that eventually
killed him, aged twenty-five.

*

Finn and I were almost asleep. This was a week ago now.

"Finn?"

"Mm."

"I just want to say something."

"Okay."

"I think I've got the balance right. It's like, he'll always be missing, but I have to keep living, and maybe we don't need the truth?"

"Mm," Finn said into his pillow.

"Maybe truth is not beauty. Maybe there's beauty in ambiguity. It's a form of imagination, ambiguity. It *is* truth. Half-truth *is* truth. As long as there's mystery, there's possibility. Imagination is beauty is truth."

Finn opened his eyes and smiled at me. We faced each other across the gap.

"I'm through my crisis," I said. "I'm sorry I talk about Robert so much."

"Talk about your brother whenever you like," Finn said. "I *like* hearing about your brother. More interesting than my complaints about Tia."

Finn finds Tia—the sister of my friend, Natalia—something of a princess at work.

"I like hearing tales of Tia. I'm the impartial adjudicator; I determine which of you is being unreasonable."

"Her. Always her. What about when I talk about font sizes and Pantone color numbers?"

"You do talk about Pantone color numbers," I conceded.

"Too much?"

"No. I like it," I said. "Expertise is sexy. Go back to sleep."

He closed his eyes. I closed my eyes.

I lay beside Finn and my mind roved over defamatory hyperlinks.

Messages in bottles, I thought. What are you *saying*, what is wrapped up in your words and in your orange rind?

You sit by the road and point to a sign. You didn't write the sign. You didn't hang it there. You don't say a word. You simply point.

I drifted toward sleep.

There was Carly Grimshaw, opposite me. Telling me how Robert would creep into her room late at night, leaving early the next morning.

I took the lunch with Carly and folded it, ready to store in the archives. Pushed it to the back of a shelf, calm folding over me. *Complete, complete, complete*, all the little pieces of that conversation, Carly and her plait, and her sister, and her flute, Carly and her four-poster bed, Carly and her hilarious passport story, Carly's forehead pressed against the window glass, waiting for my brother to come visit—tie it off, tie it off—

I opened my eyes and sat up.

*

Carly and her hilarious story.

Her brother's passport had been missing the day he was due to fly to Japan.

My brother used to borrow her brother's ID. My brother resembled Andrew Grimshaw. My brother had been secretly spending time in Carly's house.

I phoned Matilda the next morning. "What if Robert had a passport?" I asked. "An adult passport under another name?"

In the last week, here is what Matilda has uncovered: three days before we realized Robert was missing, the morning after he visited Carly for the last time, a passenger named Andrew Grimshaw flew to London.

We had never imagined before that Robert could have left Australia; he was a child without a passport. Back then, he and I had never left the country. Our family holidays were always to Queensland or the snow.

But he flew to London. We have cracked open the world.

PART 8

1.

Niall and I agreed to have a drink on Friday night.

I made an appointment with Jennie at Hair to the Throne for a cut and style on Friday afternoon.

I arranged a babysitter—my regular, Radhi, was busy, and I didn't like to ask Dad and Lynette now they had Oscar on Tuesdays, but then I remembered Rhianna, who used to babysit but had gone overseas for a year. A year had passed!

That meant I had to text with a preamble about how I thought she'd be back, apologies if not, and I hoped she'd had a wonderful trip. But it was worth it: she responded to say that she'd love to babysit.

I made a pot of Bolognese, ready for Oscar and Rhianna's dinner.

Thursday night, I ran my hand along the clothes in my wardrobe, assessing. Tried on a few outfits, but there was no soundtrack, no zippy friend shaking her head no, or exclaiming yes! Only Oscar in his Thomas the Tank Engine pajamas saying, "Mummy? Mummy? Look!" and doing somersaults across my bed. Now and then he'd fall off the edge and then there'd be a delay while I scooped him up, comforted him, agreed that the bed was "stupid," and so on. Then he'd start the somersaults again.

My mother used to snap when I hurt myself as a child, which I found mystifying. As I grew older, I understood that her exasperation was an expression of her love and concern for me. Now, however, I see that it was pure irritation: the time-consuming distraction of stubbed toes and bumped knees.

In the end, I chose the pencil skirt and the sort of meshy-see-through top.

"Do I look pretty?" I asked Oscar.

Oscar sat up from his latest somersault. Crossed his legs and leaned forward. A smile formed. Slowly, the smile grew.

Wow, I thought, I must look fantastic!

But Oscar was drawing his hand from his pajama pocket, and opening his fingers. "Look!" A domino lay on his palm. This beautiful, surprising world!

"Time for bed," I told him.

At midnight, I went to bed myself.

I was just fading into sleep when a small voice spoke: "It's dark in here." I shrieked, which caused Oscar, standing by my bed, to shriek himself and burst into tears. "You scareded me, you scareded me." I picked him up and hugged him, explaining that, well, *he* had scareded *me*. He sniffed and shuddered, climbed into my bed and curled up on my pillow. "Go back to your own bed," I suggested, but without conviction. Oscar gave another theatrical sniff, put his thumb in his mouth, and closed his eyes.

I rolled him to the other side of the bed. Eventually, I sank into sleep, at which moment Oscar began crying.

"What's wrong? What is it?"

He didn't reply, he simply wept.

"Is something hurting?"

"No."

"Is your tummy hurting?"

"No!"

I felt his forehead. It felt fine.

"Did you have a bad dream?"

In the midst of his sobbing came a yelp. "It's all right," I soothed, "Mummy's here, no more bad dreams," and similar things, stroking him, until he hiccuped back to sleep.

I closed my eyes. My heart pattered. I turned over. Pulled up the covers. Drifted toward sleep . . . and he was sobbing again.

This continued through the night. Again and again, I would sink toward darkness and the crying would pierce through. *What's wrong? What's wrong?* I got him water. He curled up, fell asleep, then cried in long, low sentences. "Shhh," I said, patting his back. The crying faded, my eyes closed, and it started up again.

I was gentle and loving, but over time, as he twisted and kicked, shouted, *No, my tummy doesn't hurt! Stop asking if it hurts!*, as the red digits switched from two to three to four, as my temples darted with aches, as I imagined myself the followed evening, bloodshot, shadowed, my witty date-girl self dissolving, I became brisker.

"What is it?" I demanded. "Just tell me what it is!"

At one point, I heard a muffled whine: "My pajama top is hurting me!"

"Okay. Sit up. We'll take it off! See? We'll get you a new top!" Bright-efficient-mother fine veneer over fury.

In his bedroom, the dawn light touched his blind. I found another pajama top.

He slept again. I drifted. He kicked me hard in the stomach.

"Stop!" I said. "Go to sleep!"

Oscar sat up and smacked the back of my head. "I want to get up," he said. "It's daytime."

Five forty-two am.

"No," I said firmly. "No. It's too early. Go back to sleep."

"It's time to get up," he insisted.

My eyes burned, angles pressed the inside of my forehead. "Go to sleep!" I rose up, took his little shoulders, forced him to the pillow.

"You hurted me! You hurted me!" He sobbed, wailed and then, through the tears: "I have to get up. I need yogurt for my throat."

2.

I gave him Children's Tylenol for his throat.

I canceled the date.

"No problem," Niall said.

"I am so sorry," I told him.

"Seriously, no problem," he said. "I hope your boy gets better."

"Another time."

"You bet," he agreed.

I canceled the hair appointment and the sitter. I called work to let them know I wouldn't be in.

Oscar curled up on the couch beneath his quilt. His cheeks flared pink, eyes flashed wild. I sat beside him watching ABC for Kids.

"Why didn't you tell me your throat was hurting?" I asked. "I thought you were just having bad dreams!"

"I *was* having bad dreams."

He outlined his dreams. In one, nobody at preschool liked him. In another, there was a puppy and the puppy took his most special toy. This, it turned out, was the penlight a doctor had given him months before. I had no idea where the penlight was.

"Any more dreams?" I urged, because I could see his thoughts progressing step by step toward: *Where is my penlight?*

"There was a swing," he said. "And it went like this." He thrust his hand through the air, much like the motion of a swing. "It was bad," he whispered.

"Huh. I can see that."

"Oh, this was a funny one. I was inside an orange."

"You were inside an orange!"

"Yes."

"How did you get there?"

He was silent.

"It must have been funny being in the orange!" I prattled. "Sticky and sweet! But plenty to eat!"

Still silent. I looked at him.

"Were you scared?" I wondered, eventually.

"Yes. It was dark inside the orange," he said, "and I didn't know where you were."

3.

That night, he was coughing, breathless, a hollow cough. I ran a hot bath and blasted the hot shower, the bathroom door closed, while he sat in the bath and asked repeatedly, "Why is it blurry in here?" and then, "Why does the steam make my cough better?" followed by, "Why is it blurry in here?"

"Is that rain?" I asked. And he said, "No, it's just the shower," but when I turned off the shower, the rain was blasting, pounding on the skylight, furious on the skylight.

And then thunder!

"What does that sound like?" I asked, and he said it sounded like fire, like a crackling fire, which, surprisingly, it did.

"Will the thunder hurt us?"

"No, it can't get inside."

"Why not? Why can it not get inside?"

I put him to bed, Vicks on his chest, and lay looking at him, finding him so sweet and adorable, conscious of the loss unfolding between us, because he will grow up, this little boy will disappear. There's no such thing as this baby, this toddler, this little person, because it's quicksilver, there's no such thing as anybody. We shouldn't have children, it's impossible, but if you want children, and you can't have them, then that's its own impossible. It's impossible to lose them, but it happens, it happened to my mother, it's happening all the time.

His eyes closed, he breathed his crackling breaths. "Oh," he said, opening his eyes. "Oh, I thought that a monster had taken you. I was looking in this direction so I couldn't see you, so . . ."

"So you naturally assumed that a monster had taken me."

"But a monster didn't take you," he said, pleased. "You're still here."

4.

H e was sick for a week.

This is how it works with Oscar. First, he gets a cold. This usually takes place on a Thursday and I think: I will keep him home tomorrow and by Monday he'll be fine. Easy!

On Friday, he is sweet, soft and warm, snuggling into my arms, large eyes, pale face, reaching out and saying, "I love you, Mummy."

The next day, Saturday, he is brittle, bright, and mad. He demands a cinnamon doughnut. There is no cinnamon doughnut. He throws couch cushions and toys. He pinches my arm. He slaps the side of my head. He picks up a picture book and tears a page in two.

He is awake for most of Saturday night screaming with an ear infection.

I took him up to the Big Bear Medical Centre on a Sunday turned ocean-gray with flicks of ice-cold rain. We waited for an hour and a half, and Dr. Seoh, whom I hadn't met before, shone a light into his ears.

I told her about Oscar's ENT specialist, Dr. Koby, and how he had said that Oscar was cured.

"He's not cured," I said now. Dr. Seoh's manner was stern, but with unexpected dimples.

"Seems not," she agreed.

"Maybe we should try a new specialist?"

I thought of Lera on the island in Bass Strait, Lera's careful steps. Hundreds of tonsils, thousands of adenoids.

"There's one named Lera," I said.

"Lera?"

"That's her first name. I don't know her last. She's a surgeon. She has great posture."

The doctor dimpled. She was typing at her computer. She prescribed antibiotics. Plenty of fluids, she said. She spun her chair around, folding the papers, instructing me to keep him at home.

5.

Each day it rained and the wind complained.

On Tuesday afternoon, I texted Niall.

Hey, how're things? I'm not going to flight school tonight. Kid's still sick. Take notes for me? A.

He replied: *Will do.*

That left me nowhere to go. In a house with a fractious child and nowhere to go.

I texted anyway. *Thanks!*

Of course, I regretted it. I knew I would, as I typed it. *Thanks!*

But, listen, if you've ever been trapped in a house for five days with a fractious child, your mind a trapped, wild animal—*you can't walk out of the door.*

You can walk out of the door if you dress your child warmly, strap your child in the car seat, drive to the Big Bear Medical Centre, pick up antibiotics from the pharmacy, take your child home.

You can walk out for that. Otherwise, you rattle the windows and doors. Your mind rattles your skull. Outside, the rain falls. You watch children's television, read children's books, play-act children's games, place soft toys in a circle, play pass-the-parcel, soft toys as imaginary friends. Help him paint a cardboard airplane, grate an apple.

You go to throw out an old tea bag lying on the kitchen sink. You realize it's not a tea bag but a toy, a plastic stingray. Ha! A little stingray! You pour Children's Tylenol into the medicine cup, measure antibiotics in a plastic syringe, beg your child to take the medicine, coax and bribe and chase your child, hide the medicine in strawberry milk, watch your child sip the strawberry milk once and say, "No more." Beg your child to drink his strawberry milk. Run out of Children's Tylenol at ten o'clock at night, slam your head against the wall because you were right there at the pharmacy, picking up the antibiotics, but you didn't get more Children's Tylenol. Measure antibiotics with syringe, beg and coax your child. Your child slaps the medicine out of your hand, spits the medicine onto his pajamas. You reach for the used tea bag on the kitchen sink, realize it's not a tea bag. Ha. Not a tea bag. It's a stingray.

So I texted: *Thanks!* and waited.

But Niall did not reply. What could he have said, anyway? *You're welcome?*

6.

The final book in my stack was about cybernetics.

It reminded me of *The Secret* because, once again, you don't have to do anything except issue instructions. Here, however, you issue them to the *machine* that is *you*, rather than the universe. Your machine is your central nervous system. It can do anything you want.

Around page 38, my concentration faded and I began to think about multiple sclerosis. In case you do not know, here is a simplistic outline of how that disease works.

Two systems are involved: the central nervous system and the immune system.

The central nervous system is your brain and spinal cord. It sends messages and secrets from your brain to your body. It's in charge.

The immune system is the tough guy. If a disease tries to get in, it takes the disease down.

When you have MS, the immune system tries to take down your central nervous system. It runs around making little rips in the central nervous system, tearing it like paper. It's spiteful and childish. It leaves scars everywhere, multiple scars, and now the central nervous system can no longer send messages.

Robert wants to walk along the shore: the message is scrambled, and he falls.

When he was diagnosed, I tried to speak to his immune system telepathically each night. I set things out logically. "The central nervous system is *not* a disease," I told it, speaking as distinctly as I could. "Think about it. It's been here *all along*."

It also occurred to me that we should try to distract his immune system. Give it other diseases to cure, for example. Or train up the CNS so it could fight back, like Mr. Miyagi with Daniel-san.

Or get the two of them sitting down and *talking*, find out what the trouble is; most likely it was all a misunderstanding.

What about when the machine malfunctions? I asked the book on cybernetics. What then?

I found the book absurd, and stopped reading.

Then I set to work outlining goals for the machine that is me: please arrange success of the kind Xuang predicted for my café; please arrange for world peace; warm, dry homes for everyone with hot and cold running water; cures for all cruel and insidious diseases; also, please arrange for the past to be unraveled and restrung so that Robert never disappeared and here he is, swinging by to visit, swinging Oscar by the hands in a circle in a park; and arrange also for the past to be unraveled and restrung so that Finnegan is here, both of us glowing with our good and golden hearts. You may have to call for backup from the universe.

PART 9

REFLECTIONS ON 2005

By Abigail Sorensen

In January this year, Finnegan and I moved to Montreal.

It started as a dare. We were at dinner, celebrating our third wedding anniversary. I was in my hostile phase.

*

After we discovered that my brother had stolen the neighbor's passport and used it to travel to London as "Andrew Grimshaw," there was, in my family, an extraordinary surge of adrenaline and hope, one that even briefly affected my father.

My mother and I flew to London ourselves, and met with agencies, missing persons associations, media outlets. We transferred our campaign of notices, ads, and inquiries to Europe for three months, and then hired a private detective to take charge.

Over the next two years, the detective sent us regular, detailed reports of his activities—he was very thorough. "London is a gateway to the Continent," he often pointed out, and he would ask if Robert had any interest in a particular European country. Italy, we told him, remembering how Robert used to rhapsodize over pizza and pasta. I also recalled his brief fascination with Montepulciano and its barrel-racing. The detective pointed out that Robert could have changed planes the moment he arrived at Heathrow, and he tracked down the passenger lists of every connecting airplane for the next forty-eight hours after Robert's arrival. But neither Robert Sorensen nor Andrew Grimshaw had taken any of these.

"There was a flight to Helsinki that day," the detective told us. "But that airline has since gone under, so I can't confirm if he was on it. Might he have had an interest in Finland?"

"He's not in Finland," my mother said.

"Why would he go to Finland?" I concurred.

Still, we agreed that our detective's assistant could take a trip to Helsinki, tape Robert's updated photograph on telegraph poles and hand out leaflets. His expenses were out of control. Eventually, we canceled his contract.

*

The internet contains the whole world, all information, all truth, if you can just crack its code, if you can click the right link.

As a lawyer, I never quit: I follow the thread of legislation, case law, precedents; open enough books and eventually the answer will be there. I'm a good lawyer except that clients aren't always keen on the hours I clock up never-quitting. It should work on Google, too, and social media. Eventually, the answer should be there. So I clicked and clicked, googled: *Where is my brother?* or *Hello Robert, where are you?* Sent emails, set up pages, blogs, made comments, followed threads. *This one will work*, the flash of hope, excitement, the spinning wheel. Nights I fell asleep with my head on the keyboard.

I read *The Old Man and the Sea*, because Hemingway is one of Finnegan's favorites, and there it was, my hunt—the fish on the hook, the giant fish, grappling with it—you think that catching a fish is easy, but Hemingway gets inside the enormity, the terrible, desperate anguish of catching a fish, the brutality of it, alone, alone, alone, in this ocean, this immensity.

*

Hope is like a giant soap bubble, and you roll around inside it, smiling while it deflates, slowly, cruelly, until you're walking around with this sticky consistency, wrapped across your flesh.

Robert's gone and I will never find him, never know.

Deflated hope becomes self-loathing. I hated myself for every flash of excitement, request for help, notification, every click, every phone call, every conversation I had ever held about Robert.

*

I phoned my mother in Maroochydore. "He's nowhere," I said. "I think something happened to him after he got to London. He's not—alive."

The sound of her breathing, rasping almost.

"I don't feel him alive in the world," I confessed. A half-gasp. I felt as if I'd taken the hat from my mother's head and punched through its crown.

Then she spoke, her voice strange and distant, a voice stripped back, her old-woman self exposed: "I don't think I've felt him alive in the world for a long time, Abi."

Now she'd punched me back.

But she was still speaking: "Your relationship with him was too special. He'd never choose not to speak to you again."

"Don't make this *my* fault," I snapped, illogically.

"But I *need* to know that he didn't hurt," Mum whispered—a strand now, a filament of voice. "I *need* to know the truth. And as long as there's even the faintest . . . I can't give up on him."

"We don't always get what we need," I informed her. "I think we have to let go."

*

My self-loathing clawed its way out into the world in search of other people: family, friends, missing persons organizations. Why are you looking for missing people? I sneered. There is no such thing as a missing person. It's all an illusion, false hope.

Anybody who hoped for anything deserved contempt.

Anybody with ambition, anybody who expected a response: people who sent me emails or asked if I wanted coffee; the junior lawyers, the rotators, the idea of rotation, statements of claim, defenses, particulars, all of it was a nasty, livid joke.

I read more Hemingway, hoping to recognize myself again, and loathed Hemingway: always verging, often crossing, into this goddamn grandiosity—and sometimes he'd get silly and drunken, and he overused the words *love* and *beautiful*, and he loved pieces of wood, and his sentences were unwieldy and winding, but there was a self-importance to this, the self-importance of the tango dancer, the giant fish, the boats, the alcohol, the women, pages and pages without women, and then a woman shows up to be beautiful, sassy, to love, to want, to be wanted—the guns, the sugarless daiquiris. I loathed it all.

I began to loathe Balmain, the inner-west suburb where Finn and I lived, particularly the tall glasses in which they served lattes at our favorite café, and the onion bhaji at our regular Indian place, which, previously, I had loved.

I loathed my state for being a state: Who had even heard of New South Wales? It was duplication, duplicity, it was *not* South Wales, it was no part of Wales, it was a lie!

Most of all, I hated Australia, because it was parochial, suffered from cultural inferiority, was racist, sexist, bombastic, it wept over sports but threw desperate people onto island prisons, voted not to become a republic, not to have its own bill of rights, and because it hadn't been able to keep hold of Robert.

*

So, it was pretty comprehensive, my hostile phase.

*

Even though I hated everyone, I still loved Finnegan.

I loved his thin frame, the shape of his legs, the hair on his legs and his arms and wrists, his thick eyebrows, his dark blue eyes, the shape of his eyebrows, the pattern of largish freckles on his back.

I loved the way he shaded his drawings with a pencil on its side, the way he left me illustrated notes around the flat, the way he poured a glass of wine, the way he scrubbed a frying pan, the way he said "swasher" instead of dishwasher, the way he spoke to the elderly woman who lived in the apartment next door, listened to her stories and, in response, told corny, dry jokes that made her laugh and flick her handbag at his arm.

*

Anyhow, at this anniversary dinner, I said, "Finn, I hate everyone except you."

He considered this. "Is that an issue, do you think?"

Then he dared me to take a year's leave without pay and move across the world with him.

"It's a dare," I said, amazed. "So I have to do it."

"You do."

It turned out that the tenants had moved out of his mother's apartment in Montreal. The apartment needed repairs, refurbishment, redecorating, and repainting, Finn explained, and his mother had asked whether we might like to live there rent-free in exchange for supervising, or undertaking, all that *re*-ing.

"Now I'm thinking we should do it," he finished. "We could visit with my cousins; they're someplace remote in Quebec. You could try something completely new—like screenwriting. Didn't you always want to try that? This is what you need."

*

I didn't tell Finn this, but I had grown to hate his mother also, for her stubborn, ridiculous refusal to return to Canada—the thing you are missing is *there*, right there!—and for her hatred of Australia, and how that affected Finnegan. "It's cruel," I told friends. "And it's a *lie* to hate a place completely." The friends argued that there was plenty to hate about this country, that hatred is subjective, it could not be a lie.

I got myself so tangled. Was I only disgruntled because of patriotism, because *I* was the only one entitled to hate my country? But it's not a truth, it's a half-truth; I know Australia is imperfect, but it's *not* to be written off—

*

"If we go to Montreal," Finnegan added, "maybe my mother will come and visit us. And when she's there, she might even realize Australia's not that bad."

The flash of a wince behind his smile, covered with a sideways shrug.

"Your selflessness," I said, "is kind of breathtaking. You'd move across the world for me and for your mother?"

"I'll take my laptop," he shrugged. "I can work remotely. It'll be an adventure."

*

His depressed mother, his hostile wife. Finn and his thin shoulders—always trying to build those shoulders up in the swimming pool—his thin waist, his occasional stutter, his passion for the abstract in art. Always trying to carry us, his mother, his wife.

A man on the side of the road trying to steer a fridge into the back of his truck; other people walk by, glancing over with interest. Finn will pull over his car and offer to help. He will joke with the man. The muscles in his back will strain against his shirt as he hefts the fridge into the truck.

*

My dad and Lynette came to the airport to see us off.

Finnegan loves my dad, and my dad is fond of Finn, despite finding him a little too artistic and thin-shouldered.

After my parents broke up, I scarcely spoke to my dad for years, but I heard about him from friends and, apparently, he fell apart for a while. Stopped taking the garbage out or shaving. Walked out of his job. In the end, a woman in his apartment block rescued him. She cleaned out his cupboards and bought him a fancy electric shaver. This rescue continued for a year but then another woman stepped in and took over—which was unfair, the first woman having scrubbed the algae from his bathtub, and treated his fungal nail infection—and then another and another, until he married one named Lynette. She seems okay.

This is a scenario you often see with sad men, I think: the rescue women. Whereas a sad woman who sits alone unshaven in her garbage, fungus in her toenails, will almost certainly remain un-rescued. A sweet young ingenue with giant teary eyes *might* be the exception, but even then it will depend on the extent and nature of garbage, and just how hirsute she has become.

*

Finn's mother's apartment is in the historical part of town. Old Montreal, they call it. It's on the third floor of a stone building with blue-painted wooden shutters. Through the double-glazed windows, we heard horses and carriages clattering on cobblestones, tourists shouting, locals swearing, trucks reversing, a piano being played at a Polish restaurant on the corner.

In my first week, I signed up for two courses, one was Screenwriting for Beginners, the other The Art of the Story.

Finn set up the laptop on the dining room table, and carried on designing ads and pamphlets.

It turned out that an old school friend of Finn's named David Chin was living in Montreal with his wife. We met up with David often, although his wife always seemed to be busy.

The apartment itself had stone walls, an open fireplace and polished floorboards. It also had turquoise-and-rose-striped wallpaper, and a plastic grapevine nailed along the mantelpiece.

"It doesn't need renovation," Finnegan told his mother on the phone. "Just *revamping*. New furniture and appliances. A few cosmetic changes."

We started by shopping for a stainless-steel dishwasher, gourmet oven, and double-door fridge at La Baie. May as well make our lives pleasant.

*

As usual, I filled in the change-of-address form that comes with every chapter of *The Guidebook*.

The first time I saw the familiar envelope, curled into the locked box in the foyer of our building, I felt both weary and relieved. I'd been pretty sure the authors would not pay international postage. This was it, I'd thought: by moving to Canada, I'd killed off *The Guidebook*.

Yet here it was. Intrepid. And I felt fond of it, and proud.

Yet, as I mentioned, also weary.

The first to arrive was Chapter 268. It touched on the subject of *knowledge*.

For many years I have carried around a vast absence of knowledge. My brother's disappearance is an epistemological wasteland. I carry this wasteland in my arms, piled before me, or I drag it behind me.

*

Chapter 268

Hume was into knowledge! David Hume, Scottish philosopher, was a skeptic. I imagine he walked around his life saying, "Hmm," doubt scribbled over his face. Infuriating at dinner parties. "But how can you be *sure*?" he must have said. Or, "Wait. Let me stop you there. Do you *know* this for a *fact*?"

"We can only know the things that we experience," he said. "If you haven't felt it, touched it, tasted it, well, how can you be sure it *is*?"

As a tribute to Hume, we would like you to head out now and *feel* something, *touch* something, *taste* something, *smell* something, *hear* something, *see* something! Keep a diary of your observations.

*

I didn't keep a journal of my sensory experiences, but I do recall noticing the things I saw, smelled, touched, and tasted for the few days after I received that chapter. But we were new to this city, so our senses were heightened anyway.

Snow everywhere when we arrived.

We had trouble finding wood for our fireplace. It's too late, people told us, too late in the season. We ordered a cord of wood, and it arrived damp through. The apartment reeked of wet wood.

Finn's friend David Chin came by and laughed. "Chuck it out," he advised. "That'll never burn." The wood hissed damply in the fireplace. David organized a fresh delivery for us, solid, dry wood. Also, he gave us his coffee machine. "Cindy and I just got a new one," he explained.

We competed, Finn and I, to see who could make the best and creamiest latte.

Outside, the snow looked creamy to me. It looked like frosting, too, of course: thick, generous frosting on a wedding cake. Although, in some places, it was rumpled and dry, like crumbled mashed potato.

*

Chapter 269

```
There is no such thing as cause and effect, Hume
said. We can never know that one thing caused an-
other. All we know is that this happened and then
that: one thing followed another.
    You cannot experience the act of causation and
thus you cannot know that it took place.
    (He killed off metaphysics.)
```

*

The death of metaphysics did not bother me in the slightest. Causation, however—when I read that part, there was an almost-pleasant corkscrew turn in my stomach. I thought I was an expert on causation, having studied *the law*, and having set up and analyzed the following sequences of cause and effect:

(a)   He was diagnosed with MS. (b) He ran away.

(a)   I refused to let him be sad. (b) He ran away.

(a)   Our parents were super-relaxed. (b) He ran away.

(a)   His secret girlfriend next door—my so-called best friend—broke up with him. (b) He ran away.

(a)   I told him he was not funny. (b) He ran away.

(a)   He was born. (b) He ran away.

Which is the relevant cause and effect?

It depends on your degree of self-loathing, your tendency to blame. It depends on your time frame, too.

But if Hume were reading over my shoulder, he would point to the spaces between (a) and (b) and say: *All we know, for certain, is that one thing follows another. Dive into the space between. Take a mask and snorkel.*

*

Spring in Montreal, it remained cold.

Snow was melting, and the streets were gray rather than white. Smears and patches of snow everywhere so that the city seemed like an abandoned construction site; someone had made a perfunctory attempt to tidy before they left. Dirty-white fill left behind, piled into little hills; smears of plaster and spilled paint.

We walked the streets, trying to find clear paths, or pebbly, gravelly, salted paths, trying to walk between slick patches of ice. Trying to find the sun.

*

Peeling away the wallpaper—soaking it with water, then finding its edges and peeling it away—was soothing to me. Finnegan found it exasperating because it was inconceivable to him that anyone could have chosen this pattern.

*

In German, nouns begin with capital letters, but not in French.

I tried to learn French by reading the cereal boxes and milk cartons in the mornings. Also, I learned French every time I opened a door. TIREZ. PULL.

I tried reading a movie magazine in French. Meg Ryan was giving her opinion on plastic surgery. I thought maybe she was opposed but, quite honestly, I couldn't understand enough. Meg's French was full of apostrophes and of *ques*.

*

I kept an eye out for Robert, of course, but he wasn't there. I had known that, and yet I hadn't known.

One day, out walking, I saw police tape across a street. DANGER DO NOT ENTER, it said. Police cars were parked in crisscross patterns both inside and outside the tape. On the street corner, a cluster of people, all with their chins tilted up.

I followed their gaze. A high-rise apartment block. A crane. A man stood at the very end of this crane like somebody walking the plank. Another man—I guess he was a police officer—also stood on the crane, but closer to the building, safer.

We all watched, the silent people and I, tilting our chins. The two men stood perfectly still, also apparently silent. High in the blue of the sky, they were tiny puppets.

After a few minutes I thought: *What am I doing? What if he jumps?* This, I did not want to see.

So I put my chin back down and headed home.

*

Often, we played pool with Finn's friend David Chin in a place on St. Denis. His wife, Cindy, always sent her apologies, and swore that she'd come "next time." Then, next time, we would watch for David to arrive, see him appear alone in the doorway of the pub, and he'd shake his head and hold out his palms. "She's not feeling up to it," or, "too much on," or, "a bit under the weather—next time, she swears."

"Her oaths are cheap," Finn pointed out.

David spat his beer, laughing. "I hope not. She vowed to love and honor me for life."

It was always noisy in the pub, and crowded. When we weren't playing pool, we'd chat near the tables, ready for our turn. Often, without meaning to, we'd block the players. They'd push their cues behind them, and hit us in the face or in the shoulder blade. They'd turn to see, and their faces would go perfectly blank. In their minds, I believe, they were both apologetic for stabbing us with a pool cue, and annoyed with us for being in position to be stabbed. The two things canceled each other out; hence, the perfect blankness.

David was large and he seemed unafraid to use his big, loud, Australian laugh and voice.

His wife, meanwhile, was a shadowy figure, an imaginary friend, a vibrant silhouette.

*

Chapter 274

Yet still we hanker to know! Not just one thing
but *all* of it, to pack it all inside a bag and
carry it on our back. An explanation. A theory of
the universe. A template for life.

All templates have leaks. Life is too buoyant
to pin down.

*

The screenwriting course was full of diagrams and arcs, rules, bullet points and three-part structures. According to the Rule of Three, things that come in threes are inherently funnier, more satisfying, more effective.

All this makes me want to break the rules, crack the structure, collect things into seven parts, or two, or twenty-eight.

I preferred The Art of the Story. That was taught by a prize-winning Canadian author. Ideas floated around us in that course. I can no longer remember what they were; however, at the time, they struck my soul.

The first lesson, the teacher counted the students in the room, and looked at the list on his table. Suddenly, I recalled a one-day writing course I took with Robert. The teacher had been a disappointment to me: not a *writer*, but a regular, anxious, middle-aged woman, knobbly fingers twisting. She'd spent fifteen minutes staring at the door, waiting for three missing students.

This teacher, by contrast, was short with a long face, a handsome basset hound with his drooping, upside-down smile. He glanced at his student list, gave a languid shrug, and began to read aloud from a book. He liked to begin each class by reading passages of fine literature, piping these into the silence of our awe.

I made friends with a girl in my class named Becky, who was from

Saskatchewan originally, and who told me she had once kissed our teacher.

"At a party," she said. She told me that all women fall in love with the teacher for exactly twenty-four hours. She was very precise about this.

I watched the teacher, waiting for my twenty-four hours to begin.

I read one of his books and felt a slippage between lines. One character would speak and the other would reply, but the words slipped out of the characters' mouths and landed on the next line down. It was something to do with punctuation, and its absence. Quote marks were missing and apostrophes.

I recommended that Finn read the book. He loved it!

"But what about the punctuation?" I said.

"What punctuation?"

"Exactly! What did you think?"

But Finn was not being clever. He hadn't even noticed.

"He does what?" he asked, surprised.

"He skips punctuation!" I opened the book and showed him.

Finn ran a finger down the page to an image he had liked. He read this out to me.

"Shall I have an affair with the teacher?" I asked.

"Do you want to?"

"Not yet," I replied. "But apparently everybody falls in love with him. And he's open to kissing his students at parties."

"Well then, by all means," Finn replied. "Be my guest."

I raised an eyebrow. His smile fell. He leaned forward, studying me closely.

"If you did have an affair," he said, "I'd forgive you."

*

There's no punctuation when somebody is missing. This was why my teacher's book bothered me.

There are semicolons, I suppose. When Robert became "long-term missing." Each time Matilda aged his photograph for us.

But now, like my father—and in her heart, my mother—I knew Robert was dead. I had fashioned my own final punctuation. In the darkest night, I'd wake breathless: What if I was wrong, what if he was just around the corner, what if he sensed that I had quit?

"Twenty years after a person disappears," Matilda had told us, "the file is usually closed."

That's 2010. Five years from now. That will be another form of punctuation, I suppose, another lie.

*

In Montreal, I wanted, more than anything, to bake. I baked caramel cakes, banana loaves, ginger cookies. Dustings and sprayings of flour between me and the world.

I'd never shown much interest before, but here I panicked into baking.

Also, Finn and I spent a lot of time wandering through Indigo or Chapters—those are bookshops—and once I remember him calling me over to the poetry section. He had found a poem addressed to a man without a sense of smell. It was by a Scottish poet, Kate Clanchy. I read it while Finn watched my face.

"Everything about this is perfect," I said.

Finn replied, "I know."

He said it made him sad, thinking of my baking, thinking of working at the table and slowly becoming aware of faint drifts of baking, or arriving home, opening the door and the blast of it, an instant immersion in baking, and these were things that the man in this poem would never experience. "Unless the poet describes them for him," I pointed out.

"I'll email her," said Finn, "and suggest she write a follow-up."

*

We painted the apartment walls, congratulating each other on the transformation. If you want to double the size and light of a place, replace the turquoise-and-rose-striped wallpaper with eggshell paint. If you want to revitalize a living room, tear down the plastic grapevine. Weekends, we scoured designer furniture stores and tried out couches.

"Wait until my mother sees this!" Finnegan breathed.

*

Finnegan's mother never visited.

But in the summer, friends visited from Sydney!

Natalia and her sister, Tia, to be precise. They slept on air mattresses in our living room. We took them biking to Atwater Market, to our favorite bar, Cobalt, where there was a free *Pac-Man* game, and hiking on Mount Royal.

We wandered around the Jazz Festival with them, and saw comedy at Just for Laughs. Natalia and I were so smitten by one comedian, we bought tickets to his show the following night. It was all the same jokes, even the "improvised" bits. Though disillusioned, we remained fond of him. We all went on a road trip to Tadoussac and saw beluga whales from a Zodiac. Finnegan's cousins invited us to spend a couple of nights in their cottage by a lake on the way back.

Much of that stay was spent helping the cousins clear the thatching from the roof of their boatshed. You peeled the thatching in chunks and sent it sliding down the slope of the roof. There were pliers for removing the nails, and burlap bags for gathering the thatch.

When chunks of thatch slid down the roof they could hit you in the eye.

At night, we swam in the lake. Natalia and I chatted on the wharf, while Finn and Tia sat in the rowboat drinking beer. The moon was bouncing like a puppet on a string, they said, like they'd never seen the moon bounce before. Natalia and I climbed into the boat, but the moon was still.

Mostly we ate hamburgers and corn on the cob, and the Canadians used words like *fixings* and *makings*.

The sisters stayed in Montreal three weeks altogether.

"Three weeks is maybe a little too long," Finn and I agreed, folding the air out of the mattresses.

*

Chapter 279

```
Also, it can be wrong, knowledge. Consider folk
etymology, false accusations, hypercorrection,
wrongful imprisonment, errors, mistakes, and
false starts.
   So many things we think we know, and then it
turns out we don't! Cigarettes were once consid-
ered good for your health! Carbohydrates, like
overalls, tumble in and out of our good graces.
Everything proved is eventually disproved, cures
stop working, diseases find loopholes, there are
sharp intakes of breath.
```

*

We both joined the YMCA. Finn loves to swim. All through high school, he used to win at Zone in backstroke and butterfly.

"You should be swimming in the Olympics!" I had urged when the Athens Olympics approached last year. "Get your swimmers! Let's go to Greece!"

But he explained that he'd always come second-last when he got to Regionals. Second-last. Every single race at Regionals.

"You never told me that bit," I said, interested. He'd told me often, with great modesty, how he used to win at Zone, but we'd never got past that stage.

A few times, I accompanied Finn to the Y, but mostly I just low-level loathed myself for not going. I couldn't understand the French well enough to do the classes, treadmills and elliptical machines depress me, and I find lap-swimming indescribably boring. Nothing happens. You reach the end of the pool, turn, and start again. At least when you play scales, you can switch keys. (Now you're going to tell me that you can switch strokes while swimming, but it's not the same at all.)

Also, the slow lanes at the Y were always crowded, toes tickling my nose, hands slapping down on the soles of my feet, a woman in a candy-pink bathing suit bobbing up and down at the end of the lane. Over in the fast lane, Finn tore up and down the length of the pool.

*

We had a lot of sex, Finn and I, this year. We were both working at home, we were both bored, and we wanted a baby.

It was always athletic and excellent. Sometimes my throat was raspy from shrieking so much.

"You have a sore throat?" Finn inquired once, hearing my husky, raw voice.

I reminded him why.

"Oh, sorry," he said, genuinely contrite. He was the one providing my orgasms, so we agreed that it made sense for him to take the blame.

*

Some days, actually, we had so much sex I started to feel delusional.

This is like being at a holiday resort, I thought, and eating slice after slice of rich chocolate cake, the kind of cake with creamy layers, a cherry liqueur center. It's great, the cake, it's delicious, but after a while, you start to think: Shall we try the tennis or the paddle boats instead?

*

It was strange living in Montreal without friends. I had Finnegan, and we both had David Chin, and I formed acquaintanceships with people in my writing classes. But the courses ended, and we lost touch.

Some days I imagined David Chin's wife, Cindy, arriving in a dazzle of bright smiles and warmth, arms outstretched, and she and I would talk fast, becoming friends instantly, overlapping words and laughter, arranging to catch up over coffee.

Other days, I saw her as sharp and haughty, or raucous, or pale with nerves. Quite soon, Finn and I decided that she didn't exist at all, and that David had invented her.

*

I got pregnant three times this year.

The first time was in April. I did the test and we stared at each other, dizzy. But by waiting until the end of the first trimester, I was bleeding and it was done.

I felt foolish for believing that pregnancy would lead to a baby. I had known about miscarriage, I just hadn't found it very likely.

"That's fine," we agreed. "That was a test run. Now we're all set."

All set was something we'd picked up from the Canadians. *You're all set now?* they'd say, after placing our order before us in a diner, and we'd say, *Yes, thanks*, and smiled at each other.

The second time was in August. Finn and I were on a road trip across America: beautiful! magnificent! breathtaking! We smiled at rock formations and majestic trees, found cheap motels, gathered ice for our esky—our *icebox*, as they call it, more prosaically—and we stopped at a pharmacy in Denver, Colorado, to buy a test.

We were celebrating at Applebee's that night when a friendly couple from Florida began chatting with us. Finn got drunk and told them I was pregnant.

"It's okay," he explained to me. "We'll never see them again."

They laughed at this.

I didn't care. I like to break rules. Also, it seemed to me, superstitiously speaking, that *telling* people would make the pregnancy work out. Our error the last time had been in *not* telling. By waiting three months, slavishly following the rules of superstition, we had defeated ourselves.

This was reverse superstition.

We outlined this theory between us while the couple watched. They laughed again.

Later, they laughed at my accent. "It was a dare," I said, telling the story of our move to Montreal, and they looked at each other and chortled.

"What?" I said.

"What?" Finn said.

"Your accent," they laughed. "It's so cute." The word *dare*, they explained, had been left incomplete, I had left them in suspense, they were waiting for the final *r*.

Later that night, I couldn't get to sleep. *I don't have an accent*, I thought at the couple. *YOU do.* Over and over, no variation: *I don't have an accent. YOU do.*

The next day the pregnancy was over.

"I don't know if this is too early even to call it a miscarriage," I said, crying into Finn's chest. "I'm embarrassed to be crying."

He said, "You were pregnant and now you're not. There was a baby and now there's not. That's a miscarriage. You can cry."

Grateful, I cried harder.

We lay side by side on the bed for a while. I said, "Tell me your secrets, Finnegan. Tell me all about you."

He laughed. "You're always asking that. Look. Here I am, beside you."

The motel room that night was small and shadowy and the internet would not work. Finn spent hours trying to make it work and eventually demanded a cut in our room rate. I went to the fitness room and ran on the treadmill. A crack ran down the paintwork from the ceiling to the floor, and a hook dangled loose from the window frame. I pounded the treadmill, holding both it and my accent responsible.

*

While on our road trip, we listened to talkback radio to get a sense of where we were. "Somebody has to teach the left wing what free speech really means!" and "I'm going to send you a copy of this book:

Why Liberalism is a Mental Disorder," and a lot of talk about "illegals." Conversations about Iraq merged into talk of illegals, the topics not discrete. "Illegals are biological weapons," a caller said, "'cause they're bringing in disease." "I think it's safe to say," the host replied, "that each illegal is responsible, in some way, for a thousand American deaths."

"Jesus," we said to each other.

Another guy was talking about affirmative action. "So now," he said, "if I'm in the hospital, and the doctor is black? I'm not going to lie to you. I'm going to ask that doctor for his credentials. 'Cause if he's only there on account of this affirmative action, I want *another* doctor, thank you."

"Holy shit," we said.

But we were driving through beautiful countryside, canyons and deserts, pulling over, taking photos, meeting friendly people, smart people, good people. You can't judge a country by its talkback radio.

Another day, we pulled over at a beach in Oregon and saw a gathering of little wooden crosses in the sand, each with a picture of a lost soldier, impossibly young, smiling for his photograph.

We drove by pro-life demonstrations, with huge photographs of impossibly cute, plump-cheeked babies.

It all seemed connected to me: the soldiers, the illegals, the plump smiling babies with hands reaching out to be taken, to grow up, join the army, shoot illegals, my cut-off words, my lost babies. And I was angry with Americans whenever they said *water*, or *later*, anything with a final *r*; the rounding of that *r* struck me as superfluous, an embellishment, unnecessary.

*

After our road trip, we decided to take a break from sex. "To refresh the system," we suggested. "To hit the restart button."

Around this time, things became strange with me. Everything made me cry. The ends of novels and TV shows. When there was no milk, or plenty of milk. When there was tuna in the fridge, mixed with mayonnaise, enough for me to put on a baguette.

I started watching sports programs and the coverage made me cry. When small girls vaulted perfectly then landed and hopped three times. When people knocked over hurdles or landed awkwardly in the sand; when rowers slowed, almost at the finish line, and gave up. When young men executed dives with high levels of difficulty and the commentator gasped, "He nailed it!"

Those divers and their tiny splashes. They made a small opening into the water with their hands and inched their whole bodies through.

At night, I got out of bed and stood at the window. In the darkness, I saw the absence of knowledge as a great dark pool.

Not a pool; if it was a pool you would at least know it was *water*, and you could touch it, put your hand inside it, feel the cold or the unexpected warmth, reach down even to a sandy, muddy, silty bottom, to pebbles or starfish or weeds.

Not a shadow either, because then at least you'd know that somewhere light was being blocked.

The absence of knowledge reared from behind me, defining my past, and another absence, an absence of children, loomed ahead of me. The two reached out and tugged at each other.

*

Finn went to the Y every afternoon to swim his laps. He often picked up dinner on the way back and he would stand at the door, his hair ruffled and wet, singing down the hall: "I am the purchaser of chili peppers!"

Stupid things like that always made me laugh.

*

I talked to my mother on the phone and she told me Xuang had got himself a dog, a Newfoundland named Bartholomew. Only she pronounced each syllable in turn, so that each took a line of its own:

New

Found

Land

I thought of the teacher from The Art of the Story, how the words slipped their lines in his book, a Slinky descending a flight of concrete steps. I loved how my mother weighed each syllable in turn, placing each before me, as if the land had been found anew.

Here, they say it in one thrust, *newfendland*, a dart puffed quickly through a slender blowpipe.

The next day, coincidentally, The Art of the Story teacher sent me an email. He mentioned that a bunch of people were attending his book launch party in October, and would I like to come?

I would say a bunch of grapes, or a bunch of flowers. Never a bunch of people. But I liked the way he, and various other North Americans, use this expression.

*

Across the road from our apartment was a convenience store called a *dep*. They call them deps here in Quebec, David Chin explained.

We would buy David drinks, to thank him for his insights into Montreal, and he would rush to the bar to buy us drinks in return, and so we plied each other with drinks all night, and the pool cues hit our faces, and we laughed, and I wondered what he'd done with his wife.

The guy in our dep went to Australia once. He wanted to tell us about it. No offense, he said, but he found the people unfriendly. He wasn't expecting that. "Maybe it was because summer was nearly over so they were depressed?" he wondered.

"Beautiful beaches," he said, "but you can't swim!"

"What do you mean, you can't swim?" Finn asked.

"The sharks and the jellyfish."

"Oh yeah," I said. "Box jellyfish up north. But in Sydney—"

He said he was in Darling Harbour and he and his friends looked in the water and saw jellyfish everywhere!

"But those jellyfish—" I began, but he was laughing at the absurdity of beaches where you could not swim. He went to a nude beach, he said, but he only walked into the water up to his knees. He couldn't believe the people swimming! In that water, with those sharks and jellyfish!

"But the jellyfish—" Finn and I began in unison. "And there hasn't been a shark attack since—"

But now he wanted to talk about how difficult it was to find your way to the Sydney Harbour Bridge for the bridge climb.

"You can see it," he said. "You can see the bridge, but you can't reach it." He had stood beneath the bridge swearing in French.

He was right there, I said to Finn later, *he was right there in Australia and he missed it.*

*

One night, we were supposed to be going out to watch an ice hockey game with David Chin and then, after the game, back to David's place for a drink.

But I was sneezing and my eyes had turned to slits. My head had that floaty, achy feeling.

"You have to stay home," Finn told me, and I knew that he was right.

Of course, I waited up for Finn. "You met the wife?" I pounced, while he was still opening the door.

No, he said, he didn't meet her, she was sleeping by the time they arrived at David's place after the game. But he saw her boots. "So it turns out," he said, "she exists."

"He could have *bought* a pair of woman's boots," I said, skeptical.

Finn said the boots had looked worn.

I didn't know what to say to that.

*

My cold stayed around for a while. It got into my sinuses. I felt desperate, tragic, weary.

Finn frowned at me.

"What's wrong?" I asked, referring to the frown, and he replied, exasperated, "I'm worried about you!"

"But it's just a cold."

"Tell me how you feel," he prompted. "Describe the way you feel."

I thought about how solicitous we were of one another. How we encouraged the other to rest. *You sleep, I'll wake you in an hour.*

You rest and I'll get breakfast.

I wondered how our interaction would itself interact with the presence of a third, a baby. Once we decided to resume our efforts in that direction, I mean, and assuming our efforts ever succeeded. Whether we would carry on the kindness.

"Of course we will," Finn said, surprised by the question.

He said, "Look at this cappuccino I've made you." The foam was whipped up into a creamy hillock, and when I stirred with a teaspoon I found it resilient and generous.

*

Suddenly, one morning, I felt better.

The cold was gone. I could breathe through my nostrils.

Suddenly! I thought, and it occurred to me that fine things, great things, magnificent things could happen suddenly! I ran down the stairs thinking of the French word for "suddenly"—*soudainement*—and, as I reached the bottom step, I remembered the German word, and I burst through the door into the foyer shouting, *"Plötzlich!"*

A young woman stood in the foyer and stared. I had just shouted, *"Plötzlich!"* into her face.

"Oh, I'm sorry," I said, "I'm sorry." I was so frantic with embarrassment I couldn't remember the French, which is ridiculous. *Je suis désolée.* I had practiced it!

But the woman seemed amused. There was amusement in the way she turned from me and pushed the front door open.

I told Finn about this later, and we got takeaway to celebrate how suddenly funny things could be.

*

One night while we were playing pool, David Chin told us that his wife was pregnant. That was why she never came along. She'd had two or three miscarriages, he added, so she was being "super careful."

"Which?" Finn asked. "Two or three?"

David shrugged. "Three, I guess," he said, frowning slightly.

*

October turned up, and Finn and I went along to my former teacher's book launch party.

The party seemed to have a rich blue glow, the blue that a traffic light would be, if it were blue; a luminescent blue. The blue bathed the walnut wood and the staircase, which was sparse and winding, each step a fine golden slat, so that the staircase was mostly air, and this air carried you up through the pulsing blue to the roof terrace.

There was not much you could talk about on the terrace except how grand the terrace itself was. Such a luxurious space, the view a black and starry sky over Montreal lights and buildings.

It was cold, though. I got so cold my face stiffened up. I had to shake it to talk. Finn drifted away to make conversation with strangers. I heard them laughing at what he said. My former teacher approached to say hello. "You don't need to talk to me!" I said. "You're the important person tonight! You're the celebrity!"

But he laughed and said that I was exactly the person he wanted to be talking to. In the dim light, I saw just how handsome he was. And everything he said seemed lit from below. His words moved up a staircase, each step a fine golden slat! He was telling me about the rough and dangerous life he had once led up north, watching me closely as he talked, as if my reaction to his words was the only thing that mattered. I wondered if he had me confused with someone else. I began to see what my friend from the class had meant when she said that every woman fell in love with him for twenty-four hours.

But why only twenty-four? I wondered.

After a while, somebody took my former teacher by the arm and led him away into the crowd. He kept his smile fixed on me, and his gaze, as he disappeared into the dark.

After that I spoke to several handsome Canadians. I began to see that all Canadians are handsome. Also, that Canadian men will look you in the eye in a frank and intelligent way. A young Australian man will only do this for a brief, startling moment, and only now and then, to flirt.

"You think?" Finn said. "Do I not look you in the eye?"

"You're half Canadian," I explained. "So you're different."

This was later. A truck was reversing outside. We heard them all day in Montreal, those reversing trucks. They delivered milk and office furniture, collected garbage, but that still didn't seem to us to justify their numbers.

"That's the song of Old Montreal," Finn said, and he sang it himself, the *beep-beep-beep* of reversing trucks.

"Okay, that's enough now," I suggested.

Finn sings a lot. He sings the *bling-bling!* of a scene transition in *Law & Order*. He sings the sounds of the elevator arriving and the subway train departing.

Once, he drew the coastline of the Great Ocean Road along the inside of my arm.

"Try to wrap your mind around how perfect this latte is," he said, placing a coffee before me.

*

One day, late in October, Finn had gone to the Y and I was home, when the phone rang. It was one of Finn's clients, asking if he could speak to Finn urgently.

I tried calling Finn on his cell but it went straight to voicemail. So I put on my coat and set out to find him.

As I walked along St. Catherine, I saw him approaching me, deep in his coat and thought.

He looked up. He saw me.

And I knew.

I had absolutely no idea what it was that I knew, but for the faintest crack of time, I knew.

"You're coming back already?" I said, surprised.

"Pool was too crowded."

I gave him the message and he said, "Ah, that guy. Not urgent at all. Let's get coffee."

*

A few days after this, I was suddenly frantic for chocolate and banana.

Snow was threatening but I spun my scarf around my neck, threw on an overcoat and boots, and ran through the streets, skidded through the streets, to the IGA at Complex Desjardins, where I bought bananas.

(I already had chocolate.)

I returned to the apartment and made banana loaf with chocolate chunks, chocolate-banana tart with flaky crust, and, finally, your basic bananas dipped in melted chocolate.

Finn was a little annoyed, as he'd been trying to cut back on sugar. Thoughtless of me to fill an apartment with the fragrances of baking. However, he forgave me and tried them all.

Afterward, I surveyed the stack of dirty bowls, beaters, measuring cups, spoons, the flour glued to the counter tops, and the cake mix splattering the floor.

"Visualize how happy you'll be," Finn suggested, "once it's clean."

"There must be better routes to happiness," I said.

To prove this, I sat at his computer and googled: *What is the key to happiness?*

Seven foods that are guaranteed to make you happy! Google offered, along with a list of foods that stimulate serotonin.

Nice! I thought. *Perfect!*

Because I like eating. Also, eating seemed a simpler route to happiness than exercise, say, or meditation, or cleaning up the mess in the kitchen.

I looked at the list.

Item one was bananas.

Item two? Chocolate.

Seriously! It gave me a chill.

*

"I have an idea," I said to Finn, a few days later. "A Happiness Café. It only serves food that stimulates serotonins."

"So all chocolate and bananas?"

"There are others. Broccoli, for one."

"Well then. Serve broccoli, you'll make a killing."

Later that night, we saw David Chin in the bar. He said his wife was seven months along now, and "so over it."

I told David my idea for a Happiness Café.

He was very enthusiastic. He said I had captured the zeitgeist. Everyone's into happiness these days, he said. Only, what would become of me when the zeitgeist changed?

I'd just change the café name, I said. I'd change it regularly. At any point in time, my café would be the emotion most embraced by the zeitgeist. The Melancholy Café. The Café of Heady Outrage.

I was only joking about all this, of course. It was the kind of game we played, the game of whimsy.

*

The last day of November, it snowed.

It was cheerful, the snow. It was one of those days when all seems to teeter in gleeful suspense. Each window ledge held a pillow of snow, and it seemed that someone had reached out a tender hand and stroked the snow pillows into soft flourishes and cheeky billows.

I unlatched the bedroom window, pushed it open, knocking puffs of snow awry, and looked down into the alley. Footsteps wide and deep in the fresh, fresh white below.

A key in the door. Finn was home from the grocery store.

The phone rang as I walked down the hall. Finn was sitting on the entry bench, pulling off his boots, grocery bags around him.

"Getting the phone," I sang, passing him, and he glanced up at me, and I knew.

*

"What?" I said, hesitating. "What's going on?"

The phone continued ringing.

He stopped, one boot on, and looked up at me.

"What?" I said again.

"Nothing!" He sounded angry! His face became hunted, wounded.

All of this was new. You may find this difficult to believe, but I had never, in five years, seen Finn truly angry, hunted, or wounded.

At last the phone gave up and stopped its noise.

"You've cheated on me!" I said. It blasted at me sideways, the thing that I knew. Suddenly I knew that he had cheated.

I felt power in my knowledge, good and strong. At this point, things were good. My intuition shone. I was proud as a ledge of snow, swooped like perfect latte foam. Fresh and new, fine-cut and gleaming like suspense.

His whole face furrowed. Meanwhile, I was trying to calculate the timing. I mean, he and I were together so much! How could he have had found the time to pick up a girl? On the way home from the grocery store one day? It must have been like lightning! His eyes met hers over the capsicums—peppers, they called them here—and they hooked up behind the dairy section?

"It's okay," I said. "I mean, it's pretty distressing. But we'll work it out."

Finn ducked his head like a schoolboy, and again I stared, having never once seen him behave like this.

"You're still seeing her?" I hazarded, and the knowledge slipped down another, different rung. *Clang.*

His head kept swaying there, on his neck, not denying, so then I knew.

"Who is she?" I whispered.

He whispered his reply. I couldn't hear. I was still in charge, standing up in the hall, while he was seated among boots and groceries.

"Who?" I repeated.

"Tia," he said.

I laughed at that.

"You don't like her! She's a princess! And she's not even here anymore! She's gone home!"

The whole thing unraveled. A practical joke. My unhinged emotions! I knew nothing. I fell against the wall in relief.

But his head remained bowed. The back of his neck.

Clang! Clang! Clang! I hadn't known my stomach went so deep. It was a well in there!

"Something happened when she was here over the summer?" I breathed.

"While you and Natalia saw that comedian a second time."

I was breathing hard now. Strangely exhilarated.

"That day that Tia stayed back here because she had a headache?"

He nodded.

"And you had work to do, so you stayed home too."

No movement.

"You didn't have work to do! And she didn't have a headache!"

Again, the downcast eyes.

"Oh, Finn," I said, still in charge, but Finn picked at the laces of his boots, and on it fell, the knowledge. Clanging ever more acutely.

"And before?" I said, icicles forming on the edges of my words. "Did anything happen with Tia *before* we came to Montreal?"

His head swung up. "Before I met you," he said, a flash of pride, defiance. "We had a thing before you and I even met. I've worked with her for years, remember?"

"What? What? What?" Now I was one of those gaping fish. "You did not!"

He stared at me.

"You did *not*! Because you'd have told me! Why would you not have told me that?"

"She didn't want you to know."

Oh, now the icicles looped over my ears, my lungs, my fingernails! "It's not up to Tia what I know!"

He shrugged. I almost slapped him. I actually raised my hand to slap away that shrug.

But the defiance was still in his eyes. It shot through everything we said as we talked in circles. This was his escape route, his loophole. There'd been something going on before he'd even met me. It was out of my jurisdiction!

"How long before you met me?" I said.

"Right before. We'd been sleeping together for the few weeks just before I met you at that party."

"No!"

"Yes."

"But then why did you start things with me!"

He shrugged, surly boy. "I liked you."

"And you didn't like her?" Not a question, more relieved confirmation. Except that he stared at me, unblinking.

"You did like her," I said.

"She didn't want anything serious. To be honest, I thought picking you up might make her jealous."

I couldn't speak. I was horror-movie moving my mouth around, trying to make words.

"You still like her," I whispered.

"I suggested you and I move to Montreal," he said, voice hoarse, "because I was afraid for us. To save us."

"*Tia*," I said. "*Tia* is why we came to Canada?"

"But then she and Natalia came to visit," he complained, as if the rules of the game had been unfairly changed. "And now Tia wants to come again. To see if we can . . . make things work."

I stared at him. There was nothing left of me now. No fresh swoops, no gleaming suspense, not even any icicles. Only a sound: a high-pitched, searing sound, located somewhere at the base of my spine.

I hadn't known at all.

*

"You have to go," I said eventually.

Following a rulebook.

We were in our bedroom, and he was tipping out the swimming gear from his gym bag. He threw some other things in it instead. Clothes, toiletries.

"What are you doing?" I asked.

"You told me I have to go." He looked up and caught my eye. The sulkiness dropped and it was him again. "The night I met you, I fell in love with you," he whispered. "Abi, I love you so much. We're supposed to be together. It's inconceivable, us breaking up. Abi . . . Abi." And he was reaching his hands toward me, crying.

"It's okay," I said, desperate with relief, wrapping my arms around him. "We'll figure it out. Stupid *Tia* can—"

Abruptly he stopped weeping, pulled back, and shook his head.

"I'm sorry," he said, packing his bag again. "She's not stupid."

And then I was breaking the rules. "Don't you go anywhere," I said. "Don't you dare leave this room. Don't you touch that door handle! We will work it out! Put that bag away! Put it away!"

"I have to go," he said gently, peeling my arms from around him. "I'll stay with David Chin."

"You can't go there! They're having a baby!"

"I have to go," he said. "I'm in love with Tia." Then he ducked his head, his wounded eyes, and I thought suddenly, with another fall, a clang: Here he is at last. Finnegan. Found and lost at exactly the same time.

*

A week went by.

He didn't call.

I waited.

I was waiting for flowers and apologies. These were in the rulebook.

In turn, I planned to break the pattern. At first, of course, I would be the woman who "cannot forgive." Our sad eyes at the table. But then I'd look up! And forgive him!

I called him in the end, and we both wept on the phone. "When are you coming back?" I said.

Now he became irritated. "This is hard for me!" he said. As if something had happened *to* him, unconnected to me.

"What are you doing?" I whispered, or maybe I only mouthed the words.

He cleared his throat. "You were very needy."

"I was what?"

"I mean, I don't blame you. But you were very needy. And she's . . . she's not."

"She's here? In Montreal?"

He didn't answer, so then I knew she was.

"She's in pieces," he said. "She feels terrible."

After I hung up I thought, *Oh, cry me a river, Tia.*

I wished I'd said that.

*

Late that night, I stood in the living room looking through the window.

In the street below, two men stood together in the rain and smoked cigarettes. One wore a dark jacket; the other rustled in a transparent raincoat. He was animated, or the wind had the raincoat; either way, it coruscated, rippled with light and frenzy. Everything out there was lit up by his raincoat, so it seemed.

I pulled on my boots, buttoned up my coat, and walked out into the streets. Strode along the emptiness. Ran my hands along the air, tracing the rain, imaginary fence posts, hedges, walls.

At an intersection, I urgently wanted to scoop out the warmth of the red traffic lights.

Eventually, I turned into a nightclub on St. Denis.

I stood at the bar and drank Crantinis, chewing on the straw. I thought about things. Specifically, I thought: Can they do this? If you lose your brother, aren't you covered? Don't you get immunity? If someone takes away the best friend of your youth, can they send you a new best friend named Finnegan, handsome with his pale skin, his dark hair, generous with his listening eyes, and can they then say: *We'll take him too?*

What are the rules? I wondered.

I was pretty sure that they had been broken.

*

After a while, I looked around and saw men who were also looking around. I remembered what you do. You call them to you, the men, with your eyes and your hips.

A man with dark blond hair approached and took the seat next to mine. I don't remember what we talked about. I think I was chewing on the straw suggestively and letting him know what I intended with my eyes. He seemed pretty keen on the idea.

We went back to my place. He appraised the apartment, nodding to himself, found the stereo, chose music. In fact, he unplugged the stereo and carried it down the hall to the bedroom.

This is a man who takes action! I thought.

This is how you heal, I thought next, reaching for the man as he reached for me. We met in the middle of the reaching. The strange shape of his shoulders, a dryness to his lips, the dent of his stomach, the music. He was kissing me so skillfully! Expertly moving us onto the bed!

I said: "Do you have any protection?"

He chuckled. "Not on me."

"Oh," I said. "Well then, we can't, because—"

He laughed again, a bigger laugh, his arms wrapped around me. "Don't worry," he murmured. There was something loose and strange about his arms. Finn's arms and shoulders have so much definition, from his swimming. I'd forgotten it was possible for arms to be soft, to have to press to feel the bone and muscle.

The hair on this man's body was fine and fair, and his skin was tanned. I'd forgotten that this was possible too; Finn's skin is almost translucent white so that the black hair on his chest, arms, calves, is startling.

The music played, and we were naked, and then he was inside me. "Oh," I said. "But . . ." And he chuckled again and repeated, "Don't worry." He moved differently from Finn, his knees were fiercer, his movements were fiercer; more traditional, I thought. I loved the selfish way this man moved: this was about him, not me, and that was how it should be, I decided. Primal! His eyes went sideways, looking sideways, not at me.

He moved faster, and faster.

"I'm going to come inside you," he said, urgently.

My mind seared into blankness. *What?!* I thought. *You're what? You can do that?!*

The thoughts collapsed into a single point, and he did.

Afterward I lay beside him, my heart thudding with calculations about what he just did, the thing that just happened, whether what he did, just now, was acceptable.

He seemed to think it was. The air in the room was breathless, sweaty, but nobody seemed to be shouting at him: *Wait, what did you just do?*

He did apologize, the way you might for knocking something over with your elbow.

*

He fell asleep beside me, which I found unexpected. I thought that one-night stands were supposed to blow you a kiss and vanish?

Early the next morning, he pressed two fingers to my lips and said, "See you soon."

The front door closed behind him.

I lay in bed.

After a while, there were shouts from outside. I got out of bed, wrapped the quilt around me, and watched through the window. In the snowy alley below, a carriage driver and two people in a car were having some kind of altercation. I was convinced it was connected to my one-night stand, but I couldn't see him anywhere out there. Raised, angry voices and then, abruptly, calm. The people got back into their car, the car reversed, and drove away.

"Back up, back up," called the driver, speaking English to the horse. Such a good horse, I thought. Such a good, calm, beautiful, bilingual horse, walking slowly backward while the passengers stayed quiet. Then the driver spoke to the passengers in French and they all cried, "No! No!" and laughed.

I stood at the window and watched this. The altercation, the calm, and then only the snow.

*

Later, I built a fire. I turned the wood over when the fire had buried itself, and blew on the embers.

I folded the laundry and put it away. Finn's khaki trousers, Finn's T-shirts, Finn's socks, Finn's swimming towel.

I tried reading Kierkegaard. Finn had left behind a copy of a book called *Either/Or: A Fragment of Life*. He'd drawn on Kierkegaard to impress me the first night I met him. Cheap trick, I thought now, although when I started reading I decided it was a reasonably expensive trick.

Music is the end of language, he had told me at the party—meanwhile, Tia down the hall somewhere—and also the beginning. Music as parentheses of language. Now Kierkegaard himself, I decided, could be the parentheses around my relationship with Finn.

I grew bored of Kierkegaard. I flicked through pages. I found these lines:

My soul is so heavy that no longer can any thought sustain it, no wingbeat lift it up into the ether. If it moves, it only sweeps along the ground like the low flight of birds when a thunderstorm is brewing.

I opened the mail and there was a fine for putting the garbage out on the wrong day. I slammed the laundry door, opened it and slammed it again. I did this repeatedly, until a long thin thread of wood peeled away and slithered to the floor of Finnegan's mother's apartment.

*

I felt quite dreamy about the fact that I was pregnant. I never stayed pregnant, so it wasn't real. I had considered taking the morning-after pill but I was certain, I knew, that I wouldn't get pregnant from a one-night stand. Life was more important and serious; life was not quite so hilarious. Besides, like I said, I never stayed pregnant.

Sometimes I thought I should call Finnegan and tell him I was expecting, let him think it was his, and then I'd smirk at Tia: *Ha, I win*, reeling him in with the promise of a child. This made me feel like someone ugly, snarling, poisonous, and the air took on a brutality, while, meantime, a small truth washed forlornly by: *What if he stays with her anyway?*

A bigger truth, of course, was the fact that Finnegan was capable of arithmetic.

I watched TV. *Canadian Idol. American Idol. The Apprentice.* The cruelty of that man's gruff jaw, his curling lip, his ridiculous hair.

Reruns of *Sex and the City* or *NYPD Blue*, the volume turned low, the lights dimmed. There was a quiet pointlessness to the programs—why all this fretting about that character? We know that, in the future, he's been shot by an underground crime figure, buried in a field with his badge, and replaced by an exuberant detective with an excellent work ethic—and in the dim, closed light, I felt as if I were on an airplane. The faint buzz of earphones, canned laughter, the poignancy of altitude. Such a vulnerable state to be in, watching television with your belt loosely fastened across your lap.

I chatted to Mum on the phone. She was reading a magazine article about Bec and Lleyton Hewitt's baby girl, she said. Also, there were race riots on Cronulla Beach.

I told her I was coming home for Christmas.

I said nothing about Finnegan, or Finnegan and Tia, or the fact that I was pregnant with a stranger's child.

I saw a reader survey on ninemsn.com.au. *Do you think the worst of the race riots is over?* Strange question for a survey, I thought, staring at this a while.

*

It's also strange the way I write these reflections in exactly the same format each year. Moments separated by dots. Impressionistic glances, that long-ago creative writing teacher called them. Like fish darting by in an aquarium.

I'll tell you who I want to be.

I want to be a shadow, a silhouette, the girl who stays at home, the girl who waits patiently, an anchor, not the girl out in the pub with the pool cues in her face, making jokes. I should have stayed at home and let Finn have his time out with his friend, I should have stayed at home, a princess, a mystery, a silence, making the baby, drawing him back home, my worn boots at the door.

Instead, I chatted, sat up high on bar stools, walked outside through the cigarette smoke, slipped on ice, and I talked and talked to Finn so he was drained dry, white with it, pale with it, desperate to go and replenish.

*

Anyway, the other day I came home to Sydney on an airplane, the way
that you do.

The accents on the plane were strange. Flat Australian, like voices
from old TV shows. I thought: *Where do they get these flight attendants?
Have they flown back to the seventies to fetch them?*

I dreamed of a small, white desk lamp. Its head was bowed, ashamed.
I lifted it up, tilted it up, as if by its chin, and it looked at me, startled.

At that moment, in the dream, and with sudden clarity, I was walking hand in hand with Finnegan. Faster and faster we walked through
the Montreal snow. "By the time we get to that lamppost up ahead?"
Finn said. "We will be warm."

I woke with a powerful feeling, as of dread.

PART 10

1.

They seemed happy to see me, the students of flight class.

"Abigail! We missed you last week!" Antony opened his arms, and the others, even Wilbur, agreed that things had not been the same.

I was surprised. I didn't think I was especially present in these classes; in fact, part of their appeal was the opportunity to be absent, passive, an observer. As a single parent, you make every decision. You get plenty of advice, of course, but it's up to me alone to determine how I deal with this tantrum, which day care I choose, whether I continue allowing favorite sticks to be brought home from the park, a giant stack of kindling forming in the corner of the living room.

Better than having to squabble with an adult whose child-rearing philosophies clash with mine, of course—but it can astonish me. *Again?* I think. Nobody responsible here but me?

Still, maybe I'd been passive in flight class because I was too shy around Niall to be anything at all.

Niall himself smiled quietly at the enthusiasm of the others.

They wanted to know how Oscar was, and Nicole told me that her third child was sick all the time. Anything going around, he'll pick it up, she said. Whereas her first two kids? Healthy as cows.

"I don't associate the cow with health, especially," Antony told her.

Pete Aldridge nodded gravely. "Mad cow disease."

"All right," Nicole complained. "What do people say? Healthy as an ox, which is like a cousin of the cow, so leave me alone. My point is, I'd never have known what it was like to have sick kids if I'd stopped at two. I'd have been secretly judging Abi, trying to figure out what she was doing wrong. *Are you getting him enough fresh air? Are you feeding him orange vegetables?* But see, I'm not saying a word."

"You're saying plenty of words," Frangipani declared, and Nicole laughed. Everyone did.

They told me that I'd missed a class on Sensory Development.

"We did the sense of taste," Frangipani said. "Not to be confused with the sense of flavor."

"But we did that too," Antony put in.

Now they became excited again. They knew so much about "taste"! Flies and butterflies have taste organs on their feet, Nicole told me. Every time they land on an object they taste it.

"Catfish have more than a hundred thousand tastebuds," Antony offered. "All over their bodies. They taste everything they touch."

Wilbur was pleased. "You guys *listen* to me!"

He had prepared treats, "flavor sensations," and they'd played guessing games with blindfolds, as well as practiced "mindful eating," chewing each mouthful eighty times.

"Very hard work," Pete Aldridge informed me, strolling across the room to study the line of ants still trailing along Wilbur's wall.

"Don't worry," Frangipani reassured me. "You can probably catch up on the missed class at home. The five basic tastes are sweet, bitter, sour, salty, and—what was the other one, Wilbur?"

But Wilbur was studying his phone. "Umami," he said. "Fish, mushrooms, green tea. Anyway. Meditation tonight."

"What about the bit where we stand at the windows?" Nicole asked, and Wilbur blinked. "Of course. Please."

We lined up at the windows, and stared out at the darkening blue.

I can honestly say that I did not see a flight wave that night. But it was relaxing, rocking on the soles of my feet, staring at the sky. It's not something you have the time or inclination to do when you're taking care of a four-year-old with an ear infection.

Everyone else seemed similarly happy at the windows.

"I was thinking something," Nicole said, pressing her forehead to the glass. "Wilbur, when you say flight waves, are you just thinking of thermals?"

"There's a sale on thermals at Aldi this weekend," Frangipani said, and I noticed Niall's eyes disappearing into his smile.

"Not thermal underwear," Nicole explained. "I mean those air currents that rise up, and birds glide on them. Is that the idea, Wilbur? That we ride on the wind the way birds and gliders do? My husband, Marcin, is a birdwatcher, and he was telling me about them. Obstruction currents happen when air hits the side of a cliff, and you can do slope soaring. Dynamic soaring is where the wind is moving at different speeds and you keep crossing back and forth."

"Dynamic soaring," I breathed. "I like that idea."

Niall turned to me. "I think you would excel at dynamic soaring, Abigail," he offered.

Wilbur sighed. "No, Nicole," he said. "No. Flight waves are something more than updrafts."

Then he began pulling out the purple yoga mats. The embroidered cushions were tossed about, the mystical music was switched on, and Wilbur instructed us to lie down. He seemed a little brusque.

"Consider this," he began, the moment we were on the floor. He himself sat cross-legged, leaning against the wall.

"Wait," Antony said. "I don't feel in the zone at all."

"Consider this," Wilbur repeated, more loudly. "I'm about to put you in the zone, Antony. If you'll just *consider this*."

"Go ahead," Pete Aldridge said. "We're right now." I heard him wriggling around.

Niall was beside me. His profile in the dim light. The pleasing shape of his nose. Our hands tapped the floor, side by side.

"Consider the splendor of height," Wilbur said.

"Oh yes," Frangipani said. "I like a tall man. I put that on my RSVP profile. *Preference for men at or above five-eleven.*"

Everybody giggled.

Wilbur hesitated. "I'm not referring to people," he said. "But to the sky."

"Are you doing online dating?" Nicole whispered to Frangipani. "Seriously?"

"Yes," she whispered back. "But not seriously. In a lighthearted way."

More giggles. Wilbur cleared his throat. We quieted.

"I forgot to tell you to breathe tonight, didn't I?" Wilbur asked, abruptly disappointed in himself.

"That's all right," I said. "We do that automatically."

"The splendor of height," Wilbur continued, returning to his meditation tone. "Thank you, Abi, you are kind. Picture yourselves down on the ground, the low ground, amid the clutter and clamor. You are jostled, battered, buttressed, your senses assaulted. There's no space! Yes, that's good, Pete, good job being discomforted by the crowds."

"It's my shoulder," Pete Aldrige growled.

Wilbur apologized. "Now picture yourself stepping off the path," he instructed. "Stepping *away* from the crowds, the cars, the streets. You are in a park. The grass is soft and green. There are trees. Consider these trees. Choose a tree. Perhaps it is a palm tree."

"Mine's a jacaranda," Pete Aldridge declared.

"All right. Look up. You are looking up at the tree. It's so tall!"

"No. Not that tall."

"Maybe try a different tree then, Pete," Wilbur suggested evenly. "A tall one. Focus on the tall tree. Consider the splendor of its height!"

"I just thought of something." Nicole's voice was loud and chatty in the musical quiet. "Is anybody here afraid of heights?"

There was a sharp intake of breath from Wilbur. "Should have asked that sooner," he muttered. "A fear of heights." He chuckled, and the chuckle grew, turned into laughter, and now Wilbur was slapping his knees.

We all joined in the laughter, although Wilbur's carried loudest and longest.

"Anyway," he said at last. "Is anyone? Afraid of heights?"

"We surely would have mentioned it by now," Antony pointed out.

"Unless," Nicole mused, "somebody here hopes to cure a fear of heights by learning how to fly?"

*

But none of us was here for that reason. We sat back up on our mats to discuss this. It's easier to talk in dim light.

Nicole said she'd never been bothered by heights before she had kids, but now she had a sort of fear of heights by proxy.

I said I had the exact same thing! When Oscar was two, I took him on a chairlift in the Blue Mountains. Suddenly, I realized how simple it would be for him to wriggle and slip from the chair, plummeting to the rocky chasm below. I spent the rest of the ride holding Oscar so tight that he had my fingernail marks on his arms.

"And yet if he'd learned to fly as a baby," Frangipani pointed out, "he'd have been fine!"

There was a moment's pause before we realized she was making a joke, and we laughed to reward her.

A friend of Niall's had attended a course on "fear of flying" at the airport. They'd been instructed to board an airplane sitting on the tarmac, but the man climbing the plane steps ahead of Niall's friend had stopped, swung around, and thrown up everywhere. She'd had to go back to the terminal to clean herself up.

For much of that story, I'd assumed Niall's friend was a man, and when we got to the end, I was disconcerted. *Who was she?* I wanted to snap. I imagined she was rather darling, what with her fear of flight.

Antony said that his partner, Rick, was afraid of heights. On their first date, not knowing about this fear, Antony had taken Rick to 360 Bar and Dining, a revolving restaurant at the top of the Sydney Tower. Rick had not wanted to spoil the date by telling Antony about his fear, but he'd ended up slithering out of his seat, crouching by the table and crawling back to the lift. It took him ages to crawl back, Antony said, because the restaurant kept spinning him away. Antony had wanted to scoop Rick into his arms and carry him, but that had seemed too forward for a first date.

Antony had never mentioned a partner before, and I felt a jolt because I'd assumed him to be single, whereas in fact he was a winer-and-diner, capable of scooping partners into his arms, or wanting to do so anyway.

"Acrophobia," he added. "That's what you call a fear of heights. Ancraophobia is a fear of winds or drafts, which would be a problem if Nicole's theory is right—flight waves turning out to be updrafts."

"The theory is not right," Wilbur said. "With all due respect to Nicole."

Nicole seemed pleased. "Thank you," she said, nodding, "for the due respect."

Later, we stretched sleepily.

"I like a good meditation," Frangipani announced, and Pete Aldridge said, "I thought you liked a tall man?" which was another sort of joke from an unexpected source.

Wilbur said he'd have to cancel next Tuesday's class, as something had come up, and he frowned vaguely toward his phone.

2.

On the way home, I replayed the line about myself excelling at dynamic soaring. My phone beeped with a text and I checked it at a traffic light.

It was from Niall.

No class next Tuesday night. I'll miss you! Can I take you to dinner instead?

3.

Oscar outlined the activities he had undertaken at the play center as we walked inside. Just your usual bouncy things and swimming among plastic balls (a concept I find both compelling and disturbing). I asked if Lynette had found his socks tonight, and Oscar looked startled. He sat on the bottom step, pulled up his trouser leg, and pointed: "They're on my foots!"

"Of course they are!" It was colder now, so he'd worn shoes and socks instead of sandals.

I decided to make a joke of my forgetfulness. "Where *are* your socks?" I said. "Oh, here they are!" Pointing to his feet. "And where is your backpack? Oh, here it is!" Swinging it around from my own shoulder. "Where are your ears? Oh, here they are!" And so on. He laughed along, relieved that I was back in control. "Where is your kiss?" I said next. "Oh, here it is!" And I kissed him on the cheek.

I hadn't planned that, I just said it. He laughed so hard! We had to play the game the entire time I was putting him to bed, me inquiring as to the location of his kiss, and then kissing him. He wanted a turn: *Where's your kiss? Oh, here it is!* Kissing my arm, my head, the wall, the pillow, the sheet.

Eventually, he fell asleep in a state of jubilation.

4.

After returning my self-help books to the library, I remembered there is more to self-help than a handful of relatively recent bestsellers.

There are entire movements, many of them rooted in the wisdom of the ancients, many stolen, Westernized, and simplified from the East. It's all right, though, social media will reduce them to a pithy pair of lines.

I borrowed more books, followed trails on Facebook, and each new sphere set my heart pumping at how much I had missed. Never looking sideways from *The Guidebook*, I might have missed the answer: the whereabouts of Robert, the story of what happened to him, how to save my marriage, a cure for this bewildering sadness.

For example, with the right feng shui I might have lured Robert home, and kept Finnegan safe in a harmonious Montreal apartment.

I read about feng shui online: *Don't clutter the space around your doorway because the chi will be distracted and not enter.*

Also: *Do not have a flight of steps at your front door or the chi will head directly up the stairs, forgetting the ground floor.*

It occurred to me that chi might share some characteristics with the universe: all-knowing, all-wise, all-magical, yet also a bit daft.

If you have a room in your house that you don't use very much, you should put a living thing in there.

What, I thought, like a child? An old person you don't have much use for anymore?

But the writer went on to explain that it could be a potted plant or a clock. With great respect to the internet, a clock is not in fact a living thing.

5.

Niall and I went to dinner at a Thai place in Newtown.

As I approached—as I walked along King Street in my clicking high-heeled boots, and my tight blue jeans, with my hair long and feathery so I felt it brush my skin as if it was excited too—I suddenly found myself too obvious. Transparent! Striding toward him with my hair loose!

Niall watched me approach and then I was standing beside him and it's almost too much, isn't it, when you both know it's a date, and you're smiling at each other in the street, your eyes sparkling, people moving around you, traffic going by, sun falling pale, and it's about to begin, about to begin.

Then you turn toward the restaurant door. "Shall we go in?"

6.

It was a good night, is what I'm trying to say.

The shine kept up through dinner, and our eyes carried on sparkling. Anyway, his eyes sparkled, and I sensed that mine did too.

We talked about Wilbur and Flight School, of course, and the others in the class. Why had *they* agreed to attend?

Nicole wanted a break from her four children? I suggested.

"So many better ways to have a break," Niall said. "She could see a movie or learn to surf."

I liked that he didn't suggest Nicole could get a facial or have her nails done—the sort of thing people always recommend for women taking breaks. A little free time? Get to work making yourself prettier! Also, I always have to curl my fingers under, hiding my torn and bitten nails, when people mention getting "nails done." There's nothing here to "do."

We decided that kindness was Antony's motivation, and that Sasha—I remembered to call her Sasha, not Frangipani—was still knotted up with *The Guidebook*, possibly even believing that she would learn to fly.

"And Pete Aldridge wants to protect us," I finished. I was looking at the last curry puff. I love curry puffs. Why give us an odd number? Should I offer it to Niall? Ask if he wanted to share? Leave it there like a lost treasure?

Niall followed my eyes. He tipped the final curry puff onto my plate.

"That's not why Pete Aldridge is coming," he said. "I can tell you why."

"Why?"

"He's got a crush on Sasha."

"No chance," I said.

"Trust me," he said.

We paused. We'd just disagreed on something of no particular consequence. I liked his certainty, and I liked that he'd mentioned a man having a crush, and I liked that he'd just read my mind and given me the curry puff.

"Anyway, who else is there?" Niall held up his hand, which was big, and each of his fingers seemed big and broad too. He murmured our classmates' names, ticking them off. "You just wanted to see what would happen," he said, when he reached my name. "And *I* wanted to see you again."

This time he didn't look sideways at a tree. He leaned on his elbows, watching my face.

"Thank you," I said. I couldn't figure out what else to say.

We both drank from our wineglasses and picked up the conversation again.

Afterward, Niall walked me to my car and there was a big notice flapping under the wiper. THIS CAR DOES NOT CONTAIN VALUABLES, the notice said, followed by a list of valuables "this car" did not contain. Satnav, radio, CDs, purse, and so on. Clipped to this was a little explanation from Newtown Police, suggesting that I place this notice on my windscreen every time I parked my car, as thieves had been operating in the neighborhood.

Niall and I read all this under a streetlight.

"So if I ever do have valuables in the car," I said, "I should cross out the *not*? Maybe put a checkmark next to the relevant valuables?"

"And if it's not listed, just write it in," Niall said. "*Grandmother's emerald ring.* Check."

"It's the only way the system can work," I agreed. "The thieves have to be able to trust us."

Niall's shoulders tipped sideways, as if a ship had tacked unexpectedly, and then he was kissing me.

It was the good kind of kiss, the right kind, gentle but not whispery, and it lasted a suitable length of time, so I wasn't gasping for breath.

We smiled at each other again.

"Better go and get the kid," I said.

7.

After that, winter got underway.

Niall and I went on five more dates while babysitters took care of Oscar. I stayed out later each time, and we spent longer kissing each other goodnight. We took turns paying for dinner, and the whole thing was costing me a goddamn fortune.

It turned out that Niall had been in a relationship with a woman named Rhami for thirteen years. They had lived together, but never seen a reason to get married. Last year, Rhami had said she needed to move on, to get to know herself, see other men.

Niall was very adult, very calm, in his narration. "It wasn't a surprise," he said. "We were so young when we got together. It was always going to happen. Best thing for both of us."

Rhami had moved out two days before Niall received the letter about the weekend retreat to the island.

"Any other time," he said, "I'd have chucked it, but now I thought, *Why not just go?* It was great. Like a reminder that things ending with Rhami meant freedom. She was a contemporary dancer, and used to perform most weekends. I'd help her set up the stage. But this time I could just pack up and go."

We smiled at each other.

I told him about Finnegan and Tia, and laughed—because it's funny, the way Tia had been part of our relationship all along—and Niall said, "I'm glad *you* find it funny. Because I don't! He's a prick!" Then: "I hope it's okay for me to say that."

I said it was fine. He should say whatever he liked.

On the fifth date, while we were making out under a streetlight, leaning up against my car—and that's what it was, making out; I recommend it—he invited me back to his place. It was the point of all this, surely.

But I couldn't figure out what to do. I declined the invitation and began to spend most of my time trying to solve this puzzle. Should I ask the babysitter to stay until morning? Am I *made* out of money? Plus, how would it work when Oscar crept into my room, as he sometimes does, and found the sitter in my bed? Maybe he'd just slink back to his own room, but he is capable of howling until he makes himself sick.

You're thinking: What! Oscar? No way! He's cute!

But he can slap me hard across the face while I'm strapping him into his car seat. He can throw himself against a door screaming. He once reached up and pulled out a handful of my hair, then pushed his face close to mine and said, "That's what you get." Because I had told him to eat his vegetables.

I took Oscar to the zoo once—I've taken him many times, we have annual passes—but on this day, he threw a book out of the open car window, told me I was a fat monster, refused to get out of the car when we arrived, burst into tears when I said, "Okay, we're going back home"— "But I wanna go to the zoo!" "Then you have to get out of the car!" "I don't want to get out of the car!" And so on.

I knew I should punish him by taking him home. But I wanted to go to the zoo, I needed to go the zoo, *he* needed to go the zoo because it wears him out and he sleeps all afternoon. So we went to the zoo, where he begged for an ice cream, until I gave in and bought him an ice cream, which he immediately threw onto the road screaming that it was "wrong! The wrong ice cream!"

Here, I lost my mind and shouted, "That's it! We are going home right now! We are *not* going to see the lions! That's what happens! You miss out on the lions!" while Oscar sobbed, brokenhearted—he *loves* the lions! He wants to *be* a lion!—and a young couple walked by, arms linked, and glanced at each other—and there went time, it was Finnegan and me, the year 2000. "These are the memories," Finn had said.

I was wiping Oscar's face roughly, cleaning off the ice cream, and those stupid, self-righteous idiots, Finnegan and Abigail, they didn't have a clue.

Of course, you'll purse your lips: "Don't let him get away with it!" Or: "*My* child would never behave like that! Try DIS-CI-PLINE!"

As if I hadn't thought of that. Brilliant! Punish his misbehavior! Let him know his conduct is unacceptable!

Don't you think I've tried that? Points systems, star charts, naughty stairs! Long, stern discussions. Removal of special treats.

You think because you've raised a child, you know how children work?

Children are as various as people.

Same with marriages.

Anyway, I was keen to figure out how to spend a night with Niall. I considered asking Lynette and Dad to keep Oscar overnight. But the very day I was considering this, Lynette said to me, "You know, when Oscar is seven or eight, he could have a sleepover with us!"

Preemptive strike. She had seen my plan in my eyes.

I can't wait until he's seven or eight, I thought in a small, forlorn voice.

Around this time, I watched an episode of a TV show in which the single mother of a teenage daughter says: *In all the years that my daughter was growing up, I've never spent a night with a man.* Now she *could* do this because the teenager was going away to college.

On the couch, I wept.

Never? I sobbed. *Never?* In all that time, she has *never* spent a night with a man?

I could see that we, the viewers, were supposed to approve—yes, that's correct, the morality, the purity, child protection—while, meanwhile I rocked back and forth in my anguish. Dizzy with it, ice-cold with it, the idea that I would not spend a night with a man until Oscar grew up and left home.

You think that I exaggerate. I don't.

8.

In my café, there is a noticeboard where people can pin their happy thoughts. I have stacks of cards printed with: *Happiness is . . .*

That's the prompt. Customers can use it to specify what makes them happy right now, or define what happiness means to them.

Turns out people seem to think that happiness is love, or a holiday by the sea, or family, or *my new nail color!!!* or a Maserati. I like it when they refer to menu items: *Happiness is this Spinach, Red Pepper, Strawberry, and Candied Walnut Salad!* Although sometimes that seems a little ingratiating. Also, too literal, because spinach and red peppers are full of vitamin B6, which boosts serotonin, and strawberries contain vitamin C, which reduces the stress hormone cortisone, and walnuts contain omega-3 fatty acids, which keep nerve cell membranes healthy. So yes, happiness *is* that salad. That's why it's on the menu.

Around this time, I read the noticeboard every day. I was waiting for somebody to write *Happiness is a Child-free Night with my New Lover.* Nobody did. A couple of interesting ones I saw included: *Happiness is my kid eating healthy food without screaming or throwing it across the room (i.e. elusive).* Also: *Happiness is . . . not available. I just want the world to be all right. Just, everyone be all right. I can't stand it anymore.*

I took that last one down; it struck me as likely to lower the mood. Then I pinned it back up, because what if the person returned and saw that his/her voice had been silenced?

Luckily it was quickly covered by a teenage boy who wrote, *Happiness is . . . my new gaming mouse.*

9.

We did another Meditation session at Flight School.

Wilbur took us soaring into the sky (with his voice), "without the trappings of machinery or wings," through clouds and fog, dodging peaks and doing loop-the-loops under rainbows and suchlike. We all enjoyed that one. Pete Aldridge said it reminded him of a ride he'd been on at Universal Studios. A dimple appeared in Wilbur's left cheek when Pete said that, but then he resumed his grave expression and nodded. "Thank you, Pete." I was always surprised by Wilbur's dimple; his face was defined by its cheekbones, a strong nose, a scar on his chin like a chipped piece of wood.

In Flight Immersion, Wilbur taught us the language of pilots. From now on, he suggested, we should say *negative* for no and *affirmative* for yes; also *say again* if we didn't hear something properly, *copy that* if we did, and *disregard* if we changed our minds.

We learned that *skyclr* means good weather for flying, and *cavok* means cloud and visibility okay.

Cumulonimbus is thunderclouds; *cumulous* is the little, white, fluffy clouds; *stratus* is the low blankets of cloud.

"The ones you don't want," Wilbur told us, "are cumulo-granulous."

We waited.

"That means you've run into a mountain."

Funny. We all laughed.

We're all in a peppermint mood, I thought, and that sent a twirl through my heart. *Peppermint mood* is something Robert used to say, when he was about six years old. I think it came from a picture book his teacher had read to his class. Until that moment, in Wilbur's living room, I had completely forgotten.

Also in Flight Immersion, we had to recite the aviation alphabet until we all had it memorized (Antony already did)—Alpha, Bravo, Charlie, Delta, Echo, and so on—and we learned that UK and US flyers used to have different alphabets (Apple, Beer, Charlie; Abel, Baker, Charlie), until a universal language was agreed upon.

Frangipani interrupted to say that she had met a man named Abel online.

"What's that got to do with the universal language of flight?" Pete Aldridge barked.

"Sex is a universal language," Nicole put in.

"Wilbur just said *Abel*," Frangipani explained. "Abel, Baker, Charlie."

"Is his name Abel Baker?" Antony inquired.

Frangipani admitted that she did not know her new man's last name, at which Pete Aldridge *tched*, and Nicole sighed, "I miss the days of having sex with men whose name I don't know. I *like* sex." Her arms stretched languorously, and I loved how open she could be. But then her eyes darted around the group. "Is that wrong? That I just said that?"

"No!" I said. "It's not wrong to say that!"

Then Nicole, Frangipani, and I had an intense discussion about how a woman's sex drive is considered unseemly, or laughable; how a woman frustrated, especially an older woman, is an object to be mocked. A cranky woman must need to get laid! Funny! But if a man wants sex, nobody says, *Oho, he wants sex! Funny!* Of course he does. It's biological.

The men in the room listened quietly.

After a pause, Pete Aldridge instructed Wilbur: "Carry on then."

Wilbur cleared his throat and told us that *Bravo Zulu* means "well done," and *Foxtrot Oscar* means "no!" or "eff off."

But then he glanced up from his notes and said, "Pilots in Australia don't actually use those expressions. I think my parents got them from a book."

10.

I carried on seeking out wisdom.

For example, I learned about chakras, the art of face-reading, and Tantric sex.

Tantric sex came up when I had brunch with an old school friend, Mish Choo, at Thelma & Louise, the café at the Neutral Bay ferry wharf.

Mish and her husband had just completed a Tantric sex retreat. It had changed her life. A revelation.

"Did your husband like it too?" I asked.

"Not sure. Who cares?" Dreamily, she twirled spaghetti around her fork. She was always absent-minded at school, too.

11.

I was excited when we did the next Sensory Development session at Flight School because I'd missed the first one. Sense of smell was a *companion class*, Wilbur told us, to the one on taste. He had set out a line of small, covered bowls, and he handed around blindfolds.

"We are going to identify these smells," he said.

Niall informed us, in his quiet, low voice, that he had no sense of smell.

Everyone was interested, and I was startled. Also jealous. Here was a personal aspect of Niall that should have been shared with me first, maybe in bed, if we ever got into a bed.

"I remember you saying that on the first weekend," Wilbur said, and now I felt ashamed. I should have remembered myself. I'd been too busy scoping the room for other men.

Wilbur had considered eliminating Niall from this course, he told us: sensory capacity was an integral element of flight.

"But if you're missing a particular sense, doesn't that make your *other* senses stronger?" Frangipani demanded, and Wilbur said, "Exactly why I kept him."

"Appreciate it," Niall said, his voice faintly ironic.

"How'd you make that first decision anyway?" Antony asked. "The chosen ones?"

There was a frisson. Everyone turned to Wilbur.

I'd never wanted to ask this, afraid it would (a) sound like I wanted praise—*You were chosen because of your beauty! Your talent! Because I saw magical potential in you!*—or (b) lead to Wilbur saying he'd chosen the most gullible, the fools.

"My parents' instructions are highly detailed on most things," Wilbur said, "but on that, they were vague. Anyway, the sense of smell and taste are intricately linked, but Niall seemed—"

"Eh," Pete Aldridge said. "Answer the man's question."

Wilbur sighed. "The instructions said to choose the people who most *needed* to fly. I was supposed to be able to tell this by watching how you approached the activities."

"So if we were useless at the three-legged race," Nicole said, "that meant we belonged in the sky?"

"Ha," Wilbur said. "No. I took it to mean the people who seemed sad. Anyway, Niall did well in the tasting sessions, and—"

"*I'm* not sad!" Frangipani cried out. "I'm a very happy person!"

"Me too," Antony put in, surprised.

Faces were surprised or bewildered; personally, I felt hostile, exposed.

Yet also I felt the exquisite despair of recognition. *Of course I am sad. How did Wilbur know this?*

"That's a technique used by a lot of cults," Nicole said thoughtfully. "You tell people you can *see* they've been hurt, and they feel acknowledged and cry and join your cult."

Now I felt foolish.

"I didn't mean it that way," Wilbur murmured. "I'm sure I got it wrong. I was sad myself that weekend, so I probably projected that randomly—or I just chose the people I liked. Niall, have you ever had a sense of smell?"

Niall said he remembered the smell of seaweed from a beach trip when he was four, but that was all.

After that, the lesson had an element of strangeness because we were conscious of Niall. I think we felt pride each time we recognized a scent—*look! look what I can do, Niall, and you can't!*—at the same time as conscious that this was brazenly ableist of us.

A few times people said, "You must be able to smell *this* one! Here, try it."

All his life, Niall told us, people had been saying, "No, seriously, smell *this*," as if they could somehow crack open his olfactory nerves.

"I guess people don't play super loud music for deaf people and say you *must* be able to hear *this*," Wilbur pointed out.

We identified various scents—cinnamon, chocolate, vanilla, rosemary, whisky, sage, onion, coffee. Pete Aldridge and Frangipani were the best of the group, both correctly identifying wood shavings, ice cubes, celery, black tea, and turmeric.

Wilbur told us we should walk up and down the corridors at the supermarket, stopping to smell every product. We should eat food that looks like itself, so that our brain connects the food and its fragrance. We should drink water regularly, blow our noses, use saline spray, and eat lentils, oysters, and pecans.

Walking down the street after the flight class, I told Niall about a poem I'd once read, which was addressed to a man without a sense of smell.

I felt shy telling him this, and forward. I offered to find the poem for him and he said, "Sure." But an expression crossed his face: surprise, amusement, maybe disappointment. Or none of those. I didn't know.

At home, when I found the poem online, it seemed to speak a language that Niall himself would not comprehend. It was written for a *particular* man with no sense of smell, I realized, and Niall was not that man. More, the poem was contained within a moment in a Chapters bookshop, on a snowy day in Montreal that, at the time, had seemed immense, a moment-stopping time, but which was just a speck riding an updraft.

Also, on this reading, I did not understand how the poet had managed to sniff the nape of her own neck.

12.

Eventually, I invited Niall to have dinner at my place and meet Oscar. He arrived at the door with a severed hand.

It turned out that Niall's older brother Patrick was in town for a quick visit—this Patrick, also a property developer, lived in Brisbane—and the two of them had been to the Paddington Markets that day. Patrick had suggested that a severed hand made of rubber would be a fun thing to bring to Niall's first meeting with Oscar.

I had time for a few thoughts: *You didn't tell me your brother was in town!* And: *You haven't suggested that I meet your brother!* But: *At least you told your brother about me, prompting him to consider what might amuse a four-year-old.*

Niall was wearing this rubbery, gruesome, withered hand over his own hand, like a glove.

"What do you think?" he asked, stepping through the door. He looked nervous. "Will he like it?"

"Well," I began, but Oscar was in the hallway staring up at Niall.

"Hey, buddy," Niall said, holding out the rubber hand. It looked pretty real, emerging from his sleeve like that. "Want to shake my hand?"

Oscar turned to me in frank alarm, so I grinned at him, and *I* shook Niall's rubber hand and made a show of saying, "Ew! Yuk! Gross!" to indicate that it was all a joke, a game. Oscar relaxed and also laughed. He reached out and shook the hand, imitating me: "Ew! Gross!" and so on.

This is great! I thought. *This is going well!* Then the toy came away and now Oscar was holding a severed hand.

Oh, the expression on Oscar's face. The blank dismay, the horror.

"It's not his *real* hand," I said quickly, realizing.

"It's not my real hand, buddy!" Niall crouched down on his knees, holding out his own hands. "Look! These are my real hands! This one's just a joke hand!"

Oscar was quiet, looking from the rubber hand to the real one, back and forth.

We had pizza for dinner and ice cream for dessert, and Oscar, at my prompting, showed Niall various toys. Niall admired them, and revealed to Oscar some inbuilt spinning mechanism in a toy car that he hadn't known about.

Afterward, when Niall drove away, Oscar and I spent a long time discussing the severed hand. How Oscar never wanted to see that hand again. Never. How it was a silly thing, a *very* silly thing, how it was stupid, what its *point* was exactly, that there *was* no point to it, *why* that man had brought it along, and why that man ("Niall," I said) had even *bought* it in the first place, and so on.

It was a terrible shock we had inflicted upon a small boy, I saw. He believed he had broken off a man's hand.

Of course, this also meant that, in Oscar's eyes, we'd been standing in a doorway jeering at a stranger's hand. We'd been saying, "Gross!

Ew!" as we shook an actual hand, a deformed, withered, diseased, broken hand.

I tried to raise this subject but it only confused him, and we returned to *why* that man brought a rubber hand along tonight, no, but *why*.

13.

The next flying class after Niall's visit was Meditation again. There is a reason I remember this class in vivid detail, but I'm embarrassed to say it.

Wilbur had acquired scented candles and they flickered, the scent of wild fig and cassis weaving around us. (I knew it was wild fig and cassis from reading the label.) I turned to Niall and studied his face for signs of the absence of scent. I felt unaccountably sad that he was missing out on this fragrance, and I wanted to *talk* about it, to write a poem for him, to uncover what dimension of experience he was missing. At the same time, I wanted to explore what *added* dimension there might be for Niall, the same way that blindness and deafness open alternative spaces.

Wilbur was quiet that night, speaking only for long enough to issue instructions, and we found ourselves briskly moved from the windows— where nobody spotted any flight waves—to our mats on the floor.

I had become accustomed to spending our Meditation sessions in the sky. Wilbur would have us close our eyes and send us soaring, varying the terrain below, and taking us on occasional detours—around volcanic peaks, say. He had the sort of voice that moved around the room at a different level to other voices; a compelling voice. You believed it.

However, on this night, he asked us to fly through the centuries, and land in the hills surrounding Florence.

Unexpected!

Here, Wilbur said, we would find Leonardo da Vinci studying birds.

"Leonardo has the secret to everything," Antony said, "locked into a code."

"It's all the Fibonacci sequence," Pete Aldridge informed us.

"What's Fibonacci?" Nicole asked.

"You don't know who Fibonacci is!" Frangipani exclaimed. "Have you been *living under a rock*?"

Pete Aldridge chuckled and began to talk about the golden ratio, the golden spiral, how you find it in leaves, beehives, pineapples, sunflowers, in the eyes, fin and tail of a dolphin, in pine cones, shells, spiral galaxies, hurricanes.

"And in the uterus," Frangipani added.

"Yes," said Pete Aldridge, not missing a beat. They nodded at each other with mutual respect.

"I still don't get it," Nicole whispered to me, and we both giggled.

Again, Wilbur was silent. There was a lengthy pause. The candlelight swayed. In a distant apartment, a toilet flushed.

"Breathe in," Wilbur said. "Be aware of your breath. Breathe out. Focus your awareness on your arms. Focus your awareness on your toes. Focus your awareness on Leonardo da Vinci, standing on a hill outside of Florence, locking all the secrets into codes, and studying birds."

After that, Wilbur used an almost everyday voice, just as compelling, to describe Leonardo's fascination with flight, the intensity of his quest for flight. How Leonardo da Vinci studied proportion, physics, symmetry, the flight of birds, insects, and flying fish, even the gallop of horses.

Leonardo studied the geometry of flight, the dynamics of the human body, the use of the wind. He considered parachutes, fans, and kites.

Now Wilbur roamed off-topic and talked about Hindu mythology, Sufism, yogic levitation, and transcendental meditation. I think, based on the sound of his breathing, that Pete Aldridge fell asleep.

But Wilbur carried on. He told the story of St. Joseph of Cupertino who, in the seventeenth century, was famous for having flown through the air, overcome by rapture, at least seventy times. He flew up to an olive tree and hovered there a good half-hour! In the eighteenth century, St. Gerard Majella flew like a bird, or was carried like a feather, over three-quarters of a mile.

Next Wilbur referred, vaguely, to the infinite possibilities of alchemy, and how compatible alchemical ideas are with quantum physics. Many mystics believe that we only need to access our core, he said, the center of our being, let it merge with the universe. In such a way, we will step out of limitations like gravity.

At last he circled back to Leonardo da Vinci.

"Leonardo designed many flying machines," he told us, "but he always returned to the idea of the *center*."

There was a pause. A door slamming somewhere down the corridor.

"He saw us as having a central point. A central pole, a center soul. *The force behind movement is in the bones and the nerves*, he wrote, *however motion comes from the spirit, the center and soul of everything*."

Another pause. "Leonardo was moving slowly, inexorably, toward the central truth," Wilbur said. "When our soul is ready, we can fly."

There was a long silence. I think Nicole was also fast asleep.

Now I will tell you the reason I remember this class so particularly.

For a moment, I believed. Right into the center of my heart, into my center, came a thought that took my breath: *It's true that we can fly*.

14.

Two things happened the day after that class.

One was that I saw Wilbur walking into my local Woolworths in Neutral Bay. He was with a woman in a turquoise jacket, her dark hair pulled into a ponytail, sunglasses propped onto her head.

I was leaving by one set of sliding doors, distracted by the shopping bags looped over my wrists, and by Oscar, who was rifling through the bags, trying to find the tray of sushi I'd bought, so I only caught a glimpse. They were stepping through the other sliding doors, their faces close, talking.

It was disconcerting. Wilbur belonged across the Harbour Bridge, in his flat in Newtown, taking his class to the sky! Not here, shopping for groceries with a stylish woman!

I flicked a finger hard against my thumb, flicking away the residue of last night's belief in flight.

The other thing was that my mother telephoned to say she and Xuang were coming down to Sydney to house-sit for her friend Trish in Crows Nest again. They were bringing Xuang's Newfoundland, Bartholomew. Should they take Oscar for a sleepover that weekend?

"Yes," I said, and almost shouted, *"Yes! Yes, you shall!"*

I'd been reading the Tantric sex book that Mish Choo had recommended. It was very encouraging. It seemed to think that sex could be *brilliant*, more brilliant than you ever imagined, and also that men were the positive charge and women the negative. I believe these were battery metaphors.

I was troubled, from a feminist perspective, because the book seemed keen on the woman being *passive* and the man *active* (how did same-sex Tantric sex work?). My most intense feminist phase had been at university, when I became conscious of discourses of pursuit and of white/black, male/female, active/passive, dominant/submissive dichotomies, and so forth.

Back then, I carried my feminist framework everywhere, pressing it onto situations, movies, books, conversations, everything. It always fit perfectly, but I grew tired of carrying it and threw it in my backpack.

Now I don't need to get it out, I just know it fits. I can still call up the language. I can even differentiate between first-, second-, whatever-wave feminism, and can acknowledge my limitations, my privileges, as a straight, white woman. Anyway, I was pretty sure that this Tantric sex book was problematic.

On the other hand, if a man wanted to make active love to me, while I relaxed and experienced *astonishing* pleasure? Well. That sounded fine.

15.

Niall said he'd make dinner at his place.

He seemed not quite to grasp the enormity of this child-free weekend. I mean, he used contractions and full stops—"I'll make dinner." Not: "I *will* make dinner!" I myself was giddy, overwhelmed by possibilities! We should fly to Paris! No. Too far. We should have a Romantic Weekend Getaway in the Blue Mountains, the Hunter Valley, the sylvan South Coast!

But he said he'd make dinner at his place. "You can help me paint," he suggested, and my heart slumped like a sandbag.

"I'm kidding," he said into my silence.

16.

On Friday afternoon, I got Jennie's Deluxe Facial Special, including eyebrow shaping and eyelash tinting.

Beauty might be truth but I was not a Grecian urn; I was a woman and I wanted to feel pretty.

When I closed my eyes, Jennie was a shadow moving around me, chewing gum as quietly as she could. "There's a lot of congestion around your forehead here," she said.

"You mean in my celestial zone?" I asked. "That's also my brow chakra and my third eye."

I opened my (regular) eyes and she was shining a torch onto my face, frowning. "You need to pay attention to your T-zone."

She got to work digging out my blackheads.

17.

Later, while I was bringing banana bread to a table, quietly conscious that my face radiated with fresh new beauty, it occurred to me that my approach to self-help was flawed. I'd focused on universal guidelines, but it's also split into categories: How to Be Beautiful, Healthy, Raise Children, Get Rich, Own a Home-Without-Clutter!

Each is also split into subcategories: Beauty branches off into How to Look Youthful and How to Be Slim (beauty and age/plumpness being mutually exclusive, of course).

You could embrace How to Be Slim. That could be your life force. Enter a jungle of exercise regimes, gym memberships, boot camps, personal trainers, this-one-bizarre-tricks, fasts, fads, shortcuts, Fitbits, calorie counters, stomach staples, nutritionists, therapists, mirrors and bathroom scales, and never leave.

You might find yourself growing smaller, your face disappearing, your shoulders dwindling, your ribs emerging.

"You're so little I had trouble finding you," someone says, and you glow. For this is the essence of How to Be Slim, this delight in being elusive, not quite there.

18.

Niall's place was a Federation cottage, battered floorboards lined with nails, unhinged doors leaning up against walls. I praised the moldings and light fittings, and as I talked I saw that all the detritus, the paint tins and toolboxes, had been pushed against the walls in an effort to tidy.

He gave me a tour, then reached for his house keys and jacket, and we stepped back out again. I supposed he had changed his mind about making dinner. First we had a drink in a bar with aquamarine lighting, next we had dinner at a Mexican place.

"Can I say something?" Niall asked.

"Certainly."

He smiled. "When I first saw you—at the weekend retreat—I felt like I'd seen you before."

"Me too!"

In fact, when I saw him, I thought: *That's the kind of guy I like.*

I didn't tell Niall that. Nor did I enter into a chain of inquiry about where we might have met before. That was how my marriage began and look how it turned out. Instead, taking a divergent path, I suggested it was misfiring neurons: we saw each other, blinked, saw each other again, and our brains were confused into thinking: *I've seen you before!*

"Like with déjà vu," Niall said agreeably.

I drank sangria and the music was loud enough to talk beneath, so I became reckless. "Do you know anything about Tantric sex?" I asked.

Not much, he replied, so I told him about it. We laughed, but it turned out that talking about Tantric sex is excellent foreplay, especially when you have both been shy and cautious up to this point. By the time we got back to his place we were like those movie couples, tearing off clothes, hands all over the place, breathing heavily, tripping over paint tins and bumping into walls.

It was extremely exciting, and not remotely Tantric.

The next morning, I woke up and studied the shape of his back and shoulders in the bed.

"Do you exist?" I asked.

He turned over and studied me through sleepy eyes.

19.

The next Tuesday we had a Flight Immersion class.

Antony arrived late, pulled a bottle of Slivovitz out of his backpack, and announced that tonight he needed a real drink and he needed us to drink it with him.

We were all amenable to the idea. We sat on cushions on the floor, drank Slivovitz, split into teams and brainstormed superheroes who could fly. Superman, the Human Torch, Hawkman, Green Lantern, Storm, Iron Man: those are the ones I can remember now.

At Antony's suggestion, we divided the superheroes up into those who fly using biological skills and those who require wings or a suit.

Next, the teams had to brainstorm songs about flight. The teams were: The Kookaburras (Niall, Nicole, me) and The Velociraptors (Antony, Frangipani, Pete), and the Velociraptors smashed us. Not surprising: way cooler name.

Wilbur was effusive in his praise and suggested we lie on the floor while he played us a scratchy recording of Frank Sinatra's "Fly Me to the Moon" as a reward.

"How are things going with that guy you started dating?" Nicole asked Frangipani while the song played. "What was his name again?"

"Abel," Pete Aldridge grunted.

Frangipani sighed. "It didn't work out. The sex was terrible. So quick! I barely had time to lie back, let alone start thinking of England."

Everyone guffawed, Pete Aldridge most loudly, but Frangipani was tranquil. "Shh," she said. "Let's listen to the song."

Since our night together, Niall and I had spoken on the phone each day, conversing in a shy, hesitant way about things like a blown fuse in my café and a delivery of mismatched kitchen tiles to Niall's place. Tonight, we behaved as we ordinarily would, but the air between us was charged with zigs and zags. I kept expecting somebody to notice and say, "Hold up! I think I see a flight wave!"

Also, now, as we lay on Wilbur's floor, eyes closed, the room's laughter fading, Sinatra singing, Niall brushed his hand against mine, and I thought I might cry from the intensity.

Next, we played with a remote-control airplane. Wilbur unpacked this from a box, peeling away tape, studying instructions and inserting batteries. I imagined him going into Kmart to buy this, and I wondered if the woman in turquoise had accompanied him. Had Wilbur described us to his turquoise friend, and had he done so disparagingly (*They think they can fly! Idiots!*) or affectionately (*For my sake, they pretend to think they can fly*)?

Niall was the best in the class at flying the remote-control plane. I watched the toy soar and turn and I felt it soar and turn in my heart. (Later, I texted Niall to congratulate him on his technique and then we exchanged messages along the same theme. I hadn't meant the double entendre in my first text, but I played along as if I had. *Sexting*, it's called.)

Pete Aldridge kept crashing the plane into walls and making "Kerpow!" sound effects. Frangipani, concentrating fiercely, rotated the plane in a tiny circle at knee height.

Finally, Wilbur had us face his computer while he flicked through multiple images of people parasailing and parachuting, using jetpacks or rocket boots, hang-gliding or flying in kite suits. From this, we skipped to YouTube videos of parkour, followed by a series of short extracts from movies and TV shows about flight. The criteria seemed pretty loose: Santa Claus swooped by in his sleigh, Harry Potter and his buddies zoomed about on brooms, E.T. rode in a bicycle basket, and George Clooney stood at an airport studying the departure board.

Martial arts movies, especially the Wuxia genre, featured heavily, and the scenes from *Crouching Tiger, Hidden Dragon* convinced us *all* that we could fly. I suppose the Slivovitz helped.

I ended up taking Oscar home in a cab.

20.

Niall started coming over to our place for dinner and staying over— no more than once or twice a week, as we did not want Oscar to get muddled and think Niall was a father figure. Or, you know, get attached.

The dinner part was tricky, as I usually make a cheese omelette for myself and kid food for Oscar, but now I had to make grown-up food for Niall and pretend this was usual. Exhausting. On Niall's first visit, I set him up on the couch with a glass of wine while I put Oscar to bed.

"Will you be all right?" I asked, and he pointed to his phone and said, "I'll make some calls." We heard the murmur of his voice while I bathed Oscar, and while I sang, chatted, scratched his back and so on. It was important not to cut Oscar's bedtime ritual short. I interrupted "Twinkle, Twinkle" to mention that our friend Niall would be having a sleepover.

"Why?" Oscar asked. "Why doesn't he go to his own home?"

"Well," I said, "it's a long drive."

Oscar accepted this, not being a fan of long drives himself.

Back downstairs, Niall was asleep on the couch, so I cleaned up the kitchen, brushed my teeth, then I kissed Niall on the cheek and he opened his eyes and smiled. "Shall we go to bed?"

So that became the pattern. Once or twice, Oscar came into my room in the night when Niall was there, but I just shifted to the middle of the bed and Oscar curled up beside me. It was important that Oscar have the same space he usually had; and Niall, as a guest, and a big man, must have sufficient territory. So I turned onto my side, made myself a dart, a ledge between them.

21.

I read about kundalini, an energy that is coiled, trapped within us— like a hyperlink, I suppose. You must keep your chakras clear, ready for it. If you are *not* ready when kundalini arrives, you get a stiff neck and headache, and you hear curious sounds such as a flute playing in the mornings. However, if you *are* ready, the kundalini offers high-voltage power, infinite potential, enabling you to experience heightened awareness and increased capabilities.

It seemed to me that this must be the way you learn to fly.

I raised the issue at the following flight class, suggesting Wilbur add a session on this topic. Wilbur seemed pleased and curious, but he firmly and politely explained that the course outline was already set. We were working on sound (identifying instruments, discussing sonic booms) and touch (blindfolded, we ran our hands over velvet, corduroy, sandpaper, walked through silk curtains and sat with our bare feet in tubs of warm water).

22.

Also at Flight School, we did a Meditation during which Wilbur played recordings of birdsong. When the recording moved on to kookaburras laughing, we all rolled around laughing. Wilbur tried to incorporate this into the meditation: the contagion of laughter, the *buoyancy* of laughter—he referred to the scene in *Mary Poppins* in which laughter rose them to the ceiling—how laughter and flight are closely connected; how laughter is sideways, it's upside down, defiance, it's a lightening, a universal language. Like flight, it is a peculiar thing we can do with our bodies that serves no obvious purpose—although flight, he noted, reconsidering, would actually serve plenty of purposes, but anyway, moving on . . . We laughed right over him.

Another time at Flight School, we talked about flight in everyday discourse; hidden flight in dance, in drugs, in dreams; flights of the imagination, taking flight. "The flight/fight response," I suggested. Wilbur was delighted with me.

We analyzed the nature of flight in our dreams. In Antony's dream life, he has to crawl along the floor to fly.

"That makes no sense," grumbled Pete Aldridge, in a mood.

But Antony got down on the floor and demonstrated: a commando crawl, using his elbows. "If I dig my elbows in hard enough," he said, "eventually I start to lift off."

Pete Aldridge said, "Nonsense," and we all scolded him for disrespecting others' dreams.

The same evening, Wilbur produced a toy that projected the solar system onto the ceiling, and we tipped back our heads while he moved the laser pointer around, describing planets and stars.

He switched the projector off. "Close your eyes and dream about fireflies," he said.

23.

One evening, we did a Flight Immersion class in which we learned aircraft marshaling signals: all clear, insert chocks, pull chocks, start engines, cut engines, turn left.

Very few of these would be useful when we flew ourselves, Wilbur noted. For example, we did not have chocks. (These are wedged behind the wheels to stop the plane from moving.)

"We don't have engines either," I pointed out.

"And yet we are learning the signals." Pete Aldridge rolled his eyes. He was especially cranky that night, and made no effort to hide it.

"It's in the course outline," Wilbur said, rubbing his forehead absently. "I think this is part of . . ."

"It's Flight Immersion, Pete," Nicole said. "We're *immersing* ourselves in things to do with flight."

"Right," Wilbur agreed. "Exactly."

Sometimes people did not show up, and we missed them. Pete Aldridge missed a week because he was getting shoulder surgery, but he gave us all a month's advance notice of this. Others would fail to appear without explanation. When we lined up at the windows, staring out into the black—it was deep winter now, always dark when we arrived, but Wilbur said you could still see flight waves; could possibly even see them *better* at night ("I think," he added under his breath. "Who knows, to be honest?")—we would talk about our week, our work, our children, and wonder where the missing classmate was.

Flight classes were always tinged with suspense, particularly when somebody was absent. They were built on such a gossamer web, on a pattern of fine glass, and could snap or crack at any moment. It only needed one person to say, "Shall we wrap up now?" or to turn to Wilbur and say, "Buddy," or, "Mate, do you think we've played long enough?" and everything would dwindle or shatter.

So when Antony was absent for three weeks in a row, the tone of the class was noisy, mildly panicked.

I don't know. I might have imagined that.

24.

One of the mothers at Oscar's day care told me that she practices witchcraft.

We were having a play date at the Phillip Street park, and Oscar had chosen to bring everyone along. By "everyone" he meant several small objects, including: one piece of Lego; a broken book light; and a tiny plastic motorbike, which, on arrival at the park, he handed back to me. "I only need things that *do* things," he said.

I pointed to the Lego brick. "What does that do?"

"Shoots electrical rays."

"Okay, have fun!"

He hardly glanced at me he was so keen to start playing, running to join Amber, arms full of objects that did things. But then, as I watched, he slowed to an uncertain jog.

Beside me, Amber's mother also watched. I suppose she was watching Amber, rather than Oscar, but I always find it hard to comprehend that anyone would watch another child but mine.

"We can only stay until twelve, I'm afraid," she told me. "I have a meeting."

Rather than respecting her privacy, I asked, "What sort of meeting?"

"A meeting of my coven."

Surprising! She had always struck me as harried, this woman, and I thought a witch ought to be more serene. Also, she was blond, and Amber wore pink sparkle clips, not spiders or newts. (Also: *hee hee hee*, she said when she laughed, not *cackle, cackle, cackle*.)

I expressed interest in witchcraft, which seemed to please Amber's mother, and the next time I saw her, at day care, she gave me a book of spells. It almost made me cry, this generosity.

She said I could borrow it for up to seven days, so I stopped wanting to cry. The book took on an urgency—I only had a *week* in which to perform these spells!—so I read it that night. *Magick*, said the introduction, *helps us to appreciate the power of coincidence.* (Coincidence again! What a coincidence!)

I scoured the book for spells that help you find people who are lost, but there were only spells for love, money, healing, and to give you confidence.

With three strands of blue cord, you can knot the wind, raise the wind, and call the wind. I wondered if I should bring this to Wilbur's attention.

25.

When I read the spells for love, I thought proudly: *I don't need these. I have Niall.*

But then I paused.

Did I have Niall?

One thing I've noticed is that romantic relationships are like life.

You start life as a miraculous little thing: a baby! And you get cuter and cuter: a darling! Strangers smile as you are wheeled by in your stroller. This continues through toddler and preschool years, everybody finding you fascinating, bringing you treats and toys.

Then you grow longer and bonier, fewer people smile at the sight of you, many regard you as one of an interchangeable swarm, some purse their lips in preemptive disapproval or scold you for being your own peculiar self.

The taller you get, the better you learn to form sentences and walk without error, the more resounding the indifference with which you are observed, many failing even to register your presence in the room.

The same is true with relationships. A person meets you and is enchanted, finding you miraculous, and then, over several dates, falls in love with you, finding you cuter and cuter: a darling! Over time, however, he/she begins to accept your presence, even to purse lips in preemptive disapproval, to scold you for being your own peculiar self. Sometimes he/she fails to register your presence in a room.

With Finnegan, of course, we mostly gazed at one another in wonder. Right up until the day he slouched in the hall, taking off his boots and scowling about his affair.

With Niall, however, I found myself waiting for things to begin. We were sleeping together, chatting or texting, but in no way was he gazing, or murmuring that I was exquisite.

Instead, we grinned, looked away, reached for each other uncertainly.

Perhaps, I thought, this is just as it should be? If he never finds me miraculous, he will never take the next step to indifference, we will simply carry on with happy chatting.

I took care not to gaze at him adoringly myself. When he realigned my sliding wardrobe door, which had got unhooked from its track a year before, or helped Oscar onto his chair at dinner, or enthused about the fact that Oscar's day care had introduced Mandarin lessons—when he did these things, it was difficult to avoid.

26.

On the fourth week, Antony was back. He was very quiet. Everyone was excited to see him, and keen to know where he'd been, but he said, "Oh, well, things, you know," and pressed his forehead to the window, gazing out at the stars, the chimneys, the moonlight.

That night, Wilbur told a story about a famous pilot named Harry Hawker. One day, Harry and his navigator took off in their Sopwith airplane to fly the Atlantic.

They disappeared.

Back in London, there was sadness at the loss of Harry Hawker. The *Daily Mail* offered to provide for Hawker's daughter. King George V sent a message of condolence to Hawker's wife.

Days later, a Danish freighter signaled to the shore: *Saved Hands. Sopwith Airplane.*

Is it Hawker? was signaled in reply.

Yes.

It turned out Harry Hawker's engine had overheated; he and the navigator had ditched, landed in the ocean, and been picked up by the passing Danish freighter.

It seemed to me that Wilbur was telling us this story because Antony was back. Our missing Antony returned. A miracle!

Afterward, as we walked slowly to our cars, I said to Niall, "My brother went missing when I was sixteen."

"For how long?" he asked.

"He never came back."

Niall was distracted, looking into the window of a shop. It was cold. We both wore overcoats, and scuffed dead leaves along the ground as we walked.

"*Never?*" he said suddenly.

We had reached my car. Niall's brow creased in the darkness. "That's terrible," he said. He faced me; moonlight, streetlight, ice-cold wind. He was waiting for me to speak. Trying to figure out: What did it mean, this lost brother? It depended on a lot of things. The age gap between us, how close we'd been, steps I had taken to locate him. He was waiting for me to clarify.

"Ah, well, things, you know," I said.

PART 11

1.

I almost blinded a teacher once.

This happened a few months after Robert went missing.

I'd written a novella about a bunch of people drifting around on a life raft. The idea was that these were minor characters from an (imaginary) novel, a fat book set on a cruise ship, who'd been lost overboard, presumed drowned. By writing my novella, I'd saved them, scooped them up onto a life raft. In the twist, one of my characters, a boy, is reeled back in, towed back to the novel, saved!

"Oh, Abigail," Mrs. Nicholls, my English teacher, said, handing my novella back to me. I'd asked her to read it. "It was so much fun!"

We were in her office. I smiled modestly. I wasn't sure why she was giving the novella back: she should be binding it, readying it for publication.

"You were inspired by Stoppard, I assume?"

"Who?"

"Tom Stoppard? *Rosencrantz and Guildenstern Are Dead*? That was an influence here?"

"No," I said.

Mrs. Nicholls smiled a warm smile, a wry smile, conspiratorial, glints of her teeth in each. All the smiles meant she didn't believe me.

"That was not an influence," I clarified. "I haven't read it. They did that in Mr. Carson's class, but I was in Ms. Richardson's. We did *Summer of the Seventeenth Doll.*"

Mrs. Nicholls still had the smile, but it kept sliding away and reforming. "It's a similar idea, though, isn't it? In Stoppard's play, Rosencrantz and Guildenstern are lost characters—they've wandered out of Shakespeare's play, you see. Out of *Hamlet.*"

"I haven't even read *Hamlet!*" I pounced.

"There's this line at the end of *Hamlet,*" she continued. "This offhand line: that *Rosencrantz!* and *Guildenstern!* are dead!"

That's how she said it. The exclamation marks. They're not in the original text; I've checked.

I was going to slap her across the face, but I *stopped* myself. I restrained myself. I chose, instead, to wave my novella at her face.

Paper cut to the eye. *Corneal abrasion.* It's agony, apparently. Also, it got infected, but I blame her for not going straight to an ophthalmologist and getting antibiotics. In the end, she had to stay in a dark room for a week.

"A week!" my mother said. "Was that really necessary?"

This was at our meeting in the principal's office, when I got suspended. The principal frowned at my mother's question, and the school counselor looked sad. Mrs. Nicholls herself was affronted.

"It's true, Abigail, that you are hurting," Mrs. Nicholls said. "I get that. But you know that *others* suffer too?"

Then she mentioned her recent divorce. My mother and I became very still, communicating with each other through our stillness. Later, when we were driving home from the meeting, Mum said: "You'd better write a letter of apology."

"How will she *read* it," I said, "if she can't use her *eyes*?"

"And what with all her suffering," Mum added. "Divorce, you know. It's *hard.*"

We both laughed. You can be pretty mean from inside your own tragedy.

2.

Mrs. Nicholls had killed my novella, a cruelty far greater than a corneal abrasion.

The boy was my brother. That was the truth. I wrote that novella just after Robert got diagnosed with MS. He was floating out there, separate from life, a sick kid in a raft with a bunch of old people. Old people are *supposed* to get sick, not kids. I was going to tow Robert back, reel him back to the master plot of life. Cure him of MS, or at the very least cure the medical profession of their poppycock idea that he *had* MS at all.

So, of course, when he went missing, it was right there in my novella, the structure that I needed. I'd require a longer rope, of course, but I could still reel him in, back from wherever he was, back to his life, his story and mine.

But here comes Mrs. Nicholls, smirking and insisting that the novella wasn't mine, that the idea, the conceit, was stolen, and that Rosencrantz! and Guildenstern! were dead!

3.

Is it Hawker?
    Yes.

PART 12

1.

In Sensory Flight, we did sight and talked about the electromagnetic spectrum, and the fact that bees and dragonflies see ultraviolet light, while pit vipers, rattlesnakes, pythons see infrared. To develop our sense of color, Wilbur spread a drop cloth on the floor, opened tins of paint, and encouraged us to paint pictures on his wall.

"Are you sure?" Pete Aldridge demanded, and Niall looked quizzically from the paint tins to Wilbur and back again.

Wilbur nodded.

However: "I'm beginning to regret this," he said reflectively, looking at the splatters on his furniture, the garish mess on his wall, once we were done.

Pete Aldridge offered to repaint but Wilbur said, "No, no, I'll do it." He ran his hand through his dark curls, streaking paint along his forehead. He glanced at his hand then and he chuckled, realizing, I suppose, what he'd just done.

2.

Niall and I chatted about our days, items in the news, Flight School and the people in our class. Sometimes, we asked each other questions.

I asked about Rhami, whether he kept in contact, if he missed her.

"Thirteen years is a long time," he said, shrugging. "You fall into patterns, you know? It can be good to break them."

"I think," I said, "that you're a *lot* wiser and more grown-up than I am."

"Me? You're practically an *owl*, you're so wise."

Which I found both flattering and distressing. If I had to be a bird, maybe a flamingo?

Niall asked whether I'd dated at all, since my marriage broke up.

"Too busy," I said. "I'd have *liked* to meet somebody, but the baby, the café."

I'd have liked to meet somebody. I had a curious urge to be with somebody big. Someone big enough for the mountains of sadness, mountains of happiness, the strangeness of me, the inconsistencies. When I thought back to Finnegan, I saw that all along he'd been small. He'd seemed plenty big, but he was just a skinny kid, playing make-believe.

I wanted a man who would tell me his darkest secrets, break down and cry while I held him. I wanted a man who would do the same for me.

Niall asked about what it was like coming back to Sydney after the marriage broke up.

"That must have been hell," he said.

"The rental market was hell," I said. "I saw about fifteen places before I found this one."

At every open house, there were crowds of couples, beckoning each other: "Come see this bathroom," or "Not much storage space."

I could not bear light or noise. Everything about me was too bruised.

"And did you have people to talk to," Niall asked next, "when you got back?"

"Oh yeah," I said. "Some."

*

Some friends were great. Shocked, sad, angry with Finnegan.

Others were trickier. "Sounds like you dodged a bullet there," one friend said, so that I stared at her, the gunshot wound a ragged hole—but she meant not having a child with Finnegan.

Another friend was happy because she had never liked Finnegan. "I couldn't say it before, but I always hated him! Pretentious prat!" and I was dismal, protective of my lovely Finnegan, another bullet shooting through five years of my life.

A third was philosophical: "I guess Tia was his soul mate after all, and that's something. He's with his soul mate?"

Her, I wanted to shoot myself. I only smiled, noncommittal.

Natalia was bright-eyed, cautious, walking the fine line between support—how could Tia have done this? She, Natalia, hadn't known a thing! She's thunderstruck!—and loyalty to her sister. I tried to be adult, objective, to separate Natalia from Tia, but when I saw her approach, I saw contained within her all the knowledge she must now have about Finnegan and Tia, and I wanted to take her by the shoulders and shake her, shouting: "END THINGS WITH YOUR SISTER! NEVER SPEAK TO HER AGAIN!"

Also, when I explained the pregnancy, there was so much in her expression, relief and judgment, conclusions drawn: you can't have cared that much for Finn, you cheated too, it's canceled out. She folded this away at once: "Of course! You were heartbroken! You didn't know what you were doing!" But there it was, her sister excused.

Eventually, I couldn't stand to be in the same room as Natalia; there was too much of a disconnection between the words in my head and our actual dialogue. Plus, her face, a simulacrum of Tia's, sent scalding water running down my spine.

I wanted to tell my friends that Finn had called me needy. I wanted them to protest, to recoil in shock as I had. I never did. They would wonder to themselves, Is it true? Was she needy? Even as they denied it, a small part of their mind would clunk into place with this new truth: Huh, she was needy. So that explains it.

*

"And your marriage was good, you thought?"

"Yeah. I guess, well, yeah."

Because, listen, I don't think I was needy.

I paid my own way. Never clamored for attention. Never pouted: "I need a massage." (That is not to say I didn't appreciate massages.) I was excited to be in Montreal. I could be cranky, tired, disconsolate. I could be weary, hopeless, and fatigued. I could sit on the window ledge, feel sorry for myself, I could look for my lost brother, and not look. I could be uneasy. I could become addicted to roast vegetables: butternut pumpkin, tomatoes, eggplant, onion, garlic with olive oil and capsicum, blackened at the edges. I could watch a horror movie again for the first time in years. I could be a good sport, easygoing, I could be happy beyond reason.

But I don't think I was needy.

Once, when a man in my café said to his friend, "It's always fifty-fifty, the fault, when a relationship breaks up," my rage snapped open like a dragon's mouth.

"So, it was just a straight-out shock, your husband telling you about this other woman?"

"Yeah. Because it was good. We had a good marriage, I thought."

I spent five years with Finn, but not with Finn.

"You think you know a guy," people said, shaking their heads.

Also: "He wasn't who you thought he was, was he?"

He was, though. He was exactly who I thought he was, just a whole lot more.

I thought a lot, when I got back, about the men who did not exist, the missing people in my life, and when the baby first started shifting about, the fluttering, like light rain drumming, here I was creating another absence. My child had a missing father.

I tried not to be too melodramatic about this. I could go back to that nightclub. Once the child was born, I could walk the streets of Montreal. Put notices up: DID YOU HAVE A ONE-NIGHT STAND WITH ME? DOES THIS CHILD RESEMBLE YOU?

I was pretty good at looking, if not, so far, at finding.

"Well, you're amazing, to get through all that. These things that happened to you."

But, in fact, my brother, my husband, my baby—it's my fault. It has always been my fault.

3.

We practiced techniques for taking off and landing. For the latter, we jumped from the couches to the floor and flung out our arms like gymnasts.

Pete Aldridge refused to take part in the landing exercises, on account of his recovering shoulder. We all worried about what would happen to him when he flew. How would he get down from the sky?

"You'll just have to stay up there forever," we said, clambering back onto the couch so we could jump again.

Eventually, somebody in the apartment below pounded on their ceiling. With a broom, we thought. Nicole got down on her knees, cupped her hands around her mouth and shouted to the floorboards, "We need to learn to *land*."

4.

One night, I dreamed that Niall gave me a plate of scented soap. I was so grateful! Such a sweet array of shell shapes, each a fizzy sherbet color: lemon, lime, pistachio, apricot. However, before I got to eat any of it (this was a dream), a young man approached, explained that he was Niall's personal assistant, and took my plate of scented soap away.

I woke up knowing that Niall had lost interest.

I sent him a text: *Do you have a personal assistant?*

I wish, he replied.

Good, I texted back.

I drafted a long follow-up explaining about the dream, but decided this would be needy, or might prompt him to confront his lack of interest—he might not yet have noticed it—and deleted it.

5.

I was puzzling out the concept of *love*. How did you pin it down?

I started watching sitcoms and movies, and reading romance novels, in search of guidance. I read both male and female authors so I could get a broad spectrum. Of course, if women write about love, it's *chick lit* or, at most, *domestic drama*. Novels about love by men, on the other hand, are just plain novels, or possibly masterpieces. This is because their love takes place in the course of road trips, drug-addled, or while cheating on their wives during savage existential crises.

Anyway, none of the films or books were helpful. The characters just got on with things. In the literary novels, they always ended up alone, presumably because romantic love is a cheap/female concept. Also, in the books by men, the relationships were *deeply dysfunctional*.

6.

"Listen," Wilbur said, leaning forward. "Some people are *super-tasters*. This means their sense of taste is vastly superior. Super-tasters, or hyper-tasters, recognize the bitterness of phenylthiocarbamide, whereas most of us would find it tasteless."

"We already did taste," Frangipani informed him.

Wilbur ignored her. "With every sense," he said, "there are extremes. Variations. Synesthetes merge senses, tasting sounds, seeing the colors of numbers. Children and dogs hear sounds at a higher pitch; seals com-municate by infrasound, which is lower than the human ear can hear."

"So do volcanoes," Antony said.

"What?"

"Communicate by infrasound."

"I mean," Wilbur said, arching an eyebrow in Antony's direction, "the boundaries around senses are not clear, bold lines. Your senses can be stretched just as your body can be changed, molded, improved. Records are consistently broken in swimming, running, high jump. We move faster, lift heavier objects, leap farther. Do you see what I'm saying?"

We were all thoughtful, seeing or not seeing. I don't know. I was lost in thought about love and where its borders are.

7.

In the bath, Oscar told me the Mandarin words for *red* and *white*. They sounded cool to me: his accent struck me as exceptional. Of course, I had no basis for this assessment.

"What about *hello*?" I asked. "And *goodbye*?"

But he couldn't remember those.

"Can't remember," he said, and I realized that somebody had taught him to say *remember*, rather than *me-member*, or that he'd figured it out himself. Either way, I felt sad.

8.

Plato's *Symposium* is a discussion of love but I found it most compelling on cures for hiccups.

Socrates once came upon a group of people who were discussing love.

"Right," said Socrates at once. "Tell me what you've been saying to your lover and I'll decide if it's appropriate."

"Socrates strikes me as insufferable," I told Oscar, who agreed with a quick, sharp nod.

"Whereas you, I love *so, so* much," I continued.

"Yes, and I love my birthday," he said. "I love turning five." So we enjoyed musing on what he might get for his birthday: a pirate sword, a pirate knife, a pirate ship. After that we discussed his imaginary friend, Jessie, and her birthday party.

"What will I go as?" he wondered, before answering his own question: "As Santa Claus."

"Makes sense. What about me?"

"What are those things on reindeers' heads?" he asked.

"Antlers?"

"Yes, you can go as antlers."

9.

At Flight School, we discussed electrical wires and how to avoid them, the wind and how to use it, the dangers of frostbite and of flying too high.

Wilbur told stories about the effect of oxygen deprivation on pilots.

Early on in balloon flight, two men took a journey: they rose so high, so fast, that both men collapsed from lack of oxygen. One regained consciousness but his hands were so frostbitten he could not release the gas valve line. Eventually, he did so with his teeth. They landed safely.

"Before you fall unconscious," Wilbur said, "your mood changes. Some people get angry, some laugh. Some become giddy, like they're drunk."

"Maybe that's what was up with your parents," Pete Aldridge suggested. "Too much flying too high."

Everyone stared, and Wilbur blinked.

"I'm kidding, of course," Pete said, annoyed.

Antony leaned back and spun Wilbur's CD stand. "What were they like, Wilbur?" he asked. "Your parents?"

"They *were* funny," Wilbur said. "Hilarious. But they never seemed unstable to me. I mean, small things. Dad was terrible on the trumpet but he played every day, and Mum hummed along like she thought he was a genius. Mum was obsessive about her garden. New neighbors moved in once, and lined the border between their properties with plants in pots. Mum threw them away. One at a time, working under moonlight. They were rubbish, she said; weeds really. And purple pots! She never wanted purple in her garden."

We all laughed.

"How did your parents die?" Frangipani asked. "If I may ask?"

"My mother got lymphoma," Wilbur said, speaking smoothly, though his hands were fists. "It moved very fast. Dad had a stroke a few days after we lost Mum. The shock, I guess." He smiled around at us in a desperate, determined way. "Mum worked in her garden right up until the last week. Dad sat on the veranda playing his trumpet for her."

10.

At another class, Wilbur showed us DVDs of pole dancers and bal-
lerinas, freezing the image at certain interesting moments. "Prac-
tise these positions," he said vaguely. "You'll need them in the sky."

"I don't know if I can *do* that," Antony said, and Wilbur scratched
the side of his nose, pretending not to hear.

However, it turned out that Frangipani had studied ballet as a child
and she demonstrated positions: *glissade, split leap, tour jeté, arabesque.*
Her instructions were delivered stridently and we concentrated, springing up and kicking out our legs.

Nicole kicked so vigorously that a postcard fell from the TV stand.
I caught the words, *W, you know that I'm crazy about you, but*—before
Wilbur scooped it up and placed it face down on the table. It was one of
those free postcards, advertising a local theatrical production.

11.

Elsewhere, Socrates suggests that we *not* praise the one whose heart
we wish to win, because it will go to their head, making them harder
to catch.

That's a fair point. Some days Finnegan used to lavish praise on
me—I was breathtaking, sexy as hell!—and I would think: Really? Am
I? In that case, should I not be trying for Matt Damon?

The thing to do, Socrates said, is to let your lover see that they are
nobody.

12.

In one class, we talked about why birds can fly—hinged wings, hollow bones, light feathers, efficient lungs—and how they navigate take-off and landing. Wilbur told the story of a French zoologist who concluded, after many years of study, that the flight of bumblebees made no sense.

"It's the speed of their wing beats," Pete Aldridge asserted, shaking his head at numbskull French zoologists. He added that midges beat their wings a thousand times a second.

"But how do they do that?" Niall asked.

"Their muscles are like a machine."

Wilbur allowed Pete Aldridge to carry on.

"Butterflies can only fly when they're warm," Pete told us. "On cold days they must lie in the sun before they fly."

"Yeah, I can't play the piano when my fingers are cold either," I said.

"And playing the piano is a form of flight," Antony said, nodding. I thought he was joking but his eyes caught mine, serious.

"Do you play?" Wilbur asked me.

"Used to."

Pete went on to tell a lyrical tale about the flight of termite couples, setting out to start a new colony.

"They can only fly in very specific conditions," Pete said. "There has to be moisture in the air or they dry out, but if it rains, they drown. You know that suspenseful weather, just before a storm? That's the idea."

"It's a sort of love story," Nicole said, "the courageous termite lovers," and I focused again, having drifted. What could I learn from the love stories of termites?

It was too late. We were back to birds: Antony was inquiring whether flightless birds—the ostrich, emu, cassowary—might benefit from Wilbur's Flight School?

Wilbur smiled mildly as we hooted, a teacher with a rowdy class.

For the next two weeks, he sent us text messages canceling the class. I finally added his number to my contacts, naming him: *Wilbur: Flight instructor.*

13.

Oscar's fifth birthday party took place at Wizzy World. We invited his five best friends from day care.

On his actual birthday, I gave him a *Ben 10* bike with training wheels. It stood in the living room, draped in red tissue paper. I made a cake and invited Niall over.

"Why is *your* friend here on my birthday?" Oscar asked, reasonably enough.

"He's your friend too," I said.

"No, he's not."

But Niall gave him a styrofoam rocket that flew into the air when you stomped on a rubber base, so ultimately we were both forgiven.

14.

Researching love, I found a book called *He's Just Not That into You.* This advises women to stop imagining a man is not calling her because he is busy. No. It's because he doesn't fancy you.

Initially, I was most bothered by the word *just*. It's like *pop, jump, toss*, undercuts truth, diminishes immensity, contains a shrug, both affected and earnest. Next, I disliked the universal "guy" permeating the text: *This is how we think. We're simple. We like sex.* (Setting aside the ways men change as they age, accumulate tragedies, read more, think more—setting aside cultural differences, varieties in intellect—maybe other men are *different* to you and your buddies?) After this, I loathed the suggestion that women have a use-by date and the stories of men mistreating women but being excused as simply *not into* them.

Also, listen, when women comfort friends, offering excuses for the lover who hasn't called, it's just their way of saying: *Of course he's into you. How could anybody not be?*

A truth more profound than the lover's loss of interest.

As Socrates says, I would rather have a good friend than the best cock or quail in the world.

15.

At Primrose Park, there is a bike track where children do circuits on scooters and trikes.

One Sunday afternoon, Oscar rode his new *Ben 10* bike-with-training-wheels around and around, calling, "Mummy? Mummy?" whenever the bike slowed, as it did each time it hit the shallow slope.

"Turn the pedals," I called. "Turn the pedals harder!"

Other children rode by, staring at him.

I had a picnic blanket, a container of freshly baked muffins, mandarins, and even a thermos of tea. The sky was high blue, the sun warm, shadows crisp around the trees. Other families sat on blankets, helped children ride, kicked balls across the grass. A tall man jogged by on the path, caught a runaway ball with the side of his sneaker, and sent it back to a father and child.

"Cheers," called the father.

The tall man nodded, slowed, gazed across the park, and turned into Wilbur. I shielded my eyes to stare. It *was* Wilbur, his flying curls, staring back at me. Now what? I thought. Do we pretend not to see each other?

But Wilbur was striding toward me, grinning. "*Hello*, Abi!" he said.

"Wilbur!" I said. "What are you doing in *my* neighborhood?"

He sat down on my rug. Quite suddenly, he stood again. "Is this okay? Can I join you?"

"Sure, but seriously, what are you *doing* here? You belong on the *other* side of the bridge." I was only joking, but my voice had a mild intensity.

Wilbur sat again and told me that his girlfriend lived in Neutral Bay. "Which one's Oscar?" he asked, so I didn't get a chance to inquire about the girlfriend. I might have asked whether she dressed in turquoise and how he, a Newtown guy, had got himself a Neutral Bay girlfriend. Also, I had a confusing sense that I should object to this girlfriend: the northern side belonged to me.

I pointed out Oscar. "Red shirt, *Ben 10* bike."

Wilbur nodded and we both watched Oscar's slow cycling. Around and around.

"He's good," Wilbur said.

"No," I said. "He's not. See that? He can't get up the hill."

"He's hopeless," Wilbur conceded. "It's not even a hill."

"Cute, though," I said.

"Cutest kid I ever saw."

I offered Wilbur a muffin to reward him for that comment. As he accepted this, he looked me in the eye. "It's very kind of you," he said, "to come to Flight School."

"Nah." I shrugged. "I like it."

Wilbur shook his head, but he'd just taken a bite of the muffin and now he studied it, turning it around to catch the light, as if it were a Grecian urn. "This is fantastic," he said eventually. "But seriously, I wake in the night and ask myself what I'm doing. It's not like my parents' instructions were legally binding. I just thought I needed to do it. Because it's what they wanted. And for me, I guess. You know, I actually googled, *What was I thinking?* when I got home from that weekend retreat?"

"And what did Google say?"

"Well, its answers weren't on point. You people are so generous, giving up your Tuesday nights. What's it doing to your minds? The way we keep pretending?"

"I think we'll be all right," I said. "Life is full of disjunctions."

He ate the muffin a while, considering this. "See," he said eventually, "I used to think my parents were writing *The Guidebook* just for me, like a private joke between us. Intensive parenting." He turned back to the bike track, brushing the crumbs away. "That was easily the best muffin I ever ate. Where's Oscar now?" He leaned right, trying to see around a cluster of kids.

I pointed. "Behind the girl in the pink helmet."

More families had arrived and there were crowds of wheels on the track, traffic jams at intersections.

"Peak hour on the bike path," Wilbur observed.

"So when you found out your parents had been sending the book to strangers," I prompted, "I guess you felt . . ."

"Strange, angry, upset, embarrassed, confused, light-headed." He smiled. I smiled back.

"Honestly," I said, "I wish I could take credit for being generous, but I like Flight School. The other people, the night out, the food and wine, the games. Life doesn't have enough games. And it's educational! We're learning about flight! I love hearing you talk."

He was listening closely so I tried to clarify. "Sometimes you tell stories, Wilbur, and I think: *When I get home, I'll write that down.* But I lose the words, they melt, like . . ." I pointed at children blowing soap bubbles, and watched as the bubbles vanished softly.

Wilbur was quiet. "Thanks," he said.

We turned back to the track. Oscar waved at me and frowned at Wilbur, stranger on our picnic rug. Very slowly, his bike tipped sideways and he spilled with a soft thud to the path. I watched to see what he would do. He lay still on the path, a little curl.

Wilbur began to stand, but I stood faster, and ran across. Oscar held out the palms of his hands to me, just faintly grazed.

"Oh no!" I said. "Did you fall?"

At which he fell into sobs, so I reached out and let him cling to me, his helmet clunking against my chin, while other children, biking by, turned their gazes on to us.

I know you're supposed to say: *You're okay! Up you get!*

But I held on to him anyway, and a moment later he scrambled down and climbed onto his bike again.

He pedaled away, wiping his nose.

Wilbur was still standing, waiting for an update.

"That's the first time he's fallen from his bike," I explained, and we sat down.

I returned to our conversation. "It's also about *The Guidebook*," I said. "I mean, I used to laugh at it, but I also kind of loved your parents—and the book wove itself into my life."

He nodded. "Mine too."

"Like, I did a wine appreciation course at university because *The Guidebook* told me to. And I made a friend there named Natalia who later invited me to the party where I met my husband. He and I connected because we recognized each other. Guess why?"

"Why?"

"We'd both been to the same Italian cooking class. And guess why I'd signed up for that?"

"*The Guidebook*."

I nodded. "But causation is complicated. I also signed up for that wine appreciation course because a cute guy was looking at the ad. It's usually a collection of factors. Cause and effect: depends how you structure the narrative."

Wilbur's mouth quirked.

"I'm not being funny," I said.

"I know. I just like what you're saying." He shifted his gaze back to the bike track. "You never mention your husband."

"Oh, he's not around. We're not together anymore."

"Does he spend much time with Oscar?"

"Oscar's dad," I said carefully, "is also not around."

This is always a complicated conversation. People naturally conflate my ex-husband with the father of my child. But Wilbur's face did not crumple with consternation, he only nodded again.

"Sometimes," I said, changing the subject, "*The Guidebook* seemed like it was meant just for me. Directly connected to events in my life."

"Me too," Wilbur said. "If something's universal enough, eventually it'll fit."

"Like horoscopes."

"Exactly. Here comes your boy now."

Oscar was approaching, pushing his bike over bumpy grass. Wilbur stood, stepped toward him and said, "Can I help?" He lifted the bike, swinging it high, and placed it alongside the blanket. Oscar watched all this, part dubious, part impressed by the height and the mighty swing.

I introduced them.

"You were on fire on that track," Wilbur told him, and Oscar nodded, agreeing that yes, he'd been on fire. "Coolest kid there." Wilbur clicked his fingers, indicating coolness.

"I don't know how to click," Oscar confessed. "I know how to do everything except click."

"Everything?" Wilbur asked, impressed.

"Everything," Oscar agreed and then corrected himself: "Everything except how to say *hello* and *goodbye* in Mandarin."

"Easily fixed."

Wilbur taught Oscar the Mandarin for *hello* and *goodbye*, and then proclaimed: "There, now you know how to do everything."

Content, Oscar curled into my side, resting his head. The sun was going down, shadows growing.

16.

The following Tuesday night, Frangipani told us she'd been studying numerology.

Of course you have, I thought.

"I used to think I didn't need anything else," she explained, tapping her nails on the window. (We were looking for flight waves.) "Because I had *The Guidebook*."

Something fluttered in my chest.

"You know why I never went into your Happiness Café, Abigail?" she continued. "Because I thought, *I don't need that. I've got* The Guidebook!" She chuckled. "But when it turned out *The Guidebook* wasn't real, I realized I'd missed so much! So I've been trying to catch up. I've been to a course in spiritual awakening, learned how to face-read, and now I'm studying numerology."

Life! Honestly! It's just a series of rebukes from the universe for judgmental thoughts.

"But that's exactly what I've been doing!" I said. "That's *exactly* what I thought!"

We compared rapid notes on our inquiries into self-help, while the others listened with interest. Niall, I noticed, continued staring through the window, but he smiled faintly.

"And numerology?" I said. "How's that working out?"

Frangipani explained that it is important to harmonize your child's name with its date of birth.

"Too late," Nicole and I said simultaneously. We'd already named our children.

Frangipani offered to check our children's numerology so that, if necessary, we could change their names. "Here . . ." She reached for her handbag and pulled out a notepad. "I'll check *all* your numerology! Is that okay, Wilbur?"

"Perfectly all right," Wilbur said.

That was a fun night! Frangipani drew up charts, counting on her fingers, informing us of our ruling numbers, destiny numbers, the *reservoir of power* in our middle names—Oscar's middle name is Robert—and something about arrows. I remember arrows of intellect and hypersensitivity—I was pretty sure I had the arrow of confusion but Frangipani told me I did not.

Nicknames should also be considered, Frangipani said. "I mean, you're not just Abigail, are you?" she asked me. "You're also Abi."

I always think that Abi sounds like someone drunk, or with a cold, saying *happy*.

"Which must be a good thing?" I tried, but Frangipani was dismissive.

She promised she would read our faces one day too. Niall, she said, had a Fire face. Niall was delighted. He wanted to change his name to *Fire Face*. Pete Aldridge told him that Niall was just fine, as a name. But Niall said he'd never liked it. As a teenager, he'd changed it constantly: "Different movie star names," he said. "But Fire Face, I think that one could stick."

Feeling reckless on Shiraz, I admitted to Frangipani that I often forgot her name was Sasha. In my head, she was Frangipani, I said, because of the flower she wore in her hair that first weekend.

"You think my name is Frangipani!" she exclaimed. "I love frangipanis!"

We smiled at each other, and it was lucky, I thought, that she did not know that *inside* the word *frangipani* was the contempt I'd once felt for her earnestness, her competitiveness, that flouncy flower in her hair.

But then, as we carried on smiling, I thought maybe she did know, but was setting this aside, allowing frangipani to glide on its own surface, its soft petals, its summer white-and-yellow, its intoxicating fragrance.

Although, then she told me I have a Bucket face.

17.

O scar was sick with a stomach bug for a week and I missed another class.

By the following Tuesday he was well again, and I flew up the stairs to Wilbur's apartment, fizzy with desire to see everybody, and especially to confirm that Niall existed.

I had exchanged texts with him, setting out descriptions of long, scattered nights and days, vomit on sheets, quilts, carpet, mattress, toys, myself flying through the darkness of Oscar's bedroom to whisk his blankie out of the way, failing to save blankie, the washing machine and dryer running through the night. I tried to make the texts poetic.

Niall had responded with exclamation marks and sad faces, but eventually we had settled into silence. There was nothing to tell him. I was slowly introducing toast and rice, rehydrating the child, despising myself for running out of Hydralyte; I was reading picture books, watching children's TV. Sure, there was a jolt of elation when I recognized Judi Dench's voice as Miss Lilly, the Dacovian teacher in *Angelina Ballerina*, but otherwise I was violent with boredom, desperate at the sight of closed doors.

Like I said, nothing to report.

But now I was leaping two steps at a time, hands on the flaking iron railings, skidding along the corridor, my hair washed and shiny, bursting with relief at Wilbur's opening door, the freedom! the adults! the treats! soft light!

Niall was not there.

The others turned from their circle of chairs, welcomed me back, asked after Oscar.

It was a strange class. Wilbur had baked a huge chocolate cake, layered and rich, creamy with frosting. He sliced pieces that fell with quiet thuds onto plates. He offered wine, coffee, tea.

"Tonight," he said, "we will not look for flight waves."

Nicole made an *aww* sound. She likes that part. As do I.

"Tonight is too significant for windows," Wilbur continued sternly. (Nicole apologized. Wilbur accepted this with a nod.) "Remember our first night when I said we would cover four units—Meditation, Flight Immersion, Sensory Development, and Practical Flight—and then move on to Emotional Flight?"

We all nodded.

"It is time," he said, with beautiful drama. "We are ready for Emotional Flight."

I looked at the door. At the intercom buzzer.

"But Niall's not here," Frangipani complained, plucking the words from my mind. Nobody, so far, had acknowledged Niall's absence and this had added to my unease. *Does* he exist? I was thinking.

"He can catch up next week," Wilbur promised. "In some ways, Emotional Flight is a continuation of Sensory Development. To reach the sense of flight we need to move beyond the exteroceptive senses, the proprioceptive senses. Beyond thermoception, magnetoception, equilibrioception, past the interoceptive. To push beyond the Buddhist notion of *Ayatana*."

"Okay, I'm out." Nicole reached for her handbag and jacket, as if to go home. She's funny like that.

"Have I missed a class?" Frangipani wondered. "I thought I'd come every time."

Wilbur looked around at us, expression innocent.

"He's been on Wikipedia," Antony decided. He seemed more himself today, Antony; calmer, quicker. In fact, he had even arrived wearing his flat cap.

Wilbur stretched his arms above his head. "Antony's right," he said. "I thought there was more to senses than we've covered, and there is. It's a science."

"Isn't everything?" I said sagely, although I don't know. Is it?

Wilbur sighed cheerfully. "I'll get back to the course outline," he said, picking up a folder. He glanced down. "*The components of Emotional Flight are these: a sense of pleasure, of the impossible, of defiance, of play, of sideways glances and crooked thinking, a sense of the sky and wonder, a sense beyond the edge of all these senses, a sense of magic, of imagination, of your heart, your soul, your self.*"

This was an impressive speech, and Wilbur allowed his voice to swell, punching the final *self* into the air.

We gave him a round of applause.

"Thank you," he said, pleased, and looked back at his folder.

"*We ask that you call to mind,*" he read aloud, "*the stories you have heard of extraordinary feats, of people crossing impossible boundaries—Bolt flies a hundred meters in under ten seconds, Bruce Lee snatches grains of rice from the air using chopsticks, a man* . . ." there's a note here in my father's handwriting that says, *find out this guy's name*—I haven't done that, sorry. Anyway, apparently he caught a cannonball with his bare hands. I think that's probably a crock of—" Wilbur reached for his coffee, and sipped from it.

He continued reading: "*Mysteries remain unsolved: the merest skeleton of facts, a structure in which to place selective truths. Consider mind-reading, psychic powers, time travel, black holes, evolution, travel through space. The Guidebook has encouraged off-kilter thinking, laying the groundwork, but to question an absolute truth—a truth that has physics, logic, history, biology behind it—you need a highly developed sense of defiance.*"

"This absolute truth being that people cannot fly?" Pete Aldridge checked.

There was a pause as Wilbur flipped through the folder, then he looked at Pete Aldridge and nodded. "Right. Where was I?"

We glanced at each other. Occasionally Wilbur had consulted notes before, but now he was reading them verbatim, head down. I was missing his eye contact. He has dark eyes, circled in gold.

"*Can you step into the silence of the sky?*" he read. "*This is the heart of defiance. Can you dismantle all you thought you knew? You also need . . .*"

he turned the page ". . . *a belief in the sky: the essential wrongness of the ground.*"

He closed the folder. "The moment you doubt that you can fly," he said, "you cease forever to be able to do it."

There was a long silence.

"So if we're in the sky," Nicole clarified, "and we think, *Holy shit, how is this even possible! I can't be* doing *this!*—we come crashing to the ground?"

"Oh, I'm just quoting *Peter Pan*." Wilbur sighed. "I have no idea if J. M. Barrie knew how flight works. That bit, I improvised."

He tapped his fingernails on the folder, opened it again. "*What is it that stops us flying?*" he read.

"Gravity," Antony said promptly.

"Gravity, right," Wilbur agreed. "Not just Isaac Newton's gravity, but being *too* grave, too serious. Being weighed down by science, trapped by solemnity. Fear of authority—"

"Fear of falling," Nicole pointed out.

"Right. It's also about finding your center. On the island, two men sat facing one another on opposite sides of the road, and pointed to the sky."

"They were there because of *you*?" I gaped at him. Like a fish.

"I have no memory of any such men," Frangipani said. "Is that good or bad?"

"Good, I would say," Pete Aldridge reasoned.

"I paid them a lot of money to sit there," Wilbur said. "So I think it's *bad* that you've forgotten. But I'll be okay."

"They seemed familiar to me," I said. "I've got it! A defamation case I once read—a man sat by the side of the road and pointed to a banner!"

The others seemed happy for me.

Wilbur returned to his notes. "The Guidebook *pointed to the absurdity of self-help manuals, of philosophy, authority, of any universal rule. Flight defies a universal rule. To fly, you must de-ice your wings, for they are heavy with the weight of frozen thought.*"

Wilbur's eyes strayed to his phone.

"It sounds like we still have a lot to cover," Nicole mused.

"Well, no." Wilbur flicked his eyes back. "We'll do one topic. It *fuses* all of . . . what I just said."

Frangipani crunched on a chocolate curl. "What topic?" she asked, jaunty.

"Letting go."

I noticed a curious sound. A little burr.

"If you let go of authority, science, fear, preconceptions, gravity—things that weigh on you, things you cling to—the sense of flight will finally kick in."

"We'll see the flight waves?" Nicole looked longingly at the dark windows.

"Right. It's a very specific form of letting go. Letting go and holding on at the same time, I guess—finding the impossible balance. There are suggested activities." Here, Wilbur's phone *ding*ed and he surged for it, studied it, and replaced it on the table. I tried to read the message but the screen was dark.

He turned another page and read aloud: *"Students lift heavy objects, hold them in air for count of thirty, then drop. Students don heavy coats, walk around room in them for unreasonable time, then remove. Students hold hands and fall backward onto mattress."*

That strange sound again, but Wilbur was smiling. "It goes on like that," he said. "Fun. See, you can leap higher after you've been pressed down deep."

The sound was Antony crying. We all realized at once. He'd been resting his elbow on his knee, his face muffled by his fist, but now the cries broke free. He tried to shield his face with his arms.

"Can't . . . keep . . ." There were yelps between the words. "It's . . . *fun* . . . but there's . . . no . . . such . . . thing . . . as . . ."

No such thing as—

We waited.

"Fun," he sobbed.

No such thing as fun. We looked at one another grimly as Antony tore his cap from his head and tried to hide behind it. You can't hide behind a flat cap.

Yoop came to my mind: a word to describe the sounds made in convulsive sobbing. *There shouldn't be a word for that. Don't intrude on anguish with your frantic classification.*

Some leaned forward, hands out, others sat back, worried or distraught.

Abruptly, Wilbur leaped up and crouched beside Antony. He took him, like a child, into his arms. Antony's face was now buried in Wilbur's chest.

We waited. The sobbing quieted.

Eventually, Antony straightened, wiped his face with the back of his own hand, and Wilbur sat back on his haunches.

"Sorry." Antony glanced quickly around at us.

Everybody reassured him that he had nothing to be sorry for.

"It's just all the talk about letting go," he explained. He aimed for smiling and frank. "Friends have been saying that exact thing to me for months—that I have to let go, that he's holding me down."

"Who?" whispered Nicole.

"My partner. Rick. He has a problem with addiction." Antony was using a matter-of-fact voice now. "Crystal meth mostly—" (Frangipani gasped) "—and he's . . . been disappearing, days at a time, left his job, or lost it, stealing from family and friends."

"From you?" Pete Aldridge asked.

"From me. And yes, of course I have to let go, but it's *Rick*, and letting go of him is not . . ." He laughed, almost raucously. "Well, it's not a game."

"Of course it's not," Wilbur said at once. "I'm sorry, Antony."

"We all carry an invisible burden," Frangipani said.

"For some people," said Nicole, "it's the size of an elephant."

Here come the elephants, I thought.

18.

Later that night, I sent a text to Niall: *You missed a big class at Flight School!*

Then I decided that was callous, reducing Antony's breakdown to an exclamation point. I remembered that these little machines facilitated talking, in addition to texting, so I telephoned.

There was no answer. I left a message.

By the following night, there had been no reply from Niall. I worried about him, alone in his house, hammering things, messing with wires. He could have electrocuted himself; a chunk of plaster could have worked loose and knocked him out.

You okay there? I texted.

As I looked at the text I'd just sent, this appeared: *Read 10:35 pm*.

If he was lying on the floor, half strangled by a power cord, it seemed he was still capable of *reading*.

19.

Oscar said, "Do you want to know the thought I just thinked?"

"What did you just think?"

"It was eighteen o'clock and I was fast in bed, and you were in bed too, we were both fast in bed, and a fairy came and woke me up with a magical bell and took me to fairyland."

"What was fairyland like?" I wondered.

"Oh." He was dismissive. "A lot of fairies." Waving a vague hand.

20.

After three days, Niall replied: *All good. See you soon.*
I started a text in reply, and stopped. I scrolled for his name, to call him, and stopped. All the voices clamored in my head: the young men shrugging their shoulders, *He's just not that into you*, reminding me that he'd never been keen, that *I'd* asked him out the first time, that he'd never bought me flowers or told me I was a goddess; Socrates telling me to treat him like a slave.

Another week went by. Wilbur canceled Tuesday's class.

21.

Every word has consequences. *Every silence, too.* Jean-Paul Sartre said that.

I'll tell you about silence; breathing, sneering silence; the lethargy of the telephone, the way it watches you, heavy-lidded.

It follows you around the house, just behind you, a reprimand, reproof. You do this, and this, and nobody knows what you are doing, the silence accumulating around each thing. It pours in like concrete, getting heavier.

You sit in your living room and, through the window, there's the girl from next door in a white dress. Her silence is barefoot, she's carrying a bag of rubbish to the garbage bin.

There's silence when an email you've sent is unanswered, and scorn in the silence, or dismay or offense.

There's silence from the oven, the cake slowly burning; silence from the alarm clock you forgot to set.

A minute's silence, immense, then day-to-day comes jostling back in.

Silence before the key turns, or the door knocker sounds; silence in the hallway after the boots are removed.

Silence when you can't think of anything to say, panicked silences.

The silence of an early morning, and the hope in it, before sounds step in, tentative.

Come here, he said. *Come be with me in the silence.* But that was only a dream I once had, in which Robert held out his hand. Water splashed, stroking the silence, wind running its hand over the silence.

Silence from the baby's room at last, the beauty of that, stretching across the house.

It was beautiful, in splinters, Robert's silence. It meant, *No news is good news; if there was something wrong, I'd have heard.*

There is something smug about silence, or sad and pale and wistful, something *lazy* about it. Implacable, like death. But silence is the possibility of noise. Death is ear-splitting, it's shattering with absence; over time, it's quieter.

22.

Headlights flared through the window, flaring in my chest, and I understood why Emily Dickinson's poetry is so terse. It hurts too much to carry on. You keep coming up against the sharp, you need a break, a fence.

Niall's silence, like Robert's, grew from reprimand to something more like punishment, a scourging.

23.

Eventually, he called and said he was sorry for not being in touch. He'd been confused, he said, figuring things out, and didn't want to speak until everything was clear. The upshot was that he was moving to Brisbane.

His brother, Patrick, had invited him. They would go into partnership. In fact, when Patrick had visited a few months before, his purpose had been mostly persuasion.

We had a long conversation then, about the property market in Brisbane. Next we discussed his relationship with his brother, and their complementary skill sets.

Until I felt something crack in my throat—afterward I realized that might have been my throat chakra, my *Vishuddha*, splitting open to let these words loose—and I said, "Well, I'm going to miss you."

Niall was quiet. Breathing. Eventually he said, "You will?"

"Of course I will!"

"It's just, I never really thought you were into it," he said. "When I came over, you spent a long time putting Oscar to bed. And you only ever spent that one night at my place."

"But Oscar . . ."

"I know. Oscar has to come first. I was fine with you having Oscar. It's just, I felt like I wasn't a priority. And even when you were with me, I never really thought you were *there* . . . if that makes sense. And you haven't exactly been chasing me."

At this, I became former-lawyer strident: "*I* was never there? But that's exactly what I thought about you! I thought you didn't *exist*! I thought you didn't want to be chased! I mean you never said that I was . . . pretty."

Niall breathed laughter down the phone. "But you *are* pretty. I was nuts about you. I didn't think you'd want to hear that. I thought that would . . . scare you away."

My heart was tumbling high speed, ribbons of hot and cold crisscrossing my face.

"But, Niall," I said—and it was strange to use his name; I never used it —"I was crazy about *you*. I mean, when you smile . . ."

"We should have talked, I guess," he said. Then he reached into the pause to say, "I'm flying out Sunday."

"What if I chased you through the airport?" I said. "And caught up with you *just before* you handed over your boarding pass?"

He laughed. We both did. But I was actually serious. Imagining the sprint.

I made a decision. "Please change your mind," I said.

He made a sound, something desperate or pleading in it, a small laugh, or cry.

"Abigail," he said, "thirteen years is a long time."

Thirteen years? I thought. *What's he on about?*

The length of his previous relationship, I realized.

Then I saw that, the whole time we'd been dating, all the truth had been trapped in blocks of unspoken words.

He asked me to let the flight class know he would miss them. "Wish them luck with . . ." he began, but he couldn't be bothered with a joke, or maybe he couldn't come up with one.

24.

Oscar reached into his shoe, grasped the tongue and tugged on it. It came away in his hand. I startled, looking at the tongue of the shoe, wrenched out, torn out, here in the open air.

Oscar seemed unsurprised.

"Here's this thing," he said, tossing it aside.

25.

The final session of Flight School took place the following Tuesday. We peered through sunset-gold-pink windows, but Wilbur cleared his throat and we turned to look at him. He wore a threadbare gray sweater today, and he tugged at the neckline so we could see his collarbone. The skin there was sun-darkened.

"Antony telephoned me yesterday," he began, even-voiced. "He says he's very sorry and he'll miss us all, but he won't be coming anymore."

I told them that Niall was moving to Brisbane, and had also asked me to say he'd miss them.

"Oh, he's going to Brisbane!" Nicole exclaimed. "I was thinking that . . ." She paused, surprised by herself, and then carried on. "I was thinking that you and Niall might get together, Abi."

I was pleased with her. It meant Niall's interest in me had been visible, palpable, and therefore that Niall had, in some small way, existed. It also meant I could refer to our relationship.

"Well, actually," I said, "we've been seeing each other for the last few months."

Everybody seemed so delighted to hear this that I had to correct myself quickly. "But not anymore," I said. "He's moving to Brisbane."

"Oh." They drooped. "So you've broken up?"

"Was it serious?" Nicole asked.

I considered. "In a way," I decided. "This is going to sound stupid, but the first time I saw Niall, on the weekend retreat, I felt like I knew him already. And Niall said he thought that too. So, it kind of seemed like we were *meant* to be."

"And now he's gone," Frangipani murmured.

"Secret romance!" Nicole said, trying to rally the mood.

Now Pete Aldridge and Frangipani glanced at each other and Pete declared, gruffly, that he and Sasha had started seeing each other. They were about to spend six months driving around Australia in Pete's campervan. So they'd have to quit flight classes too, he said apologetically.

"Seeing each other!" Nicole and I said in unison.

Pete had signed up for the same online dating service as Frangipani, it turned out, tracked her down and sent her a kiss.

"That's how you indicate interest in someone," Frangipani clarified.

"A virtual kiss," Pete agreed, frowning to show the gravity of a virtual kiss. "I took down my profile the moment she agreed to a date."

We demanded more details and they seemed pleased by the attention at first, and then irritated, so we stopped and turned back to the windows.

It was like falling dominoes, because next thing Nicole announced that she too would not be coming anymore. She went on to explain, surprising us—although afterward I realized it made sense—that she'd been in crisis this last year. Questioning her life, her marriage, asking herself *how* she'd ended up in this house with four children, this husband with his accent and so on.

"I think a Polish accent would be great!" Frangipani chimed in. "I'd love a guy with a Polish accent!"

Pete Aldridge sighed stoically.

Nicole said she loved her husband's accent, it was just this weird thing she'd been doing where she was seeing her life through a haze and she didn't get it, none of it made sense. She had voices in her head saying things like, *Who cast the Polish dude in the husband role?* and *Why's that kid obsessed with lizards?*

She kept comparing this to the life offered to her by the fortune teller, the one with the goats.

"That's why I went on that retreat," she said, "and came to these classes. To take a side swipe at my life."

We all nodded, almost understanding.

Wilbur was smiling at her; we all were, I guess.

"Anyway, the other night," Nicole continued, "I dreamed that the ceiling of my room was swarming with insects. They kept swooping down, biting and stinging, and I was going *Ow! Ow! Ow!* Until I *screamed*: STOP IT! I must have screamed in my sleep because Marcin was sitting up beside me in bed. *Stop what?* he asked."

"In his accent," Frangipani put in.

"Yes, he was using his accent. And he said, *Stop what?* And I told him my dream and he praised me for shouting, *Stop it!* And he kissed my forehead right here"—she pointed to the center of her forehead—"and we lay down and went back to sleep. And the next day I woke up and felt like I'd come back from somewhere, like I was sinking slowly back into my life."

Nicole scratched her wrist. "I *could* have another crisis," she admitted. "I mean, he could easily do everything wrong in another situation.

But I love my husband, my children, my work, and I don't *want* to raise goats. I have no interest in them."

We all agreed vigorously that a life raising goats was not for us, and congratulated Nicole on her breakthrough.

Now they turned to me, and there I was in the fading golden light, the spotlight, everybody asking: "What about you, Abigail?"

Wilbur was perfectly still, watching me.

"I think I'll stop too," I said. "If that's okay, Wilbur?"

Wilbur's face was inscrutable, sad, soft, lovely, kind. It seemed to surge with something for a moment then relaxed.

"Of course," he said, and smiled.

And that was the end of Flight School.

PART 13

1.

Except that I ran back.

I was almost at my car when I pivoted, sprinted back and pressed the doorbell.

Wilbur opened his apartment door, looking interested.

"You missed three!" I cried.

He startled, but then raised an eyebrow. "Three?" And he stepped aside to let me in.

In the living room, music played on the stereo, the lights were dim. Armchairs still stood in their circle, but the coffee table had been cleared, except for a single glass of red.

"You missed three," I repeated.

"Yes, you said. What did I miss? You want to sit down?"

I noted that he was not the kind of person who rises up, claws out: *I did not! I did not even miss one!*

He was the kind of person who inquired politely what he'd missed.

"I don't mean *you* missed three."

"That's a relief."

"When we went to the island retreat," I explained, "someone put a note under my door that said, *You missed three.* It was never followed up."

Wilbur nodded, understanding. "Would you like a drink?"

I shook my head, impatient for an answer.

"Remember we were supposed to write reflections each year," Wilbur began, "and send them to *The Guidebook*?"

"Yes."

"Well, you missed three, Abi. You did them every year, except three. I was supposed to check how many years everyone missed, and put notes under their doors. Some people had missed most. Sasha missed none."

"Of course," I murmured and then, because I have a competitive streak, I told him that I *had* written reflections every year! Like Sasha, I'd missed *none*. But three I'd never mailed in: the first because I got distracted by my brother going missing, the second because I thought we might find him, and the third because my marriage broke up. But I sent *all* the others in. "Are you saying," I finished, suddenly mortified, "that you *have* those reflections? You've . . . *read* them?"

"No!" he said. "God, no. They're sealed in envelopes. Are you sure you don't want something to drink? Also, I made a banana treacle cake for tonight, but I never brought it out, with everything going on."

I looked at the windows. It had started to rain.

"Maybe I should wait until that stops," I decided.

Wilbur disappeared to the kitchen. I texted Dad that I was running late. He sent back a smiley face, which I found disconcerting. What was smiley-faced about me running late?

"How about Pete Aldridge and Sasha?" I said, once Wilbur was back with cake and cream, coffee in a pot, and mugs.

Wilbur nodded. "I tried to be smooth and teacherly, but I practically needed to lie down."

"Actually," I said, "Niall always thought Pete did this course so he could hit on Sasha."

"I thought Pete did the course to stop me throwing you all off a cliff."

I laughed. The cake was warm. It sent a shiver right through me.

"But why the notes under the door anyway?" I asked. "Was it meant as a reprimand?"

"It was going to come up in a class on letting go," Wilbur explained.

He tilted his wineglass this way and that, and replaced it on the table. "We were going to burn all the reflections we'd written. *Letting go* of our misconceptions and troubled times, see."

A crumb of cake jammed in my throat. Wilbur offered me water.

He was smiling, but it occurred to me that there was nothing left to say. "I might see you around my neighborhood," I suggested, "when you're visiting your girlfriend."

"Oh." Wilbur shook his head. "We broke up. Recently."

He told me about the turquoise girlfriend. Her name was Danika, which made my lip curl. (But I was being unfair to Danika, based on the color of her jacket, and uncurled it.) He'd been seeing her for the last couple of years, he said, and it had been magic at first, but then his parents had died and things with Danika began to unravel.

"She was wonderful about my parents," he said, "but when I found the material about *The Guidebook*, well . . ."

"She didn't think you should run the course?"

"She understood why it was important to me, but she was strongly opposed to me doing it."

"So she *didn't* understand."

"No, she did. She thought my wanting to do it was an expression of my grief and bewilderment."

"What's wrong with expressing your grief and bewilderment?"

"I wanted to follow their instructions step by step, untangling it as I went along. But Danika said that was the wrong way to grieve. She said I should acknowledge that my parents must have been unhinged, confront what that meant for me, and *then* let go of it."

At this point I curled my lip at Danika with abandon. "Who is she to be telling you the *right way to grieve*! You can grieve however you like, Wilbur! There's no *right* way!"

I surprised myself then, by telling him about my own complicated relationship with grief: how I'd never been allowed to grieve properly for the people I'd lost. First, my brother went missing, but I couldn't grieve for him because he might be coming back.

"I thought his disappearance was connected with *The Guidebook*," I admitted, "since he vanished the same year *The Guidebook* started arriving. That's the real reason I went on the retreat, and even why I started coming here—I thought the *truth* might mean the truth about Robert. About why he went, and where, and how he died . . . I know he's dead." I paused.

"Oh, Abigail," Wilbur said quietly.

"And when my marriage broke up, I'd lost the love of my life. If he'd *died*, people would have been coming around, sharing memories and bringing casseroles, but he'd had an affair, so I wasn't allowed to be fond and misty about him. If I was, I wasn't *confronting* the truth. And I wasn't allowed to be angry. That was being *bitter*. And I wasn't allowed to miss him, because I'd *never actually had him*, and . . ."

I might have carried on, but Wilbur was listening with such compassion on his face that I almost burst into tears.

"Now I'm denying your right to grieve," I told him, ashamed, "by going on about myself. My point is, you should grieve the way you want."

"Thank you." He smiled warmly. "But to be fair to Danika, she was only trying to think of what was best for me."

"Oh, *Danika*," I said, exasperated.

Wilbur tipped back his wineglass, hiding his face, so I couldn't see if he was annoyed or if that was a glint in his eye.

"So," he continued, "I had to cancel classes sometimes because Danika kept arranging things for Tuesday nights, getting tickets to shows. She sent texts during our classes, trying to distract me. In the end, she gave me an ultimatum: her or the class. And I . . . chose the class."

"But now the class is over!"

Wilbur smiled. "It was the right choice for Danika and me."

There was a rain-falling, music-playing quiet.

"The funniest thing," Wilbur said eventually. I was looking at the windows, and thought he must be eating cake. I assumed he would take up the sentence again in his own time.

But the quiet had returned.

"The funniest thing?" I prompted, turning back, and then I saw that he was going to cry. He was trying to get hold of his facial muscles to prevent this.

"Sorry," he said. "Just, the funniest thing." And there it was again: the silence.

I pushed my chair closer, ready to—could you hug your flight instructor?

"Can I tell you something?" he tried, coming at it fresh. "I know this was a dream or false memory, but the funniest thing is, I once saw my parents fly."

He had taken control of his tears now. He looked at me steadily.

"You did?" I faltered.

"I was small, maybe four or five, and I woke in the night and looked outside. There was the streetlight and the letter box, a car parked beside it. The eucalyptus tree with branches that opened around an electrical wire. And just above this wire were my parents. Holding hands. Hovering in the air."

I laughed. He did too.

"It was a dream or my imagination," he said. "Maybe I overheard my parents talking about flying and so I constructed the image? Or it was two images, superimposed—my parents were probably out the front holding hands, and my four-year-old mind positioned them in the sky." He looked at me carefully. "I know that my parents never hovered above electrical wires. I never mentioned this in class because, well, Pete Aldridge would have pounded me—but I also think a part of me wanted the memory to be true."

I studied his smile and I saw that two unstable people had built a gossamer house and left it to their son, who had got to work plastering the walls with his own loss. These classes had been built on bewilderment: our own, Wilbur's parents, Wilbur's.

"Because otherwise," Wilbur continued, "I had to admit that they were insane."

At this point, he began to cry properly, and I stood up and put my arms around him. I could feel the bones in his shoulders, the scratchiness of his chin against my chest.

He stopped fast and apologized.

"No," I said. "Never apologize for crying. I feel honored that you cried."

He looked a bit grim and uncertain about that.

"I figured something out," I said, and Wilbur wiped his eyes, surreptitiously almost. Now you couldn't tell he'd been crying at all.

"I don't believe your parents were insane," I pronounced. "I believe they were writing a self-help book. Flight really *was* a metaphor. Think about it. We had to—to follow the path into flight, to *lose ourselves* in the fantasy. That final class about *letting go*, wasn't that the point? Your parents were offering their own unique route to the . . . flight of the human spirit?"

Wilbur raised an eyebrow. I could tell he was unconvinced, but tentatively pleased with my theory.

"Seriously," I said. "I think that's exactly it!"

The quiet now had a deeper quality, with occasional drips in it, and I looked at the windows.

"Has the rain stopped?"

Wilbur peered out, like somebody looking for flight waves.

I picked up my handbag. I was preparing a new speech—one in which I thanked him, not only for the cake and coffee, but for *all* the Tuesdays, because they *had* been something special, and he must never listen to Danika, he must—

"But you probably *had* seen him before!" Wilbur said suddenly.

I blinked.

"Niall! When you met, you felt like you'd seen each other before. You probably *had*, when you were teenagers."

"What?"

"Do you know how my parents got all your names and addresses?

Through me. They wanted teenagers, but strangers, not my friends. So they enrolled me in holiday courses and camps, drama and hiking, that kind of thing, with other teenagers. Then they got the enrollment details—my dad could be charming, my mother could lie beautifully. You and Niall were in one of those courses, probably the same one!"

I found this unlikely. I never did any holiday courses or camps.

"Creative writing," Wilbur said, snapping his fingers. "Workshop for Young Writers."

"I *did* do that course," I whispered. "With my brother. You were there too?"

He nodded. "We had to say our favorite foods and I said that it depended on the ocean. I thought I could impress girls by being enigmatic. Niall was in that class too, but he signed up under the name River."

"River!" I yelled. "I remember him! I *liked* him! His favorite food was Special Fried Rice!"

Wilbur sighed. "Some boys figure things out sooner than others."

But River? Why River? "Niall said he used to call himself movie star names," I recalled. "River Phoenix!"

That's why I knew Niall. He wasn't the kind of boy I liked, he *was* the boy I had liked!

A blaze of excitement abruptly dwindled. My intuition that Niall was *the guy* was not the universe, nor fate. It was prosaic, easily explained.

"Well," I said—and then one last accusation. "You also promised snow."

Wilbur took a length of red wool from the couch beside him and wound it slowly around his thumb. "A local had told me the clouds looked like snow clouds. I've hardly ever seen snow, I was excited." He shrugged. "I'm sorry I misled you."

The wool wound tightly around his thumb. We both watched it.

He'd been just as disappointed, I realized. He'd stood on the beach, facing the wind, eyes closed, wanting snow.

Now he let the red wool slip from his thumb, and smiled. I looked around his apartment.

The Guidebook was over. Flight class was over. This was the last time I would see Wilbur, and I knew almost nothing about him. Despite spending a year of Tuesday evenings in his apartment, I didn't even know what his day job was.

I considered asking him now, but then my eyes ran over the bank of windows, the prints of hang gliders, the tiny hot-air balloons, the patch of wall that Wilbur had repainted in a slightly darker shade, the circle of armchairs, and at Wilbur himself, in his jeans and T-shirt, his bare feet, his rumpled curls, and I decided it was better to keep him like that, to remember him this way, his name in my phone: *Wilbur: Flight instructor.*

"Goodbye, Wilbur," I said.

"Goodbye, Abigail."

He closed the door behind me.

PART 14

1.

Now I have to tell you about Tuesday.

I woke from a dream that spun with sorrow. Then I frowned, seeing that it hadn't been sorrow at all, in the dream, but a roll of paper towel.

It seemed to me, as I lay in bed, wondering why I'd dreamed of paper towel, that it was time to reach conclusions. I had read so much self-help! I'd googled, followed Facebook trails, collected instruction manuals! I was surely an expert now.

For example, I knew exactly what you must do when you wake up in the morning.

You wake up in the morning and you write your dreams down in a diary.

No. You wake up in the morning and drink a glass of water.

You wake up, you greet the sun. You send out a note of joy to your god or the universe.

You wake up, you go back to sleep. You need more sleep.

You wake up and you list all the things you're grateful for in life.

You wake up and, first thing, you exercise. Answer emails. See to your skin routine. Self-focus. Think about your goals.

Wake up and hang out with your kids! Let them choose their clothes for the day!

Or, like Winston Churchill, stay in bed and read the newspaper.

Wake up and ask yourself: If today were the last day of my life, would I do what I am doing today? (But then you'd never go to the dentist.)

Wake up and make the bed at once.

First thing, squeeze lemon juice into hot water.

First thing, water your plants.

First thing, consider what you're going to have for dinner. Get out the necessary pots and pans.

First thing, meditate.

First thing, drink a green juice, spinach or kale.

First thing, jump on a mini-trampoline.

There goes the day. Full of its first-things.

I pulled the quilt higher. From Oscar's room, I heard giggles, and I turned my head to look at the pillow beside me. I'm always turning sideways, looking for somebody who loves him, and loves me, ready to share a smile at the sound of his giggles.

The giggles drifted closer and here was Oscar himself, climbing onto my bed with Bumblebee. My mother keeps sending him Transformers.

"Why are Decepticons bad?" he asked, his opening gambit for the day.

"Well," I said. "Do you mean, how have they acquired that reputation? Or why have they become bad: was it intrinsic, biological, or was it their upbringing? Or do you mean, to what end—what do the Decepticons hope to achieve by their misdeeds?"

Oscar looked at me with disapproval. He twisted Bumblebee in various directions and told me he'd dreamed a monster was chasing him down a street. Him and his friend Lachlan, from day care.

"You were there," he added, jutting his chin in my direction. "But you just walked away."

Often, when he tells me his dreams, he refers to me in the third person. Mummy is a character. "What's going on here?" Mummy often says, in a friendly-enough voice.

But in this dream it was me, abandoning him and Lachlan to a monster!

"You know I would *never* do that," I said. "I'd always protect you from monsters!"

I tried to wrap him in a fierce hug, to demonstrate my protectiveness, but he wriggled away. "Well, you didn't this time."

We came downstairs and ants had got into the honey.

It was crowded with them.

I couldn't stop staring at the honey. Dead ants poised like prehistoric insects in resin. *Add a heaped handful of ants to the honey.*

While I stared, Oscar fell off a chair.

I scooped him from the floor and he scolded me.

"You didn't catch me! Why didn't you catch me?"

"Well, I was over there," I explained.

He found this an unsatisfactory defense.

"Here," I tried. "I'll give you a hug. Hugs make everything better."

We had learned this from a cartoon on TV. Formally, we hugged.

"It didn't work," he said. "It still hurts." He pointed to his elbow. "Why didn't you catch me?" he repeated. "Why weren't you standing right here?"

At breakfast, we played with everyone.

"Let's get everyone and bring them downstairs," Oscar suggested, so we went upstairs and gathered handfuls of toys.

As usual, he got the good guys: Buzz Lightyear, an adult digital watch I'd bought for him in a pharmacy (he begged for it; it was only three dollars), a plastic spoon. I got the baddie—there was only one this morning: a small, wooden roof that belonged on a toy house. It was bright red.

I held up Roof-guy and had him say, *Ha ha! What wicked deeds shall I do today?*

This was a return to form. Prior to this, I'd been in a phase of having my baddies send invitations to the good guys to join them for peppermint tea. Oscar's good guys accepted the invitation and used the opportunity to take out my baddies. I queried the ethics of this.

Ha ha ha! cackled my baddie now, striding toward the good guys, and Oscar said, "That's not how he walks." He showed me how to hold the little roof on its side.

"Could we enter into peace negotiations?" I suggested. "Could we discuss a ceasefire?"

But the goodies stormed me back to my own compound.

"Oscar," I said, "we have to collapse the goodie/baddie distinction. We have to ask, what is it that makes this guy a baddie and all your guys goodies? Those plastic passengers from the bus, that salad server, the dinosaurs, all presumably from privileged backgrounds, technically goodies, and yet always killing my little guys. Today I only have *one* little guy, not even any friends to help him strategize. We have to question the distinction," I said.

"Yes, we do," Oscar agreed, and he killed my red-roof baddie.

He decided to bring everyone to day care, but this was a different everyone. A plush lion dressed like a mad scientist, a bath-toy shark, Woody's cowboy hat. I checked everyone, and they seemed safe enough.

We stood at the open door while he counted these toys into his day care bag and I looked at the sky, deciding how I should approach my day.

2.

How you approach your day depends on what you've been reading. If you've been reading *I'm OK—You're OK*, you go to the bus stop. The bus is late.

Your Child stamps your foot. Not fair!

Your Parent says, *Well, ain't that always the way?* Your Parent's voice is hokey.

Be an Adult! Seek out other sources of information, study the timetable, consult your watch, weigh up the factors. On the bus, a stranger laments that it never stops raining these days. Calmly disagree. Point out to the stranger that it was sunny the day before yesterday.

If you've been reading *The Celestine Prophecy*, go to the bus stop. Be still, be dreamy. Draw some energy from the universe and offer it to the roadside plants.

If Socrates is your guy, ask yourself relentless questions about the bus.

Or sit at the bus stop and be mindful. There is a breeze on your face. A blister on your heel. The sound of the approaching bus. Its gear changes. Old gum on the path.

Or don't go to the bus stop at all. Stay at home. Focus on placing wood elements by your front door.

You go nowhere. You are nothing. You don't exist. There is no bus, nor stop. Time is nothing more than intuition.

Call in sick. Take a day off. Have some me-time.

Stop on the way to the bus stop and get your hair done. It will give you such a boost! Do that every day. Nails and hair.

Stay home and cut pictures out of magazines of places you'd like to visit and luxury automobiles you'd like to own. Glue these to a large piece of cardboard.

Miss the bus. Deliberately miss the bus. Go to the airport instead and fly somewhere remote. Sit in the desert and think about things and stars.

Miss the bus. Go to the airport instead and fly to a third world country. Help the local villagers dig a well.

Enroll in a college course! Make an appointment with a hypnotherapist to help you give up smoking! Do some yoga! Consult a tarot reader!

Do nothing. Wait for the full moon. Walk beneath it.

3.

The café was full when I arrived. Oliver lounged on the counter, chin in his hands, face morose, while banana bread burned beside him.

"He's in one of his moods," Shreya told me gleefully. She's always sunny when Oliver is low.

The balanced universe.

Considering I'm his boss, Oliver is not remotely bothered by me.

"I'm in a funk," he confided, as I skirted around him, reaching for tongs, tossing the burnt bread, starting another slice.

"That's fine," I said. "There's no need to fear unhappiness."

"What are you talking about?"

"Don't fear unhappiness. I read it somewhere."

"That sort of talk," Oliver said, rallying enough to push me away from the kitchen space, "is going to put us out of business."

"I think it might be the new zeitgeist," I said.

"It's ridiculous. Of course you should fear unhappiness. It hurts."

I told him I was going to figure everything out today.

"Everything?"

"I'm reaching my conclusions."

Oliver said that was good news. It was! I set my mind the task of sorting out the chaos of self-help, while I got on with more practical tasks.

Self-help is built on fear and hope, with splinters of truth to catch you.

Categories of self-help: assistance with issues (love, sex, money, career, health, beauty, death); improvement of the self (character, soul, essence); explanations of the universe (its point).

There is self-help that requires you to lie to yourself. It's not the situation but your thoughts about the situation that make you unhappy! Straighten up, smile, declare that it is what it is. Acknowledge it and let it go. My brother is gone, my husband is gone. Here, let me feel that, and release.

There is a recurring promise of limitless potential, either out there or within you: ANYTHING is possible, ANYTHING! (So why not flight?)

A sound like trolleys colliding in a supermarket turned out to be a toppled tin of cutlery on the counter. Shreya had knocked it over as she swept by.

Also: a lot of talk about the moment.

We all need to be in the moment. Everyone rushing there. It must be crowded there, in the moment.

At table six, an elderly woman entwined her hands. "It's hard," she said. "Well, it's hard. Forty years is a long time to wake up next to the same person. To look forward to chatting at night. Cinnamon toast and so on."

There is always a tone. Wise and gentle, or wise and sad, or wise and happy, or shazam! Or fierce. A lot have a shrug to them: Here it is. Take it or leave it. Or sensible as Mary Poppins, spit-spot, clap-clip, or the ancient art of men telling women what to do.

At table five, a toddler turned page after page of our bumper coloring book, swiping each with a single stroke of green. Wasteful. Her mother played with packets of sugar.

Popular self-help teaches you to ask for help, accept help, set boundaries, say no.

So you ask for help and the person you ask politely refuses. Because he or she has learned to set boundaries and say no.

Two women, both thirtyish, at table eight.

"The piano is half a tone out. It's by a hot window. It can never be properly in tune."

"That's it, isn't it? We expect the four classic elements of balance, restraint, form, and clarity." Their words fell beautifully, like stars.

If you're sad it could be that you have unresolved abandonment issues, or it could be an imbalance in chemistry, or not enough sunshine.

Or a reaction to the chemicals in food, or your kundalini energy is awakening too soon—before your nadis are pure enough—or blockages in your chakras, tears in your aura, mistakes from your past life.

It could be that your blood sugar levels are awry and you need a banana.

It could be that you're tired, or you're a woman at a particular point in the cycle. It could be the darkness of the clouds, the colors or absence of color, the placement of your couch. It could be you are lonely, or not meeting your full potential.

It could be that you're a member of a minority and have suffered centuries of oppression, a lifetime of cruel slights. Or your sex life might not be up to scratch. Or it could be that you felt insufficiently loved by a parent, have unresolved anger toward an ex, have consumed too much alcohol. You may have brought this sadness on yourself by sending inappropriate messages to the universe—inadvertently, you've requested sadness!—or you need exercise, a cup of tea, or the social order is awry, an inflammation of your brain, an infection, a virus, pollution.

There could be residues of sadness caught up in your joints, your veins, your knuckles, from times when you had reason to be sad.

You could be sad because you've inadvertently misfiled your sadness, labeling it "self" rather than "memory," so that memory becomes the essence of you.

Or your sadness has been passed down in your DNA, from your ancestors, accumulated over generations. Or there is leftover sadness imprinted in the air, and you've gone and walked through it, got yourself enmeshed in it, strands of the past now wending through your heart.

We must take care where we walk. There should be signposts.

A teenage boy in a school uniform ordered a banana smoothie, and his mother, checking her phone, said, "A long black, thanks . . . You know what? No. I'll have a smoothie too."

Quantum physics is a handy tool for self-help, largely because of the metaphors, and because nobody really understands it.

A group of regulars arrived and set to dragging tables and chairs around in their usual proprietorial way. I asked for the latest news—Joachim needed a root canal, and Rohinta had just been evicted. "So we *really* need happiness today, Abi!" They make this joke often, always with an edge of: *No, but seriously.*

A lot is about getting. Money, beauty, friends, love.

For a while, "how to get" was tied to elaborate instructions: a fellow should wear a hat and a tie; a fellow should work hard and buy his girl flowers.

However, we got fed up with how much a fellow had to do, and things became simpler. These days, a fellow can get someone to fall in love with him in ten minutes. (Mirror their gestures, check their reactions when another person speaks.) Or even in two. (Gaze into their eyes.)

Just ask. Snap your fingers. Ask the universe.

The teenage boy with the banana smoothie fetched a pair of our *Happiness is . . .* cards and handed one to his mother. As they left, they pinned the cards to the board. *Happiness is . . . getting my braces off,* said one. The other: *Happiness is . . . time off for banana smoothies with my boy.*

*

The universe features prominently.

Sometimes it's busy sorting things out and you just have to be ready to say: Why, yes! Thank you! *when it makes an offer. Or else:* Now I see why you did that terrible thing to me! It was so this good thing could happen! It all makes sense. Thanks, I guess, universe.

Sometimes you have to set it tasks to do on your behalf.

There is a real abundance to the universe. There are also exclamation marks!

Sentences leaping from one thing to the next! Casual twirls in logic!

Three young women sat at table two, one telling the others about a job she once had at a magazine.

"There were these advice sections and I had to write pieces on, like"—she lowered her voice so it almost disappeared—"how to give a good blow job. And I thought, *Who am I? How did my life come to this?*"

The others laughed.

There's no room left to live—you can't swing a cat in this life—instead you must deal with your teeth (brush, floss, strengthen with this product, rinse with this mouthwash), your face (cleanse, tone, moisturize, sunscreen, night cream, eye cream, Botox), your body, your mind, your spirit, your relationships (this is how you give a good blow job).

Just spend five minutes a day learning a language, doing crosswords, doing sudoku! Just spend thirty minutes a day walking, meditating, praying, swimming laps, learning a musical instrument, volunteering, having quality time with your children! Just the price of a cup of coffee. Line-dry in shade. Pop it in the freezer. Jump in a cab. Wash in warm, soapy water. Eat this, consider this, you MUST. READ. THIS.

*

"Have you sorted it all out?" Oliver asked, as I packed up to leave. He had recovered and was lively again, whereas Shreya was now sullen and scuffing.

"You bet," I replied.

4.

Of course, all I'd done was circle back to chaos. I would have to choose a belief system and immerse myself in it. Otherwise I'd always be springing from one to the next, playing on surfaces, a postmodern frolic. Crowding myself out of my own life.

If you're going to get into Tantra, for instance, you have to consult a Tantric goddess, do seminars, read *all* the books, follow *all* the instructions, including those that make you hysterical.

Melancholy, I drove along Blues Point Road.

I suspected other people were better at living than me. Did others elbow their way through fog, rising out of it some days, relief blending with terror of its return?

Of course others did.

Maybe others fear silence, and absent punctuation too, for their own complicated reasons. Maybe, by a certain age, we have all encountered some impossible loss, or at least the accumulation of small sufferings.

During sad patches, you are expected to wrench, drag, extract, syphon, tweeze some happiness out. "Black dogs" are what Winston Churchill called the sad patches, but dogs are too small. They're elephants.

Oscar seemed pleased enough to see me.

As I signed him out, he began to tell me a funny story, and I drifted, half listening, aware that it was amusing only because he signaled this by interrupting himself to laugh.

"And then Donatello fell down a pizza chute!" he finished.

I laughed along. "So funny!"

Abruptly, he looked up at me: "Why?"

I decided to focus. Mindful parenting. Be in the moment with your child. It is not enough to murmur and chuckle: one must *listen* to the plot of a *Teenage Mutant Ninja Turtles* episode that has been recited to my child by another child at day care.

"How do you say the word *bibblepop*?" he asked, as we drove home.

That was an easy one. "Bibblepop," I replied.

"No, but how do you say it?"

"Well, you just—you say it. It's just . . . *bibblepop*."

"But *how* do you say it?"

"Are you asking what it means?"

I hoped not. I had no clue.

"No! How do you say it?"

We circled this for the rest of the trip.

Conversation, when done properly, is music.

Disjunctions, miscommunications, conversations at cross purposes, pretension, artifice, vicious jibes, and, most especially, silence, all these things excoriate your soul.

At home, I considered dinner.

There were moths in the kitchen cupboards, in the pasta and the rice. Dead moths faced me, pressed flat against transparent plastic.

Meanwhile, ants crossed the kitchen sink. The smell of dead ants, the smell of dead moths, the sweet drops of Antkill that I dripped along the back of the sink. Intense excitement among the ants, a rush to these pools of deliciousness.

Remorseful, I tried to warn them: "Stay away! It's poison!"

Oscar explained that, when you jump on a trampoline in the rain, you go higher.

"You do?" I said. "I didn't know that."

"It's because the rainwater bounces you up. It acts like a rocket booster."

"I see what you mean!" I said, and then I saw why Oscar had misunderstood this phrase. *I see what you mean* is a phrase I use for: *Interesting, darling, but you're wrong.*

My child won't eat, my child refuses to bathe, my child is biting and hitting me, my child has been whining all day . . . But this pain doesn't count—just you wait until the kid learns to drive and do drugs! You think one kid is hard? Try three! You brought this on yourself—like a hangover: you haven't raised him properly, you haven't used this technique, just say no, implement consequences, easy! Plus, they'll grow out of it anyway.

As if the "real" problems don't have solutions too. Stop basing your decisions on profit margins. Stop selling guns. Stop flying your drones and your private jets. Stop stamping out your cigarettes on other people's flesh. Let the lost and broken people into your big wealthy country. Let the children into their mother's arms, stop with the shiny, plastic things. Toss these weapons into the garbage. Pop these frightened people into a warm house. It's simple. Easy. Stop complaining.

I sliced up carrot and cucumber sticks, and sat down with Oscar to read him a story about a jester. "Move the couch so we can play Jester," Oscar commanded.

"No, please . . ." Because I really did not want to play Jester, it rolled through me, actual anguish, at the idea of playing Jester.

But I rallied: "Okay, yes, we can do it." I imagined that we would dance. And juggle!

But he wanted to be a jester-knight, it turned out, and fight with jousting sticks. He gave me the pink fairy wand as my jousting stick, and he used the candy cane.

Luckily, after a few minutes, he was ready to begin the story.

I looked down at his soft hair, soft cheeks and thought I could die of this exquisiteness.

The story got off to a good start. A young prince, it seemed, wanted to be a jester.

"Have a carrot stick," I suggested, turning a page.

"No thanks. Why did the prince want to be a jester?"

"He just . . . it was his ambition."

"Why?"

"Maybe he was funny?"

"How do you know?"

"I don't know. I'm speculating."

"Why was the prince funny?"

"He just . . . some people are funny."

"Why?"

"Some people are just—well, maybe he had a finely tuned sense of the ridiculous, a defiant turn of mind, a gift for physical comedy."

"How do you know?"

Partly, it's the pointlessness. It's imaginary! A story! There is no prince, no jester, no sense of humor!

Oscar was suddenly furious. *But why?* he shrieked. *Why was the prince funny?*

This small boy raging in my arms. Anger like a paintball pelted hard against a window, the multicolored paints streaking down the glass. Deep crimsons and purples streaking down the front of my mind, I can't see for the—

I stood up.

"Let's go out for dinner!" I said.

5.

It's strange, isn't it, how people love their children?

It's a form of insanity. I was watching a mother at the table next to us in Maisy's, as she gazed adoringly at her perfectly ordinary son, who looked to be about seven.

I feel sad for the mothers of seven-year-olds. Their generic children. No longer soft and sweet like my little five-year-old.

Yet this mother seemed so keen on her child! He was relishing his Bolognese and spilling some, and she was reaching over to dab it up, smiling at him as she did.

Does biology distort a mother's vision, or *clear* her vision so she can truly see?

I mean, they're a dime a dozen, children. I took Oscar to a Hi-5 concert once, children *everywhere*, like a generous sprinkling of ants in honey, and it struck me: children are a dime a dozen!

Nevertheless, Oscar swaying in time to the music (more or less), Oscar shout-whispering song names, pointing out "Kellie" and "Kathleen" (repeatedly, knowledgeably), Oscar was all the manna, all the treasure, the *point to everything*.

And I assume other parents see their children the same way. Mystifying.

We shared the nachos. Oscar had brought everyone along—a Ping-pong ball, the digital watch again (new toys get frequent rotation), Optimus Prime, a pull-back-and-go Shrek on wheels—and everyone had Oscar's attention.

This gave me time to draw conclusions.

Men speak in absolutes, women in uncertainties, and this often strikes us as a weakness in women, but it's knowledge: a knowledge that we cannot know, not ever.

Oscar suggested that Shrek and the Ping-pong ball could be my baddies, while the watch and Optimus Prime were his goodies.

"No, no," I said, appalled, not physically capable of goodies and baddies. "Let's eat our dinner."

*

You hide behind a lamppost. You stand on a street corner: by the time we reach that lamppost, we'll be warm. You hold his hand and run through winter streets in Montreal. You are all the blog posts, comments, status updates, billboard posters, books, advice, lampposts you've ever read or seen. The swing flies through the air, and you are inside an orange, the juice and sticky pulp of it, the seeds.

Heaviness is only lightness in disguise, overdressed—

I looked across at Oscar, scooping up a corn chip, studying his toys. Clearing his throat quietly, and clearing it again. The watch lay on its face now, and the back had fallen off. Cheap trash.

But look at that beautiful face. How he picks up his water glass with both hands, his fingers curling around. Look at him studying his toys again, his little head a storm of images, of genies, lamps, Transformers, spaceships, robots, airplanes, fire at the end of a tunnel. Consider the wrench of the disconnect, the boredom, repetition, loneliness, the child not eating, the child not sleeping, the real despair, the real euphoria, both set firmly outside the real. The child is happiness inside a frame, framed happiness, but the weariness, the sweetness, his little nod—

The strangest expression crossed Oscar's face.

"What's wrong?" I said.

He stared at me. "I want to go home."

"Here," I said, suddenly needing to hold him, comfort him. "Let me pick you up." I stood, reached around the table, and he reached his hands to me. Then his arms fell to his side, and he gave a cry, such a curious cry, a dry, shrieking, furious cry. His face, now that I studied it, was white and crinkled with anger.

I gathered him up. "What's the matter?" I asked, calm and panic side by side.

I looked down at the table. The scattering of toys. The watch lying open.

"What's happened to the back of the watch?" I asked. "Did *you* take it off, Oscar? With these little fingers?" I curled his fingers open, and we both looked at his palms.

He cleared his throat, coughed, and scratched at his chest.

"Oscar," I said.

I stared at the watch lying on the table. The watch burned my face.

"Oscar," I said. "Where's the watch battery?"

He started to cry. "Why are you *mad* at me?"

I looked on the floor. I lifted the plates, the glasses, the cutlery.

"Oscar, the battery? Was the battery here? Did it fall out of the watch?"

"What battery? What battery? Stop being mad at me!"

Had the back of the watch been missing this morning? When the watch came by to kill my rooftop baddie, had the watch been naked like this? I had no idea.

"I'm not mad at you, darling. Was there a silver disc in the back of that watch?"

"What's a disc?"

"A circle. Like a flat circle."

"Why are you *mad* at me?"

"I'm not mad! It's fine! Just tell me. Do you remember seeing it? Was it here right now?"

He cried again.

I made my voice bright. "I just need to know. I'm not mad at you. I just want to know if maybe you *ate* the battery! You didn't eat it, did you? A little silver circle? Did you think to yourself: *Yum! This must be chocolate!*"

"No."

My face calmed. My heart slowed.

"I didn't think, *This must be chocolate*. I thinked, *I'll just eat this now*."

"You ate the silver circle?"

"Yes."

"When? Just now?"

"On the other day."

"Do you mean this morning, Oscar? Did you eat it this morning at breakfast? Or do you mean yesterday? Which do you mean?"

"Yes," he said. His nod.

PART 15

1.

A complete memory presented itself: a pediatric ENT surgeon named Lera with a strange and careful stride, walking beside me on an island in Bass Strait: *The button batteries. Kids swallow them. They stick them up their noses. They'll burn a kid's esophagus irreparably.*

I swooped everybody into my handbag. Everybody spilled and trailed behind me. Oscar, meanwhile, juddered in my arm, swinging with me this way and that as I negotiated chairs, tipped over a chair, left it lying, tossed a fifty-dollar note on the table, pushed open the door.

The waitress chased us up Military Road. "Your change!"

I was carrying Oscar on my hip. Striding. I ignored her.

"Your *change*! Wait!"

"That's okay!" I called back, grinning madly. "Keep it!"

Doggedly, she followed. "Excuse me! You've left way too much!"

"Mummy!" Oscar complained. People turned to stare. Me with the child in my arms. The waitress scurrying behind us.

Right away, they start burning through, those lithium batteries.

"Your change!" shouted the waitress.

There seemed nothing else to do. I stopped. She gave me the change. The traffic lights opposite the post office are inconceivably slow.

While we waited, a teenager beside me pulled the wrapping from a Magnum.

"Can I have an ice cream?" Oscar suggested.

My arm was aching from the weight of him. I swiveled him around to my front, so both my arms could share his weight.

Did the button battery *always* get lodged in the esophagus? Maybe it slid right down to his stomach? So then what? Was it floating around in there innocently? He probably didn't even eat it. I probably just made him *think* he ate it, in my panic just now.

If he swallowed it yesterday, and nothing had happened, did that mean he was okay? Or was it slowly, steadily burning through his esophagus, or his stomach, or his bowels?

I don't understand chemistry, the human body, biology, life, or anything at all.

We crossed the road. I swung him onto my right hip.

"I can walk," he said.

I clung to him more tightly.

My car was on Yeo Street. Here was my car.

Strange! It's so strange, the fine film of life. You move around inside it then the horror burns a hole in the film.

You don't believe it. You can stand at your car, searching for your car keys while the horror burns its hole. Fumble for your keys, transfixed by the burning, not believing it.

Vanished brothers, scowling husbands, and here it is again: my little boy has swallowed a lithium battery.

Or not. Or maybe not.

If we don't get to them in time, the kid will die.

Was I supposed to call an ambulance?

I buckled him into his car seat. He wanted Shrek.

"Not now," I said.

"But I need him!"

Or never talk again. Never breathe on their own again.

But if he swallowed it yesterday, or even the day before, then time has already accumulated. Time is already here with us, sluggish and irrelevant, or rushing to a point.

And I'm rummaging in my handbag for Shrek.

"Why are you smiling, Mummy?"

"Shrek is not here, darling. I think we left Shrek at Maisy's. Never mind!"

You still have to buckle your seatbelt. You still have to negotiate out of the tight car spot. Back a little, forward a little, back a little, forward a little, while your heart thrums faster than a glissando on the piano. You still have to signal. Wait for cars to pass. You have to stop at red lights. Change lanes. You have to tackle the sudden blockage in your memory: *How do I get to the Pacific Highway from here?* Drag the geography of your neighborhood into place again. Through Crows Nest. Drive through Crows Nest. The glissando smashes up and down your chest, a man's large hands, knuckles over piano keys, flaring up, flaring down, while all the time, Oscar howls: *"Go back for Shrek! Go back right now!"*

I pulled up at emergency.

What were you supposed to do with your car?

I spilled myself out. Ordinary dusk here. Two orderlies chatting. A man with a briefcase hitched high beneath his arm.

A doctor walking through sliding doors, handbag over her shoulder.

Elegant posture, a curious gait.

I stood at Oscar's open door, staring at the woman.

Oscar cried quietly for Shrek. My child might be dying in the back seat of our car, or he might be perfectly all right. Meanwhile, I was staring at a woman with short, sharp hair, dark skin, reaching out each foot as she walked, as if to test the ground ahead of her. She walked right by me, I felt the breeze of her. She followed a path, around a curve, disappearing in shadows.

It wasn't her, of course. I'd imagined her into being.

I pulled Oscar from his car seat. He was quiet now, listless after his tantrum, bored by it even, but perfectly well.

I would need my Medicare card. I would need ... triage? I would need to convey the urgency of this situation without alarming Oscar, press through administration, despite Oscar seeming perfectly fine. Maybe he *was* perfectly fine. Maybe the battery was safely encased in some kind of harmless material? Maybe it was long gone. How much was I supposed to panic?

Somebody was approaching, a man in uniform, busy, efficient, grinning at Oscar, curious, detached, but with a kindly face.

And then a different kind of horror, more like astonishment.

Because it *had* been her. Or anyway, it *could* have been her.

"She lives in Crows Nest," I said. "She could *easily* work here!"

The man smiled and tilted his head.

I was pointing at the corner. "Lera?" I called. "Lera!"

The man rocked back, but I bellowed, "LERA!"

She was there again, the woman, coming back around the corner, peering at me.

"Is it her?" I said.

The air was full of patterns now. Oscar, in my arms, looked up at me, perplexed. His hair tickled my face. The air was clustered with crystals. I couldn't see the woman's face for the patterns. I reached out to scrape these away, the cobweb tracings, icicle networks, but my hands were scooping at nothing.

She walked toward me, pushing through the muddled strands. One foot, the next, one foot, the next, her handbag swinging. Keys in her hands, I saw now.

"Abigail!" she said.

It was Lera. She remembered me.

"This is Oscar." I pivoted to present him to her. "I think he's swallowed a battery. A button battery from a watch."

She nodded once, a quick clip, and smiled at Oscar.

"When?"

"I don't know," I said. "Maybe this morning. Maybe yesterday. We got the watch a week ago. It could have been any time in the last week."

"A new watch?"

"*My* new watch," Oscar interjected, annoyed. He'd had enough of sitting in my arms. He slithered to the ground.

"How old are you, Oscar?"

"Five."

"And have you been feeling well?" she asked him. "Any trouble breathing? Or eating your dinner? Any tummy aches?"

Oscar stared at her.

"He's been a bit cranky today," I said. "But otherwise he's fine. Your tummy's okay, isn't it, Oscar?"

We both smiled down at him.

"My tummy *hurted* today," he said.

"It's probably fine," Lera told me. "It's probably gone straight through his system."

I thought she was going to send us home. I was looking inside the car, at Oscar's car seat, the mood lightening immeasurably.

"But we'll take him inside and make sure," she added, reaching for Oscar's hand and marching him toward the sliding doors.

2.

Everything was calm and brisk. There was paperwork. They took him for X-rays and blood tests. I was along for the ride, and Lera was driving, bypassing everything for us.

"The scans will probably show nothing," Lera told me. She asked me how I'd been since the weekend retreat. I remembered she'd left before the "truth" was revealed. She didn't ask me for the truth.

She was so relaxed I kept expecting her to leave. *I'll leave you in these people's capable hands*, I imagined her saying.

The scan showed a disc battery caught in Oscar's esophagus.

"Oh, right," I said, interested, when they pointed it out on the image.

Lera remained chatty, calm, but the pace picked up. She explained that she would do an endoscopy now. To get it out.

More paperwork.

I had to kiss him goodbye in the operating theater.

"Give him a kiss," Lera instructed me. "We'll keep you up to date."

Oscar himself was quiet, but pleased with the attention. He smiled shyly whenever anybody spoke to him. "Five," he answered in his small, shy voice, when people asked his age.

I stepped back out of the operating theater.

"Where's Oscar's mum? Here she is." A nurse approached me, smiling. "Here's the thing," she said.

She told me that the battery was wedged in the esophageal wall, that there was damage there, a deep ulceration, that it was bleeding.

"Uh-huh," I said.

"Here's the thing," she repeated. "You have to be super careful, taking out a battery in this situation. You want to minimize the damage. What you don't want is a hemorrhage. You don't want a heart attack."

"Hm," I agreed.

Both of us were nodding, the nurse and I, then abruptly I stopped.

"What? You don't want what?"

"Here's the thing," she said—a third time now—"with these removals of disc batteries, complications can happen days, even weeks later. Serious complications. You've got to get it right."

I was only staring now.

"Dr. Jalloh has called in a cardiovascular surgeon. Her idea is that they'll work together, to minimize—"

"Who's Dr. Jalloh?"

"You know her, don't you? Lera. Lera Jalloh."

Here a new burst of panic almost throttled me. "I don't know her *well*! I mean, is she good? Is she any good?!"

I was only assuming she was good. Based on the elegant manner in which she walked, the pleasing way in which she talked, months ago, an afternoon on an island.

"Oh, the best," the nurse said. "She's usually at Randwick—at the Sydney Children's Hospital. She was only here for a consultation today. Which is lucky, isn't it? A pediatric ENT surgeon in the house? This is the best possible care for your little boy. I can assure you of *that*."

ATTENTION, said a sign on the wall. *If your child or family have been in contact with someone who has* CHICKEN POX *in the last 3 weeks, please notify a staff member* IMMEDIATELY.

A sketch of a face covered in specks, lines shooting out of it, like a picture of the sun.

Don't you dare, I said to the face.

I didn't beg, plead, or bargain. I just threatened. The face was the universe and God. I was taking them both on.

The number three sidled at me: your brother, your husband, your child!

I trampled it with: *Don't you dare!*

If you have a cough, sneeze, or other sign of respiratory tract infection, another sign told me, *please let a staff member know*.

Do we really have to let a staff member know we have a cold?

Those ones, the life-threatening surgeries—I come out of those ones bathed in sweat.

A yellow formica table with tubular legs. A rocking horse. Pump bottles of hand sanitizer.

I telephoned my mother.

"Abigail!" she answered, proud that she understood how phones work. The person whose name appears is calling you.

I read the signs on the wall again. I was standing, having refused to sit down. The chicken pox sketch, the child's speckled face.

"Hello?" sang my mother. "Abigail? You there?"

A child complained, a trolley rolled by.

"Hello? Hello? Abi?"

A woman passed me, carrying a baby. "Hush," she crooned. "Hush now." The baby blinked, perfectly silent.

"Hello?" my mother tried again, and then she was speaking to someone else: "It's Abi. She must have dialed by mistake. She's at a party or something." She hung up.

I looked at the chairs. If I didn't sit down, it would be okay.

The clock on the wall carried on. One hour. Two.

This is silence, I thought, amid the rattling wheels, clanging beds, children crying.

This is silence.

I started a text to Niall. *Hey, I'm—*

Then I tapped back and amended it to: *Hey, how's Brisbane? Found somewhere to live? I'm—*

I deleted the text.

I scrolled through the numbers. I hit *Wilbur: Flight instructor.*

"Abigail," he stated, answering almost at once. I imagined him in his apartment, seated on one of his chairs, holding his phone ready to pick up. A calm, pleased voice. "How are you?"

"Good!" I said. "Well. Okay, I guess. Listen, I wanted to tell you the funniest thing. I'm at the hospital and guess who I just saw?"

"At the hospital? Are you okay?"

"Guess who I saw?" I repeated impatiently.

"Who did you see?"

"Lera! You remember Lera?"

"Lera," he echoed, thoughtful.

"From your island retreat!"

Wilbur breathed laughter. "I remember her. I liked her. And you just saw her?"

"Yes! She lives in Crows Nest and she's a surgeon, so it makes sense she'd work at Royal North Shore, but she doesn't! She just happened to be here! So, I wanted you to know that the whole thing wasn't madness. It wasn't a waste of everybody's time, because Lera's here!"

He laughed again. "Thank you," he said. "I appreciate that. But why are you at the hospital?"

I studied the chicken pox sign again, chewing on my nails. A sink with a soap dispenser, paper towel on a roll, press-button bin—I had dreamed about paper towel last night.

"Abigail?" Wilbur said.

Don't you dare, I thought, hanging up.

Weary at my own ferocity, I remembered, with a terrified surge, that the universe might think I *wanted* the worst, that *don't you dare* could mean: *please, do dare*.

He will be okay, I begged. *He will be fine!* Urging the universe to comprehend my message.

Lera appeared across the room. She didn't see me at first, so I had time to examine her face, and I knew then, from her forlorn mouth, the line on her brow.

I tipped backward, caught by the wall.

She moved toward me, touched my shoulder.

"He's okay," she said.

She stepped closer. Her face was bathed in sweat.

3.

He opened his eyes once, in the night, lying very still, and looked across at me. All the questions in his eyes, his fear, his deep, deep questions. He was wired up, a puppet, in a veil of tubes and wires, small boy tangled in fish net. The color of his pillowcase matched the bandaging taped across his throat, a tube snaked out of his little nose.

He closed his eyes again.

Later, I woke abruptly, fell out of my chair in a lunge to stand up, but Oscar was still sleeping, machines beeping steadily.

A man sat beside me, straight-backed.

I blinked.

It was Wilbur.

"What time is it?" I asked. Couldn't think of anything else to say.

"Just after two."

I looked at him steadily.

"I was in Cairns when you called," he said—apologized. "So I've only just got here."

The ICU moved dark and steady around us.

"But why—" I stopped. Cairns. Slowly my mind followed the coastline of New South Wales, jiggling up to Queensland, halting at Brisbane, on and on to Cairns.

"I flew back," he said. "Came straight here. Told them I was your flying instructor. Ha, no I didn't really, I said I was a friend." He smiled crookedly. "Can I get you anything? Coffee? Food?"

"But why . . ." I tried to rephrase the question.

"Your voice on the phone," he explained, fixing his eyes on Oscar.

We both stared at Oscar.

"What do they say?" he asked me.

"They'll keep monitoring him," I replied. "They'll keep doing X-rays. They'll keep him on antibiotics. There are—"

Here Wilbur nodded slowly, then spoke in his own low murmur: "He'll get better. Kids are good at getting better. Kids are—"

I guess I was half asleep. I found myself falling into my words the same way you fall into dreams. "But it's all my fault! Because we play with *everybody*! We're always playing with *everybody*!"

Wilbur watched me intently, trying to keep up, as I babbled.

I'm not a mindful parent, I wasn't *in the moment*, I hate goodies and baddies, I was deliberately *not looking* at everybody, but I *know* that watches have batteries, I know those are dangerous, I'm always letting my mind wander, and it's my fault, it's my fault—

That my brother ran away—I told Robert he wasn't *funny*! And I was needy about Robert so Finnegan left, and it all comes back to me—the starting point is *me*. I don't take steps to *stop* bad things, I never say *no*, you *cannot*, to the boys, to the men, to Samuel, to the one-night stand, to Robert, to Finnegan, to my little boy. Why didn't I say, *no*, you can't run away, you can't leave me, you can't bring home the sticks, you can't have this cheap watch, I never say *no* when I should be saying no, but I *refused* to laugh at Robert's joke and that started *everything*.

At this point, I was crying into Wilbur's chest, trying to cry softly so I wouldn't wake Oscar or disturb the quietly beeping patients, the quietly chatting nurses. I don't know how much Wilbur heard or understood.

Probably just: *It's all my fault*, the shape of that phrase garbled, muffled by his shirt.

4.

But Oscar did recover. He was transferred to the Sydney Children's Hospital where, slowly, his esophagus healed. The X-rays were clear. The tubes were removed. His voice returned, his color.

Sometimes, the tear in the fabric is sewn together.

He was in hospital for five weeks. I got used to the cluttered ward, with its sinking-heart of economy class on long-haul flights, wheeling tables of Rediwipe multipurpose cloths, stacks of styrofoam cups, posters about Children's Immunization and Not Being Abusive to Nurses.

I slept in an armchair beside Oscar, or not slept so much as drifted, all the time a strange pressure high in my chest: relief and fear, or dismay for Oscar and his confusion—the cheap, dry gauze of his breathing, the gagging sounds he made, how he cried in fury at the pain, and how crying made it hurt more, his throat breathing fire, dragon-fire, monster-fire.

The other adults in the room, their closely guarded terror, cheerful voices, the closeness of loss, its impossibility, and the sweet intensity of gratitude for these people taking care of our children, the people speaking in measured tones, moving around the hospital explaining things, studying charts, gazing at little faces, thoughts running back and forth behind their eyes as they smiled at the children.

Lera—or Dr. Jalloh—visited Oscar every day the first few weeks. A nurse told me that, ordinarily, the surgeon and her cardiothoracic colleague would do daily post op visits for the first few days, then drop back to alternate days, handing management over to the pediatric intensivist team. So Lera was giving us special treatment. She didn't look at me as she spoke to him, but she always placed one hand firmly on my shoulder, which intensified the pressure in my chest.

"Do you know," she said to Oscar one day, "there is a playroom down the corridor there?" She pointed. "When you are well, you can play there. And do you know what you'll find?"

Oscar shook his head.

"A castle! With a door! And windows! So, get well, and you can play there."

Oscar turned to me, astonished.

My parents came. I phoned them eventually. Mum and Xuang, Dad and Lynette, in a friendly circle. On their first visit, Oscar was sleeping. He opened his eyes, stared at one face at a time. There was blood on his nose. He wiped it away with his sheet. Then he turned to me and whispered, "Tell them about the castle."

Children arrived and stayed, or left after a day or two. A little girl named Dara was in the bed beside Oscar a while—she had reached into the babysitter's scalding coffee—and she woke the ward with screaming nightmares each night. Her mother apologized frantically.

Dara was replaced by a boy named Dylan, who was six and had Kawasaki disease. There was a lot of talk about Vaseline for Dylan's lips, and about the rash on his face and chest. "My lips are sore," he complained often.

Once, a boy around eight turned up across from Oscar. He was exhilarated by the hospital. He could watch TV and play computer games *all day long*, he told his sisters when they visited. His sisters asked if he would ever walk again. It *hurts* too much to walk, he explained, but that's just for the moment. The sisters seemed relieved. The father arrived with spring rolls.

"When I get home," Oscar told me one day, "I will be too sick to go into my bed. I will need to go in your bed. I am *very* unwell." His dark-circled eyes huge in his pale face, his ribs, his skinny little body.

"Yes, you are," I agreed. "But you'll get better."

And his color returned, his brightness.

5.

Wilbur visited Oscar regularly, sometimes bringing gifts: a stuffed rabbit with fur so soft Oscar and I took turns holding it against our cheeks; a book of stickers from the movie *Cars* (these ended up all over the bedhead, table, drawers). Wilbur would sit alongside Oscar and set to work playing with him, and I'd lean back and watch, relieved to see him entertained. A few times, Wilbur produced foil-wrapped meals he'd prepared for us, dessert in a separate container. He said he liked to cook, it was no trouble.

One night, Oscar was sleeping when Wilbur arrived.

He'd brought along chocolate chip cookies, which we ate with coffee, speaking softly in the dark ward. They were warm and delicious. He mentioned he'd got the recipe from a client.

"A client?" I asked. "You know, I don't actually know what you do?"

He smiled broadly, the dimple in his left cheek deepening. "Flight instructor," he said.

I smiled too. "No, but what do you *really* do?"

"Flight instructor."

My stomach fell. *Thud*, it went, hitting the floor. He really *is* mad! I have to cancel these visits! Delete him from my phone!

But he explained, gently, that he taught people to fly airplanes. He owned his own plane, and kept it at Bankstown. He also used this for charter flights, which explained why he'd been in Cairns the night I called.

"My parents got a lot wrong about airplanes," he confided. "I think they found the material in old library books. I used to worry that I'd undermine their lessons when I corrected their mistakes, and that we'd end up not being able to fly. And then I'd think: *Oh, wait*."

We both laughed. Partly I was laughing in relief that he was sane, and partly because there was a certain beautiful insanity about the fact that he really was a flight instructor.

"I grew up wanting to be a pilot," he explained. "Sometimes now I wonder if I was subliminally affected by my parents' obsession with flight—or if I'd have done it anyway. I'd also like to be a chef, and maybe that's my *real* dream? But it was a course in Japanese cooking that got me interested in cooking, and I did that course—"

"Because *The Guidebook* told you to?"

"Right."

"Causation is complex."

"Yes!" He surprised me with his sudden intensity. He swiveled the chair so he faced me, knees almost touching mine. "We've had this conversation before—that day in the bike park, remember?"

I shrugged. I remembered the day in the bike park, but not what I'd said. I was embarrassed, though, because I often tell people causation is complex. It's one of my favorite, empty phrases.

"But it's not empty," Wilbur argued. And he reminded me of what I'd said in the ICU, that first night.

Again, I was embarrassed—to be reminded of my hysteria—but he spoke kindly. He was sorting through my words: it seemed he'd understood more than I'd imagined.

He did ask me to clarify a few things. Who exactly was the *everybody* Oscar had brought along to Maisy's, for example? And everything was somehow my fault? *Everything?*

Briefly, I outlined the disappearance of my brother, the loss of my husband, the reasons that these things, and Oscar's accident, were my responsibility.

Wilbur considered. His silence was lengthy and measured.

"About Oscar's accident," he said eventually. "You could tell that story in a different way. The watch manufacturer who cut costs so that five-year-olds can open battery compartments. A mother who was patient with her child's imaginative play, and generous in her definition of *toy*, who couldn't have known about the manufacturer's negligence."

I gave him a doubtful look, but he wrapped his hand around my knee and squeezed. "Sorry," he said, realizing what he was doing. "I was trying to get that expression off your face. Can I talk about your former husband?"

"If you like."

"It sounds like that other woman was stringing him along before you met, and you rescued him. But here she came again, and there was nothing anybody could have done."

"You mean because she was his soul mate," I said flatly.

"Doubt it. She sounds awful. You don't have to be someone's soul mate to get addicted to them. I just mean it was nothing to do with you talking about your missing brother—if you'd never said a word about your brother you'd probably have decided *that* was the reason. You'd have blamed yourself for keeping yourself from your husband."

I looked away.

Along the wall behind Oscar's bed was a call button, the word *cancel* underneath. I studied this: call, *cancel*, call, *cancel*. Not for any particular reason.

"And can I say something about your brother?"

"All right."

"In all honesty," he said, "I find the causal connection between you telling your brother that his joke about elephants wasn't funny and his running away from home extremely tenuous."

I frowned.

"No offense," Wilbur added, "but you must have been a pretty crap lawyer."

"I was a *great* lawyer!"

He shook his head. "Not with arguments like that, you weren't. What *I* think is that life is full of memories, stories, and facts, and we push our way through them—"

In the dim light of the sleeping ward, a nurse stood at the foot of a child's bed, writing something on a chart.

Wilbur gestured, as if pushing through curtains: "—and now and then, we pluck one, pull on the seam and make *that* responsible for everything."

The nurse stepped to the next bed along, brushing past a pair of *Get Well!* helium balloons.

"Which," Wilbur murmured, "is wrong."

The balloons knocked together gently, a small reprimand, and settled back into place.

6.

On Oscar's last night in the hospital, Wilbur came by to celebrate. Oscar fell asleep with a slice of cake slipping from his hand.

Wilbur picked up his bag, placed it on his lap. "I've been packing up the Flight School," he said. "All my parents' archives. And something occurred to me."

He cleared his throat, his expression odd and formal.

"You remember I mentioned they got your contact details from the creative writing course?" he continued. "Well, I decided to look through the archives to check—and then . . ."

Again, he paused. My heart fluttered. I didn't know why.

"Your brother," Wilbur said.

Now my heart stopped altogether.

"You mentioned you did that course with him. So I was thinking, what if my parents sent the first chapter to him, as well?"

"But . . ." I thought fast. The big envelope in the rusty frying pan. If there'd been a second envelope, one addressed to Robert, I'd have seen that too.

"I don't think so," I said. "There was only one." And then I remembered that Robert had been home from school that day. He could have already opened his, he could have read it, and—

"But," I repeated, shaking my head, "even if they did send him one, he must have thrown it out. If he'd sent back a *yes*, well, *The Guidebook* would have come for him too."

"Right," Wilbur said. "That occurred to me too, but I looked anyway. I found all the replies to the first chapters. They'd kept everything, my parents. Even the stack of papers and postcards that only said: *Yes!* And I found this."

Wilbur reached into his bag. He drew out a small, open envelope. He held it out to me.

"I'll go," he said, standing. "So you can read this alone."

He glanced at Oscar, curled and sleeping, blankie pressed beneath his arm, and smiled. Then he leaned down and kissed the top of my head. He'd never done that before. I could feel warmth through my hair. He walked out of the ward.

7.

Inside the envelope was a worn piece of paper.

Robert's handwriting. It stopped my breath. There's more of Robert in his handwriting than in close-up photographs of his face.

It was his formal style, his neatest cursive, and this is what it said.

Dear Rufus and Isabelle,

Thank you for sending me the first chapter of your guidebook.

It made me laugh so hard I spat out my orange juice. I love it. It's exactly the kind of guidebook I'd want to read, if I decided to start reading guidebooks.

However, I can't accept your offer because I'm going to be leaving pretty soon, and I won't be here to receive them.

The reason I'm leaving is this. Recently, I was diagnosed with MS. Now, the man who first discovered MS had a son who was a doctor. And after his father died, this son became a polar explorer. POLAR regions: the regions of long dark and long light.

Whenever I read about MS, there's talk about light and dark. Not enough exposure to sunshine: a deficiency of vitamin D.

Why did the son become a polar explorer? I think I know why. He was on to something.

So I'm going to the North Pole to see if the patterns of light there are the cure. The short days of winter, long days of summer, the aurora borealis. Flying to London, then straight to Finland, where I plan to get a job on a Russian trawler. I've researched, and this seems a cheap and sensible way to reach the North Pole.

I get to Helsinki on my sister's birthday. I'll send her a postcard to wish her a happy birthday from the north side.

Speaking of my sister, I can see that you've sent the same envelope to her. So of all the people, in all the world, she's been chosen, too. Hopefully, she'll say yes.

Yours sincerely,
Robert Sorensen

8.

You know what's extraordinary? How quickly this letter uncovered the truth.

A single turn of the spade almost. Within a few weeks, Matilda, still technically our caseworker, had sorted it out. She came over to my place to meet with me, my parents and their partners, and sat on my couch, a black coffee growing cold in front of her. As she spoke, I stared at her face and thought how it had widened and softened, and how her eyelids had grown heavier, her voice deeper, but that she was otherwise exactly the same.

Here is what she said.

In December 1990, a young man was found drowned in Lake Saari-järvi, one of the many small lakes outside Helsinki, Finland. The papers in his coat pocket were so water-damaged they were illegible. It seemed he had broken into an old holiday cottage that day, probably planning to sleep there, walked outside to explore, stepped onto the frozen lake, and fallen through the too-fragile ice.

A shopkeeper a few kilometers away said that he had spoken to the young man earlier that day when he bought provisions and postcards. The boy had told him he was from Montepulciano in Italy and that it was his nineteenth birthday. They had chatted about barrel-racing and gelato.

Nobody claimed the young man, he matched no missing persons pro-file, and he was listed on police files as an unknown Italian youth, aged nineteen.

"It's not Robert," my father said, annoyed. "Robert was only fifteen."

"He had the neighbour's passport," Matilda reminded him. "Andrew Grimshaw's passport, remember?"

It was Robert, it turned out. The local police had stored his dental and fingerprint records. We also recognized the list of possessions left in the cottage: his brown corduroy trousers, the baggy black trousers that narrowed at the ankle, his button-up shirts with tiny, sharp collars, his white sandshoes, his favorite black duffel coat with chunky wooden buttons (not given away after all), gray T-shirts, a toothbrush, unwritten postcards, a bottle of my mother's sixteen-year-old Lagavulin, and a mixtape that I remembered making for him: the Cure, Depeche Mode, Madness, Talking Heads, Joy Division, the Triffids, the Church.

Matilda finished reciting the possessions, the playlist. She had memorized it all. She looked around at us. We stared at her, silent.

"But where's he been," my mother asked, baffled, "all this time?"

"They kept him in a morgue for two years," Matilda explained. "But they could never identify him. His passport wasn't on him or with his things—they think it must have been lost in the lake. Eventually, they gave him a small state funeral and he was buried in a special section of a local graveyard reserved for unknowns."

"Who would have been at the funeral?" my father asked.

"Well . . ." But here Matilda, whose voice had been neutral, practical, kind, began to splinter. My mother moved closer to comfort her. My father and I sat listening to Matilda sob because nobody had attended Robert's funeral, and stared at our palms, at the truth we had just been handed.

Robert had flown to London, immediately on to Helsinki, taken a bus to Saarijärvi, broken into a cottage, and stepped onto the ice.

PART 16

1.

After Matilda left, my father howled.

It turned out he'd never truly believed that Robert was dead. He'd just pretended, to us and to himself. Trying to force Seneca's approach: believe the worst and you will be prepared when it takes place; by believing the worst, he actually thought he was *earning* a happy surprise. That's what you call a misreading of Seneca. Dad tried to stand up and his legs gave way beneath him.

For my mother, it was terrible and strange. All this time, I realized, she'd been carrying the burden of the search and the hope for us. Now her face and shoulders settled into quiet, desperate anguish. Watching her was like seeing an unnatural shift in a landscape: real-life time-lapse photography.

I was okay.

"This is good," I said. "Now we know the truth."

He hasn't been alone, trapped, suffering somewhere, for years, I pointed out. Also, drowning was supposed to be an almost euphoric death, and Robert had died in a generally happy, adventurous state, play-acting that he was Italian, buying himself food for a picnic in a stranger's cottage. Nobody had taken his life. It was sad and stupid, but I had already grieved for him. I had grieved for *years*. Now we could all move on.

The next couple of days, I hurried around making lists. I was back at my café and Oscar was back at day care. Oliver and Shreya had looked after the place well in my absence, but all its deficiencies—the peeling paint, the worn table edges—were now startling. So there was plenty to list.

On the third day, I decided to walk up to Greenwood Plaza myself, to pick up some fresh avocados and tomatoes, as we were low. I waved to Jennie in Hair to the Throne, and we both pantomimed in our usual way. It's possible that she knows what we mean by the pantomime, but I certainly don't.

It was a Thursday afternoon, a bright sky, and Blues Point Road was busy. I skirted around tables of outdoor cafés and a curious thought occurred to me.

My marriage had been over before it began, and my brother had died before I even knew that he was missing.

My imaginary husband, I thought, smiling to myself, observing the parallels, and my imaginary brother.

These last twenty years, since Robert had disappeared, he had been with me all the time, a growing-older brother. I'd seen him around corners and underneath hats, I'd seen him pulling gloves onto his hands.

I'd seen Robert with a girlfriend or a boyfriend, leaning on a partner's shoulder, looking through a window; Robert rolling a pen—

And now I was howling.

Standing on the corner of Blues Point Road and Lavender Street, wailing.

Robert rolled a pen along a table and it felt good beneath his palm. He thought about skipping the song on his stereo. He grew older. He figured out how to live with his multiple sclerosis. Some days he was exhausted, but some days he felt great. He even jogged when he could. He thought about getting gas for the barbecue, and how to be bigger than all this, and whether there was any point in being bigger.

I was standing in the daylight, wailing, and I didn't see how I could stop.

Whenever I drove in my car, Robert was always pulling up beside me at the lights, in a Land Rover, or a ute, a Mini—he was always turning to look at me, the stranger in the car alongside, and his eyes were always lighting up, a wild grin: *Abigail! There you are!* The whole enormous joke of it. *Look! It's me! I'm back!*

I stood on the corner, and now it wasn't sobbing, it was shrieking, it was *caterwauling*.

People stared at me in horror, or quickly looked away. They stepped around me, clutching their grocery bags higher. A woman pushing a baby in a pram briskly crossed the road to avoid me.

My throat stung from the terrible sounds it was making, my body shook with it, and I knew this was wrong, I had to stop—I'd be arrested, sedated, restrained; this *screaming*, it was unseemly, uncivilized, illegal—but here came Robert, grinning in my direction, here was Robert carrying a saxophone, here was Robert taking to an orange with his fingernails . . .

A Toyota Corolla pulled over alongside me. Its door opened. A woman in a sundress, a stranger, climbed out. Behind my own screams, I heard a voice calling, "Mum? What are you doing?" A teenager sat in the passenger seat, plucking at her seatbelt: "Mum? What are you *doing*?"

But the woman ignored the girl, and ran across to me. Astonishingly, she flung open her arms and wrapped them around my shoulders, and she pulled me closer, the smell of her perfume, her shampoo, the warmth of her hands on my back.

"It's okay," she said firmly. "It's okay."

"My brother," I sobbed. "My brother is dead."

The woman cried out herself and drew me closer, and here I was standing on the corner of Blues Point Road and Lavender Street, and there was no such thing as hope, no such thing as Robert, and there was my brother, a little boy, fifteen years old, a blue sky day, a frozen lake, there he was, stepping out, full of hope, onto the ice, and here was a stranger, murmuring *shhh*, and *hush*, and patting my back while I wept in her arms, and there he was, my brother, stepping out, full of hope—

2.

For a while, my parents and I looked for someone to blame. It was Andrew Grimshaw's fault for leaving his passport unattended; it was Carly's fault for inviting Robert over. It was Wilbur's parents' fault, we decided, in a flash of inspiration, for not contacting us when they received Robert's letter outlining his plan.

Only, it was not their fault: it was implausible, a fifteen-year-old boy running away to the North Pole. They would have dismissed it as fantastical.

Next, we began to claim fault for ourselves: it was my fault for not allowing Robert to be frightened; it was my mother's fault for ever telling him about Jean-Martin Charcot; my father's fault for not sitting Robert down and sorting through viable treatment options.

This led us all into silence—*viable treatment options* was a gentle way of pointing out that Robert was an idiot. Looking for a cure for MS in the North Pole. Which led to our agreeing that Robert was a *boy*, a kid, fifteen years old, flawed, brave, terrified. My mother said that *I*, Abigail, had been just a girl myself, almost exactly Robert's age, doing my best to help him.

My mother whispered, "I should have paid more attention."

"*I* should have paid attention," Dad said, his hand on her hand.

For a moment, I thought that was the moral of the story: pay attention. Stop thinking about self-help and sex! Concentrate! *Watch* your child, be vigilant! Don't let him run away to the North Pole! Don't let him take apart his digital watch!

But then I remembered that I can be standing in the kitchen beside Oscar and he can fall from a chair. Just as it is psychically impossible (for me, at least) to focus on goodies and baddies for more than five minutes, it is physically impossible to monitor a child as if you were a CCTV camera. Sometimes you have to set a saucepan on the stove. It only takes a fraction of a second for a child to eat a battery.

And I might never have considered the absence of the watch battery, or its significance, if I hadn't left Oscar for a weekend away, walked beside Lera, listening to her talk about her work.

I told my parents that Robert had been a creative soul, a free spirit, and that if they'd closed him down, or trapped him, or tried to shape him, they'd only have lost him sooner. I watched my mother straighten, as I spoke, while my father's shoulders relaxed.

One day, our family would fly to Finland and retrace his journey, visit the cottage, the lake, his grave, take a sauna, try ice-fishing, eat warm Leipäjuusto with cloudberry jam.

For now, we held a party to remember and farewell Robert, with collages of photographs and old video footage. His old friends and mine turned up—Carly and Andrew Grimshaw and their parents, little Rabbit-all-grown-up, Robert's friend Bing, even Clarissa, his old girlfriend. My mother's best friend Barbara came too; they'd made up a few years ago, after Barbara's husband died of motor neurone disease. We played Joy Division, Robert's favorite band, and told stories about the wild way he hurtled down a ski slope, laughed about his astonishing courage—secretly saving the money to fly alone to Finland—and read aloud some of his high school poetry. Oscar jiggled, ecstatic, beside me. For him, it was like a party for a superhero, only one where he himself was junior superhero: his own middle name was Robert, he was Robert's *spitting image*.

Xuang gave an unexpectedly poignant speech about how he wished he had met Robert, and he recounted stories my mother had shared with him about Robert and Abigail as children. "Such a special bond they had," he said, which made me cry with gratitude. "They used to have a ceremony on Abi's birthday each year, toast each other with their parents' whisky . . ." Everyone laughed, but Xuang was looking right at me, lowering his voice, raising an imaginary glass and wishing me well on my journey ahead. Through another rush of tears, I saw Robert in a cottage on a lake outside Helsinki, and I understood that he had not brought my mother's Lagavulin along to keep him warm, as we had hypothesized.

I gave a speech in which I mentioned Robert's peppermint mood. People in the audience nodded, remembering. "I hope he's in a peppermint mood," I said, "wherever he is right now."

Later that night, my mother phoned and informed me: "We are designed to recover."

"I mean, I know not everybody does," she added, "but that's the design." And she expressed irritation with the number of people who say you never recover from the loss of a child.

"Of course, I'll never stop missing him. Some days I feel like a cake tin, pieces of baking paper stuck in patches to the bottom. Or I'm an ice cube tray that somebody is twisting, and ice is clattering into the sink, and the sink is also my heart."

"These are good," I said. "Unexpected metaphors."

"Or I'll be in bed," she continued, "thinking: break glass with hammer, and my chest is the glass."

"Uh-huh," I said, understanding.

"But often I'm happy," she said. "You can be happy, Abigail. I myself am happy with my new frangipani tree and Xuang."

"In that order?"

"He's driving me crazy today—he's got this idea I could make a killing knitting jackets for dogs. I only wanted to knit the *one* jacket, for Bartholomew, not a production line of jackets! So yes, in that order."

PART 17

1.

Today, I am walking to the Barry Street park with Oscar. For no particular reason, he is dressed as Spider-Man.

"Are you ready to see my shadow?" he asks, pride and suspense in his voice.

"Yes," I say, and we emerge from the shade of a tree into the sun and there it is, beside me, his shadow. Our two shadows walking side by side, the littleness of his compared to mine, his shoulders pronounced by the padding in his Spider-Man suit.

For a moment, I think I have figured it out: you can ask the universe or God or legal texts, you can try the gym or shopping malls, numerology, philosophy, politics, witchcraft, Tantra, tango, the exotic, the erotic, psychotherapy, religion, adages-printed-on-stickers-and-attached-to-scented-candles, Facebook, television, Centers of Spiritual Wellbeing, football, personality tests—you can try any of those, but mostly it comes down to what you do with fears and hopes.

Pass them out to friends and family. Howl them to strangers on street corners. *I think he doesn't love me, I saw my parents fly once, this is all my fault.*

Hand them over and, between you, sort them out.

The right sort of people will let you hold on to false hope and impossible dreams (*Of course he's* into *you! Of* course *he's coming back!*) until the time is right to gently take them from you. They will dispel your fears and help you see or carry truth.

Meanwhile, whatever you do, here comes the future, thundering toward you.

Regardless of the approach you choose, you can take a good guess, from one moment to the next, what will happen.

You can guess, for example, that this small Spider-Man will start school in a week. On his step-grandmother's advice, he will wear two pairs of socks to prevent blisters from his new shoes. You will photograph him waving at the doorway to the classroom, return to your car and cry.

And then, over the days, weeks, months and years to follow, his little boy body will stretch up and up, his chest broadening, his chin growing square.

He'll get certificates of merit at assembly—walk up to the stage to collect them, his back very straight—and he will read his first chapter book, drink his first soft drink, learn to tie shoelaces, to wobble teeth, blow up balloons, click his fingers, dance, spell, and make a paper airplane. Karate, hip hop, loom bands, Beyblades, hoverboards, *Clash of Clans*, *Minecraft*, bottle-flipping, dabbing, *Pokémon Go*, fidget spinners—each of these will be a passion, a religion, in his life, before he swings abruptly to disdain—disdain not only for the passion, but for his former self. "Be kind," you will beg him, "to your former self."

One rainy day, when he's six, he'll run to fill his water bottle in the park, while his new friend Ely trips and lands face first in the mud.

And Wilbur, often around, will stand with his umbrella over Ely and Ely's mother, while the mother, crouching, says: *Okay, it's okay*, her face pale, the child's mouth bleeding. There will be a quiet distance between Ely's mother's panic and our calm, Wilbur and I standing alongside, Oscar staring, the sky heavy with rain, the playground slippery, the boy with the blood in his mouth.

Wilbur will give Ely and his mother a ride to the medical center, where the doctor will give the boy a single stitch, and send him home.

You can also take a guess that there will be cranky moments, and quiet. Terrible things will happen in the news, and moments of horror will tear into your life. Cars will turn corners, lights will come on and switch off, and alarms will sound. People will play chess and *Candy Crush* on their computers. They will update their status. Pipes will leak under bathtubs and stain the ceilings of the rooms below. Water will pour from bottles into glasses, washing machines will *bleep!* when wet towels are caught and unbalanced.

You will be surprised by an invitation to the wedding of Pete and Sasha, and will be seated at a table with Wilbur, Nicole and Antony, plus three pest control guys. These guys will joke about being second-tier pest control friends, and will ask how you know the happy couple. You will glance at each other, and Nicole will shrug and say, "Flight School."

Power outages will darken neighborhoods and the torch will be missing from the kitchen drawer. You will light scented candles instead. You will soak up leftover soup with bread. You will decide, now and then, to stop eating bread.

Oscar will dream and not dream; he will be afraid of dogs and then beg for a dog. One day he will tell you that he does not like a boy in his class named Reuben, because Reuben does not sing as beautifully as he himself sings. You will wonder whether you should point out that this is not a basis for character judgment, or it's a *teeny* bit conceited, or even that Oscar is, in fact, fairly tuneless. You will only say you understand. Oscar, meanwhile, will sit cross-legged on the edge of the water and think his own private thoughts.

After the wedding of Pete and Sasha, you will find yourself meeting your friends from Flight School every month or so. At restaurants, cafés, on Sundays, with the kids, and with Nicole's shy husband, Marcin, at

Balmoral Beach. Nicole's girls will take charge of Oscar, pushing him on the swing.

"Oh, Abi," Nicole will say on a picnic rug at Centennial Gardens one day. "I lied to my dentist. I had a chipped tooth and the dentist said, *Just out of interest, what were you eating when you did this?* And I said, *A nut.* But it wasn't, Abi. I was eating a sweet."

You will laugh, and love Nicole.

You and Nicole will find yourselves sharing stories of former boyfriends, former sexual experiences, and together sorting through the strangeness of how we blame ourselves when we could have set stronger borders, when you whispered *no* but you could have shouted it, how you begin to see yourself as a person without substance: the world not within your control. How this shades into every crisis, every loss, how you look for the place where you could have shouted *no*, and made it stop, you make everything your fault.

Later, you will consider the evolution of sex in your life, from the confusion of it being *his* choice, his urgency, to playing along with his rules, his ideas of foreplay, his ideas of who you are, to the ideas you both have, from movies or magazines, of what sex is meant to be—a flinging about, a yoga class, sweat and breathlessness—to a stripped-back primitive recklessness, to shy simulations of romance, to something that you know you haven't found yet.

Another day, you will tell Pete Aldridge that there are moths and ants at your home, and his face will light up. He will draw out his business card and place it on the table of the Indian restaurant. Frangipani will snap it back and promise that Pete will take care of your pests free of charge.

"Will I?" Pete will say, disgruntled. "Why's that then?"

You will invite your flight class, and old friends from Oscar's day care, and new friends from Oscar's school, to your house for drinks, or tea and cake, or wine and cheese, and you will be invited to other people's houses and parties.

One day, redheaded Niall will send you a friend request on Facebook, and you will exchange witty messages. Later that night, you will put on an apple-green dress and remember Niall saying, "I was fine with you having Oscar." *What do you mean, "fine"?* you will think. My having Oscar was fine?

You will remember Niall lying on the couch, and how you made him dinner, and cleaned up after dinner, and how "that was fine," he accepted that. It will occur to you that he could have offered to bring takeaway, or offered to tidy while you put Oscar to bed, or offered to take you both out. These occurrences will surprise you.

You will be afraid, sometimes, of small sharp chicken bones, the sound of a bath running, rising static; afraid of yourself and who you might become. You will be afraid as you watch small boys on scooters almost colliding, or boys doing the backstroke down swimming pool lanes.

You might find yourself afraid of change, or loss, of industries collapsing, American elections, of terrorists, contempt and pedantry; afraid of the noise of heels scratching floorboards; afraid of the dark, other people, phone calls, traffic jams, muffled voices, a spider on the wall. You might be afraid of the lines of age, afraid that you will forget to have Oscar draw a picture and enclose it in a thank-you card for Auntie Gem, who sends him a twenty-dollar note every birthday. You will be afraid that your guests are bored, afraid that you've hurt feelings, that you've been selfish, or childish, or that you're missing something perfectly obvious.

Some days you will be afraid that there's nothing left now, that you are ugly but, out of courtesy, nobody has pointed this out to you. You will fear that love, the possibility of love, will dissipate, that you will become a quiet, smiling person, smiling wryly, disappearing, forming part of nobody's dreams.

One day, you will receive an email from someone named Cindy Chin, which you will almost delete, thinking it is junk mail, but instead you will open it and read:

Dear Abigail,

I've never met you, and I hope you don't mind me writing to you now. My husband, David, used to hang out with you and Finn, when you two lived in Montreal. I always wanted to come along, but I was so sick with my pregnancy that I could never do it. I was sorry about that. I really wanted to meet you.

Anyway, this is none of my business and you might not want to hear this, and it might not be relevant anymore, because I'm sure you've moved on—but I wanted to say that David and I were SO MAD at Finnegan for what he did to you.

David is still good friends with Finn, so he can't say any of this stuff to you himself, but I can. (I think.) We see Finn and Tia sometimes, and look, Tia's sort of awful. She's just very self-satisfied. And what David keeps saying to me is that you were awesome. He loved you! He thought you and Finn were so much fun, and he says that you made Finn the best person he could be, while with Tia he's half that person.

It's just really sad.

Anyway, but I hope you are happy! And I hope you don't mind me writing this! And maybe one day we will meet up after all.

Best wishes,

Cindy Chin

After that, you and Cindy will exchange emails for years.

I can let it go now, you will think with midnight clarity, *because it wasn't a lie, not all of it, Finnegan and I—just as Robert and I were not a lie.* Such a special bond they had. *Somewhere in the world, people know that.*

Eventually, you will find the kindness to forgive your former self for hope, and for mistakes, and the courage to angle the anger in the right direction.

You can take a guess that there will be moments of toxicity, that people will ask favors, that you will stand on chairs to fix blinds, change light globes, reach for things on top of the fridge. That there will be a sticker chart on the fridge, with stars for good behavior, that the plumber will smile as he says goodbye, that friends will say, *Don't come close, I've got a terrible cold.*

At Nielsen Park, Wilbur will stand at the water's edge, his back to you, and raise his hand to his forehead, and you will study the tall man with the wild curls, the muscles in his back and his shoulders, and feel a curious jolt.

Later, you will be chatting to Antony, but half your mind will be listening to Wilbur, telling stories about airplanes to the others: "You focus on the circle in front of you," Wilbur is explaining, "four or five things you have to scan—you set up a continual scan—instead of looking out at the big sky."

You tune back into Antony, who is still sad, but calmly sad now, and beginning to be hopeful, having just met someone new.

"The first time you put your hand out into the slipstream, you can't believe how strong it is," Wilbur says.

Both you and Antony turn to listen.

One day, in passing, you will tell Wilbur that Finnegan said you were needy. This will be the first time you ever told anybody this.

"Wait," Wilbur will say. "Wait, I thought that was *your* interpretation. That *you* thought you talked too much about your brother. I didn't know *Finnegan* said it himself."

And then he will rage at Finnegan, an unexpected rage. He will not take it with him, inside of him, curling it up to consider later—perhaps Abigail *was* needy?—he will rage. His rage will take the last of your doubt; you will watch it drift, a soap bubble, and fade against a tree.

Oscar will turn seven and you will sit with him in a café while he drinks a milkshake, and gaze at him, drink in his sweet voice, the bones in his cheeks, his long, bony legs swinging underneath the table, his humor, his stories, his own unique turn of mind.

Another day, you will watch as he tries to force a broken piece back into a toy, his fierceness, his whole body shaking with the effort, and there, for a moment, is Robert, the same exact fierceness, the trembling when he tried to fix a broken Rubik's Cube.

Another day, Wilbur will tell you a story about that ex-girlfriend, the turquoise girl, and how she did not know how to swim. He tried to teach her once and it was the funniest thing. She was doing everything right, listening to every word he said, her arms are going, her legs are kicking (Wilbur here demonstrating), but no matter what she did, she would *sink*. Sink to the bottom of the water. *God* (Wilbur will say), *I never laughed so hard*.

And you will feel, at that moment, enormously sad.

Later you will decide that this is sadness for women who sink despite doing all they can. Then you will realize that your sadness is for Wilbur, because his eyes shone with gentle affection as he spoke. Some time later you will see exactly what the sadness means.

One night, Oscar's eyes, golden-green, will follow a glass of water as it drifts along the slant of the coffee table. Wilbur, visiting, will point to the tree shadow in the front door glass, and say, "It looks like a person leaning in to peer through the glass, one hand raised to his forehead." You and Oscar will say, "Yes! It *does*!" and Wilbur will open the front door suddenly, to catch it out, the tree, all three of you breathless for a moment, but the tree will be back where it belongs.

Another day, you will buy a kitchen clock, and Wilbur will crouch beside Oscar, explaining how to tell the time. Oscar will grow fretful, confused, until Wilbur says, "Tell you what, we'll start on the small hills in the snow."

And into that moment will slide another moment—my brother Robert on a family ski trip, flying down a slope in the reckless way he skied, wobbling side-to-side at speed, face snow-burnt and vivid with glee, scarf flying, jacket flying—and as Wilbur draws circles on paper, taking Oscar back to the basics of time, back to how numbers fit together, you will glimpse how it all fits together, the small hills, the snow, flight.

Some days you will feel like a silver fish, a flying fish. You will wake in the morning and think, *What a dream, what a dream*, and walking to the café, you will think, *I must write that dream down*, but the dream will already be gone, sliding down the window glass, gone.

Wilbur will walk into the café that same day, and you will recall that the dream was about him. He will see you remember, your eyes will exchange dreams.

He will cross the room and say, "Abigail."

You will find out what Tantric sex is like, with a tall man with wild curls who knows how to look you in the eye.

Or not Tantric sex, but something more than that, more humor, more passion, his palm running slow down your inner thigh, more about Wilbur and Abigail, and all the truths coiled within them.

Later, at home, a flying fox will soar over palm trees into the magenta light.

Later still, you will telephone Wilbur to tell him that Oscar chose the butterfly gingerbread at My Little Cupcake today. But when the woman reached her tongs into the jar, the butterfly wings snapped away. "You can have the broken one for free," the woman said, reaching her tongs into the jar again. But the *next* one also broke, and the next, and you and Oscar walked home from the shop with a bag full of butterfly wings.

"There are tiny gold coins in the cracks between my floorboards," you will say to Wilbur, "spilled from Oscar's pirate ship. A handful of glow-in-the-dark stars are caught in the lint compartment of the dryer. And dragon eggs in the kitchen sink."

"And butterfly wings," Wilbur will add. "Where is the bag of butterfly wings?"

"Oh, well; those, we ate."

And you will both laugh quietly, sleepily, and you will have the strangest feeling that he is resting his forehead against yours as he speaks, that you are resting your forehead against his, and there will be a long pause, and you will lie back on your pillow, the phone still at your ear, and fall asleep into the gold coins, the stars, the dragon eggs, the butterfly wings, fall asleep into the absence of fear, into truth and hope, friendship and love, all of it there in that pause.

You can also take a guess that one night, while you are standing beside Wilbur at his place, staring through his windows into the night, something will glint, catching your eye. "Do you see that?" you will say.

Wilbur will wrench the window open and lean out. A faint sound will drift into the apartment, like a hushed breeze that sighs and exhales, as if the air were breathing. You will open the next window along and lean out too, and you will turn to look at each other, disbelieving. Now a fragrance will brush against you, something with pieces of eucalyptus in it, faint notes of vanilla. And in every direction, as far as you can see, tracings will surge and fall, drifting in sets, crossing each other, almost transparent but silver-lined. A little like water crossed with mist. You will both reach out, touch a wave as it passes, and it will glide by your hands, soft as cloth but with an unexpected firmness.

Again, you will glance at each other. Because you are not blockheads, you will not leap out of the window.

You will run down three flights of stairs, out into the dark street, the parked cars, the streetlights, and they will still be there, the air alive, bustling, almost laughing with flight waves. A low wave will pass by your hip and you will touch it and, without deciding, will find yourself riding it, your body slung across it, and it will carry you steadily along the street until you panic and slide back to the road, running a few steps, exhilarated.

You will both fly. You will practice on the low waves, then learn how to cross, higher and higher, until you are up among the trees, the icy freshness of the air up there. At first you will hold yourself awkwardly and your lower back will twinge, and then you will remember the positions you rehearsed in Practical Flight. You will relax your shoulders, hold your arms steady.

At times, you will panic at the fact that you are high in the sky, but images will return to you from Flight Immersion, and you will accept that the sky is for you.

You will call advice to each other. You will shout, "Is this real?" Wilbur will fly close to you, and you will reach for each other's hands.

You will fly through the dampness of clouds, swing over electrical wires. You will soar over city lights, across grids of suburban roads.

You will knock on doors and collect your flight class—Frangipani will fly neatly and gracefully, a ballerina; Pete Aldridge will surprise you by shouting and whooping. Antony will weep, Nicole will frown, anxious and swearing until her face brightens and then she'll tear higher and higher, swimming through the air, reaching for stars.

You will circle a children's playground, gazing down at the moonlit slides, the dandelions, the ridged mud, broken gate. And there, on the path running alongside this playground, a man will be walking, hands in his pockets, head bowed in thought. He will look up and see you flying above him. To your surprise, it will be Robert. Back again, never stepped onto the ice, but sailed to the North Pole, was cured by the northern lights, and now he's back to cure the world of all its cruellest illnesses. You will know him at once; he will still have his hair, finer than it was, a darker blond, and he is well and tall and his face is broader, more rectangular, but he's looking up, laughing at all of you swooping about, especially happy to see you, his sister; hands in his pockets, waiting while you skim the waves down to him—waiting to tell you his story—

Like I said, you can take a guess.

Most of these things will happen.

ACKNOWLEDGMENTS

To my publishers, Emily Griffin (in the US), and Claire Craig (in Australia), for extraordinary insight and wisdom in the editing of this novel; to everyone else at HarperCollins (especially Katherine Beitner, Sarah Lambert, Leah Wasielewski, Christina Polizoto, and Cassiopeia Neely); and to my superb agents, Jill Grinberg (in the US) and Tara Wynne (in Australia).

To the Australian Arts Council, whose generous grant took a great weight from my shoulders at just the right time and made it possible for me to complete this novel.

To the café owners and managers who answered my questions and chatted with me about café life, especially at Maisy's and at Café ZoZo in Neutral Bay, and at Oski in Kirribilli.

To Kalle Manner, a *rikosylikonstaapeli* (detective sergeant) at Itä-Uudenmaan poliisilaitos (the Eastern Uusimaa Police Department) in Finland, who was enormously generous with his expertise and even emailed me location photographs, and to his sister, Anu Pietilainen, who provided very helpful Finnish expertise of her own.

To the two kind doctors who reviewed the medical sections of this book, and to all the extraordinary people who work in the public and private health systems, especially in pediatrics.

To Kate Clancy, for all her poetry but especially Poem for Man with No Sense of Smell, which I have always admired (and about which I do not share Abi's reservations).

To Nigel Wood, who is endlessly patient with my crises of confidence and my questions about life with anosmia, and who tells (quite seriously) fascinating stories about termites.

To all my friends, including but not limited to Natalie, Libby, Rachel, Suzy, Sandra, Jane, Jayne, Jo, Cathy, Sophie, Gaynor, Anna, Hannah, Elizabeth, Melita, and Stephen, and with particular thanks to Laura, for exquisite emails and encouragement; Kathryn, for the mentoring, wit, and sagacity; Michael, for late-night texts *containing* wit and sagacity; Maria, Deborah, and Rebecca, for making Coco Chocolate a dreamland; Limor, who shared with me her powerful poetry; Corrie, who sends gifts that basically write books for me; and Lesley, whose mother once pulled over her car to comfort a stranger weeping on the side of the road.

To my sisters: Liane (who lit up when I said I wanted to write a book about flight, which is why I wrote it, and who generously applauded every draft, which is why I didn't give up on it), Kati (whose many talents include proofreading all our novels), Fiona (who lets me crash her family beach holidays), and Nicola (for her beautiful enthusiasm and GIFs).

To my mum, who makes me laugh, believes in magic, and never quits; and to my dad, who as a boy dreamed of flying planes, made his dream come true, and still talks about flight with a gleam in his eye. (Dad has always told mesmerizing stories about the sky and was hugely helpful with technical questions, although, to be clear, he would never "step out of a perfectly good airplane.")

To my son, Charlie, who is hilarious and a master of sideways-crooked thinking.

Finally, special mention to Loren O'Keeffe, who was generous enough to read this novel, and to respond to it with kindness. Loren's brother Dan went missing in July 2011, and she established the Missing Persons Advocacy Network (MPAN) in 2013. MPAN does important work creating awareness around missing people, and providing practical support to their families. It operates without funding and tax-deductible donations are welcome at www.mpan.com.au.

This book is dedicated to my family and friends, but I'd also like to dedicate it to those people with missing family members or friends. The strength required to live with ambiguous loss, with the absence of the one truth that matters the most, is breathtaking.

ABOUT THE AUTHOR

Jaclyn Moriarty is the prize-winning and bestselling author of novels for adults, children, and young adults, including the Ashbury-Brookfield books and The Colours of Madeleine trilogy. Jaclyn grew up in Sydney; lived in the US, England, and Canada; and now lives in Sydney again.